## "I've never had to ... um ... I'm not too familiar with this type of machinery."

*Machinery?* Daniel used his thumb to push the brim of his Stetson higher on his forehead. "It's a washer," he said with a grin. "Not a nuclear reactor."

Zara rubbed a palm on her thigh as she spoke. "I just haven't used one be—in a very long time." She looked totally lost as she contemplated the simple, everyday appliance.

"It's a fairly easy task. First you sort the clothes by type—jeans and heavy stuff like towels, then another pile of lighter colors, maybe T-shirts and bed linens. But keep the reds with the other dark colors or everything will turn pink."

Zara picked through her box and pulled out a minuscule black triangle of elastic and lace. "And which category of clothing might this fall into?"

After swallowing his surprise with a huge gulp of coffee, Daniel stuttered, "Um ... that w-would be delicates. Do you have a lot of that ... in there?"

She brought out a handful of the flimsy-looking underwear. "It's all new, but I thought it should be washed before I wore it. Since it's going to be close to my skin, I want it to be really clean."

Daniel felt his face go warm as his don't-get-involved resolve flew straight out the Washeteria window. If Zara liked clean, he could be the most spotless man in Texas. Hell, he'd shower twice a day and three times on Sunday if that's what it would take to get as close to her as her unmentionables ...

# JUDI McCOY

## WANTED:
### *One Perfect*
# MAN

AVON BOOKS
*An Imprint* of HarperCollins*Publishers*

This is a work of fiction. Names, characters, places, and incidents are products of the author's imagination or are used fictitiously and are not to be construed as real. Any resemblance to actual events, locales, organizations, or persons, living or dead, is entirely coincidental.

AVON BOOKS
*An Imprint of* HarperCollins*Publishers*
10 East 53rd Street
New York, New York 10022-5299

Copyright © 2004 by Judi McCoy
ISBN: 0-06-056079-7
**www.avonromance.com**

First Avon Books paperback printing: February 2004

Avon Trademark Reg. U.S. Pat. Off. and in Other Countries, Marca Registrada, Hecho en U.S.A.
HarperCollins® is a registered trademark of HarperCollins Publishers Inc.

Printed in the U.S.A.

10  9  8  7  6  5  4  3  2  1

*To my agent, Helen Breitwieser:*
*Thank you for believing*
*in this book and all my work,*
*no matter how unusual or outlandish the idea.*

*To my editor, Erika Tsang,*
*and Avon Books/HarperCollins:*
*Thank you for having the courage to publish*
*a very different book.*

*This story is for all the dreamers in the world.*
*May you live long and prosper*
*on your journey through life.*

only be reached by crawling out of Will's bedroom window. Though the boy loved sitting on the roof and gazing at the sky, it worried Daniel that one night his son might get so excited by what he saw through the Meade he'd flip right over the guardrail onto the ground below.

"Yeah. I like it, too," said Will, concentrating on the telescope lens. "If we lived in a city, I bet we'd never see anything this great."

Pleased at the boy's candid musings, Daniel grinned. He'd come to cherish moments like this, when he and his son could share ideas and discuss things freely, safe from the intrusion of Rebecca's parents. Six years ago, when he'd been a new, fumble-fingered dad, he didn't have a clue of what to do with a two-year-old. That was the reason he'd jumped at the chance to buy this hole-in-the-wall combination grocery store/gas station when he'd first stumbled on it. It gave his boy an anchor, but it was also the last place the Warfields would think to look for an up-and-coming astronomy professor. Will's waxing poetic over their isolation was just icing on the cake.

"I know what you mean." Daniel peered into the sky in the direction Will was scanning. "See anything yet?"

"Nuh-uh. But it's still early. They'll be here."

"You said the lights were closer last night, but there were fewer of them? Maybe the show's over."

"Know what I think? I think tonight's the night they're gonna hit ground. If we're lucky, they'll land near the creek or—"

A burst of panic flared in Daniel's chest. "The

creek? Will, please tell me you're careful down there. It's one thing to be chasing after frogs, but the rain we had last week could have kicked up a few of those poisonous snakes Jeremiah keeps talking about. And your asthma—"

"Da-aad. I'm not a baby. I know which snakes to stay away from. And I take my inhaler. Jeez."

Daniel frowned but kept his tongue in check. Sometimes it was hard to remember Will was a growing boy and not the gap-toothed toddler he'd been when they first met. He might have been robbed of his son's babyhood, but now that they were a family he planned to enjoy every moment of the rest of their life together. As long as the Warfields didn't find them, he silently amended.

"Can I ask you something?"

Daniel tapped Will's behind with the toe of his boot. The kid always had a question. "What?"

"What do you think the lights are? Really?"

Daniel heaved a sigh. It had been so long since he'd used his brain for anything more difficult than calibrating the settings on a carburetor, he'd grown rusty as a worn-out radiator. If he'd had his instruments and charts, he wouldn't have to sound stupid in front of his own son.

"Darned if I know. Let's just enjoy them while they're out there, okay?"

As if refusing to give credence to such a simple idea, Will spun around to face him. "I know you don't like me talking about the things you did before we moved here, but—"

"You're going to bring them up anyway." He reached out and ruffled the boy's mop of dark brown curls. "I'm feeling mellow tonight, so go ahead. It's all right."

Will flashed the glimmer of a smile. "Did you ever see anything like these lights when you were teaching at the university?"

Daniel crossed his feet at the ankles and continued to rest them on the rail. It was clear where Will got his love of the stars, as well as his inquisitive nature. Daniel had spent the first third of his life with a crick in his neck because his eyes had been trained on the heavens. He'd been forced to run from the Warfields, but he didn't regret giving up his lifelong dream for the everyday joy of a better one—the right to raise his child. There was nothing he hated more than keeping secrets from the boy.

"Not that I can remember, but I've been checking the newspaper. If those lights were anything special, we'd have heard about them by now."

Will shrugged. "I guess so. But maybe they somehow managed to sneak by all those space stations and satellites floating around up there. I mean, what if these falling stars aren't really stars at all? And what if they had some kind of cloaking device that let 'em pass by all our heavy artillery without being noticed, and once they entered our atmosphere they thought it was safe to drop their shields?" He took a huge gasp of air. "What if we were the only ones who saw them after they did it, and—"

"Whoa, hold on a second. Catch your breath and

think about what you're saying. With all the organizations out there who do nothing but monitor the skies, your theory isn't plausible. I know you believe there's life in other solar systems, but I have yet to make up my mind, even if there are enough stories about Roswell to fill a set of encyclopedia. Though I find it hard to believe we're the only intelligent beings in the universe, I don't want you jumping to any conclusions."

Will fisted his hands on his hips. "Okay then, if you were really such a hotshot astronomer, what do you think they are?"

Daniel swung his feet from the rail and set the front legs of the chair down with a solid *thwack*. He never told Will he'd been the proud owner of a brand-new Ph.D. when he'd left his chosen profession. The fact that he'd never seen anything like the lights intrigued him, too. If it were seven years ago, he would have been documenting the find, calling NASA, and raising a ruckus so loud they would have named whatever the phenomenon was after him. Only it would have been called—

Frustrated, he blew out a breath. It didn't matter what they would have called the lights. He'd given up everything to protect his son, and it was going to stay that way. If his real name ended up in the wrong hands, Rebecca's parents would be after them so fast even a shooting star wouldn't be able to carry them away.

"I can't tell you because I don't know," he said, reining in his temper. "Your Meade is top-notch amateur equipment, but it's not powerful enough to get a clear view. And your being a little snotnose is not a quality I admire. Now I suggest you glue your eyeball to that lens before you find yourself grounded."

The quiet words of chastisement were all Will needed. "Yes, sir," he said, slowly turning back to the telescope.

"How about you sidle over and let me have a peek?" Daniel teased, trying to smooth ruffled feathers. Standing, he nudged Will's shoulder and trained his eye on the lens. Adjusting the coordinates, he zeroed in on Cassiopeia A, the remains of a huge star that scientists calculated had exploded 320 years earlier. From there, he swung to the southwestern corner of Upsilon Andromedae, under the Great Square of Pegasus, the direction from which the lights had originated.

Moving to the side, he let Will have a turn at the lens. "You did good. It just needed a hair's worth of correction."

Will again concentrated on the Meade. In a scant second his thin shoulders quivered, his voice grew shrill. "Wow. Here they come! And they're really moving."

Though it seemed a lifetime since he'd left his position at Columbia, Daniel still remembered how awe-inspiring it was to search the sky for a new discovery. Caught up in his son's enthusiasm, he laid a hand on Will's back. "Seems to me they look a whole lot brighter tonight."

Before he could say more, a single, skittering dot of

light caught the corner of his eye. Separating from the pack, it moved quickly in an arcing trajectory toward the trees at the back of his property. Amazingly, the phenomenon was close enough to be seen by the naked eye. All Daniel could compare it to was the small but brilliant glitter of energy the Disney studios used to portray Tinkerbell in their animated version of *Peter Pan*.

And for some unknown reason, the sight of it made him wary.

"Look . . . they're flying away." Will raised his gaze from the Meade and pointed heavenward. "All except that one."

"I see, son. I see." Training his eyes on the falling light, Daniel watched it dance and tumble at will. Then it winked out over the stand of trees at the rear of their property. Father and son stared in wonder, until Will took him by surprise and scrambled toward his bedroom window.

"Just where do you thing you're going?" Daniel asked, catching Will by his collar.

Hanging half in–half out of the window, Will stared up pleadingly as he struggled. "We haf'ta get to the creek and see where it landed."

"Not tonight we don't," said Daniel. "First thing tomorrow morning is soon enough. Besides being way past your bedtime, it's pitch-dark out there." He almost added that he would get up early and accompany the boy, but thought better of it. By the time they hit ground, there was usually nothing left of a falling star. He'd only ruin the boy's fun if he tagged along and was proved right.

"Aw, Dad. Please?"

"Tomorrow," he said again, chucking Will's chin. "And you have to promise you'll leave the snakes be."

"I promise." Will threw him a look of mischief. "How early can I leave the house?"

"First light," said Daniel, knowing he'd regret it come dawn. "Now off to bed."

Two days later, on a Thursday morning, Daniel walked catty-corner across the intersection to Coombs's Luncheonette in search of some company. At the center of Button Creek, the diner was haven to the workers at Pepperdine's Feed and Grain as well as most of the truckers, ranchers, and farmers who found their way into the tiny hamlet. Knowing the locals liked to keep their business in town, Daniel made a trip to the restaurant several times a week to stay in touch and promote goodwill.

The luncheonette was crowded that morning, as if every man within a five-mile radius had decided to swallow a gallon of caffeine and one of Lucy's steak-and-egg sandwiches to jump start his day.

Daniel called a greeting to a group in the corner as he removed his sweat-stained Stetson. He nodded at a couple of boys he knew worked at the Feed and Grain and a few more who bought gas from him on a regular basis when they stopped by Zetmer's Mercantile to order supplies. Settling himself on a vacant stool at the counter so he could keep an eye on the pumps, he nodded at a short, rotund woman holding a coffeepot.

"Looks like a full house, Lucy. You giving the motor oil away today?"

Lucy Coombs, owner of the restaurant for as long as anyone could remember, set a cup of her special brew in front of him. "Dan'l. Ain't seen you in a couple days. You've been missin' all the excitement."

He glanced out the dusty plate-glass window and sipped at his coffee. "Someone moving in next to Doc's?" he guessed, staring at the beehive of activity taking place adjacent to the veterinary clinic across the street. Oddly, no one else in the diner seemed to take much notice. Instead, the other customers' eyes, all male, were fixed on the rest room door.

Lucy swiped at the counter with a worn, greasy rag. "Looks that way. Couple of fellas stopped by a few days ago, then again yesterday. Said they're surveyors, come to see if the bridge over the creek needs repair. They're supposed to sit here a while and decide whether or not we need a traffic light and a bit of road widenin' afore they leave." Shrugging, she patted at her iron gray hair. "Seemed like nice enough fellas to me."

Daniel watched as the men made several trips from a black van to the office and back again, their arms loaded with what looked to be computer equipment. The hairs at the back of his neck rose, but he dismissed the eerie feeling. He'd done a damn fine job of covering his and Will's tracks and hadn't varied their boring routine since they'd moved here. Besides, if the Warfields had found them, he was fairly certain they would simply charge in with a sheriff and a court order. The sheriff would handcuff him, and the Warfields would take Will. They wouldn't bother with setting up surveillance or stocking an office.

The door to the rest room opened, then closed with a bang and Daniel whipped his head around. Coffee mug halfway to his mouth, he froze at the sight of the girl, a young woman, really, standing with her back against the diner wall.

"Hey, Zara."

"Morning, Zara."

"Zara darlin', I sure could use a refill."

As if stunned by the number of admirers and their requests, the woman sucked in a breath, calling attention to the fullness of her breasts as they pushed against the cotton of her modestly cut T-shirt.

"Just ignore them bozos and come on over here, honey." Lucy waved a callused hand. "This here's one of the local fellas I was tellin' you about."

The woman threw Lucy a megawatt smile, showing perfect white teeth. "Yes, ma'am."

Daniel felt his throat close up as the prickle in the back of his neck amplified to the tenth power. Zara walked—no—she glided across the pitted, black-and-white linoleum, her long denim-clad legs extending much like a Thoroughbred's did when it made its way down the stretch.

"Close yer mouth, Dan'l," he thought he heard Lucy snort.

Zara held out a pale, ringless hand and, robotlike, he grasped it in his own. Her hand was smooth and cool and . . . tingly? And the feel of it caused his stomach to tighten.

"I'm Zara. It's a pleasure to meet you."

Feeling gutshot, he inhaled to the sound of Lucy's mulish laughter. "Daniel Murphy," he muttered.

"What'd I tell you, honey?" Lucy continued. "Men in these parts'll have their tongues on the ground and their peckers pointin' due north for days, once word you're workin' here gets out. Now you set to helping Tomas scrub the grill like I taught you last night, hear?"

Her face flushed scarlet, but Zara's brilliant smile never wavered. "Yes, ma'am."

"Don't let her boss you around, Zara," Daniel commented, testing her name on his tongue. The unusual word called up the memory of a serene yet breathtakingly beautiful constellation he'd once studied. All blushing pinks and brilliant blues, the star cluster had enthralled him throughout college and into graduate school. It had become a distant memory until that moment when he saw this woman and heard her name.

"I don't mind," Zara answered. "It's my job, and I have a lot to learn." She turned and walked around the counter into the kitchen, accompanied by another round of admiring glances.

Lucy shook her head, and the bun at the nape of her neck swayed from side to side. Raising her lively brown eyes, she scolded the room in general. "You fellas should be ashamed of yourselves, tauntin' a poor girl like that. She's a respectable young lady, and I'll slap the first man who says she ain't. Now drink yer coffee and get to work afore I call Jay and tell him what a bunch of lazy jackasses he's got on his payroll. Tomas is makin' chili today, so y'all better step quick around lunchtime."

Sheepishly, the men downed their coffee, laid money on the tables and counter, and moved as one, making their way out of the diner. The last stragglers gazed longingly over the pickup ledge into the kitchen as they walked out the door backward.

Lucy brayed again. "Men. The lot of 'em ain't worth the spit it takes to lick a stamp." She eyed Daniel shrewdly. "Thought someone might have told you about my new waitress by now. You been hidin' under a rock for the past two days or what?"

*I've been concentrating on shooting stars*, thought Daniel, though it was obvious from meeting Zara that in doing so, he'd missed the best sight to appear in this backwater town in years.

"I had a motor to pull, and Will's been spending a lot of time at the creek. Neither of us has had a chance to catch up on the local gossip." He craned his neck to stare over Lucy's stooped shoulder and got a good view of the new waitress's gently rounded hips as she scrubbed at the massive, stainless-steel griddle. "Where'd she come from?" was all he managed to croak out with his next breath.

Lucy refilled his coffee mug. "She was hitchin' her way to Denton when the truck she was riding in stopped for breakfast yesterday mornin'. Saw the sign in my window and asked if she could have the job. Being a smart woman, I said yes."

Daniel hunkered down over his coffee mug. "And you think a girl who looks like Julia Roberts's younger sister wants to work in Button Creek?" He shook his head. "Have you taken a good look at the woman?"

Lucy tossed a glance over her shoulder, then rested her arms on the counter and leaned in close, showing a set of stained teeth. "Don't know nothin' 'bout your Miss Roberts. I just know that Zara's a good girl. She don't wear makeup or fancy-smelling perfume, and she dresses more modest than most young women nowadays. Came here with nothin' but a backpack and a desire to work, and that was good enough for me."

"Where's she staying?"

"Cabin number two. But don't tell that to any of those randy bronc riders out there. I don't want any of 'em waitin' to surprise her some night after Hank's closes."

Daniel thought back to the stories he'd heard about Lucy when he'd first moved to Button Creek. Rumor had it she'd been in love with a local cowboy from the time she was seventeen. When the fellow left to ride the rodeo circuit, he broke his neck trying to tame a Brahma bull and shattered Lucy's heart in the bargain, which had blackened her opinion of cowboys to this day. Over the years, she'd become a shrewd businesswoman. Besides making a go of the luncheonette, she rented cabins to anyone needing a place to stay while passing through. It was obvious she'd seen a potential gold mine in hiring a waitress who looked like Zara.

"So why are you trusting me?" he asked. "For all you know, I could be just as randy as one of those cowboys you're always complaining about."

"Shoot," Lucy teased, "you're 'bout as much like them bronco boys as President George W. You don't smoke, cuss, or visit Hank's Hole in the Wall, and you're a family man with a little boy so cute I'd like to put him in my pocket and take him home. I'd even think about trusting you with my own daughter"— Lucy winked—"if I'da had one."

"Thanks . . . I think." Daniel frowned. Setting his cup on the counter, he turned his attention across the street. The black van was still there, but the office the men had been moving into looked as if it was shut up tight. Suddenly, he was more concerned about the would-be road surveyors than the beautiful woman in the kitchen. "Have those men been in today?"

Lucy peered in the direction Daniel's gaze had settled. "Sure have. Rented cottages one and three. So far, they've paid cash for everything and been real friendly in the bargain. Won't hear no complaints about 'em from me."

"And they said they worked for the Texas Department of Transportation?"

She scrunched up pencil-thin eyebrows. "Don't remember 'em sayin' exactly who they worked for, but a wider road and safer bridge might bring everybody in town more business. From what I see, you could use it."

"You're right about that," Daniel agreed, swirling the last of the coffee in his mug. "Guess I'd better get back to the garage. It's close to eight."

He raised his gaze to the kitchen pass-through and found Zara peering at him, her wide blue eyes intense. "If you need anything in the way of supplies, feel free to stop by Murphy's Last Chance, and I'll see what I can do."

Zara propped an elbow on the ledge and rested her softly rounded chin in the heel of her hand. "I just might do that, once I get a few days' worth of tips in my pocket."

"I don't usually issue credit, but I'd be willing to make an exception in your—" *Open mouth, insert foot,* Daniel thought, biting his tongue at the suggestive words. "Uh, if you're really strapped, I mean. That is, I'd do it for anyone new in town."

Her lips raised in a Mona Lisa smile, warming him to his hairline. "Thank you. That's a very kind offer."

Figuring his face had to be as red as Del Calverson's pickup truck, Daniel tried for a halfway-dignified exit. He laid a dollar on the counter, tipped his Stetson toward Lucy, and made his way to the door, hoping he hadn't made too big a fool of himself. It had been a long while since he'd felt anything more than passing interest in a woman, and damn if he'd just let his tongue swipe the floor over a stranger.

But he was still able-brained enough to cast a final glance at the shiny black van across the street. Since going on the run with his son, he'd learned to be suspicious of anything overtly odd. Now he had two quandaries to mull over: Why would a woman who looked like Zara show up in a two-bit diner in the middle of nowhere, and why would the Texas Department of Transportation take the time to send surveyors and their costly equipment to a tiny hole-in-the wall like Button Creek?

Zara wiped her sweaty brow and got comfortable in her cabin. When Miss Lucy had first taken her inside, she'd been surprised by the primitive cottage and its adequate living space. A worn table and chairs stood just inside the front door. The wall to the left held a row of cabinets, a sink and cooking appliance and, as she followed the wall around, a small refrigerator.

She walked into the next room to the double bed Lucy had assured her had a new mattress and clean linens. A chest of drawers with an oval mirror above it stood in the corner, then came a built-out area that housed a closet and small bathroom. Next to that was a green-and-gold plaid sofa, a standing lamp, and a low table with a television and VCR. Tucked in a back-corner window was an efficient but noisy metal box made specifically for cooling the inside air.

Luckily for her, the cabin came with the salary she earned as a waitress, because she needed her money to purchase food and additional clothing. Though she'd been told by Lucy she could take her meals at the diner, the fat, salt, and sugar served there wasn't exactly her idea of proper nutrition.

Exhausted, she walked to the bathroom and turned on the taps, then removed her pants, underthings, and shirt, and hung everything neatly in the closet. After finding a towel, soap, and washcloth, she stood in the warm spray and washed her body and hair, stepped out, dried herself off, and readied for bed. Without a sleeping gown, she had to slide naked between the sheets.

Though she was considered a healthy physical specimen, the long hours she'd worked yesterday and today were far more than the amount she would have spent toiling at home. She envied her companions, who'd been sent to the larger cities. They had been trained for more professional occupations in order to blend with their surroundings. She'd had the dubious luck to be matched with a man who lived in a remote area where women didn't have much to do except housework or farm labor. Still, it would only be for a short while. She was strong. She could handle twelve-hour days of standing on her feet and serving others.

When she'd left for the evening, Lucy had reminded her that the diner was closed Saturday morning and usually had a light crowd for lunch. Saturday night was a whole different story. People came from miles to have dinner at the restaurant, then went to the Hole in the Wall to kick up their heels and listen to the live band Hank always booked for the weekend.

When Miss Lucy had asked if she enjoyed country western and was she partial to something called the two-step, Zara had replied that she wasn't sure. The older woman had advised her to use the morning to rest up, because if Zara did decide to visit the Hole, every man there would want to take a turn teaching her how to dance. From the sound of it, she'd be so tired she'd sleep right into Monday, which meant she would miss her one day off.

Zara wondered if her fellow travelers were having the same stimulating yet confusing time as she was. They had separated two nights before and weren't allowed contact with each other again until they met at the rendezvous site. She hoped the others had found gainful employment, or at least a logical reason for being in their target areas.

Raising her hand, she was immediately comforted by the sight of her one link to home—the bracelet on her left wrist. Nine stones winked at her in the glimmer of moonlight slanting over the bed. Three green, three red, three clear as water, the emeralds, rubies, and diamonds—as they were called on Earth—were held together by a metal known here as platinum.

Touching an index finger to the stone in her right earlobe, she recalled the past few days. She had met some local women, and would have liked to ask them about their lives, but meeting women was not the reason she was in Button Creek. She had but a singular goal: meet one man, interact with him, and make the rendezvous site at the appointed time.

She needed to find Robert Lotello but, so far, there hadn't been a Robert, Bobby, Rob, or Bert in the entire group of men to whom she'd been introduced. Yet her information could not be incorrect. Her locator told her Robert Lotello lived within a mile radius of the center of Button Creek. And she had to find him in order to succeed.

Her usually organized thoughts tumbled like waves to the shore. The men she'd met thus far had been interesting and, if she'd been able to ignore her mission statement, might even have been acceptable. Some were old, many were young, a few were nice-looking, but, if she'd had the right to choose, her target would have been the one called Daniel Murphy.

Murphy was tall, with the form of a man who worked hard for a living. He had dark hair and penetrating eyes the color of the coffee she had served by the gallon these two mornings. His rough-hewn face with its impressively carved nose and squared jaw appealed to her as had no other she'd met thus far. Even with the scar that ran from his left eyebrow to his temple, a man like Daniel Murphy would be considered desirable on her planet. And he had fathered a son—the correct criterion for a viable match.

Smiling to herself, Zara thought of the way she had passed the time on her journey. All of the women had fantasized over the physical attributes of their target, saying foolish things as they'd expressed aloud their idea of the perfect subject. Murphy would have fulfilled any one of their fantasies. He certainly fulfilled hers.

Unfortunately, she did not have the right to choose. She had to remember to treat the one called Murphy exactly as she did all the others and keep him at a distance. She would give herself one week to locate Robert Lotello. If she didn't meet him in that amount of time, she would be forced to do something potentially dangerous. She would have to use her instruments.

Settling to sleep, Zara closed her eyes, but visions of Murphy crept into her thoughts. She could tell by his touch he was definitely a healthy man . . . exactly what her planet lacked at the present time.

She punched her pillow and turned on her side. Mornings on Earth came quickly. She had to erase her frivolous thoughts about the gas station owner, keep her focus, and get a good night's sleep. No matter how drawn she felt toward Daniel Murphy, her mission had one simple goal.

To become impregnated by the man named Robert Lotello.

# Two

Daniel spooned out canned string beans, careful not to let them touch the hamburger patty or rice that shared space on Will's dinner plate. A sudden memory of the way Lucy fed his son when they'd first arrived in Button Creek made him smile. The kindly older woman had made a joke of the fussy way Will wanted his food to be kept separate; she'd even used a special divided dish whenever he came to the diner for a meal.

He carried their supper to the table and waited for Will to finish chugging down his milk. "Find anything interesting at the creek today?"

Will wiped his moo-juice mustache with the back of his hand. "Just some more of that slimy yellow stuff we collected yesterday. I used a stick to scrape it into a jar and put it in the fridge, like you told me, and I put some in a plastic bag in the freezer, to be on the safe side. Want to see?"

Daniel stared at his son, who looked so eager, so bright-eyed and intelligent, and wondered if he had done the right thing when he'd taken the boy from his grandparents. Was Will missing out on the good part of having a complete family, a woman's gentle hands to tuck him in at night, or a grandmother waiting for him with homemade cookies when he returned from school?

Right now, Will reminded him so much of Rebecca it hurt Daniel's eyes, never mind his heart. If she'd been honest and told him about her pregnancy, they might have found a way to be together. They might have found a way to make it work.

"Dad? I asked if you wanted to see it," Will said a second time.

"Hm? Oh, I already got a good look at the stuff, remember?" Daniel answered with a half grimace. "Just thought you might have found something new." He lifted a forkful of rice to his mouth and recalled the check he'd made of the goo the first time he'd had a chance to inspect the creek with Will. Aside from being a little like not-quite-set Jell-O, the yellowish substance seemed to have no discernible toxic effect on the wildlife or trees, no smell, and no taste. He knew because he'd taken a lick of the slime when Will wasn't looking and found it to be bland and, so far, harmless.

"Do you think it has something to do with the shooting stars?"

The sound of hope flooding his son's voice made Daniel grin. "Only if you can give me the name of a space traveler who'd want to touch anything that disgusting."

Will rolled his eyes. "Then what do you think it is?"

Tongue in cheek, Daniel made a full-fledged effort to be serious. "Looked like snot to me."

"Ee-uuu." Will giggled. "It did to me, too, but you said I wasn't allowed to say gross stuff when we're eating."

"You're right, you're not. Now finish your supper, and I'll take you across the street for a piece of Miss Lucy's lemon meringue pie to make up for my poor table manners."

Will proceeded to devour his food like a starving man. After cleaning his plate, he said, "Dad? I've been thinking . . ."

Daniel carried their dirty dishes to the sink, turned on the hot water, and added a squirt of liquid detergent. "I thought I smelled rubber burning."

Groaning, Will cleared the table of napkins and glasses. "Funny. Real funny."

"Well, don't keep me in suspense. What were you thinking?" Daniel asked, waiting for the sink to fill.

"About the sno—I mean slime. Could we maybe take the stuff to a lab in Denton or Dallas and have it analyzed?"

Methodically, Daniel washed and rinsed the dishes, then set them in the drainer. "Guess we could send it to the county agricultural bureau and tell them we found it on our trees. That wouldn't be too far from the truth."

"We did find it on a tree. And on the ground and the rocks along the creek, too." Will propped his elbows on the counter and sighed. "If we knew what the stuff was, maybe it would tell us something about those lights."

It had been three nights since Will had last viewed the shooting stars in his telescope, and the kid was bummed. Daniel was creative, but not magician enough to make things appear in the sky that shouldn't be there just to keep the boy entertained.

"Look on the bright side. The lights are gone, but you, Grunt, and Ricky have fresh victims to pester—those two surveyors who moved in next to Doc Mayberry's office."

Will raised a shoulder. "They're not gonna be any fun."

"Oh? How can you tell?"

"This afternoon, while you were working on Mr. Beldon's truck, I ran into them on my way back from the creek. They were carrying boxes and tripods and a bunch of stuff I didn't recognize. And they weren't very friendly, either."

So that was where the two men had been, thought Daniel. When he hadn't seen them in the diner that morning he'd let himself linger over coffee as he'd covertly eyed Lucy's new waitress. Busy daydreaming, he'd forgotten to check for the men and their black van again. It figured they would head for Button Creek to start their work, but he had to ask the next question for his own peace of mind.

"Did they talk to you? Ask you about anything?"

Will quirked up a corner of his mouth, letting the dimple in his right cheek show. "They said good morning and asked what I had in the jar. I told 'em tadpoles."

Daniel tried not to lecture as he advised his son. "Will, I know you think this thing with the stars was special, but I don't want you to lie about it."

"What was I supposed to say? That I was hunting aliens or looking for a UFO landing site? Nuh-uh. If we find anything, it's gonna' be our discovery and nobody else's. I don't want to share with a bunch of dweebs."

"Dweebs?" Daniel suppressed a smile. "And what, pray tell, is your definition of a dweeb?"

"You know. Guys who try to look cool, but they're not."

"What did these men do that made you think they were trying to *look cool*?"

Will scrunched up his forehead as if thinking hard. "Well for one thing, the short guy had on dress shoes. You know, like the kind my health teacher Mr. Nesbitt wears. No one but a dweeb would wear shoes like that to stomp around in the woods or a creek."

"Is that all, or did these dweebs commit a few other fashion felonies?"

"Da-aad. I'm serious. The taller guy had on the right kind of boots, but they were brand-new, and he was wearing those thin rubber gloves, like a doctor or something. Everybody knows you need the leather kind to do outdoor work proper-like. And you should have seen their clothes. *Jeesh!*"

"All right, I'll bite. What about their clothes?"

"Nerdy. Their jeans were all stiff and clean, kind'a like when you're going camping for the first time ever and your parents buy you all new stuff. They looked like nerds trying to be cool."

Daniel filed the information away for later and worked on Will's tolerance level for those who dressed differently. "Maybe it's their first time on the job, or their old clothes wore out and they bought new just for this assignment."

"All at the same time? I do-on't think so."

"Okay, so they're fashion-challenged dweebs. Keep tabs on them if you want, but if they aren't friendly, stay out of their way. And if you don't find anything more than that yellow goo in the next day or so, I think the shooting star incident is over."

Shoulders drooping, Will hung his head, and Daniel ruffled the boy's hair. "Don't worry. There are enough sights in the heavens to keep you occupied for the whole summer—for the rest of your life, if you're lucky. We'll find something else to concentrate on really soon." Daniel hung up the dishrag and let the water out of the sink. "Now, how about that pie?"

Lucy's was even more crowded than it had been the other morning. It looked as if Daniel wasn't the only man who thought about hanging out at the luncheonette on a regular basis just to sneak a peek at the pretty new waitress. Scanning the room, he spotted Zara serving a table near the plate-glass windows. Like a beacon at the end of a dark tunnel, her smile lit up the restaurant.

Fending off the urge to go to her and demand she focus that brilliant glow on him alone, Daniel did his best to look disinterested as he sauntered to the counter and took the seat next to Will.

Cleaning rag in hand, Lucy turned from the serving ledge and made a beeline toward them. "Let me guess. Two slices of lemon meringue pie, right?"

Will stared in openmouthed amazement. "How come you always know what we're going to order, Miss Lucy? It's no fun if you keep telling us what we want."

Lucy winked at Daniel. "I'm a woman, boy. All women know what men want. It's an instinct."

"It is?" Will asked in disbelief. "How come?"

"Well, God only had so much he could pass out at creation. He gave men the muscles and women the brains. Leastways, it seems that way to me."

"Thanks, Lucy," Daniel said, deciding he wasn't in the mood for their usual banter over which was the superior sex. "That's just what I wanted my impressionable son to hear."

Lucy brought over two huge pieces of pie and set them down smartly. "Don't go gettin' your shorts in a bundle, Dan'l. Just because you're smarter than most of the men around here don't make you special. Now I got to get in the kitchen and check on tomorrow's pies. Blueberry. And Tomas is makin' his special baked ham and mashed potatoes with redeye gravy. How's that sound, Will?"

The boy turned plaintive eyes to his father. "Blueberry pie is our favorite, Dad. Maybe Miss Lucy would let me work off dinner for both of us if I asked her real nice."

Daniel nodded, as if seriously considering his son's suggestion. The last time he checked his bank balance they were living well within their budget, but he didn't want Will to take their financial situation for granted. The Warfields' abundance of money had been one of the reasons he'd been forced to take the boy in the first place. Rebecca's parents had raised their daughter to worship the stuff, which in turn had become one of the sticking points in their short-lived relationship. Daniel had vowed his son would learn to respect financial solvency, but would never use it as a weapon or a bargaining chip against those he loved.

He raised his voice just enough to carry into the kitchen. "Lucy, you got any work Will could do to earn a plate of that ham and a piece of pie for tomorrow night's supper?"

Lucy's head popped into view. "I'm sure Tomas would appreciate the chance to spend time with Maria and the baby. Hold on while I ask him if he'd like a little help."

Daniel could see the tilt of Lucy's head as she talked to Tomas Herrera, her chief cook. Tomas and his wife, Maria, had lived in a trailer behind the diner for the past three years. Maria had been Lucy's waitress until two weeks ago, when she had delivered a baby girl in the back of the trailer. Daniel liked the young couple, figuring they added a pleasant mix to the interesting characters of Button Creek.

Seconds later she ambled to the window and cracked a smile. "Tomas says thanks. There's crates that need stacking at the back of the kitchen, and I'm thinkin' Zara could use a little help filling the salt-shakers and ketchup bottles. The rest room trash bins need to be emptied, and the can in my trailer has to go out, too. Think you could handle all that?"

"Yes, ma'am," Will said quickly, as if fearful someone else would jump at the chance to perform the chores.

"All right. You stick around 'til closing time, and Zara will tell you what to do."

"Who's Zara?" Will whispered. He took a big bite of pie and tried to sit tall enough to see into the kitchen.

Daniel spun the boy's stool around until it pointed toward the back wall, where Zara stood joking with another table of men—boys really, who worked at Pepperdine's for the summer. Fighting the absurd urge to march over and drag her to his side, he bent to Will's ear. "That's Zara. Lucy's new waitress."

"Oh." Will's single syllable word held just the right amount of reverence to tell Daniel the kid felt gut-punched, exactly as he had when he'd first seen the woman. No surprise Zara would be his son's first crush.

The waitress glided to the counter and stood next

to Will. "Could I have two more slices of pie, Lucy? And is there any more chili left in back?"

"Pie, yes. Chili, no," came Lucy's muffled voice from somewhere in the kitchen.

Zara turned and shook her head at the table nearest the rest room door. "Sorry, gentlemen. Just the pie, like I thought. That okay with you?"

The good-natured moans and groans made Daniel, Will, and Zara laugh at the same time, until finally, she settled her gaze on Will. "Hello, Daniel. And who is this young man?"

Pride welling, Daniel suddenly felt the urge to show off his progeny. "This is William Daniel Murphy, but he answers to Will." He tapped Will on the shoulder. "Say hello, son."

"Hullo," the boy mumbled, his eyes glazing over at the sight of Zara's smile.

"Hi." She held out her hand to Will and waited until he found the sense to clasp it in his own. "I heard Miss Lucy say you'd be helping me tonight. You about ready?"

Will stared at his palm as if he'd just shaken hands with one of the Dallas Cowboys. "Uh-huh."

"Okay. Just let me get that pie for Skeeter and Joe, and we can get started." Touching the tip of her earlobe with one finger, she slid her sapphire gaze to Daniel. "Are you going to wait for him, or do you want me to walk him home when we're through?"

"I'll wait. Thanks."

Zara nodded, then strolled to an empty table and pocketed her tip. She loaded dishes onto a tray, wiped the table, and carried the tray to the kitchen as grace-fully as if she were serving in Buckingham Palace. Daniel felt justified making the comparison because he'd spent a year studying at Oxford while in gradu-ate school. Besides the Warfields, he'd been exposed to plenty of people who'd lived a life of wealth and privilege.

Will gobbled the last bite of his pie and jumped off the stool to tag after Zara. One by one, the patrons left their money on the tables and filed into the warm night air. Seconds later, Lucy called good night, and he heard the rear door bang shut. Will and Zara started to fill the saltshakers, leaving Daniel to peruse at his leisure.

Zara was tall, but he'd already noticed that her legs seemed to take up half of her substantial frame. And he meant substantial in the most complimentary of terms. With well-defined muscles in her arms, full breasts, and nicely curved waist and hips, she was put together like a woman who could handle herself anywhere. He could imagine her as a professional tennis player, maybe a volleyball or track star. Given the majestic aura she walked in, he figured Zara prob-ably could do whatever she set her mind to.

Her hair, pulled into a low ponytail at the back of her head, was the color of burnished gold, her skin the hue of heavy cream. A patrician nose sat above a generous mouth and rounded chin. Straight, dark brows hovered over clear, blue eyes, as if waiting to add punctuation to her thoughts.

Daniel couldn't help but think how out of place she

was in Texas, home of many cosmetically enhanced, big-haired women. Was he the only one who could see she stuck out like an orchid in a dandelion patch?

She laid a hand on Will's shoulder and guided him into the kitchen. A door slammed, then she was back at the counter.

"I sent him to Lucy's trailer to get her trash. After that, he's going to stack crates. All that's left are the bins in the rest rooms, and he'll be finished. Do you want a coffee refill while you wait?"

Daniel opened then closed his mouth, as if English had become a foreign language. "Um." There, he'd gotten out the first syllable. "No, thanks."

Zara nodded. "He's a nice little boy. You should be proud."

"I am."

She tucked a wayward strand of gold behind her ear. Her *perfect* ear, he thought, noting the good-sized diamond stud she wore in each delicate-looking lobe.

"You own the gas station across the street, right?"

"Yep. Bought it from Scooter Button's estate about four years ago. We make a good living." God, what made him want to sound like a suitor totaling his assets to a potential fiancée?

"I bet you do. And you must know just about everybody in a five-mile radius. I got the idea from Lucy that everyone who lives around here has passed through your station or the diner at one time or another. She says you're the only convenience store for quite a ways."

"Have to drive fifteen miles south or twenty miles

toward the lake to find another, and my gas is cheaper by two cents a gallon. I keep up with my competition." Great, now he was flaunting his business acumen. *You're pathetic, Murphy.*

Zara removed her apron and set it on the counter, and Daniel couldn't help but notice her only other bit of jewelry: a sparkling, gem-encrusted bracelet encircling her left wrist.

"Well, that's good to know, if I ever have the need— for gas. I don't own a car, but I could use some groceries. Things like fresh fruit, vegetables, whole grain bread. Do you carry those kinds of products at your store?"

"Sorry, all my vegetables are canned or frozen, ditto the fruit, but there's a produce stand up toward the lake. You could drive there one morning, if Lucy is willing to lend you her truck."

She wrinkled her nose. "Um. I don't think that would be a good idea."

"Sure it would. Lucy's a generous woman. She'd let you—"

"I don't have the proper license."

"Oh? Well, she could take you to Denton to apply for a new one, if you lost yours. Or maybe I could—"

"I . . . um . . . I don't know how to drive."

Daniel blinked his surprise. Shoot, didn't just about every man and woman in America over the age of seventeen know how to drive a car? The only ones who didn't, he remembered, were a few born and raised in Manhattan. But his logic had one minor flaw. He was pretty good at placing accents, and although Zara's was definitely refined, it was not quite East Coast. But that didn't mean much. She could have been an army brat, or maybe her family had done a lot of moving around when she was young.

Not wanting to come right out and ask, he took a guess. "Then you must be a city girl. New Yorkers don't need to drive when there are subways, buses, and cabs to get them where they want to go."

"Is that where you're from? New York City?"

"Yeah . . . we . . . I mean, no. I am from the East Coast, though." *Good going, Murphy, you almost revealed something no one else in town knows to a woman you just met. And isn't it interesting the way she'd turned the tables and answered your question with one of her own?*

"So tell me again the reason you don't drive?" he asked, as she swung around to clean the restaurant coffeemaker.

"Just never had a need to learn, I guess. Now, what was it you said you carried in your store?"

Daniel ran a hand through his hair. Okay, so she was politely telling him to let the question drop. He had plenty of secrets he kept under his hat. Was it really such a big deal she didn't want to list her reasons for not being able to drive? "I sell bottled water and soda, a choice of frozen meats and cold cuts, some paper goods and canned food, that kind of thing. Feel free to stop by tomorrow after the breakfast crowd thins out and take a look."

She turned and smiled at him, and though it was close to nine o'clock at night, Daniel felt as if the sun were shining.

"I just might do that."

The back door creaked, and Will raced in from the kitchen. "All done at Miss Lucy's, Zara. You want me to do the baskets in the rest rooms now?"

"That would be fine, Will. Thanks."

She disappeared into the kitchen, and Daniel waited for his son to finish his chores. When he'd brought the last of the trash from the bathrooms, they called good-bye. Zara answered, but she didn't come to the counter again.

Zara slipped into the cabin and rested her backside against the closed door. Running a hand through her hair, she finger-combed the waves as she willed her breath to calm and her heart to slow its frantic pounding. Everything had gone just fine today until Murphy walked into the diner with the child. The sight of the bright-eyed little boy with his mop of brown curls and dark, twinkling eyes had pulled a string she'd swear was tied directly to her womb. They looked so happy together, so . . . right, sitting side by side as they ate their pie and joked with one another.

How her world would have cherished a child such as Will and the man who had fathered him.

The second she touched his hand, she knew Will had a health problem, but from the impression she received it didn't seem life-threatening. Still, she couldn't remember treating anyone on her planet for the same condition.

Tugging the memory chip implanted in her earlobe, she searched for the illness. She'd sensed his lungs were involved, but the rest was a jumble. Asthma was a possibility, as well as emphysema and pneumonia, but she couldn't quite put her finger on the exact problem because those conditions had long been eradicated from her world. She sighed at the limits of the program, still fairly certain his condition wasn't severe, and tucked her concern away for later. At present, she had a more serious matter to consider.

Daniel Murphy.

It was his second visit in as many days. Perversely, it was the second time he'd made her stomach quiver and her pulse quicken. He hadn't leered or pushed, as did some of the men she waited on, but she'd felt those keen brown eyes admiring her the way she imagined a man would if he was interested in a woman.

And for some unknown reason, his curiosity had taken hold tonight. Instead of keeping the conversation impersonal, he'd asked pointed questions. It had taken quick thinking to call up the evasive tactics she'd been taught during training and avoid a direct answer. Fortunately, he'd let go when he sensed her reluctance, but something told her that, with Murphy, her mumbled excuses hadn't been enough to satisfy his need to know.

The elders had been aware the travelers would be lacking some of the basic Earth necessities when they arrived: social security cards, birth certificates, and a license to drive their motorized vehicles, to name a few. In their haste to get the mission up and running in time to meet an optimum flight path, they had concentrated on the more immediate task of matching the women to their targets and making sure they had proper instructions. It was now apparent they had erred in not giving the women a form of identification.

Leave it to an intelligent and quick-witted man like Murphy to spot the inconsistencies and question them.

She sighed as she walked across the room and got ready for bed. She'd been warned to keep her distance from everyone except her target, but with his dark wavy hair and compelling brown eyes, how could she not be drawn to Murphy? If they lived on her planet, it was probable they would be keeping company, exploring mutual interests, and planning a life together. The union would be approved because he had fathered a son, but something told her their mating would have been more than a biological act. Even now, she could recall the tension that had bubbled between them like some chemical experiment run amok.

She was not supposed to react this way to a stranger. She had no business letting her emotions erupt the second he walked into a room. Robert Lotello was the only man with whom she was supposed to interact in any personal way. The success of the mission depended on her, on each of the women, being able to conceive a male child from their targets.

Climbing into bed, she thought again of Will. How wonderful it would be to bear a child like him. But his father could not be Daniel Murphy. No matter the attraction between them, she had to control her urge to get close and concentrate her energies on locating her intended match.

She had to find the man called Robert Lotello. And she had to find him soon.

## Three

"So tell me, Zara, how come a smart gal like you never learned how to drive?"

As Murphy predicted, Miss Lucy did invite her to come along on her Saturday morning junket to the farmers' market. They were in Lucy's battered red truck, zipping along well above the speed limit. The older woman was perched on two pillows while her feet were planted firmly on what looked to be wooden blocks strapped to the pedals on the floor.

"I guess I was never interested," Zara replied, amazed at how easily she found it to lie. Though she'd been ordered to manipulate the truth to make a success of her mission, back home it wouldn't have crossed her mind to tell a falsehood for any reason. "What are those blue flowers growing along the side of the road called? They're very pretty."

"Bluebonnets, the state flower of Texas. The orange

ones are Indian paintbrush. There's black-eyed Susan and . . ."

She breathed a sigh, relieved she'd been able to get Lucy involved in a botany lesson. She knew perfectly well the names of every plant and form of wildlife one might run across in north Texas, but she had to do something to distract the woman. Lucy's tenacity in digging into Zara's private life was quite daunting. The inhabitants of Earth, it was rumored throughout the galaxies, were too wrapped up in their own existence to bother worrying about anyone else. The fact that most of them thought they were the only intelligent life-form in the universe proved that theory to be true.

Unfortunately, her instructions on learning how to deal with the people here were sadly lacking when it came to Lucy Coombs and the other residents of Button Creek.

"Where'd you say you were from again?" Lucy asked, breaking into Zara's musings.

"Um . . . Oklahoma. Northern Oklahoma. How much farther to the market?"

"A mile or so. Had some friends lived up in the panhandle. Place called Tyrone, near Hooker. You know that area?"

"I was from the eastern side of the state, toward Arkansas. Is that the market, there on the right?"

"Yup. Feel free to take a basket from the back and fill it with whatever you want. If you think you're bein' cheated, just come and get me. I wouldn't pay more than a quarter for a good-sized tomato or squash. Beans is fifty cents a pound, if they let you pick through 'em on your own. Got that?"

"Yes, ma'am." Zara came around to Lucy's side of the truck and helped her from her goose-feather throne. "Do you need me to carry anything?"

"Nope." Lucy marched to the tailgate and grabbed a stack of empty bushel baskets. "I just exchange these empties and the boys bring the full ones over. I been comin' here so long most of 'em weren't born when I made my first trip. They all do just about whatever I tell 'em. You'll see."

Zara was impressed by the woman's cockiness. Anxious to see how Lucy handled financial negotiations, she followed demurely to the first stand, set up in a semicircle under three yellow-and-white-striped umbrellas.

"Jasper, you old coon hound, what looks good today?" Lucy demanded. "And don't try and tell me everything. Those beans I brought home last week was downright puny. Had to throw most of 'em out while I was stringin' 'em."

Jasper, a skinny, wizened fellow who had to be at least as old as Lucy, spat a wad of thick, brown tobacco into the dust at his feet. "Now, Lucy, I find that hard to believe. Sam here"—he nodded to a younger version of himself—"picked those beans personally. And Sam wouldn't let us sell nothin' anyone'd consider puny. Isn't that right, Sam?"

"Right, Grandpa," replied Sam, his eyes trained on Zara. "I believe Miss Lucy's jokin' with us."

"Hmmph," Lucy grumped loudly, sifting her hands

through the huge pile of dark green vegetables on the table.

"And who might this pretty lady be?" Sam asked when Zara grinned at Lucy's bluster.

"Zara—" Lucy gave a snort. "Shoot girl, I don't even know your last name. Maybe you should do the introductions yourself."

Zara held out a hand to Jasper, then Sam, and said quickly, "Just Zara. It's a pleasure to meet you. And I think your vegetables look delicious."

The positive comment was all it took to get the best price. Unfortunately, while Lucy dickered over the choices, Zara couldn't help but stare in mild confusion. For some reason, the produce she'd studied from pictures didn't match everything displayed on the table. She recognized beans, tomatoes, and broccoli, because they were similar to vegetables on her planet, but not the long green vegetables or their yellow counterparts, or a few of the others. In the end, she copied Lucy's order on a smaller scale and hoped everything would taste good. By the time she thanked him, Sam even threw in a jar of his mother's homemade chutney and a loaf of freshly made whole wheat bread.

"Our fruit's not ready for picking yet, but Fred over there"—Jasper gestured to the stand across the way—"imports his from the southern part of the state. Just tell him I said he should take good care of you."

Zara paid with her tip money and headed toward the mounds of fruit arranged on a long rectangular wooden table. Smiling at Fred, a man who looked old enough to be an elder on her planet, she reiterated Jasper's last instructions.

"I'll do that, sweet cheeks, if you tell me your name," Fred said with a wink. His nut brown face creased into a teasing smile.

Before she could answer, Lucy, who had sneaked up from behind, tossed out a threat. "You stuff that tongue of yours right back in your mouth, Fred Smithers, or I'll tell Janine. This here's my new waitress, and she don't fool around with married men."

"Well, that's good to know, Miss Lucy. My grandson, Ronnie Paul, is fixin' to go to the Hole tonight. Maybe I'll tell him to stop by and have himself a little supper at your place. What would you say to that?"

"I'd be pleased to wait on your grandson, Mr. Smithers," Zara replied, positive the more men she met, the sooner she might find her target.

Looking the table over carefully, she was relieved to find that the fruit, especially her favorite—apples —made more sense, and dropped her choices into a bag. Satisfied with her purchases, she waited while Lucy chose several dozen baskets of berries, a bushel of apples and one of cherries, then watched the older woman proceed to another stall.

Finally on her own, she strolled to a refreshment stand for an ice-cold bottle of springwater and continued her tour of the block-long market. On the way, she stopped at a clothing stand and bought a pair of jeans, three T-shirts, and a denim skirt.

After walking back to the parking lot, she deposited her parcels in the rear of the truck and hoisted herself onto the front fender to sip at her water. It wasn't long before two men, both of whom she guessed to be in their midtwenties, sauntered over to introduce themselves.

The taller of the two removed his cowboy hat, gave a sly smile, and held out his hand. "Name's Ronnie Paul Smithers. Miss Lucy told us you were working at her restaurant. Are you gonna be at the Hole in the Wall tonight?"

Before she could answer, the second man took off his hat as well. "I'm Billy. Miss Lucy says you don't dance, and I was wondering, well, I'd be happy to teach you—if you're going to be there, that is."

"If I decide to go, you'll be the first person I look for," Zara said, trying to keep a straight face. Instead of going to the trouble of organizing a mission to Earth, it might have been more prudent if the elders had concentrated their efforts on sending a ship to beam up the men in Button Creek. If they were all as nice and well put together as the ones she'd met so far, her planet's struggles would have soon been over.

"So, maybe I'll see you tonight." Billy stared at the tips of his boots.

Ronnie Paul set his hat on his head. "Me too. It's been a pleasure." He jabbed his elbow in Billy's side, and the two men turned and walked away.

Admiring the fit of their jeans and the length of their stride, Zara finished her water. Though neither of them had appealed to her in the same visceral way as had Daniel Murphy, they were lovely males who seemed virile and strong. She was absolutely certain nothing was wrong with them physically or she would have picked up on it when their hands touched.

She took a calming breath and concentrated on the reason she was there. Her world had sent a major regiment to Earth long ago, with orders to assimilate themselves into the day-to-day existence of the planet.

Some of the explorers had become famous: a female aviatrix who disappeared without a trace; a supposed thief who parachuted from a plane and was never heard from again. They'd even retrieved groups of her people in an area known as the Bermuda Triangle. In reality, her compatriots had returned to help perpetuate the mystery the elders used to keep Earthlings aware of the possibility of aliens. When the time was right, everything would be revealed to the inhabitants of this planet. Meanwhile, all explorers who had served their purpose were brought home to share their knowledge and observations.

She was still amazed she'd been chosen as one of the nine who would save her race. Each of the travelers had been picked for her biological compatibility to an Earth male. More specifically, an Earth male who had a plethora of male sperm. Years of experimentation had rendered most of the men on her planet incapable of fathering a child. Without the male embryos with which she and each of her traveling companions hoped to return, her race would soon be but a memory. And now, it was up to her, a mere healer, to do something heroic for her world.

She'd been warned to keep her search a secret. All she knew was that Robert Lotello was in his midthirties, which would make him about ten years older than the boys she'd just met. Her search for Robert would have been easier if she'd been given his photograph, but it had been so long since the men had been chosen, the elders doubted an image would help. They had insisted she would recognize her match immediately because of the link they'd provided, and she wondered if that was true. So far, the only man to whom she'd felt connected had been Murphy, and he was not the man for her.

She tossed her empty water bottle into a trash bin. A few minutes later, Sam and Fred, along with several other helpers, began to arrive with bushels of produce. Miss Lucy trotted to the truck, her arms laden with huge bouquets of wildflowers, and Zara decided it was definitely a smart idea to hold her tongue. If the older woman found out she was looking for a man, especially one particular man, Lucy would never stop her prying questions.

Slipping from the fender, she helped with the flowers, gave Lucy a hand into the truck, and took her own seat. Once on the highway headed south, Lucy asked, "You get everything you need at Lily's clothing stand?"

Zara recalled the still-damp underwear she'd been rinsing out each night before bed. Most of the people here probably owned drawers full of the serviceable cotton stuff, instead of the single clammy set she'd been putting on each morning.

"I could use some underthings. Is there a shop we could get to and still make it back in time for lunch?"

Lucy kept her eyes on the road and her foot on the accelerator. "There's outlet stores south of Button Creek toward Denton. Tomas can manage without us for a while, if we're quick about it. You got any tip money left?"

Without thinking, Zara pulled a handful of paper and coins from her pocket and held it out. "Will this be enough?"

Lucy eyed the bills, then slanted her brown eyes in Zara's direction. "Depends on what you're buying. If it isn't, I'll advance you on your pay. It's not a problem."

Annoyed she was still having a difficult time calculating the currency on earth, Zara said a polite "thank-you," and concentrated on the passing scenery. It was nice of Lucy, offering to take her shopping when the woman had a business to run. She was beginning to like these outgoing, friendly people. Even though she'd arrived in Button Creek with little but the clothes on her back, she'd been treated with nothing but respect and kindness.

Maybe it wouldn't hurt to visit the Hole in the Wall tonight, after all. If she was lucky, Robert Lotello would be there. He might even be an expert at the two-step.

Saturday was Daniel's busiest day of the week. Most campers heading for the state park started their vacations on Saturday. Families intending to picnic or go boating on the lake usually chose that day as well.

Memorial Day would be here in a few weeks, which meant tourist season was right around the corner. His first customer of the morning stopped for gas just past dawn, and Daniel had worked steadily through the afternoon.

But no matter how hectic his day, he always closed at six in order to spend time with Will. Most nights they barbecued on the grill they kept on the overhang that held Will's telescope, but once in a while Daniel treated them to dinner at Lucy's or fast food and a movie in Denton. During the school year, he helped Will with his homework while they talked over their day. Now that school was out, Will had his horse to ride and friends to hang with, as did any normal kid. Sometimes he took the bus to the elementary school, where he could explore the library or tinker on the computers. In the evening there was television to watch while Daniel wrestled with the store's books.

Their Saturday nights were special. They played chess, read *Sky & Telescope* or other astronomy journals and talked about the stars, or better still, spent time focusing the Meade on distant planets while fantasizing what it might be like if they were able to visit. Rarely did Daniel leave his son alone in the evening to do something grown-up, like stop at the Hole in the Wall or have a friendly dinner with another adult.

But tonight was different. For the first time since they'd moved to Button Creek, Will had been invited to Ricky Pepperdine's house overnight.

"So, you're packed and ready for this sleepover

thing?" Daniel asked, trying not to sound anxious as he straightened the kitchen.

"Sleepovers are for girls. This is a campout. Can we go to Lucy's now? I have to get to Ricky's by seven."

Daniel knew he was being overprotective and just a tad too parental, but he couldn't help it. At this moment, sleepover and campout shared the same definition in his wary mind, and either one would separate him from his son. Just because his little boy was growing up didn't mean he had to like it.

"Do you have your inhaler?" he asked, voicing his biggest concern. Along with Rebecca's fine-boned features, Will had inherited one of her flaws. He was an asthmatic.

Will stared at his toes before answering. "I've been fine all month. And besides, it's sissy to carry that thing wherever I go. Grunt and Ricky don't use one."

Daniel frowned. Marching to Will's bedroom, he took the piece of molded plastic off the dresser and turned, trying not to let his anger get in the way of his words. Sitting on the edge of the bed, he set the inhaler at his side and pulled his son near.

"We've talked about this, young man. You have a physical condition that could be serious if left untreated. Remember how frightened you were the last time? You wouldn't want Grunt and Ricky to see you in the middle of an attack, would you?"

Chin set at stubborn, Will shook his head. "They won't see me because nothing bad is going to happen. We're gonna tell ghost stories around a campfire, then Ricky's great-grandfather is going to show us how to pitch a tent the way the Indians used to. Grunt says Mr. Pepperdine still remembers when whole tribes lived around here. He tells great stories, Dad, and you already said I could go. Puh-leeze."

Daniel remembered the exact moment he'd said yes to the campout. At the time, he'd had his entire body wedged under the hood of Art Ryder's ancient Ford. He knew Jeremiah Pepperdine and liked listening to the old guy's stories himself. According to the locals, the fellow was 103. He spent most of his time rocking on the front porch of his grandson's Feed and Grain, regaling anyone who'd take the time to listen with his cowboy and Indian adventures in the final days of the waning West. But Jeremiah had a way with a story that could upset a young boy with an active imagination.

"Some of his stories can scare the life out of you, if you let yourself get carried away, Will. Promise me you'll keep it light, okay?"

"Jeez, Dad, do you think I'm a baby or something? I'd never do anything to make them think I was a little kid."

Daniel hid his grin behind a stern cough. Besides being four years younger and sixty IQ points ahead of Grunt and Ricky, Will was a foot shorter and thirty pounds lighter. There'd been a few times in the recent past when the older boys had made Will the butt of their practical jokes. They had probably invited him on the sleepover because they hoped to frighten the bejeezus out of him, and his son was just too innocent to figure it out.

But he had to let go sometime. Rebecca's stifling parents had been one of the reasons she wasn't able to handle their relationship. The last thing he wanted was to smother his son or embarrass him in front of friends.

"Humor me. Take the inhaler, just in case. If you keep it in your duffel bag, no one will know it's there." He handed the inhaler to a silent Will. "Okay?"

Will nodded as he took the dreaded piece of plastic. "Okay. Now can we go to Lucy's? I'm starving."

"Finish packing and meet me at the truck. After we have dinner, I'll drive you to the Pepperdines'." Daniel heard the honk of a car horn and left to take care of his final customer of the day.

Jay Pepperdine stood in the doorway of the luncheonette. Three inches taller than Daniel, he was a bear of a man in his early fifties, and owned the local Feed and Grain, which had been built by his father on land given to him by Jeremiah. During the twenties, Scooter Button and Jeremiah had been in love with the same girl, until she'd rejected them both and married another man. Scooter, annoyed that Jay's father had the nerve to stay around and start up a business, hated the Pepperdine family so vehemently that he'd drawn up his will to exclude them from taking over any more of "his" town.

When the old guy died, Jay hired a passel of attorneys to try and break the will, but was unsuccessful.

Thanks to Scooter's hatred of the Pepperdines, Daniel was able to purchase Button's Gas and Go and rename it Murphy's Last Chance.

Daniel had always felt he owed Jay a debt for welcoming them into town. As Button Creek's main source of employment, Jay's opinion wielded influence, and the wealthy rancher had a fair head on his shoulders. He realized Daniel had nothing to do with Scooter's convoluted legacy and had encouraged other locals to patronize Murphy's garage. He'd given Daniel a chance to prove himself. Despite the age difference between his son and Will, he'd even encouraged the boys to be friends. If for no other reason than that, Daniel knew he had done the right thing in letting Will spend the night.

"Murphy," Jay said, sitting at the counter. "I thought I'd come by and pick up Will, if that's all right with you."

Daniel shook Jay's hand. "Much obliged. It'll save me a trip out to your place. What time should I come get him in the morning?"

"How's noon sound? That way the boys can sleep in a bit, and my housekeeper can fix 'em a big breakfast."

Lucy brought over a cup of coffee and a slice of blueberry pie and set them on the counter. Jay nodded his thanks, then swiveled on the stool and settled his light gray gaze on Zara. "I heard from the boys you finally hired a new waitress, Lucy. By the look of her, I'd say you did a right smart thing."

Lucy folded her arms across her plentiful bosom.

"Put your eyes back in your head, Jay Pepperdine. You already buried two wives who were way too young for you."

Daniel winced at Lucy's cut-to-the-bone remark, then sneaked a peek at Jay's reaction. Amazingly, he was smiling.

"Now, Lucy, there's no law that says I can't marry again. Besides, Ricky could use a little brother or sister to take care of. Might give the boy a sense of responsibility."

"Responsibility, my fanny," Lucy harrumphed. "And don't you be makin' any passes at my waitress, either. She's too good for the likes of you. More coffee, Dan'l?"

Hiding his grin, Daniel held up his cup and let Lucy fill it to the brim. Will, who'd finished his pie and was spinning on his stool, stopped to tug his father's sleeve. "Can I tell Zara where I'm going tonight? She's just standing over there, talking to some of the boys."

"Okay, but she's got work to do. Don't be a pest."

Will jumped down and made a beeline for the far corner. Surprisingly, the woman stopped her animated conversation and nodded encouragement as she listened to Will's prattle. Again, Daniel was gut-punched by the brightness of her smile. Zara lit the room like a high-powered flashlight, sending sparks of—

"She's a fine-looking woman, isn't she?" Jay's voice came across cool and appraising. "Wonder if she'll be going to the Hole tonight?"

A wave of emotion so foreign Daniel couldn't find the words to name it overwhelmed him. "I wouldn't know. Why don't you ask her yourself?" he snapped. Immediately, he dropped his gaze to his coffee cup and wished he could take back the harsh-sounding words. With salt-and-pepper hair and the muscular build of a man half his age, Jay was, according to Dolly Hingle, the "catch" of Button Creek. He didn't deserve animosity, and he certainly didn't need Daniel's approval to romance a woman.

"Now there's an idea. Unfortunately, I can't work on it tonight. I've got those three young'uns to supervise as well as Grandpa Jeremiah. You could ask her out yourself, Murphy. That boy of yours could use a mama."

Daniel ran a tongue over his teeth to hold back a ripple of guilt. When he'd met Zara, for the first time in a long time he'd had a powerful desire to want something totally for himself. The idea of the beautiful woman becoming a mother to his son had never entered his mind. He sat straighter on his stool. He had no right to be so possessive. Zara never treated him any differently than she did the other men who drooled over her while eating in the diner. He had no claim on her, and he wasn't in a position to make one.

"Will and I are doing fine without a woman in our lives," he said tersely.

"Are you now?" Jay gave a wicked grin. "Well, I'm mighty glad to hear that. With you out of the running, that'll leave me a clear path, now won't it? Too bad

I'm going to have to wait to make my move." Standing, he called to Will. "You ready, boy? It's past seven, and the others will be waiting."

Will said his good-byes to Zara and darted back to the counter, where he retrieved his duffel and brandnew sleeping bag. "I'm ready, Mr. Pepperdine. Bye, Dad." With that, he raced out the door.

Feeling as if he'd lost his best friend, Daniel gazed up at Jay. "Thanks again. You know where to reach me if there's a problem."

Jay nodded, then tipped his hat to Lucy and followed Will to the truck.

# Four

Zara waved her hand in front of her face in an attempt to dissipate the smoke clouding the air. It was obvious from the gray haze drifting through the dance hall that the Hole in the Wall had yet to hear of the health hazards of inhaling the noxious weed. If she let herself be talked into coming here again, she would need to spend several hours in the detox chamber as soon as she arrived back home.

"Come on, Zara. One more time around the floor." Billy held out his arms in eager supplication. He'd been enthusiastic in his efforts to teach her the two-step and something called the Cotton-Eyed Joe. Now, after what felt to Zara's aching feet like an overabundance of dances, she was fairly certain she was hopeless.

"You're just trying to be a gentleman," she said lightly. "Why don't you go on over to that nice-looking young woman standing by the bar. She's been staring at you for the past half hour. I'll bet she'd be happy to dance with you."

He squinted through the smoky haze. "Heck, that's Lizzie Beldon. Just because I asked her to the movies a couple of times, she got it in her head there was something serious between us. She's jealous 'cause you're new in town, and the guys are always talking about you, is all. Lizzie and I aren't an item or anything."

From the force of Lizzie Beldon's steely gaze, it was obvious the girl had taken those few trips to the movies seriously. Too bad she couldn't tell Lizzie it was against orders for her to entangle herself with anyone other than her target.

The band announced a break in the live music, and someone popped a tape into the sound system. A few brave couples remained on the floor, impressing Zara with their coordination and stamina. "Maybe you could go say hello to Miss Beldon, just to be polite," she coaxed. "I'd appreciate a glass of cold water before the band starts up again."

The young man reluctantly took her advice, but as soon as he disappeared into the crowd, two more customers from the restaurant sat down at her table. Zara groaned inwardly. At this rate, she was never going to make it outside for a breath of fresh air.

Smoothing her hair, she listened to the men discuss the delicate business of crossbreeding cattle and the latest prices at Pepperdine's. If she'd been sent here as an animal husbandry expert, the conversation would have been enlightening. After promising to return and dance with each of the men, she excused herself and wandered to the front of the tavern. There were benches where she could sit, breathe the fresh air, and meet people as they headed inside. Perhaps she might even meet Robert.

Spurred on by the thought, she opened the door and ran smack into a tall, hard wall of muscle.

"Oops." The man grabbed her upper arms to steady her. "Sorry. You okay?"

She tilted her head to stare into Daniel Murphy's dark-fringed eyes, jolted by the quiver of recognition she felt at the sound of his deep, resonant voice. "Daniel. I didn't see you coming in."

"I didn't think you planned on being here tonight," he muttered in return, hastily backing away.

Folding her arms across her chest, Zara walked to a wooden bench flanking the doorway, sat down, and inhaled a gulp of air. "I didn't. But Lucy came to my cabin with boots and said I should get out for a while. She practically insisted—"

"Boots?"

She stuck out her feet to show off the red leather boots foisted on her by Miss Lucy. She'd never owned anything quite like them. "Lucy said she bought them a few years ago for her niece, but the girl refused to wear them. She meant to return them and never got the chance. I don't know whether to believe her or not, but she said that after tonight they were mine. Wasn't that kind of her?"

Daniel didn't need to hear the story of Miss Lucy's generosity to see that the hand-tooled boots were perfect for Zara. They hugged her slender feet, then rose upward to caress her calves like glove to hand, making what was left of her shapely legs go on forever. Or maybe it was the Band-Aid of a denim skirt she was poured into that called attention to her mile-long legs.

Hat in hand, he wondered why in the hell he hadn't stayed home and watched television as he'd planned. Small talk had never been his strong suit, especially with women.

"Um . . . they look real . . . nice." Well great! Now he was stammering. Angry he'd been unable to concentrate on much of anything these days except Zara, he kicked himself for sounding like the village idiot.

She scooted over on the bench and gazed at him through long, sweeping lashes. "Were you planning to dance or just looking for company? I imagine it's lonely with Will gone."

Unable to resist, Daniel sat down. Resting his elbows on his knees, he twirled his hat between his fingers. "Except for the time Will spends in school or playing with friends while I work, he and I are always together, so I guess the answer is yes. I'm not exactly what you'd call a C and W fan, but I thought the noise might take a bite out of the silence. What about you? Some nights, I imagine one of Lucy's little cabins can feel as big as a cathedral."

Zara wrinkled her perfectly sculpted nose. "I'm going to do my laundry at Dolly's tomorrow, so I plan to inspect her selection of videos. I'm sure a good movie will help fill the emptiness."

Still feeling a little awkward, Daniel gestured to the

honky-tonk's front door. "Were you having a good time in there?"

She pulled at a lock of her shoulder-length hair and sniffed. "For the first five minutes. Right now, I smell worse than the bottom of an ashtray, and my feet are telling me they need a vacation. I'm not one for smoking or drinking, I guess."

"Neither am I," he confessed, thinking he'd never smelled anything as good as the smoky-sweet scent of Zara wafting toward him on the cool night air. "A beer once in a while is about it, and Will has asthma, so I wouldn't even think about taking up cigarettes, even if I wanted to. I need to set a good example for my son."

Tucking the hair back behind her ear, Zara crossed her leg and swung her foot. "I've noticed—that you're a good father, I mean. It's nice, a man being so solicitous of his child."

"Yeah, well, we're all we've got. We—" Abruptly, he pushed away the idea that maybe he'd finally found someone with whom he could share his checkered past. "What about you? Any sisters or brothers? A boyfriend back home?"

"Not really," she said, staring into the darkness. Her eyes grew wide. "Someone's in an awful big hurry to get to your store. Is that Miss Lucy?"

He followed her gaze across the parking lot. The streetlight on his side of the intersection had been out for several months, and he'd planned to discuss the problem with those surveyors from TXdot as soon as he found the time. Zara had eyes like a hawk if she was able to see the figure he could barely make out crossing the highway.

If it was Lucy, there had to be a problem, because the only other time she'd come to his house had been the night Maria Herrera had gone into labor. He stood and trotted down the sidewalk, Zara hot on his heels. "Lucy? Is that you?"

The figure turned and began a fast shuffle, meeting him in the middle of the street. "Dan'l, one of the hands at Jay's ranch said they'd been tryin' to reach you. When you didn't answer your phone, he called and asked me to find you. You've got to get over to the Pepperdine place pronto. Something's wrong with Will."

Daniel didn't bother to ask what. Heart beating in triple time, he raced across the lot to the back of the store, took the stairs two at a time, and pulled his car keys from a peg next to the door.

*Was there time to call for an ambulance from Denton?*

He remembered the last time someone in town had needed help. It had taken the ambulance so long to arrive, Bill Lawler's son had bled to death under the tines of a hay combine.

Before he made it out of the house, something menacing tugged at his gut, and he raced into Will's room. There, lying half-hidden under the boy's pillow, was his inhaler.

"Hang on!" Daniel warned, watching Zara's knuckles tighten on the door handle as he whipped the steering wheel and made a sharp left onto Jay's half-mile-long driveway. Zara had been waiting in his truck when he'd hotfooted it down the stairs, and it hadn't entered his mind to tell her she didn't need to tag along. He'd been so intent on driving, the only other word he'd managed to snap out had been "asthma" the one time she asked what he thought might be the problem with Will.

He swallowed hard when he saw the campfire up ahead. Clutching the inhaler in one hand, he steered his truck onto the lawn and jolted to a stop. Zara jumped out of her seat and raced toward the fire before he had his door open. While the ring of cowhands parted for her as if she were a female Moses, he had to practically fight his way through the crowd that gathered around his son.

Daniel finally skidded to Will's side and dropped to his knees, but it took a second to register that the boy was already cradled between Zara's hands. Kneeling next to his son, she had one palm resting on his sternum and the other on the middle of his back. Nearly petrified by the sound of Will's labored breathing, Daniel tried to shove the inhaler into his hand, but Will ignored him.

Suddenly, Will's wide-open eyes closed, as did Zara's, and Daniel stilled. Then the boy's arms dropped limply at his sides and his breathing began to slow as if he was no longer in distress.

Chest heaving, Daniel glanced up at the rancher. "What the hell's going on here?"

Jay shrugged his burly shoulders. "Damned if I know, but I think it's best you let Zara handle things.

Will had me scared half out of my mind. Thought he was gonna choke to death before you got here, but he quieted down just fine almost the second she touched him."

Still holding the inhaler, Daniel sat back on his heels, his gaze glued to his son and the woman who held him. "How long was the attack?"

Jay checked his watch. "Going on thirty minutes now."

Daniel winced. The doctors had classified Will's episodes as mildly severe, but until tonight the attacks only lasted a few minutes. He saw to it Will went for regular checkups and took his medicine, but so far he'd never found the need to take him to the emergency room. Would he have to tonight?

He found himself trying to match his breathing to Will's, as if concentrating on the steady rhythm would make him a part of the recovery. Finally, Will relaxed his rigid posture and leaned back against Zara's chest. At the sound of Jay's murmured "Well, I'll be . . ." the crowd released a single pent-up sigh. One by one, men began to drift from the campfire. Grunt and Ricky, who had clustered around Jeremiah to observe the proceedings, started to whisper.

Resting her chin on the top of Will's head, Zara hugged him close. "Better?" she asked, though her eyes were still closed.

Will nodded and blinked, then focused on his father. "Dad? What are you doing here?"

Swamped by a torrent of emotion, Daniel stood and snagged Will's wrist. "I don't know what just happened, young man," he blurted, ignoring the question, "but you have some explaining to do. Gather your things. We're leaving."

Zara rose as Will backed away. Tentatively, she reached out and placed her palm on Daniel's forearm. For a split second he thought he felt a sharp burning, but the sensation was quickly replaced by the same weird tingling he'd experienced the past two times they had touched. Jerking his arm, he reached for Will again, but the kid jumped as if struck.

"You're frightening him," Zara admonished, her voice a bare whisper.

He cut his gaze to Jay in an effort to elicit some fatherly pity. One nod was all the prompting the man needed. Grabbing the handles of Jeremiah's wheelchair, Jay issued a curt order as he herded the throng toward the house. "Okay, everyone, the show's over. Let's go talk Betty into giving us some of that leftover chocolate cake."

Daniel retrieved his hat and placed it firmly on his head. Tucking his hands into his back pockets as a way to hold on to what little self-control he'd regained, he stared at the dying fire, then looked back at his son. He'd never seen the boy make such a speedy recovery, even with a shorter attack.

"Will, come over here. Please."

The boy looked up at Zara, who nodded encouragement, and took a few steps forward. Daniel caught Will in a bear hug and raised him from the ground, not knowing whether to shake the kid or hoist him up on his shoulders in a victory dance.

"You scared the life out of me. Are you okay?"

Will wrapped his arms around his father's neck and squeezed tight. Seconds passed before Daniel remembered they were not alone and opened his eyes to find Zara smiling. "Thank you," he mouthed silently.

Setting Will on the grass, he trained his gaze on his son. "You lied to me, Will. At the very least, you disobeyed a direct order. I distinctly told you to put your inhaler in your bag."

Will's shoulders drooped under the weight of his father's glare. "Yes, sir. I know."

"What do you have to say for yourself?"

Sniffing loudly, Will muttered, "I'm sorry. It won't happen again." He shrugged as he ran the tip of his sneaker through the trampled grass. "But I guess I'll have to be punished, huh?"

The boy sounded so pathetic, Daniel almost hugged him a second time, but a transgression this serious couldn't be ignored. "You got it. Now, go into the house and thank Mr. Pepperdine for having you over and get back here so we can leave. Go on, scoot."

Will gave a feeble grin, then remembered his manners. "I don't know what you did, exactly, Zara, but it was totally awesome. I feel a whole lot better. Thank you."

Watching him trot toward the house and skip up the porch stairs, Zara shifted on her feet. "I hope you'll reconsider and let him spend the night. This camping thing seems very important to him."

"He needs to go home and take his medication,

then rest," Daniel said curtly. "What the heck did you do to him?"

She ran her fingers through her hair to push it off her face, and the light from the waning campfire danced against the golden waves, turning them the color of molten copper. Soaked with sweat, her bright red T-shirt had turned transparent, outlining her bra and jutting nipples.

"It was nothing. Just a . . . a relaxation technique I've had some luck with in the past. Will took to the transfer—the exercise—immediately, which made it easy for me to help him."

Afraid he'd be accused of ogling, Daniel tore his gaze from her chest. "A relaxation technique that's 'totally awesome'?" It was all he could do to not laugh in disbelief. "I'd love to read the book you learned it from."

She blew out a breath. "It didn't come from a book—"

"Well, whatever you did, it looks like I owe you. Much as I don't understand it, Will seems completely recovered."

Drawing up to her full height, she took a step backward. "That's not necessary. Will did most of the work. I merely guided him. It was no more than anyone else would have done in my place."

Daniel wanted to believe her, wanted to think it was a happy coincidence she'd pulled his son through what might have been a serious situation, but something gnawed at his insides. He had just witnessed a minor miracle and he suspected Zara knew it too, so why the modesty? And why would someone with her type of *relaxation* skills want to live in Button Creek?

"Okay. You did what any normal person would do to help a kid who couldn't breathe. Now let me show my thanks by cooking you dinner, say tomorrow night at my place? I know Will would enjoy it . . . and so would I," he added as an afterthought.

Before Daniel could figure out what in the hell had prompted him to issue such a harebrained invitation, Jay came ambling out of the darkness.

"The kid seems fine, Murphy. He's chowing down on a huge piece of cake and his breathing sounds better than normal. Jeremiah's getting ready to tell another ghost story, so I came out here to see if I could get you to change your mind. Let the boy stay, why don't you?"

Glancing at Zara, Daniel caught the gentle pleading in her eyes. Mini-miracle forgotten, she looked genuinely interested in Will's happiness. Feeling double-teamed, he swiped the inhaler off the ground and handed it to Jay.

"Aw, hell. I know when I'm licked. Just see to it he keeps this at his side, will you? I'll be by about noon to pick him up."

Jay smiled his approval and turned to Zara. "Don't know what you just did, little lady, but my guess is folks 'round here will be talking about it for quite a while. I'd be honored if you'd let me see you home."

Daniel tamped back a jolt of what he refused to believe was jealousy and took a step closer to her side.

He'd already committed to cooking the woman dinner; how the heck could he refuse to give her a ride home? Besides, he was the one who'd brought her here—he should be the one to take her back. The dumbest thing he could do was hand her to Jay Pepperdine.

"That won't be necessary. You have the boys to look after. I'll see to it Zara gets to her cabin safely. And thanks again."

Dolly Hingle's Washeteria and Video Rental was exactly that, plus a whole lot more. On Sunday mornings, many of the residents of Button Creek went to church, either to the Baptist Ministry up at the lake, or south to any number of services held in Denton, but sooner or later almost everyone ended up at Dolly's.

Daniel usually cooked a big breakfast, then he and Will gathered up their dirty clothes and headed to the laundromat. Today, at just past nine and with Will still at Jay's, he was at loose ends, so he collected their laundry on his own and made his way across the street.

Dolly always had hot coffee and juice, plus an assortment of fresh pastries she ordered from a Denton bakery sitting on a table in a corner of the shop. For under ten dollars, a person could satisfy his or her sweet tooth, get a hefty shot of caffeine and bring home a few bushel baskets of clean clothes and a video at the same time.

Daniel carried two plastic baskets to the center row of washers and began to sort. After filling three of the ancient machines with whites, colors, and heavy-duty, he added detergent, then placed four quarters into each slot and slid them home. Once he heard the water flow, he ambled over to the coffee stand and took out his wallet.

"Morning, Dolly. Save me a bear claw?" he asked, giving the tall, thin woman a grin. Though not as old as Miss Lucy, Dolly was a lifelong resident of Button Creek. Widowed for the past several years, she enjoyed the idea that her business had become a week-end meeting place for the locals.

"Sure did," she responded, holding out a cup of coffee. "Thought you might be here early. You sleep okay, or did you spend the night worrying about your boy?"

Daniel pulled out some cash, set it on the table, and took the proffered coffee. Darn it if gossip didn't run through Button Creek faster than mercury through a broken thermometer. If Dolly Hingle knew what had happened at Jay's ranch, sure as hell the whole town knew as well. Between thinking about Will's close call and trying to figure out what Zara had done to help him, Daniel hadn't slept more than a few hours. More than likely, Dolly knew that, too.

"I managed. I'm sure Jay would have called if any-thing else had gone wrong." The sound of a door slamming echoed from the hallway that led to the rear of the store. "Is your nephew in town again, or did you finally rent out the efficiency?"

Dolly pocketed the money, then handed over his change and a napkin-wrapped pastry. "Fella came looking for work and a place to stay the other morning, so I told him he could have the room in trade for helping out around here. Says he's a photographer on a tour of the country, and he thinks Button Creek will be a nice addition to his portfolio. With my arthritis acting up, I needed someone to sweep and run the video rack, so we struck up a deal."

The door marked PRIVATE opened and a heavyset man with a long black ponytail and a drooping mustache walked out. "Morning, Dolly. I'll be ready to work as soon as I have a cup of that fantastic-smelling coffee."

She nodded and poured him a cup. "Jack, say hello to Daniel Murphy. He runs the convenience store across the street. Daniel, Jack Farley."

He shook Jack's meaty hand and filed the man's Long Island accent and retrohippie look for later. "Nice to meet you. Dolly says you're a photographer?"

After sipping at the steaming coffee, Jack Farley gave a too-polite smile. "Yep. I'm doing a pictorial on rural America. If I'm lucky, I'll be able to turn it into one of those coffee table books that sell so well around the holidays."

"Well," Daniel said before taking a bite out of his bear claw, "you couldn't find a place more rural than Button Creek. Take any photos yet?"

"I thought I'd spend a few days getting familiar with the area first. Dolly tells me you own the barn and land behind the gas station, all the way to the creek. Mind if I walk the property in the next few days?"

Before Daniel had a chance to answer, the front

door opened, and Zara strolled in carrying a battered cardboard box. Dressed in jeans and a tucked-in, hot pink T-shirt, she flashed her brilliant smile as she took the box to the row of washers and spoke to the room in general. "Good morning."

Daniel was thrown so off-balance he forgot to answer Jack's question.

Jack whistled low under his breath.

"Hey, Zara. Thought I might see you here today." Dolly poured coffee into a styrofoam cup and ambled to the girl's side. "Lucy told me you'd be over to do some wash. Soap's on the wall. Just tell me how many boxes when we settle up."

Zara stared at the machines for a long minute, then looked back at Dolly. "Yes, ma'am."

"Heard you did a nice bit of doctoring on Daniel's son last night. Tell me, how'd you learn to do what you did for Will?"

Accepting the cup of coffee, Zara sniffed delicately, then set the drink on top of a neighboring washer. "It was just a little something I learned at a meditation seminar." Raising her gaze, she finally paid Daniel some attention. "Have you heard from Will or Mr. Pepperdine?"

Daniel, who'd been concentrating on Jack while the man listened intently to the conversation, rested his backside against the wall before he answered. "Not yet. Guess that means everything went okay."

"Ah-hem." Jack Farley loudly cleared his throat.

Dolly gave a little *tsk* and patted at her short, salt-and-pepper hair. "Where are my manners? Zara, meet Jack Farley. He's going to be helping out around here for a few weeks. He's a photographer."

"Hello," Zara answered politely, then returned her puzzled gaze to the washing machine.

Dolly went to the bakery table and picked up a clipboard. "Jack, why don't you grab a donut and follow me to the video rack? I can show you how I like things done while you finish your breakfast."

Jack finally tore his eyes off Zara and did as ordered.

Feeling like an umbrella someone had discarded in a corner, Daniel scowled as he fisted a hand on his thigh. Just who the heck did Jack Farley think he was, staring at Zara like some goggle-eyed idiot? Besides such conduct being disrespectful, he'd always thought it was flat-out rude. Women hated that type of behavior . . . didn't they?

He loosened the death grip he held on his coffee cup and heaved out a calming breath. Zara, who was standing in front of the washers and rubbing on an earlobe, had her full lips pursed into a pout. Her puzzled expression—she looked as if she was staring under the hood of a forty-year-old pickup with a blown engine—almost made him laugh out loud.

With a sudden burst of sympathy, he pushed from the wall and walked to her side. "Need some help?"

She continued to finger the diamond stud resting in her earlobe. "I've never had to . . . um . . . I'm not too familiar with this type of machinery."

*Machinery?* Daniel used his thumb to push the brim of his Stetson higher on his forehead. Hell, he'd always thought operating a washer and dryer was part of the cleaning gene that sat right next to the shopping gene on a woman's DNA chain.

"It's a washer," he said with a grin. "Not a nuclear reactor."

Zara rubbed a palm on her thigh as she spoke. "I know what it is. I just haven't used one be—in a very long while."

Folding his arms across his chest, he added Zara's reluctant pronouncement to the list of other quirky facts he just realized he'd been compiling about her. She didn't own a car or a license to drive one, she avoided talking about where she was from, and she had downright spooky medical skills. Add that to the fact she didn't know how to use something as simple as a washing machine, and the mix got downright peculiar. Combine everything with her perfect bone structure, finishing school accent, and regal bearing, and the answer was obvious. He'd been a dope not to have figured it out earlier.

She was a poor-little-rich-girl in hiding from someone, possibly her wealthy parents or an angry boyfriend—worse, an abusive husband. Zara was exactly what he *didn't* need to complicate his life.

And right now she looked totally lost as she contemplated the simple, everyday appliance.

Taking pity on her, he said, "It's a fairly easy task. First, you sort the clothes by type—jeans and heavy stuff like towels, then another pile of lighter colors, maybe T-shirts or bed linens." He snagged the red shirt she'd worn last night just before she tossed it in with her white sheets. "But keep the reds with the other dark colors or everything will turn pink. I'm speaking from experience, by the way."

Zara picked through her box and did as instructed, then pulled out a minuscule black triangle of elastic and lace. "And which category of clothing might this fall into?"

After swallowing his surprise with a huge gulp of coffee, Daniel stuttered out, "Um . . . that would be delicates. Do you have a lot of that . . . in there?"

She brought out a handful of the flimsy looking underwear. "It's all new, so I thought I'd better wash it before I wore it. Since it's going to be close to my skin, I want it to be really clean."

Then and there, Daniel's don't-get-involved resolve flew straight out the Washeteria window. If Zara liked clean, he could be the most spotless man in Texas. Hell, he'd shower twice a day and three times on Sunday if that was what it would take to get as close to her as her unmentionables.

He felt his face warm. Lifting the lid on one of his own machines, which had just finished the spin cycle, he loaded his clothes into a dryer as he spoke. "I'm pretty sure they need a washer of their own. Here— use this one. Just set the water level to low and add detergent, then slide your quarters in the slot."

She wrinkled her forehead as she did what he suggested. Daniel huffed out a breath when, out of the corner of his eye, he caught Jack Farley still checking her out as she loaded her clothes. Damned if things around town weren't getting weirder than a circus sideshow. What kind of crazy coincidence was it when a pair of supposed surveyors and a woman who looked like a cross between a movie star and a socialite show up in town on practically the same day?

Now they had an obnoxious photographer wanting to snoop, snap pictures, and put the place in a book. What in the hell was going on that had Button Creek smack in the middle of a population explosion?

Daniel put quarters in the dryer and ambled to the coffee table. "Dolly, I'm running home for a half hour or so. When my dryers stop, would you mind putting in a few more quarters if the clothes are damp?"

"Will do," answered Dolly.

He waved at Zara and walked out the door. He had to straighten the apartment and get ready for tonight. Unless he missed his guess, their dinner was going to be one hell of an interesting meal.

## Five

Zara heaved a sigh of relief when Daniel left the laundromat. The weekend certainly wasn't turning out as she expected. First, she'd helped Will get through a particularly alarming bout of asthma, when she'd been under orders not to call attention to her healing skills, then she'd nearly botched the ordinary job of cleaning her own clothes. Just now, she'd caused Daniel Murphy's face to flush as pink as her shirt by performing the simple task of sorting laundry.

Unfortunately, nothing in her indoctrination classes had led her to believe it was unacceptable to discuss, never mind hold up for scrutiny, one's underwear in public. One of the first things she was going to do on her return was see to it that the experts added a section entitled "embarrassing moments to avoid" to the next Earth-training program.

Resting her elbows on the edge of the box, she de-

cided it was time to admit to what she suspected was
a more serious breach of duty. Beside the fact that she
liked Will, she was fighting a disturbing inner longing
to get closer to Daniel Murphy. Though physical contact with humans was forbidden unless it had to do
with her target, none of the rules had mentioned anything about contact through her heart. Was she doing
the right thing by becoming involved with these two
humans?

Bewildered, she bought a donut dusted in powdered sugar while she waited for the washers to go
through their cycle. Townspeople filtered in and out
of the store, some commenting on what she had done
for Will or smiling their approval. After Dolly helped
transfer her clothes to dryers, Zara propped her bottom against an empty washer and thought about her
predicament. Instead of avoiding Daniel and his son,
she'd promised to have dinner with them. She was
supposed to arrive at six, which gave her the afternoon free. She thought to check out two videos, one of
which she'd hoped to watch this afternoon, the other
to take to the Murphys'. Now she wondered if she
shouldn't cancel the date.

Glancing around, she saw that the laundromat had
grown crowded. She stepped to the rack covering the
rear wall of the room where, seconds later, Jack Farley
appeared at her side. "Looking for anything special?"

"I'm not sure. Action adventure maybe, or science
fiction? What do you recommend?"

"Now why would a beautiful woman like you
want to see a Rambo-style shoot-'em-up or a movie

about space monsters? I'd think a nice, sedate romance would be more to your liking."

Biting back a bubble of laughter, Zara picked up a video entitled *Contact*. "It's not for me. Daniel said his son enjoyed science fiction, so I thought I'd surprise them and bring something we could watch together after dinner tonight. Are you familiar with this one?"

Jack took the video from her hand and checked the number on the spine against a list from the clipboard. "It's an oldie, but what isn't on this shelf," he confided. "Jodie Foster's in it and a few other heavyweights. Let's see—nope, Murphy hasn't rented this one yet." He tucked the pencil behind his ear. "It's pretty good as science fiction goes, but I don't think it's very realistic."

"What makes you say that?" Zara asked, perusing the shelves so she wouldn't have to look him in the eye.

"Well, the premise is a good one. I mean, the idea that aliens are out there trying to contact us is sound. I just don't think they're going to reach us the way it's depicted in this film."

"And how's that?"

"By willingly giving us a blueprint of a spaceship and instructions on how to use it."

"How do you think they would make contact—if they were here, that is?"

"I have two theories. They're either going to come down and make their presence known to the whole world, or they're already here, living among us and waiting until the time is right to do what they plan to do."

Zara tried, but she couldn't resist ignoring the order she'd been given: to avoid commenting on anything to do with life on other planets. She took the video from his hand. "You think so?"

Jack squared his shoulders and tossed her a look of condescending superiority. "Well, I don't like to brag, but researching alien sightings is a hobby of mine, so I know what I'm talking about. I imagine it's difficult for a woman to understand the concept of the vastness of the universe."

*Vastness of the universe, my fanny!* Zara almost laughed out loud at how easily she'd picked up one of Miss Lucy's favorite expressions. Biting the inside of her cheek to keep from giving Jack an abbreviated version on the laws of astrophysics when applied to interplanetary travel, she couldn't help but compare him to Murphy and the way he'd explained the operation of a washing machine. Daniel had been patient and concise; he hadn't talked down to her just because she was confused. She'd take ten men like Murphy teaching her about the simple, day-to-day happenings on earth over one "alien expert" like Jack Farley in a heartbeat.

"Can you sign this one out for me?" asked a man who walked up beside Zara. "Name's Ed Newton, and I'm kind of in a hurry."

"Sure, no problem." Jack checked off the man's name from his list, copied the video number, and pocketed the money, then nodded to Zara. "I'm sure that one will be fine."

"I'll take this one, too." She handed him a video

that proclaimed itself a classic, something called *An Affair to Remember,* along with a five-dollar bill. "And thanks for the review. See you later."

Carrying the movies to a large table, she set them aside and removed her clothes from the dryer. She placed the neatly folded items in her cardboard box just as two men she recognized as neighbors opened the door to the laundromat. Each man occupied a cabin on either side of her, and she waited on them every morning for breakfast. In her head, she'd begun to think of them as Eggs Over Easy and Short Stack.

Dolly rose from her chair at the bakery table as the surveyors walked in. "Jack, bring those two baskets of clean clothes from the storage room, would you? Gentlemen, your laundry will be right out."

Eggs Over Easy, a tall, thin man of about fifty, with a receding hairline and florid face, nodded at Dolly, then smiled at Zara. "Morning. How's it feel to have a day off?"

Zara set the box back on her washing machine. "Great. I can't believe I have the whole day to put up my feet and do nothing. What about you?"

Short Stack, a younger man with a blond crew cut and piercing green eyes, helped himself to coffee from the table and ambled to her side. "We don't take a day off until the job's done. Isn't that right, Frank?"

Frank tugged his jeans until they were cinched up well above his waist. "That's right, Chuck." He turned to Zara. "You must hear all the gossip in town. Anybody new come into the diner lately?"

Zara cocked her head, considering his question.

"I'm not sure, but I'm still pretty new myself, so I don't think I can help you much. Why don't you ask Dolly or Lucy? They're Button Creek's mainstays." Trying her best to look only mildly curious, she said, "Are you looking for anyone in particular?"

"We just like to keep track of how many newcomers gravitate to a dot on the map like Button Creek. There's always a lot of research done on an area before the state decides whether or not to install a traffic light. We'll be laying some counting lines across the road first thing tomorrow to keep tabs on the traffic that goes through here on a daily basis."

"I see. What else do men who work for the transportation office do?"

Chuck threw Frank a strange half smile. "Measure the runoff in the creek, run a few stress tests on that one-lane bridge back behind Mr. Murphy's property, check the road to see how difficult it will be to widen. The department made us responsible for the whole area."

Jack walked from the storage room carrying a plastic basket under each arm. "Here you go, fellas. Dolly says that'll be five dollars each."

Frank pulled out his wallet and handed over a twenty as he sized up Jack. "I don't remember seeing you in here the other day when we dropped off our laundry. You new to town?"

"Name's Jack Farley." The men shook hands. "I'll be taking pictures of the area for the next month or so. That creek and one-lane bridge sound interesting."

"I see," said the older surveyor. "Well, then I'll have

to ask you not to touch any of our equipment if you run across it. We use delicate instruments that don't like to be jostled."

"I'll try to remember." Jack turned to Zara. "Are you all set or do you want me to come over later and help you work the VCR? Maybe you'd let me stay and watch that movie on the aliens as a thank-you?"

"Aliens?" The muscle in Chuck's left cheek twitched. "Don't tell me a smart-looking woman like you enjoys that kind of entertainment?"

"Well, I—"

"She rented a movie about aliens to take to the Murphys' for dinner. I was just offering to help her with the setup," Jack interrupted.

"You some kind of expert on audiovisuals . . . or creatures from outer space?" Chuck asked.

The photographer drew back his shoulders. "Seeing as I've investigated my share of stories on alien sightings for newspaper articles, I'd like to think so."

"You ever see an alien?" Frank challenged with a snort.

Zara stepped out of the circle and picked up her laundry, eager to escape the pointed discussion. Backing toward the door, she waved to the trio. Frank ignored her, and Jack nodded absently as he continued to argue, but she felt Chuck's penetrating glare long after she made it to her cabin.

Will danced around the kitchen table like a kid on Christmas morning. Between running from the front windows to the kitchen and back again, he'd arranged and rearranged the glasses and silverware and folded napkins so many times Daniel lost count. Now, at one minute past six, he was sitting in his usual seat at the table staring at the clock on the microwave.

"What do you think's keeping her?" he asked, swinging his feet impatiently.

"That clock is a few minutes fast. She'll be here."

"Is supper almost done?"

Daniel lifted the lid and released the tantalizing aroma of chicken and mushrooms simmering in onions, garlic, and tomato sauce. "What do you think?"

"Hmm, smells great. How about the broccoli?"

"Everything is ready," Daniel said. He still didn't know why the boy enjoyed vegetables so much, but he wasn't going to complain. "Stop worrying."

They both jumped when they heard a knock on the downstairs door. Will shot from his chair like a bottle rocket, and Daniel slammed down the frying pan lid. Darn it if Zara hadn't done a number on his son. Will enjoyed Maria and her daughter, and he had grandmotherly friends in Lucy and Dolly, but after last night, it was obvious he was damn near in love with the new waitress. It was a schoolboy crush, but Daniel still wasn't sure he liked the idea of a stranger getting so close to his child.

The sound of voices rang out, Will's high and excited, Zara's husky and questioning. Unwilling to admit he was just as eager as his son, Daniel went to the refrigerator and took out the bottle of white wine he'd been saving for a special occasion. Zara had said she wasn't much for alcohol, but maybe she'd think tonight's dinner was important enough to have a celebratory glass.

He turned as they entered the kitchen, determined to keep his tone and his emotions light. "Glad you could make it. Will, why don't you take Zara into the living room? I'll be with you in a minute."

Zara's face flushed pink with what he thought might be embarrassment. Her hair was pulled away from her face and held in place by a white plastic clip, and she wore a navy blue T-shirt and that thigh-skimming band of denim she laughingly called a skirt.

"I'm sorry I'm late. I became so engrossed in a movie I ended up watching it twice, and the time just slipped away from me." Smiling, she handed Will a video. "I brought this for after dinner."

Before Daniel could answer, Will said, "Wow. *Contact.*"

"I realize it's a little out-of-date, but I heard Dolly's selection is a few years behind the times."

"I haven't seen this one. Thanks, Zara," said Will, tugging her through the archway that led to the living room.

Shaking his head, Daniel poured two half glasses of wine and a glass of lemonade and followed them. Zara and Will were already shoulder to shoulder on the sofa. Will had opened up one of his astronomy journals and was talking animatedly.

"And that's the constellation Upsilon Andromedae. It's only forty-four light-years from our planet.

It's one of the first pictures taken from the Chandra Observatory," he pronounced, almost as if he'd been the photographer. "I've been keeping a scrapbook. Want to see?"

"Will." Daniel handed him the glass of lemonade. "Zara just got here. Maybe she'd like to sit and relax. She might not be interested in what goes on in outer space."

Zara sat up straight and pulled at her earlobe. Then she turned on her megawatt smile. "Oh, but I am. Astronomy is one of my favorite topics."

Will gave a whoop of delight, set his drink on the coffee table, and raced toward his room.

Daniel raised a brow in warning. "You've unleashed the monster now. Once he gets on a tear about something, there's little I can do to deter him."

"He's a wonderful little boy. He seems unusually bright for an eight-year-old."

Ready to burst his buttons, Daniel swiftly confided, "He's in the gifted program at school. They had him tested, and his IQ's just about off the charts. But I don't want him to know, so I'd appreciate it if you could keep it between the two of us. I want Will to grow up a normal kid in every sense of the word."

"Thank you, and I'll honor your confidence. I've always thought it important to speak with children on a level they understand. Knowing about Will makes things easier."

Daniel realized he was still holding the wine, and placed a glass in front of her on the table. "I know you said you don't drink, but we don't get company very often. I've been saving this for a special occasion."

"White wine? I'm not sure if I should." Once again, she fingered the diamond in her earlobe. "We don't—I don't think I have much tolerance for alcohol."

"It's okay if you don't want it. I just thought—"

"No, no." She laid one hand on her throat and raised the wineglass with her other. "Do we give a toast first? I'm afraid I'm not familiar with the finer points of drinking, so you'll have to guide me."

Daniel had been so uncertain of having Zara over, he hadn't given much thought to where the night would lead. And he hadn't worried once about what the invitation might mean to her. He'd already decided that the fiddling she did with her earrings was a nervous habit. Since she'd touched her ear twice in the past five minutes, she had to be more wary than he was. Guiding her on a tour of wine etiquette never entered his mind when he thought of the things he wanted to do when they were together.

Hoping to put her at ease, he sat at the opposite end of the sofa. "You usually give a toast when there's something to celebrate."

She grinned as she raised her glass. "Do we have something to celebrate?"

Before Daniel could figure out whether or not she was flirting, Will bounded from the back hall. "I've been cutting articles out of newspapers and magazines. The United States is launching a probe at the end of the year to study some of these places."

"I know," Zara murmured. "And what they find is going to be very . . . exciting."

"NASA's gonna send a spacecraft to monitor the motion of the stars and their planets in 2005, but I won't be old enough to go." Lips set in a pout, he thrust up his chin and plopped down beside her. "I will someday though."

"Is that what you want to be when you grow up—an astronaut?"

"Yeah. Dad says my asthma will probably keep me out of the program, but I'm hoping someone will find a cure by the time I get to college."

Zara rested a hand on Will's shoulder. "Medical science is making great strides these days." She reached up to push a stray curl from his forehead. "I'm sure they'll find a cure someday soon."

Daniel swallowed hard. No one except the school authorities knew about Will's genius IQ, though he thought Lucy and Jay Pepperdine suspected it; until last night, the boy's asthma had been a secret as well. It had been years since he'd trusted another adult enough to talk about his son. The idea that Zara was so observant of Will and would be touched by his plight began to chip away at his resolve.

He sighed inwardly. He'd been burned by a woman before. What was it about this one that made him want to unburden himself? "Hey, anybody around here hungry?" he asked. "Because I know where we can get some really good food."

"Dad made our favorite." Will stood and offered Zara his arm. "Come on, I'll show you where to sit."

Zara grabbed her glass of wine, and let Will escort her to the kitchen. Daniel watched in awe as his son pulled out her chair and sat next to her at the table. Amused by the boy's chivalry, he walked to the stove. "Hope you don't mind if I serve from here. 'Fraid we don't own any fancy platters to put the food on."

Zara placed her napkin on her lap and Will did the same. "That's fine. What are we having?"

"My version of an Italian delicacy, without the red wine." He spooned rice on a plate, covered it with chunky red sauce and a chicken breast and added steamed broccoli, then turned and set the plate in front of her. "Hope you like it."

She quickly brought a hand to her earlobe and rubbed. "Oh . . . chicken . . . I . . . um . . . it smells . . . interesting."

Was it Daniel's imagination or had Zara's complexion just gone as green as the broccoli? "Something wrong? You do eat chicken, don't you?"

Shifting in her seat, she stared at the food. "I serve it at the diner, but I can't . . . I mean, I don't eat it myself. I'm a vegetarian."

The words hit Daniel like a brick. "I'm sorry. I should have asked. I just assumed . . ."

"No, it's okay, really. I should have been the one to tell you about my eating habits."

Will blinked, and Daniel thought the kid was going to burst into tears. Instead his lower lip quivered. "We could fix something else. We have lima beans in the freezer—or salad. We always have salad, don't we, Dad?"

Daniel reached over and set Zara's dinner at his own place. "Will's right. It'll only take two seconds to whip up a salad." He spooned rice and broccoli onto a fresh plate, then handed it to her.

She set it down and folded her hands primly on the table. "Please don't go to any trouble. Sharing meal-time with you is special enough. Broccoli and rice are favorites of mine."

Daniel gave Will his supper and took his seat. From the upset look on his son's face, he figured he'd better do something to make dinner a success, or Will would never speak to him again.

"Well, then, let's have a toast." He raised his wine-glass high. After a second, Zara did the same. "Come on, Will, you too. Here's to new friends and . . . vegetables."

Grudgingly, Will raised his glass of lemonade.

Zara giggled, and Will's lips worked their way up at the corners. "New friends, vegetables, and rice," he pronounced, proud of his ad-lib.

"To new friends, vegetables, and rice," Zara agreed. She watched Daniel and Will each take a swallow of their drink. When the two men grinned at her, she brought the glass to her lips and gave a re-signed sigh, then tossed back her half glass in one quick gulp.

Daniel took a second sip, enjoying the wine's smooth, fruity tang. From her bemused expression, he assumed Zara was pleased with the drink, too. He heaved a silent sigh of relief. The evening seemed to be turning out fine, after all.

\* \* \*

Daniel climbed through Will's bedroom window, cursing out loud when he nicked his shin on the ledge. Damn if he wasn't getting too old to be crawling around like a little kid just to be able to go outside and relax on the overhang. One of these days he was going to have Otis Zetmer install a door in place of the window, which would make it a lot easier for him to barbecue or sit with Will and look at the stars.

Limping, he walked to the railing and gazed toward the barn. Will and Jaybird were parading around the corral as if they were in a competition ring. Zara had propped herself against the fence and seemed to be enjoying the show. Every once in a while Will would trot Jaybird over and she'd scratch the horse's ears or pat its nose, then Will would canter off again and put the gelding through its paces.

Earlier, she'd offered to help with the dishes, but Will had looked so horrified at the thought that he'd marched Zara straight to the barn. They'd been out there for the past hour, amusing themselves while Daniel tidied the kitchen.

Once dinner was under way, things had gone well. Zara's dietary restrictions hadn't come up again, and everyone enjoyed second helpings. Their conversation had been lively, mostly because Will chattered through the entire meal like a set of windup false teeth. Zara had even finished another half glass of wine, and he'd done the same.

Then he served dessert, a freshly thawed chocolate cream pie from the downstairs freezer. Zara had spent a lot of time tugging at her ear before she'd tried that pie, but she'd grinned like a little kid tasting chocolate for the first time when she finally took a bite.

"Hey," Daniel called from the overhang. "You two going to stay out there all night? Thought we had a movie to watch."

Waving his hat like a banner, Will called out, "Okay," then said something to Zara, who turned and headed toward the house.

At the sound of Murphy's voice, a little jolt of pleasure spurted through Zara's veins. She'd had a better time tonight than she ever remembered having on her own planet. The error of not explaining her eating habits had been awkward, but only for a few moments. The wine she'd drunk didn't seem to have any unusual effects on her system, though the chocolate pie had been close to a mind-altering experience.

There were so many similarities between their two worlds, she was surprised there was no chocolate back home. She'd been told to bring back anything deemed worthy of reproduction, and cacao beans were going to be at the top of her list if she managed to find a few in their natural state. Otherwise, she would bring back a sample of chocolate and plead with the scientists to do their best.

She crossed the field of wildflowers that separated the barn and corral from Murphy's Last Chance and ordered her heart to stop pounding. Maybe it wasn't such a wise idea to go upstairs and be alone with the man. Will said he would be along as soon as he fed and rubbed down his horse. Perhaps she should wait at the back of the building until he was finished.

"Come on up, the door's open," came a voice from above.

She stood still, wondering if Daniel felt it, too, this strange, indefinable link that let him know whenever they were near one another. But that was ridiculous. The only person—man—who was supposed to be attuned to her presence was Robert Lotello.

Suppressing a smile, Zara started up the stairs. Then again, since arriving in Button Creek so many men had told her she was the light of their life or the answer to their prayers, it was difficult to imagine what the correct reaction from Robert would be once she met him.

She had to get her mind off Murphy and onto her mission. It was time, she decided, to use her locator and find her target, no matter how risky. She would be entering her first fertile period within the next twenty-four hours, and she didn't want to lose one of the three chances she had to conceive.

Thinking hard, she bumped into Daniel as she set foot on the landing. He reached out to steady her, and she ignored his touch by sidestepping into the kitchen.

"Is Will putting Jaybird to bed?" he asked, giving her room.

"He's rubbing the horse down, then feeding it. He's very responsible for an eight-year-old."

A glimmer of pride shone from Daniel's dark eyes.

"I raised him to my own set of values. Whether it be business or pleasure, a man shouldn't be allowed to shirk his duties."

"I see." Zara followed him into the living room and sat in the middle of the sofa. Suddenly curious, she couldn't help but ask, "What about Will's mother? What happened to her?"

Daniel hesitated for just a second before he settled beside her and picked up the remote control. "She's dead."

Somehow she'd known that would be his response. "How sad for you both. Was Will a baby when she died, or did it happen recently?"

Daniel took a sip of wine and she noticed he'd refilled her own glass, this time to the brim, and placed it on the table. "It was a while ago. Will was about two years old, so I'm not sure how much he remembers of her. We don't talk about Rebecca very often."

"Surely you have photographs or a video to show him?"

"Rebecca and I . . . we weren't married, so no, I don't have a thing. It's better that way," he added in a somber tone.

Surely Daniel didn't feel guilty because he and Will's mother hadn't been wed? "Doesn't he want to know what she looked like, or have questions about her death? And what if something happened to you? Aren't you worried that he would be alone? Is there family who can take care of him in case of an emergency?"

Daniel's jaw clenched. "We have each other. That's enough."

Unwilling to believe Will's relatives would shun him simply because his parents hadn't been married, she persisted. "There are no grandparents or aunts and uncles?"

"I was an only child. My mother and father have been dead a long while now." He rested his elbows on his knees and fiddled with the remote. "Rebecca's parents are dead, too. At least as far as Will and I are concerned."

"But it's a shame to keep a child and his grandparents apart. Isn't there some way you can mend the rift?"

"That's really none of your business," he bit out sharply.

*You're right*, Zara silently agreed, but it was still a shame Will didn't know all the members of his family. It was a good thing Daniel didn't reciprocate her feelings, or she would soon find herself totally drawn into the life of this man and his son. If she wasn't strong enough to control her emotions where Murphy and Will were concerned, she was relieved he could.

Before she managed a safe response, Will skipped into the room. "Is the video ready?"

"It will be after you wash your hands," chided Daniel.

"Ooh-kay." Will rolled his eyes. "Take a pill, Dad."

"Now," Daniel snapped, pointing the way to the bathroom.

Zara could tell by his harsh attitude that her questions had made things uncomfortable. "I touched Jaybird, too. Maybe I should wash?"

He sat back against the cushions and gave a weary-sounding sigh. "Petting is one thing, digging through an oat bin and grooming rigorously are entirely different. Besides, who knows what else he did in that barn. He loves to shovel manure."

She tried to take him seriously, but laughter came bubbling up from deep inside. "Shovel manure? You think that's what he's been doing?"

Daniel's stern glare softened. "Maybe not tonight, but he does it almost every day. Loves the job so much I couldn't even use it as punishment."

"What *did* you do to discipline him for not bringing his inhaler to the sleepover?"

He rubbed a hand over his face and around to the back of his neck. "When he gets back from summer school tomorrow he has to sweep the two bays and align all my tools in size order. He's probably going to enjoy it, the little stinker."

Before she could comment, Will walked back in the room, his hands raised high. "All clean. Now can we watch the movie?"

## Six

*T*he movie she'd chosen had been a success, Zara decided as she waited for Will to scramble out the window and onto the back deck. Raising her leg to follow him through, she half sat on the ledge and gazed down to her expanse of naked thigh. The fact discovery team on her planet really needed to get a better feel for the type of clothing women wore on Earth, she told herself, well aware of Daniel, who was standing beside her while silently observing her machinations.

"If I'd known I had to do gymnastics I would have worn my jeans," she muttered.

Daniel cleared his throat, but had the decency to stare at the space above the window. "Go ahead, I promise not to watch. •

She took the hand Will offered and wiggled sideways. Lifting her free leg, she hopped onto the overhang and tugged at the hem of her skirt. "Thank you."

Will pulled a second chair over to his telescope and waited for her to sit. Instead, she walked to the edge of the railing and took a deep breath, inhaling the scent of flowers on the evening breeze. From there, she could see the creek at the back of Murphy's property as well as a skyline almost as huge as the one she was used to admiring on her own planet.

She looked down at Will, who was adjusting the telescope. "You have a wonderful view."

Will nodded as he took a step back. "Want to see?"

Zara sat down and focused through the lens. When Will had asked her about sky watching, she couldn't help but admit her fascination with the stars. It was too late to pretend she wasn't interested. Automatically, she guided the instrument toward a set of coordinates she knew as well as her own name and lost herself in an almost suffocating blanket of homesickness.

After a few moments, Will's voice whispered in her ear, "They're out there, you know, just like in that movie we watched tonight. I can feel it."

Startled, Zara jumped. "Oh . . . well, you could be right. Tell me . . . um . . . which constellations fascinate you most?"

"All of them. But the past few weeks Dad and I were studying right where you're looking now. We watched something special come from that direction."

Pulling away from the lens, she looked back at Daniel. "Special? What kind of special?"

"Lights," he said, taking a step closer to her chair.

"At first, I thought they might be shooting stars or debris from a meteor, but Will thought differently. He tracked them every night until one evening last week, when they just didn't appear anymore."

"They weren't meteor fallout or shooting stars. They were something else," Will said surely. "Dad didn't want to believe me until that last night, when one of them landed by the creek."

Taking a deep breath, Zara swallowed the fear rippling up from her stomach. "Well, they're gone now, right? You haven't seen them in a while?"

"Nope," said Will sadly. "But Dad and I went to the creek the next morning to investigate."

"Will," came Daniel's voice from the darkness.

"And we found some really neat stuff."

"Enough, Will. Zara doesn't want to hear about it."

"Oh, but I do." Ignoring Daniel, she looked Will in the eye. "What did you find?"

"Want to see it?"

"Certainly, if you don't mind."

"Nuh-uh. It's in the freezer. I'll be right back." Doing a quick skip and step, he scampered around his father and made it through the window before Daniel could grab him.

Daniel ran a hand through his hair. "I didn't mean for him to get you involved in this."

"I don't mind humoring him. And I really am interested. As I said earlier, astronomy is a hobby of mine."

Daniel smiled suddenly, as if she'd given him a gift. "You are a surprise. I haven't met many women interested in that particular science."

"It's not something that comes up in everyday conversation, but I've always enjoyed studying the stars. Seeing this telescope and the kind of things you and Will read, I gather it's the same for you."

Daniel nodded. "Ever since I was Will's age."

They both turned as Will crawled through the window with a plastic bag and a flashlight in his hand. He passed the bag to Zara and turned on the light. "This is stuff we scraped from the rocks around the creek the morning after we last saw the lights. We don't know what it is but it looks like—"

"Raw egg white," she offered, finishing his sentence. "I mean, it's almost the same color. What does it feel like?"

"Slime." Will giggled. "Dad said it reminded him of—"

"That is enough, young man. Put the bag back in the freezer before the stuff thaws and gets ruined."

Dimple in his cheek flashing, Will took the bag and did as he was told. Trying to keep her curiosity in check, Zara turned to Daniel. "What do you plan to do with the contents of the bag?"

He sat in the chair next to her and gazed out over the yard. "I told Will I'd take it to a lab to be analyzed, but I really don't know how to go about finding a reputable one. I have to locate a place that has the right kind of equipment, then make up some kind of story about where I found the stuff, and what I thought it was. Until tonight, I'd hoped Will had forgotten the whole episode."

"And my being here brought it to mind all over

again. I'm sorry I encouraged him," she said on a sigh. "Maybe you should just toss it out and hope he'll forget about it."

"I doubt it," he answered, chuckling softly. "The kid's like a pup with a bone sometimes. Now that he has a new audience, he won't rest until I've taken it somewhere. Don't worry, it can't be anything more than some kind of sap from a tree, or maybe animal residue I've never seen before. I don't think it had anything to do with the lights."

Zara released a pent-up breath. Daniel's assessment was very close to the mark; any competent Earth laboratory would only come up with the most basic of chemical compounds for the life-sustaining plasma.

"You're probably right. Now tell me what made you buy such an impressive piece of equipment. This telescope must have cost a lot of money."

"When I was young, my parents weren't able to afford anything this sophisticated. I had to wait until I was in college to use a top-of-the-line instrument like Will's Meade. I vowed I would give my son the very best if he showed an interest, and that's what I've done."

"I wasn't aware auto mechanics needed a college education."

"Tinkering with cars was always a hobby of mine. I could take an automobile engine apart and put it back together again before I was thirteen. After I found—gained custody of Will, I was able to fall back on the mechanics to make a living."

"So what did you study in college?"

"Astronomy . . . astrophysics . . . a little bit of everything." He leaned over and swung the tripod around to the southwest. "Take a look and tell me what you see."

Zara refused to show her surprise at Daniel's impressive background. On her planet, education was carefully plotted for each individual according to his or her genetic code and intelligence level. From the sound of it, Murphy would fit in nicely with her world's scientific community, even if he was ninents behind in facts and data.

Aware he was trying to change the subject, she put her eye to the lens and found herself staring at a familiar constellation. "It's beautiful. I gather it's one of your favorites?"

"It is. It's called Ring Nebula M57. That faint display of dark blue mingling with the light blue halo has always intrigued me. The way the rose color hovers at the edge reminds me of the night making way for the dawn, like the start of a brand-new day."

Warmed by his poetic words, she pulled back from the eyepiece. While she'd been focusing on the constellation, Daniel had edged so near she could feel his breath feather her cheek. Her gaze was drawn to his well-defined lips, hovering so close it would only take a nod to have them touch her mouth. Slowly, their breathing took on a shared rhythm. Daniel's head bent a fraction, and his lips brushed hers in a butterfly touch.

Until the sound of Will's voice made them jerk

apart. "See anything interesting?" the boy asked, sticking his head through his bedroom window.

"What I see is bad tim . . . bedtime, young man," quipped Daniel, his voice a faint stammer.

"Aw, Dad. It's just past ten."

"It's almost ten-thirty, and you have a full day tomorrow. The school bus will be here at seven-thirty, remember? And after you get home, you have to clean the garage and sort my tools. How about you brush your teeth and get ready for bed?"

Defeated, Will shrugged. "Good night, Zara. Guess I'll see you around. And thanks for bringing the video. It was great."

Daniel stood and escorted her to the window, then helped her through it and into Will's room. "Give me a minute to see him settled, and I'll walk you to your cabin. Okay?"

Against every sensible atom in her body, Zara found the voice to say, "All right."

Zara walked from the hallway into the living room, shocked at the way she'd so easily responded to Murphy's offer. Filled with giddy panic, she gulped down the last of her wine, well aware that back home scientists still claimed most physiologies were adversely affected by the dangerous drug. Since nothing unusual had occurred with her first glass of the pale liquid, maybe they were wrong.

Thirty seconds later she realized something in those last few ounces of wine had hampered her ability to think rationally. Sitting in a corner of the sofa, she began to grow warm. Suffocatingly warm. Her heart thumped hard in her chest. Every cell in her body vibrated, as if she were connected to an energy transferal unit. She smelled a rich, sweet scent and knew it was the remains of their chocolate dessert, still sitting on the kitchen table. Suddenly, she could hear Daniel's deep voice as he spoke to Will; heard Will answer as if he were there in the room with her.

Completely at odds with the unfamiliar sensations, she catapulted to her feet as Daniel walked back into the room. "You ready?" he asked, reaching for his hat.

Zara opened her mouth to speak, but the words stuck in her throat. Not knowing what else to do, she murmured a nonsensical response and headed down the stairs at a jogger's clip. Opening the back door, she sped out of the building to the sound of Daniel's feet pounding behind her.

Still feeling a mild panic, she trotted past the gas pumps at the front of Murphy's Last Chance and crossed the highway without checking for oncoming traffic. She had no business spending time with any man other than her intended target, but there was no way she could explain that to Daniel. Escape, she decided, was the only way to let him know she wanted to be rid of him. He seemed perceptive; surely he would take the hint.

"Hey, wait up," he called, racing to her side. "What's your hurry?"

She took a calming breath and turned to face him. Walking backward, she wondered if she had misjudged his intelligence. "I'm tired, and I have to be at work by five. I can see myself to the cabin." Spinning on her heels, she plowed through the diner parking lot, around the corner, and onto the worn path between the restaurant and the Washeteria—until Daniel's hot, hard palm grasped her shoulder and stopped her in her tracks.

Moving to stand in front of her, he grabbed her hands and stepped close. "Zara. What is it? Was it something I said? Something I did?"

Anticipation sizzled up her arms with the force of an electrical jolt. While a few of the men on her planet might have pursued her to continue the conversation, never would their touch have filled her with such painful need. Scientific advancements had turned most of them into mild-mannered and impotent stoics. Something she knew Murphy could never be.

She stared at his eyes, then his mouth, then the open neck of his denim shirt, but everywhere she focused became a torment to her senses. Daniel's eyes were deep and piercing, as if they could see into her very core. His lips looked soft in the moonlight and so enticing she could almost feel them on her own. The V of his shirt showed a sprinkling of fine, dark hair, and oh, how she wanted to taste that small expanse of smooth, tanned skin.

Licking her lower lip, she tugged her hands away and forced herself to inhale. "You didn't do anything wrong. It's just—"

He folded his arms across his broad chest. "Take it easy. I'm not going to jump you or anything."

A smile twitched at her lips as she stored the colorful phrase into her memory. The fresh air had steadied her heartbeat, cooled her cheeks, and cleared her head. She realized how silly she must have looked, sprinting away from a man who was simply kind enough to want to see her home safely. She had learned from her training programs this was the way things were done here. Unlike in her world, dangerous situations abounded on Earth, forcing men to walk women to their doors at night. The act signified nothing more than good manners—apparently something Daniel had in great abundance.

She concentrated on the closures of his denim shirt, buttons of some kind that she was sure would open with a tug. "I'm sorry. It's been a long day, and I suddenly got very tired, that's all."

"I see. Well, no harm done. I'm pretty beat myself."

The gruff, throaty sound of his voice warmed her all over again, dulling her ability to think. Searching her frazzled brain for a sensible answer, she muttered, "I should go."

He continued to stare at her, his laserlike gaze holding her in place as surely as if he'd nailed her feet to the pavement. Their eyes locked as seconds passed. Finally, he took one of her hands and led her toward the row of cottages half-hidden behind the diner.

"Come on. Let's get you inside."

They walked the next ten yards in silence. Zara's arm tingled under his touch, but she refused to place any further importance on the feeling. She'd drunk alcohol, something that had disappeared from her world with the first Citizen's Unification Summit. Chocolate was a new and heady taste that had played havoc with her nervous system. The unusual vibration simply had to be her untrained physiology's adverse reaction to two unfamiliar products. Her own planet's history was rife with the evils of toxic substances. Wasn't that the reason they'd been banned by the elders in the first place?

Keeping her right hand firmly in his left, Daniel stopped at her door and held out an open palm. "Your key?"

"Key?"

"Please tell me you locked the cabin."

Tired of feeling out of control, Zara stuck out her chin. "I didn't think it was necessary since everyone I've met has been friendly and caring. Besides, I don't have much worth taking."

He shook his head, not quite snorting. "I doubt any of the longtime residents of Button Creek would be so devious, but I wouldn't put it past one of those newcomers who've blown into town. What with that Farley fellow and those nosy surveyors hanging around, this place has become as busy as rush hour on the LBJ Freeway. And I don't trust any of them."

With her free hand firmly on the doorknob, she felt secure enough to pursue Daniel's line of thought. If she had to, it would take only a second to disappear—and end the disturbing rush of emotions flooding her system.

"I serve Chuck and Frank breakfast every morning, and they seem like nice enough men. Why are you so suspicious?"

His mouth drew into a tight line. "I've mulled it over for days, and I can't think of one viable reason the Texas Department of Transportation would bother to install a traffic signal in this one-horse town. There are a lot more major arteries heading up to the lake that could use a light, and that bridge gets, at the most, five cars a day traveling over it. I agree the underpinnings are wobbly, but listening to them talk about their so-called important job just doesn't make sense."

"I'm new, and you never seemed to question my reasons for coming to town. You've even invited me to your home."

"You helped my son. And I'm positive you don't have any ulterior motives. I feel it"—he placed her hand over his heart—"right about here."

The thudding of his life source pulsed against her fingers, and she fought the urge to pull apart his shirt and lay her ear against the rapid, steady beating. Still at a loss, she swayed into his chest as she gazed into his hooded eyes.

To Zara, all time seemed to stop. An eternity passed before Daniel bent forward, letting his breath warm her lips. Her eyelids felt weighted down as they closed on her sigh. Gone were the scent of chocolate and the sound of Will's voice. Every doubt that had flooded her mind faded. There was only Daniel, there in front of her, stealing her ability to resist.

Their lips touched on a whisper, parted, then came together hard. His hand went to the back of her neck to cradle her head, and she slanted her lips to fit against his more fully. His free hand snaked around her waist and pulled her close, joining them from shoulders to hips to knees.

The taste of him was more intoxicating than alcohol, sweeter than chocolate. Hotter than a shooting star, it held her suspended.

Desire, heavy and all-encompassing, pulsed through Daniel's veins. Zara's lips were moist, her eyes so filled with wonder, he simply couldn't resist kissing her. The voice of reason that had been warning him all evening to keep his distance was suddenly drowned by the potent, heady press of her mouth against his own.

When she'd raced from the house, he'd thought her a little crazy. In the darkness of the parking lot, she'd reminded him of a doe wary of its first scent of man. Now, with her nestled so intimately against him, all he could think of was finding a way into her very core.

He ran his tongue across the seam of her mouth, and she opened like a flower to rain, eager to drink the taste of him. He sucked at her tongue and she stilled, as if she'd never experienced such a boldly sensual act. Stroking, he kept up the primal rhythm until she moaned deep in her throat.

He soothed her back, then cupped her bottom in his palms. When Zara raised her arms and wrapped them around his neck, it excited him so much he had to pull away and rest his forehead against hers. Panting like a marathon runner, he placed his lips on her brow and waited for the earth to stop spinning. Long seconds passed before he came to his senses.

"Don't ask me to say I'm sorry, Zara. That kiss was too good for an apology."

As if defeated, she dropped her arms to her sides, and he snuggled her closer, until her cheek rested on his chest. Her breathing slowed, but she continued to tremble in his arms.

"You okay? You feel a little shaky."

Jerking away, she broke from the embrace and put a finger to her earlobe. "I'm the one who should apologize. I shouldn't have let that happen. I have to go. Good night, and thank you again for dinner."

Before Daniel knew what happened, she pulled open the door and ducked inside.

Zara stumbled into her cabin, her breath a painful swelling in her chest. Resting her backside against the front door, she listened to Daniel's footsteps fade as she fought the urge to burst into tears. She exhaled slowly, her mind reeling. What had she done? Why had she done it? Worse, what would the elders say if they found out?

She'd been warned that any interaction resembling that in which she'd just engaged with Daniel Murphy was forbidden. Such contact could jeopardize the entire thrust of her mission. She had been sent to Earth to achieve one goal with one man, and only one would do.

She had to conceive a male child with Robert Lotello.

Ten Earth years ago, when Robert Lotello had become a sperm donor to help put himself through graduate school, he'd come in contact with an explorer working at a fertility clinic. Unbeknownst to him, he'd been implanted with an invisible tracking device in preparation for a visit. Then, after more careful scrutiny, Robert had been matched to a woman from Zara's own planet. He had been matched to her.

If she continued to explore this uncontrollable attraction to Murphy, there was a good chance she might never find the man. She could betray her world all for a few heady moments of frivolous pleasure.

Moving quickly through the darkness, she went to the refrigerator, took out a bottle of water, and pressed the frigid plastic to her forehead. After draining half the liquid in one swallow, she ran the side of the bottle over her throat, down to the V of her shirt and let the chill cool her senses. She needed time to think.

Raising her hand to the moonlight, she stepped to the kitchen window and examined her bracelet. Tomorrow would be her fifth day on Earth. Robert Lotello hadn't surfaced, though he was supposed to reside within a mile of Button Creek. How much more time could she take to secretly look for him? What if she never found him?

She sighed. Perhaps she had waited long enough to use one of her three energy tabs. The search would be risky and might cause her subject a small amount of pain, but his discomfort would be minimal, and it would denote for certain she had found him. It would also force her to put this disturbing attraction to Murphy in the past and allow her to get on with the job she'd been commissioned to do.

A gust of wind shook the tiny cabin, filling the room with the invigorating scent of rain. Peering into the night, Zara saw a billow of dark clouds scuttle across the moon. Thunder sounded in the distance, and a bolt of lightning split the night, proof positive of the suddenness and volatility of north Texas storms. The building shuddered as another boom filled the silence. The patter of rain, soft at first, built to a drumming cadence. More lightning and thunder shattered the sky, until there was nothing but the fury of the storm.

Methodically, she closed the windows and undressed for bed. Rain was always welcome in that part of the country; luckily, it arrived at a perfect time. When Will had proudly waved a plastic bag full of the familiar gelatinous material, she'd almost grabbed it from his hand. Thanks to the storm, the harmless, ecologically friendly compound that was the remainder of the elastic-like bubble she'd used to drop to Earth would melt and be absorbed into the ground. Even if Daniel did as he'd promised and took the substance to a laboratory for analysis, nothing unusual would be found.

Sliding between the sheets, her thoughts automatically drifted to her physical encounter with Daniel

Murphy. Her skin still tingled from his touch, her lips still felt the warmth of his kiss. Her insides ached with wanting, ready to allow him any liberty to appease the desire.

Women on her planet had long ago ceased to dream about a relationship with a man. Thinking about Murphy and all the ways they could pleasure each other, when she was honor-bound to complete her mission, was foolish and frivolous.

But oh so tempting.

Thunder cracked ominously, and she shivered. Her orders were specific: Locate her subject, interact with him enough times to ensure impregnation, and find her way to the rendezvous site on the appointed day and time. Personal contact was to be kept to a minimum, though it was reported by the explorers that humans usually required some kind of emotional entanglement to procreate.

*Easier said than done*, Zara thought as she listened to the rain beat against the cabin roof. She was already in the throes of emotional entanglement.

With the wrong man.

## Seven

*W*aking from an uncomfortable night, Daniel felt groggy and disoriented. The sound of angry drizzle drumming against the windows told him the storm was still going strong. Under the patter of the rain he heard the television in the living room and glanced at his alarm clock. Shoot, some father he was. Will had probably gotten ready for summer school on his own.

Pushing from the bed, he stepped into a clean pair of jeans and headed for the bathroom. Will met him in the hall. "I'm all set for the bus," his son said, a lone dimple creasing his little-boy cheek.

At the sight of Will, dressed in clean clothes with his mass of curls combed carefully in place, Daniel gave a nod of approval. "I see that, but don't you think you might need a slicker or maybe an umbrella and boots? It's raining to beat the band out there."

Will shrugged. "Those yellow slickers are for dorks. I bet Ricky and Grunt won't be wearing one."

Daniel placed a hand on his son's back and guided him into the kitchen. Pleased to see a used cereal bowl and spoon in the sink, he went to the coat closet and pulled out a folded umbrella. "Humor me. Don't charge through any puddles and carry this in your book bag. Did you make a lunch for yourself?"

With a roll of his eyes, Will took the umbrella and shoved it in his backpack. "Peanut butter and jelly, an apple, and a juice box. What did you and Zara talk about last night, after I went to bed?"

Daniel rubbed his hand on the back of his neck. "Grown-up stuff. Did you take your medication? What about your—"

"I took my pill, and I have my inhaler," Will answered, and returned doggedly to his first topic. "Did you invite her over again? I thought maybe we could make something she can eat next time. I'm going to check out vegetarian recipes on the library computer." A horn honked in the distance. "There's the bus. See ya'."

"See ya'," Daniel called, wishing he'd taken the time to give the kid a hug. Sometimes the reality that his son was growing up too damned fast ate a hole in his gut. If he managed to save enough money for a computer, Will wouldn't need to go to the school to amuse himself. He could stay at home where he belonged, and feed his imagination right at the kitchen table. Heck, together they could search out recipes or anything that caught his fancy.

He started the coffee, slid two slices of bread into the toaster, and strolled to the living room. Staring out the front window, he watched the surveyors race through the pelting rain into Lucy's diner. Great. It wasn't enough that thoughts of Zara and the incredible kiss they'd shared had kept him up most of the night. Now he had to stand idly by while she served those two interlopers breakfast.

He stomped back into the kitchen, poured coffee, and buttered his toast. Sitting at the table, he began his meal, but the toast tasted burnt and the coffee bitter. He was an idiot. If he'd played his cards right last night, Zara would be here right now having breakfast with him instead of strangers.

Staring at the toast, he heaved a sigh. It had been years since he'd felt an attraction as powerful as the one he had for the new waitress. Maybe it was time he stopped following his head and listened to his libido. He knew the woman had a few secrets, but how bad could they be? Certainly nothing like the storm cloud that had been hanging over his head for the past six years. If there was trust between them, the secrets could be revealed and dealt with, then forgotten.

Jay Pepperdine had been right when he'd said Will needed a mother. Maybe it was time he forgot about Rebecca's betrayal and her vengeful parents and began a real life for himself and his boy. It had been almost six years since he'd been forced to kidnap his own son, and in all that time he hadn't heard a word about the kidnapping on the radio or television or read about it in the papers. Maybe Rebecca's parents had given up, and he could let his guard down, just enough to start over again with a woman.

Daniel told himself to get a grip and come back to reality. From what he remembered of the Warfields, they weren't the type to let go. He emptied his coffee into the sink and tossed the remains of the toast in the trash. Mondays, especially rainy Mondays, were slow at the garage, with very few customers for gas or groceries, and Will would be gone until three.

A man who worked as hard as he did deserved a hearty breakfast every once in a while. Plopping his Stetson on his head, he thundered down the stairs.

"Morning, Dan'l." Lucy filled his cup to the brim with strong, dark coffee. "You look lonelier than an abandoned calf. Will gone for the day?"

Daniel sipped at his mug, his gaze glued on the counter. If Lucy knew he was there to keep an eye on Zara, the older woman would never let him hear the end of it. "Yep. His teacher said he could come in and use the computer while summer school was in session. The little traitor couldn't wait to board the bus."

Lucy nodded in sympathy. "The boy's a smart one, all right. Now, what can I get for you this morning?"

"Hot cakes and bacon," he answered automatically. "And ask Tomas to warm the syrup."

Laughter, like chiming bells, came from the far side of the restaurant. Unable to resist, Daniel turned toward the sound. Zara, her eyes glowing so brightly he could see their deep blue color from across the room, was having a high old time with those government men.

*Great!* He'd been up half the night worrying that his fast hands had frightened her, and it looked like last night's kiss hadn't disturbed her sleep one iota.

Lucy placed his breakfast order on the pass-through, then swung back to face him. "Zara looks like a new-minted penny this morning, don't she? I asked her how dinner went at your place, but she really didn't say. You three have a good time?"

Daniel dragged his gaze back to the older woman. "Things went just fine. I've been meaning to ask, have those TXdot men mentioned how long they'd be staying?"

Instead of answering, Lucy used her towel to clear the counter of invisible crumbs. Tomas rang the bell that signaled an order was up, and she waddled over to check it out. After carrying the plate to a cowboy sitting at the opposite end of the counter, she meandered back to Daniel. "Both cabins are paid to the end of June. Why?"

Shrugging, he sipped at his coffee. "I didn't think there'd be enough work for them to stay this long. They are working, aren't they?"

"Shoot if I know," Lucy muttered. "Seems to me they spend a lot more time askin' questions than they do puttin' in an honest day's labor. I went to the creek to pick poke salad yesterday afternoon and found them diggin' around like badgers huntin' grubs. Seemed real excited about somethin' they found near your property, but they clammed right up when they saw me." She put her fists on her ample hips and beetled her brow as she stared at the two men. "Still, they pay on time, and Zara says they tip well, so I can't complain."

The front door opened and Jack Farley hurried in. Closing his oversize umbrella, he propped it against the wall and shook himself like a wet dog. "Morning." He took a seat at the counter next to Daniel. "That's quite a storm we're having. What do people do to keep busy around here when it rains this hard?"

Daniel accepted his plate of pancakes and bacon from Lucy and smothered the stack in steaming maple syrup. "They work, Farley. I sell gas and dry goods, Lucy runs this place, Dolly washes clothes. I thought she needed your help, by the way."

"Not right now." Jack nodded his thanks when Lucy set a mug in front of him filled with coffee. "Most of the videos aren't due back until five, and I finished all the chores Dolly needed done yesterday. How was your dinner with the lovely Miss Zara last night?"

Well hell, did everybody in town know Zara had spent the evening at his place? Instead of answering, Daniel focused on breakfast. Jack Farley's obnoxious grin was just too damned much to handle on an empty stomach.

Jack leaned in close. "She's a very attractive woman, but I guess you already know that. I'd be cooking dinner for her myself if that efficiency at Dolly's had more than a hot plate."

Before Daniel could make up his mind whether or not to deck the guy, Zara walked around the counter. Smiling politely, she kept her gaze on Jack.

"This rain is really something, isn't it?"

Jack puffed out his chest. "Sure is." He spun on his stool as he took in the near-empty restaurant. "Say, I've got an idea. How about you and I go to my place when your shift is over and play some cards or checkers? Better yet, I could show you my portfolio. I've compiled quite an impressive group of photos over the past year."

Daniel halted in midchew. Fisting a hand around his coffee cup, he resisted the urge to snarl. "Look, Farley, Zara doesn't have time to spend playing games with you."

"I don't?" she asked, her mouth pursed into a tight knot.

"You don't," agreed Lucy, sounding like a lioness protecting her cub. "Today's the day I promised to teach you how to make cherry pie. And if you two roosters don't approve, you can take your objections outside. Now, it looks like that storm's lettin' up. Dan'l, there's someone at your pumps. Jack, I'd like to let you sit and jaw with my help, but we got work to do."

Grasping Zara by the elbow, Lucy steered her into the kitchen without a backward glance. "Come with me, little girl. We got us a passel of piecrust to roll."

"Guess she put us in our place," commented Jack, grinning from ear to ear. "I don't think Miss Lucy likes me very much."

Daniel finished his coffee and rose from his stool, relieved the older woman had found a way to keep Zara and the photographer apart. The jerk's invitation had been so obvious he might as well have asked her to view his etchings, for chrissakes.

"Mr. Murphy?" The taller, thinner surveyor appeared at his right side. "Now that the rain is slowing down, we want to lay a counting line across the highway. We'd like permission to set the box on your property."

Drawing to his full height, Daniel folded his arms across his chest. "Where are you laying the other one?"

"The other one?"

He raised a brow. "If the line on my side of the highway is for northbound traffic, I'd imagine you need one for the southbound side as well."

"Right you are, Murphy," Chuck, the surveyor with the crew cut answered. "And we're laying it in front of Mrs. Hingle's laundry. We figured if we used the Hole's lot, come Saturday night some cowboy in a pickup truck would manage to take the box out, and this place is too busy. Isn't that right, Frank?"

Frank shook his head in agreement. "So what do you say? Can we set the box up at the corner of your gas station?"

Daniel wanted to say no. He wanted to shout no, in fact, then push one of the guys up against a wall and make them confess the real reason they were in town. But he knew Lucy wouldn't appreciate his turning her diner into a boxing ring. And since he was the only one who thought it strange their one-horse burg had been turned into Grand Central Station, he doubted anyone would be on his side of the fight.

"Fine. Just make sure you keep it out of the main drive that leads away from the pumps. I won't be responsible if anyone gets it in their head to run the darned thing over."

"Sure, no problem. You ready, Chuck?" asked Frank, pulling a billowy yellow rain slicker over his head.

"Ready." Chuck nodded, doing the same. "And thanks again, Murphy. Farley, see you around."

Daniel waited until all three men were gone before he put on his Stetson and left the restaurant. Will had been right, he thought with a tight-lipped grin. Wearing those yellow rain slickers did make a man look like a dork.

Hours before dawn, awakened by her internal clock, Zara sat up straight on the side of her bed and stretched. Once the rain passed, she'd waited on a steady stream of customers straight through to closing. Wincing at the tightness in her shoulders, she recalled the taxing yet strangely fulfilling task she'd been introduced to that morning. Miss Lucy had been right when she'd said making dough for two dozen pies could give a body a powerful ache.

When Zara was younger, she had sometimes helped her mother cook a meal on special holidays, but the day-to-day preparation of food was now considered a menial task confined to androids or a replicator. Fruits and vegetables on her planet had been so manipulated in the laboratory, they tasted insubstantial and bland when compared to the interesting varieties she'd found on Earth. This afternoon, when the wonderful aroma of cherry pies baking had filled the diner, she couldn't help but think she'd accomplished a wondrous feat.

More importantly, between endless rounds of flouring, rolling, pitting, and filling, she hadn't found the time to daydream even once about Daniel Murphy and the unbelievable kiss they had shared. Toxic effects of alcohol and chocolate aside, if all went well tonight, she would never again feel compelled to rest her head against his hard-muscled chest or run her fingers through his thick, dark hair . . . or feel his lips press demandingly against her own.

Standing, she closed her mind to the erotic memory. If her calculations were correct, she would be entering her fertile period within the next few hours. She would have, at the most, three days to conceive. Nothing, not even Daniel Murphy, she reminded herself, could keep her from locating her subject and attaining her goal.

She dressed quickly, then opened the door to her cabin and peered through the alley separating the restaurant and laundry. At 3 A.M., she had little worry anyone would see her walking through town. After scanning the highway, she took the path between the buildings, stepping carefully around puddles still filled with the previous night's rain. The corner streetlamp illuminated the front of Coombs's Luncheonette, while the light across the street in the parking lot of Murphy's Last Chance was out, casting that side of the road in darkness. Hoping to keep her presence hidden, she walked to Daniel's gas station to begin her quest.

The night was warm and somewhat humid. Zara wiped her palms on her thighs, then held up her wrist and took inventory of the gemstones in her bracelet. The rubies were meant to intensify her healing skills; the diamond crystals pure energy, to be used only for protection or, in dire circumstances, retaliation if attacked. The emeralds enabled the locator disc, assisting with the search for her target and, if need be, her pickup site.

With trembling fingers, she pried out one of the emeralds, popped the catch, and slipped the stone into the indentation made especially for the gems. Once the stone was securely in place, she snapped the clasp shut and pressed. As expected, it cast a pulsing, beaconlike fan of light in front of her.

She began by walking a rectangle from south to west to north to east, intent on following the locator's signal. When the light faded just past Zetmer's Hardware, she crossed to the opposite side of the street in hopes the disc would brighten. Instead, it dulled to a glimmer and slower blink. Undeterred, she walked back in the direction of the Washeteria, then crossed over the highway again and stopped in front of the surveyors' office. When the disc grew brighter, she knew she was on the correct side of the road.

She paced the shoulder in front of the gas station,

but the farther she moved from the corner, the fainter the light shone. Heading back to Murphy's Last Chance, she realized the signal was strongest right here, in front of Daniel's business.

With hesitant steps, she neared the cinder-block and redbrick building, noting the locator's positive pulsing. Puzzled by the instrument's reaction, she worked her way around the back until she stood facing the door to the Murphys' apartment. Staring up at the overhang, then down to her wrist, she told herself the finely tuned disc had to be wrong. This was the home of Daniel Murphy—not Robert Lotello.

Walking backward, she stood in the field between the barn and the garage and watched the locator fade. Pacing ahead, she could actually feel a stronger signal as she drew closer to Daniel's back door. Completely befuddled, she could think of only two possible reasons for the instrument's actions. Either the locator had been damaged on landing, or it was experiencing some kind of internal malfunction.

If the bracelet wasn't working, she would have to question everyone she came in contact with until she found her subject—certainly not the wisest course of action. From the way the locals gossiped, she would only have to speak with two of them before the entire population of Button Creek knew she had business with Robert Lotello.

Taking a deep breath, she decided to test the integrity of the locator one final time. Moving slowly in a circle, she noted that nothing had changed. When she turned away from Murphy's Last Chance, the light dimmed. When she faced the building, the instrument began a strong, pulsing glow.

Concentrating, she tugged at her earlobe and tried to call up the instructions she'd been given on the repair of a faulty locator. Annoyed her mind was blank, she raised her gaze to Daniel's apartment and gasped.

Daniel's head ached like a son of a gun. Rising from his bed, he stumbled to the bathroom, swallowed a trio of aspirins, and returned to his room. After fifteen minutes of lying in the dark, he realized all he could think of was Zara and her soft, yielding body pressed against his groin, which only seemed to make the throbbing worse. Determined to rid his brain of her and the headache, which he suspected might be one and the same, he ordered himself to stop mooning and pulled on his jeans.

Hoping a breath of fresh air would help, he slipped into Will's room. Satisfied the boy was fast asleep, he climbed onto the overhang and took in the vastness of the heavens. Billions of stars dotted the inky blackness, their encompassing glow almost brighter than the three-quarter moon. Heaven and all its wonders had been his first love, its study his profession. Because of Rebecca's betrayal, he'd been forced to give up a job he prized and a goal he'd longed for throughout half his life to become a fugitive. He now knew their relationship had been doomed from the start, but it had been worth every second of frustration and heartache for one simple reason. It had given him Will.

Lowering his sight, he scanned his property from the left, the woods that grew right up to the stream, where the creek ran from a trickle in the summer to a small river in spring. His gaze took in the pasture and barn and, in front of it, the field of wildflowers he and Will planted when they'd first moved here.

Now, staring down into the field, he couldn't quite believe his eyes. He ran a hand over his face, but still the vision remained: a woman holding a light of some kind, swaying amidst the bluebonnets as she moved in a circle.

Unsure whether to call out or simply ignore her, he felt his gut clench when the figure stopped turning and lifted her head. What in the heck was Zara doing, standing in his field at this hour?

When she began to walk toward the house, some unexplainable inner force compelled him to meet her. In his haste, he almost fell into Will's room before trotting barefoot through the house and down the stairs. By the time he arrived at the back door, Zara was waiting for him.

"Daniel?"

Her voice, a mere whisper on the breeze, struck a chord in his heart. Rubbing the sore spot at the back of his head, he worked up a smile. "Zara? What are you doing out here?"

Holding her hands in front at her waist with her right fingers hooked over her left wrist, she met his gaze with a look of wonder. "I needed a little fresh air. The wildflowers are so beautiful I didn't think you'd mind if I—What about you? Why are you up so late?"

He descended the three stairs that led from the cement porch, until he stood directly in front of her. "Nothing serious. Woke up with a headache, so I thought the same as you—that a little fresh air might do me good."

Her eyes grew huge in the moonlight. "You have a headache?"

"I could hardly believe it myself. The darned thing dragged me from a sound sleep. I didn't know what else to do, so I popped a few pills, and now I'm waiting for them to take effect."

Daniel watched as she fumbled with her bracelet. Stuffing it in her pocket, she pursed her lips and tugged at her earlobe. "I could try to make it better, if you want."

She took a step closer, and he smelled the tantalizing aroma of cherries, overlaid with her unique, smoky-sweet scent. The thought of her soft, perfectly shaped hands touching him intimately set his heart to pounding in time with the pain in his head. Swamped by a wave of desire, he asked, "You mean that meditation stuff? Like you did for Will the other night?"

Her straight, even brows drew together, telegraphing her concern. "Yes, but not in the exact same way. I'll need to touch your head, not your chest. I could sit on the porch, and you could sit on the next step down and lean back or—Here, let me show you."

She climbed the stairs, sat down, and spread her thighs wide. Seeing what she suggested, Daniel went all jelly-legged. The idea of his body resting against her most private core with his head pillowed on her breasts was more than he could handle. "I don't want to take advantage . . ."

Madonna-like, she smiled. "Don't be silly. I enjoy making people feel good. Come over here and sit down."

The thrumming in his head increased as he shuffled toward her and sat on the bottom step. Maybe if he didn't touch her long, firm thighs or let his back rest in the V of her legs . . . or put his head against her shapely breasts . . .

"Sit up straighter and lean back." She placed her hands on his shoulders and urged him near. "This will feel good, I promise."

Telling himself he'd never been more happy to have a headache in his life, Daniel followed her instructions—and was catapulted straight to heaven.

Zara's hands went to his temples, moving in small, gentle circles. "How does this feel?"

"Um . . . nice. Real nice."

"Take a few deep breaths." Her fingers threaded through his hair. Stroking softly, they moved to the back of his head. "And this?"

He swallowed. "Good."

"Just good?" she teased, a touch of amusement turning her soft voice sassy.

It felt better than good. If felt incredible. But between the headache and being cradled against her thighs, his brain had turned to oatmeal.

"Is this where the worst of the pain is?"

She put one hand on his forehead and the other behind his left ear, and Daniel shuddered. Warmth suffused his skull, radiated down his chest to his stomach and lower. Colors danced against the backs of his eyelids as a brilliant swirl of purple, magenta, and the softest pink encompassed his brain. Without warning, the pain surged slightly and disappeared in a burst of glittering fireworks.

He closed his eyes as a feeling of utter calm filled him. God, but she could work magic. If this was what Will had felt when she'd eased his asthma attack, no wonder the boy was so enamored of her.

The night sounds stilled around them. Daniel's heartbeat echoed in his ears. The ache in his head had disappeared as quickly as it arrived, while a new more specific pain took hold. The hurt pressed against the zipper of his jeans, pulsing in rhythm with his heart.

Turning in her arms, he knelt on the step and gazed into her eyes. Her palms rested on his shoulders, giving off the same tingling vibration he felt every time they touched.

"I don't know what you did or how you did it, but the headache is gone."

She smiled, just the slightest upturn of lips. "That's good. I'd hate for you to be in pain . . . anywhere."

Daniel tried to remember if he'd experienced this same roller-coaster ride of desire with Rebecca, but simply couldn't recall. It was as if the act of being close to Zara, of being touched by her, had erased his memory and taken control of his senses.

Filled with newfound courage, he sucked in a

breath. Taking one of her hands, he placed it on the bulging placket of his jeans. "I have another hurt."

Her eyes opened wide, and her smile grew until it transformed her face. The rasp of his zipper sounded loud as a freight train rumbling through the night. Inching forward, he feathered his lips over hers, deliberately running his tongue across the seam of her mouth. When she opened on a sigh, he drank in her cherry-sweet taste and moved his hands to her waist, tugging her shirt free. With shaking fingers, he skimmed the satin of her skin, then slid up to cup her breasts. Her nipples, already hard and swollen, burned the center of his palms.

With their mouths still fused, she slipped her hands into his briefs and caressed his penis. The erotic act turned him mindless with need. He ran his palms to her underarms, then pushed the shirt up and over her head as she struggled to get free. Undoing the front clasp of her bra, he tossed the scrap of lace over his shoulder.

Reverently, he placed a fingertip on one budded breast.

"You are so beautiful."

She sighed against his lips. "And you? Are you beautiful as well?"

All doubts forgotten, he rose and took a backward step. Never more aware of the power of his body, he hooked his thumbs in the waistband of his jeans and pulled until he walked out of his clothing. Arms hanging at his sides, he let her look her fill.

Zara's gaze ran greedily over Daniel's muscular arms and flat, rippling stomach, then lower to the juncture of his thighs. She tried to call up the ancient ritual, the words she was supposed to be thinking during the mating act, but nothing came to mind. There was only Daniel, looking magnificent and profoundly male, an offering shrouded in starlight.

"Your turn," she heard him say as he returned to the bottom of the steps.

Heat rushed up from her belly to flood her cheeks as she came to her feet. Mimicking his actions, she pulled her jeans and panties down and kicked them aside. Fully naked, she quivered as the night air whispered across her skin. As soon as she'd felt the microscopic tracking device implanted behind his left ear, she knew she'd found her man. Though his name was different, the locator had to be correct. He was *the one*, and she would hold the memory close forever.

She opened her arms. "I've waited so long for you, Daniel. Please don't make me wait any longer."

His teeth flashed white as he climbed the stairs and stepped into her embrace. Like some great predatory beast, he pressed her against the wall, devouring her mouth with his own. His hot, searching hands roamed up from her belly to cup her breasts, while his lips traveled downward, found a pebbled nipple and began to suck.

Zara's bones liquefied as her knees buckled. Catching her, Daniel lifted her and crushed her to his chest. The force of his mouth tugging at her breast made her whimper low in her throat. Cradling her in his arms, he walked to a wicker settee and set her on her feet. He plucked up a folded blanket and opened it, then tossed it onto the porch. Dropping to his knees, he drew her down until they were lying side by side, his arms resting on her back.

"I swear I'm healthy," he murmured, "but we still have to think about protection. Wait here while I go into the store—"

"No! Don't leave me." She raised her fingers to his lips. "You don't need a condom."

Coming to his knees, he rested his hands at the sides of her head. "It's been a long time for me, Zara. I haven't been with anyone since Will's mother. I don't want to hurt you."

She grasped his forearms and pulled him near. "I've seen you with your son. You could never hurt me."

Tenderly, he placed his mouth on hers, and she opened to his tongue. His hands stroked, his fingers teased, until every cell of her body vibrated under his touch. Reaching out, she wrapped her fingers around his steely length and moved her palm up and down, then around to grasp his buttocks. Boldly, she pressed him down, until he was nestled in the V of her legs, hard and throbbing against her heat.

"Zara! I don't think I can hold on much longer."

"Then don't. I need you inside of me as much as you need to be there."

Raising up, he gazed into her eyes. She arched against him and clutched his sex, guiding him to the emptiness only he could fill. Daniel plunged, and the knifelike pain sliced straight to her heart, but she kept silent, knowing this was part of giving herself to a man.

"Aw, Christ, baby, why didn't you tell me?"

A tear trickled down her cheek. "Because there was nothing to tell. Now love me, Daniel, the way a man is supposed to love a woman. Please, just love me."

Stunned by her gift, Daniel held Zara close, rocking gently as she trembled in his arms. Her warm, wet core milked the center of his existence, and when her shudders came hard and fast, he drove harder, faster, longer. Covering her mouth with his, he swallowed her scream with a shout of his own, until the universe stopped spinning and the stars died in the sky.

# Eight

*A* breeze rippled across Zara's forehead, fluttering the stray curls at her temples. Chilled, she turned to her side and snuggled into the mound of muscle resting beside her. Enfolded in a hard-yet-protective embrace, her nose brushed soft, downy hair. She opened her eyes and found Daniel gazing at her with a satisfied grin.

She groaned inwardly, acutely aware that something not quite right had happened. The locator had led her here, to a man for whom she felt more than just physical attraction. And though he didn't have the proper name, he did have the implant that reacted correctly to the locator.

There could be no doubt that Daniel was Robert Lotello.

But how could she ask him why he had a different name without explaining why she was looking for him? Until she had a chance to align her thoughts, nothing made sense. Nothing, that is, but the feel of Daniel's arms holding her in a warm embrace. She could tell from his raised brow, he was about to voice a question, one she was fairly certain she couldn't answer, so she avoided his gaze and concentrated on his finely molded chest.

"I didn't hurt you, did I?" He ran a finger from her nose to her ear, until it rested on the diamond in her earlobe.

"Of course not." She peered over his shoulder, another dismissive ploy. "But the sun's coming up. I have to go—"

His sigh, one of contentment and understanding, filled her with a second wave of desire. "Not yet. I want to look at you a little longer, hear you tell me what's going on in your mind."

"My mind?" She tried to make light of the situation. "Not much, other than what I'm going to wear to work today."

He smiled. "Very funny." Placing a kiss on her forehead, he asked, "What are you really thinking about right now?"

Refusing to surrender to his probing, she thought again about her mission. Generations had passed before her world discovered that the children they'd been creating were being born with fertility problems. Many of the women were sterile, and the few men still capable of having sex could father only females. Her planet was filled with desperate people, incapable of bringing back the balance between their men and women.

She and her compatriots had been the lucky ones, born into families who had believed the only way to create a child was the natural way, and declined to have gene-altered offspring. Though a few of those children were male, the elders felt it was time to strengthen the gene pool with new blood. It was the reason she and the others had been chosen, nurtured, and trained for this journey.

Until tonight, Zara had never realized how much the coupling would mean. If she could crawl inside of him and stay that close to him forever, she would die happy. Now she knew how her parents must have felt when they'd conceived her—exhilarated, happy, and secure, all from this one sweeping act.

If she remained on the porch any longer, nestled against Daniel's warmth, she was certain they would have sex again. And she had no doubt each repetition would fuel further desire. She'd been warned that once she met her target, she would feel an inner longing to carry out the mating ritual, but she suspected this compelling attraction to Murphy came from something more than the locator's mechanical pull.

Frowning, she attempted to rise. "I'm thinking that Will might wake up. It wouldn't be right for him to find us here."

With a hand on her shoulder, Daniel gently pressed her back to the blanket. "It can't be much past four-thirty. He never gets up this early. Stay a few more minutes and tell me what you're thinking—how you feel."

"I told you—fine. What more is there to say?"

His jaw clenched. "You were a virgin, a fact I find pretty peculiar in this day and age. How old are you, anyway?"

*With the people of my world living to twice the life expectancy of Earthlings, a lot older than you think.* But this was definitely the wrong time to discuss the life span of her race. She pursed her lips, hoping to shame him into silence.

"I thought it was bad manners for a man to ask a woman such a personal question—and excuse me for being 'peculiar.' "

He huffed a sound of frustration. "You know what I mean. This is the new millennium. The way I understand it, women, at least most of the halfway-attractive ones over the age of sixteen, no longer save themselves for marriage. I'd peg you for about twenty-five. Am I close?"

"I'm a little older," she lied, thinking he could double the Earth age and be more on the mark.

"Yeah, well, it can't be much. And since I'm the guy you picked to be the first, I'd like to know why."

"I don't have an answer for you. And I didn't think I'd be questioned like a suspected criminal by the man to whom I chose to give myself." Still unable to look him in the eye, she stared at the pulse beating in his neck. "If I'd known it would be such a big deal, I would have—"

His fingers wrapped around her upper arm, just

tight enough to let her know he was upset. "You would have what? Found someone else? Christ, Zara, choosing your first lover isn't like shopping for a new pair of shoes. And that's certainly not the kind of talk a man likes to hear after doing what we just did."

*And if I'm not pregnant, we'll have to do it again.*

Struggling to regain her focus, she rose to her knees. "I'm sorry, but surely you can see how awkward this situation is. I don't know the correct rules for postcoital conversation."

"Yeah, well neither do I," he growled, kneeling to face her. "I told you I haven't been with a woman since Rebecca, and I meant it. You're not the only one new to this game." He let go of her arm and ran a hand across his nape. "Forgive me if I'm not acting the way you expected, but I thought what we did was special."

Confused by his attitude, she stood and struggled into her T-shirt, then her panties and jeans. She'd been told most humans desired some form of reassurance after they shared in the sexual act, but she'd also been warned that many men were fearful of showing emotion. Daniel's anger came as a surprise. It almost sounded as if he cared.

After slipping on her shoes, she picked up her bra and tucked it into her pocket. It would take a day to learn whether or not she was pregnant. If she wasn't, they would have to make love—no, she reminded herself—have sex—again. Which meant she needed to keep him willing.

Glancing down, she found Daniel staring through

hooded eyes, as if trying to see into the very center of her being. Sighing, she said what she could to ease the tension.

"I agree that what just happened was special. And as to why I picked you . . . well, I guess I never felt attracted enough to anyone, until tonight. I hope we can . . . I mean I'd like to do it . . . again."

His face settled into an unreadable mask. Rising to his feet, he draped the blanket around his hips. "Yeah, me too. But I want you to know I don't consider this just indiscriminate sex or anything. I apologize if I came on a little strong."

She walked down the steps and he followed. Standing under the waning moon, he bent his head until his lips brushed gently against hers. After he straightened, he tucked a stray lock of hair behind her ear. "If you wait a second, I'll get dressed and walk you home."

The gesture, so sweet and sincere, made her want to weep. She refused even to consider the way her heart pulsed or her body trembled at the idea of another mating. Being near him was causing her to lose her objectivity, and that was the last thing she needed. Her mission—her goal—had to be her first priority.

"We can talk later. Go upstairs and check on Will. If you come to Miss Lucy's after dinner, I'll buy you both a piece of cherry pie."

"Sure I can't—?"

"Yes, I'm sure. Now good-bye."

Daniel followed her to the edge of the building and waited while she crossed the street and disappeared into the pale dawn light. Her long, shapely legs and determined stride told him she was stubborn, but her unsteady gaze and nervous responses to his pointed questions had said she was vulnerable, too, and very much a rookie in the man-woman game.

Heaving a sigh, he picked up his jeans, tossed them over his shoulder, and made his way up the stairs. Making love—no, he cautioned himself—having sex with Zara had been even better than he'd imagined. Though he hadn't been with many women in his life, he had a sad suspicion she had ruined him for any others. But if things were so damned wonderful, why did he have a raft of questions still tumbling around in his mind?

For starters, she'd been a virgin, so why was she on birth control? The answer she'd given had been no answer at all, but she could have invented a few. She could have said she was taking the pill to regulate her cycle or help with her complexion; he would have bought either excuse. And if she'd lied and wasn't protected, why would she chance getting pregnant?

Now that he was clearheaded enough to think, he couldn't help but wonder if he was simply a way to unburden her of her virginity. Had he been used by Zara the same way he'd been used by Rebecca?

Aware he had a lot to think over, he tiptoed into Will's bedroom, relieved to find him still asleep. Gazing down at the person he loved most in the world, he realized Zara had been right about one thing—it would have been a disaster if the boy had found them on the porch. He was too perceptive. If he suspected something was going on, he would jump to all kinds of conclusions. The last thing Daniel wanted was to get Will's hopes up or set a bad example.

He just couldn't take the chance of bringing another person fully into their lives right now. As much as Zara seemed to fit, he also felt she was hiding something. And he had his own secrets to protect. Relationships needed to be built on honesty, something he didn't think either of them could give at the moment.

He stood at the window and watched the sun rise over the barn. It was definitely too late to go back to sleep. He had a lube job and a tune-up scheduled, and now he had a date for dessert at Miss Lucy's. Will would be thrilled.

Heading for the shower, he wondered what the evening would bring.

Chuck had just finished brewing a pot of coffee when he heard the coded knock. He'd been expecting Frank, senior agent and leader of this assignment, but not quite so soon. Eager to know if there was any news, he walked in double time to the door, unlocked it, and swung it just wide enough to let his boss slither through.

"Everything quiet, or did you get lucky?"

Frank rotated his shoulders as he made his way to the worn green-and-gold plaid sofa. Sitting heavily, he rubbed a hand over his full, ruddy face. "The woman met Murphy, but first she performed some kind of weird ritual—hell, it could have been a mating dance, for all the sense it made."

Encouraged by his superior's words, Chuck poured two cups of coffee and brought them to the table. After a week of little more than suspicion, maybe this was the break they'd been waiting for. "Ritual? Like a ceremony or something?"

"Damned if I know. But that bracelet on her wrist was a part of it. Lit up like a garden torch while she paced off steps around the highway. She walked a rectangle down the main drag, across, up, and over again, until she landed back in front of Murphy's Last Chance. Stared at the building for a few minutes, then marched to the field between the barn and the station."

"What happenêd when she got there?"

"Not much. Spun around in a circle for a while. Looked damn strange to me."

Chuck's bushy brows met over the bridge of his nose as he sat at the table. "Nothing else?"

Rising from the sofa, Frank stretched out the kinks in his back, then took a seat opposite his coworker. "She stared at the building until Murphy came out. He met her on the porch and the two of them started going at it, but I didn't stick around to watch."

Chuck leaned back and folded his arms across his chest. "You mean they had sex?"

"I told you I didn't stick around to watch, but I heard enough to know that was the general idea. Before that she did something—don't know what, exactly. Murphy complained of a headache, and she offered to take care of it. Got quiet for a few minutes, then I heard him say the headache was gone. Right after that there was a lot of moaning and panting, so I left. Poked around the Feed and Grain for a while, then circled behind the trailers. The people in this po-dunk town are so gullible you could spray paint Day-Glo orange graffiti down the middle of the highway and they wouldn't even notice."

Pinching his lower lip between two fingers, Chuck gazed at the ceiling. "Maybe the buzz around town about her bringing that little boy out of a serious asthma attack was on the money. Plenty of people we've questioned told us they've met aliens with powers way beyond ours. Maybe being a healer is hers."

Frank selected a manila folder from the pile in front of him, opened it, and tapped his knuckles on the table. "Problem is, it's all hearsay. We've never caught an alien and been able to check it out. And don't for-get those idiots we arrested in Sedona. It was damned embarrassing dragging them all the way to Washing-ton only to have Lucas Diamond laugh in our faces. There are a lot of New-Agers who practice holistic medicine, and not one of them has ever mentioned they came from Pluto or any other damned place in the universe. I'm still not convinced she's the one we're looking for."

"Stands to reason it's her," Chuck insisted. "Jack Farley came to town too late to be considered, and he doesn't make any bones about his interest in aliens. Besides, if he's an example of an extraterrestrial life-form, they'd never have the smarts to get off the ground on their own planet, never mind shuttle to ours. I already told you about the strange expression Zara had on her face when she raced out of the laundry the other morning. It has to be her."

"Then we're going to need better evidence than a glowing bracelet and her being able to cure a headache or two. I think we should move farther north, up to the lake, and check around there. We can't afford to miss anything." Frank drained his coffee mug, then walked to the door and opened it a crack. "I say we keep investigating. The lady might not be what she seems, but we can't just walk up to her and accuse her of being from another solar system. Murphy doesn't act like he belongs here either, and I don't think for a moment he's an extraterrestrial."

"Murphy is definitely a fish out of water," argued Chuck. "Gave me a hell of a time when I laid down that counting line. And he asks too many questions. Maybe we should run a check on him, too, just to see what we can stir up."

Frank peered into the morning light, then quickly shut the door. "The woman's crossing the highway. Once she's in her cabin, I'm going to get some sleep. The lab results on that slime we sent to Virginia should be ready today—make the call instead of us waiting for the mail. Wake me after you talk to them. And let's try to get a sample of her fingerprints, just to be on the safe side. She might not be an alien, but she's definitely hiding something."

"Right, boss," Chuck said to the closing door. He

walked to the pitted counter and poured another cup of coffee, hoping the bitter liquid would burn off his anger.

Never mind that Frank was the head honcho on this assignment. It didn't mean he couldn't have an opinion, or do a little sleuthing of his own. He had a brain and knew what to look for. He'd worked plenty of alien investigations before the two of them had been partnered.

Besides, ever since that damned movie had come out, he'd wanted to kick a hole in something. *Men in Black* couldn't have been further from the truth, and it had made his division in the Bureau a laughingstock. It would be a real step up the ladder if he could prove everyone wrong, maybe earn him a book and movie deal, and a host of guest appearances on Leno or Letterman to boot.

If Frank doesn't want a turn in the spotlight, thought Chuck, I'm not going to quibble. Hell, it was time he had his own chance at the big score and a little notoriety, instead of his boss. Being labeled the first man to bring in an alien was a title he could live with just fine.

*Nine*

$D$aniel ignored the ache in his lower back as he bent over Henry Danforth's pickup and made a final adjustment on the timing belt. He had a reputation to uphold as an exacting and reliable mechanic, and he'd be darned if he'd let some woman who'd dropped into his life out of the blue ruin that image. At least that's what he'd told himself every time his mind wandered from the repair of automobile engines to Zara.

The questions nagging him at sunrise had only intensified throughout the day. Though he wasn't the most experienced man in the world, he knew enough to be certain the sex with Zara had been incredible. Now, if only he could figure out why she'd treated losing her virginity more like a clinical experiment than a rite of womanhood.

He'd been so boggled by the act, he'd almost forgotten how easily she'd cured his headache. The colors he'd seen, the warmth he'd felt infusing his body had been magical, practically as mind-altering as the sex. Anyone capable of producing those reactions simply by the laying-on of hands belonged in a medical journal or one of those television tabloid shows. Yet Zara had acted as if her gift was nothing more than normal meditation.

The more he thought about it, the more it gave him pause. Hell, everything he knew or didn't know about the woman gave him pause. She'd appeared from nowhere. He didn't even know her last name. Where did she come from, and why would a woman as intelligent as Zara seemed want to live in a town like Button Creek? And what person over the age of seventeen couldn't work a washing machine or have a driver's license, even if she only used it for identification purposes?

Unfortunately, he'd been so distracted by the puzzling thoughts he'd been short-tempered with his son. After a cranky lunchtime discussion on why his father had yet to take the slime in the freezer to a lab in Dallas, Will had muttered something about going to help Tomas's wife with her baby, and Daniel quickly agreed. Now, close to the dinner hour, he felt guilty about foisting his kid on Maria for an entire afternoon. Her command of the English language was sketchy at best, and Will's nonstop questions and constant chatter would, at the very least, have her spinning in confusion.

Daniel wanted to kick himself for getting so impatient with his son. He'd been an inquisitive child, too. It was frustrating when adults didn't answer your questions. Rebecca had often complained that her parents never spent any time with her while she was growing up. With her father a well-known superior court judge and her mother on the board of every charity in New York City, she'd pretty much been raised by a string of maids and nannies.

That was one of the reasons he'd been compelled to fight for the custody of his child. The judge and his wife hadn't thought him good enough to take care of his own son, yet they'd been so callous they would have allowed the boy to be cared for by strangers.

He'd been able to justify the act of kidnapping Will by telling himself the Warfields had given him no choice. If they'd allowed him one inch in the custody battle, if they hadn't bribed a laboratory worker into falsifying the DNA test or used their influence to sway the family court judge, he would still be teaching at Columbia and Will would be living close enough for weekly visits.

Their own deceit had cost them their grandson—and forced him to become a fugitive.

He heard a scuffling noise and turned to see Will walking slowly into the garage. Guilt overwhelmed him, and he tried for a truce. "You have a good time at Maria's?"

Will's usually animated face was puckered in a frown—a sure sign there was something on his mind. "Pretty much. I played with Lucetta and took her for a walk around the trailers in her stroller, then Maria let me help change the baby's diaper. After that, I watched while Lucetta had her afternoon feeding."

*Uh-oh*, thought Daniel, *here it comes.*

Moving to his father's side, Will folded his arms and rested them on the fender. "Is that the only reason women have breasts? So they can feed a baby?"

Daniel bit the inside of his cheek before he answered. "It's the main one."

"Is that why so many women are showing their breasts on the Internet? Because they're getting ready to nurse their babies?"

Daniel straightened so fast his head cracked against the hood of the truck. Wincing at the pain, he held back a string of foul words. "The Internet? You've seen pictures of women's breasts on the Internet?"

Rubbing his nose, Will shrugged. "Sometimes. Grunt and Ricky are always fooling with stuff like that."

"I see." Daniel warned himself not to overreact and ducked back under the hood. "And do you fool around with them?"

Will moved to the front of the truck and stood on tiptoe. "Nu-uh. They turn off the monitor when I walk in the room. But once in a while I see anyway."

Daniel tried his best to act nonchalant, but inside he was fuming. How the heck was a responsible father supposed to make his son understand that pornography had a place, but it certainly wasn't on his twelve-year-old friend's PC? And what the hell was Jay Pepperdine doing, letting boys on testosterone overload look at that kind of thing in the first place?

Standing, he furrowed his fingers through his hair and checked out the bump he'd earned when he'd whacked his head. "Does Mr. Pepperdine know that's what his son is looking at on his computer?"

"Beats me. But lately, Grunt and Ricky have been doing it a lot. It's boring."

*Boring?* Daniel let out a breath, relieved he'd been given a reprieve. The boy knew the basic mechanics of how babies were made, but had yet to learn the finer points. "You might not think so when you get closer to twelve. It goes with the stuff I explained to you about what happens when a man and woman are attracted to one another. When you start thinking women's breasts are interesting, let me know, and I'll fill you in on the rest, okay?"

"Okay." Mammary glands temporarily forgotten, Will dragged a case of oil to the pickup, climbed onto it, and peered into the bowels of the truck while Daniel renewed his work. After a few seconds of silence, he asked somberly, "Do you think I'll be as tall as you when I grow up?"

Daniel muffled a laugh. How in the heck was he supposed to know? He'd been an only child, but his father and uncles had all stood right at six feet. Will very much resembled Rebecca, who'd been a fine-boned, delicate woman, but she'd had no brothers, and the few times Daniel met Judge Warfield, the frail-looking man had been seated.

Still, there was no need to let Will think he was a scrawny kid. "Right now, I'd say you're about average for an eight-year-old. If you manage to grow into those clodhoppers we laughingly refer to as feet, you could be as tall as me."

Giggling, Will glanced down at his shoes, then back to his father. "I want to have muscles, too. How long do you think it will take for my biceps to get as big as yours?"

Daniel recalled the look of approval he'd seen in Zara's eyes when he'd undressed. Few college professors were known for their stellar physiques. Until he'd started working in the garage, his build had been average at best. Lifting cases of canned goods and overhauling engines had obviously added a few notches to his buff quotient.

He slid his gaze to Will, who was waiting patiently for an answer. "A couple more years, I guess, but if you're really determined to get some muscle definition, you could start now. Step down from that box and give me a second."

After Will did as he was told, Daniel finished with the engine, slammed the hood, and wiped his hands on the rag attached to his belt loop. "Come on over here, and I'll show you what to do."

Together, they went to a far corner of the garage where he stored a box of free weights. After pulling out one of the smallest dumbbells, he positioned Will's palm and fingers around its middle, then took out two larger weights and wrapped a hand around each. "Hold it like this and work it slowly. You can do each arm separately or both at the same time."

Imitating his actions, Will did five forearm curls. "How many should I do each day?"

"Ten reps, two times a day should be a good start. And nothing heavier until I say so. Your muscles are still in the growth and development stage. I don't want you to get hurt."

Totally engrossed in the exercise, Will began to count out loud. Daniel finished twice as many reps, then set the weights back in the box. "Why are you so interested in bodybuilding all of a sudden? Grunt and Ricky aren't picking on you again, are they?"

"Nu-uh. But if I'm stronger, I might be able to fight my asthma better. Besides, astronauts have to be in top shape to pass the physical. I'm just getting ready."

"I see." Daniel went to the utility sink and lathered his hands. Using a wire brush, he tackled the grease that had worked its way into his knuckles and under his nails. It was close to six. The sooner he started supper, the sooner they could have dessert—and see Zara.

"You hungry?" he asked, making his way to the wall phone.

"Starving. Could we eat early tonight?"

"How about I dial Mr. Danforth's number? You can tell him his truck is ready. If he's not there, just leave a message. I'll go up and start the barbecue."

He handed the phone to Will, then headed up the stairs. Damn if he wasn't just as eager as his son to get to the diner. If he didn't know better, he'd think Zara had cast a spell on both of them.

Once in the shower, Daniel turned the hot water on high. Resting his hands on the white tile wall, he let the stinging spray pummel the same spots Zara had run her hands over the night before. When the near-scalding water sluiced across his weary muscles he groaned. Surrounded by a steamy cloud, he grew hard and throbbing as he recalled the way he had felt, sheathed to the hilt inside of her. Maybe she would invite him to her place tonight, after the restaurant closed and he got Will to bed.

*Get a grip, Murphy,* he warned himself, scrubbing shampoo into his hair. *Zara's new at this man-woman thing. Coming on like a sexually depraved teenager isn't the way to go if, and it's a big if, you're thinking about a relationship with the woman. Real relationships need to develop slowly, until there's trust and a sense of belonging. Remember how you let yourself get so wrapped up in Rebecca you didn't realize she'd used you until it was way too late?*

"Dad? You almost done in there?"

At the sound of his son's voice, Daniel lowered the water temperature and stuck his head under the spray, more to cool his raging desire than rinse away the shampoo. Just as he turned off the taps he heard the bathroom door open.

"I set the table and made a salad. When are you comin' out?"

Annoyed he'd almost been caught with an erection hard enough to drive nails, Daniel reached past the shower curtain and fumbled for a towel. After wrapping it loosely around his hips, he flung the plastic aside. "What have I told you about respecting another person's privacy?"

Will hung his head and stared at the floor. "When

either of us is in here or our bedroom and the door is shut, we're not supposed to come in unless we knock and the other one says it's okay." Shifting a shoulder, he peeked out from behind a fringe of dark lashes. "But I'm hungry. And I want to see Zara."

Daniel sighed. So did he, and the anticipation was making him as ill-tempered as a randy bear. Stepping over the rim of the tub, he ruffled his son's hair. "Yeah, me too. I promise I'll hurry."

By the time they arrived at the diner it was past seven. The only customers still eating were the surveyors and Jack Farley, and a table of young men who worked at the Feed and Grain. Ticked that he still felt like an overanxious teenager, Daniel tried not to let his excitement show as he and Will found places at the counter. When weekday evenings were slow, Lucy closed early. If his luck held, the few people inside would finish their meals and be out of there in a half hour or so.

"Dan'l." Eyes alight with mischief, Lucy grinned when they settled on their stools. "Zara said you might stop by. You two ready for a taste of her cherry pie?"

Will spun around on his seat before answering. "And a big glass of milk. I'm starving."

Lucy brayed out a laugh. Shoulders shaking, she turned to the kitchen window. "Hey, Tomas, cut me two double slices of pie, would you? And pass over a glass of cold milk."

Always impressed by the way Will could chow

down, Daniel raised a brow. "Correct me if I'm wrong, but aren't you the kid who just polished off a burger, salad, and a huge helping of steamed carrots?"

Wiggling like a worm on a hook, Will ignored the comment and rested his elbows on the counter. Suddenly, his brown eyes brightened. "Hey, Zara. We're here for our pie."

Daniel looked up to find the object of his afternoon fantasies staring pensively from behind the kitchen pass-through. Since he'd spent most of the day ordering himself to stay out of the diner while at the same time secretly hoping Zara would visit the garage, he wasn't surprised to find his stomach acting as if it was ready for a bungee jump. Determined to quell his nerves, he opened a napkin and tucked it into the neck of Will's T-shirt.

Lucy set forks and two giant-sized slices of pie in front of them and with a wink, turned back to Zara. "Seein' as your guests have arrived, I can take care of those two tables if you'd like to handle the counter for a while."

Finally, thought Daniel, they would have a chance to talk privately, or at least as privately as they could in front of a precocious eight-year-old. He watched as, coffee carafe in hand, Zara walked quickly from the kitchen to the counter and filled his cup.

"This pie is the best." Will loaded his fork with a second huge bite. "Isn't it great, Dad?"

Daniel eyed his still-intact slice and cut into the flaky-looking crust. Raising the fork to his lips, he grinned. "I'll let you know in a second."

The pie hit his tongue like a breath of springtime. Cherry-sweet, yet refreshingly tart, it reminded him of the way Zara had tasted last night when he'd run his lips over her lush, welcoming curves. A vision of her lying beneath him, her eyes wide, her breasts rising and falling with desire, flashed through his mind, and he swallowed hard.

"Will's right. This is good." He took a swig of coffee, hoping the hot liquid would wash away her starlit image, but all it did was fill the area below his belt with a burning ache. "I didn't know you were such a good cook," he managed, choking out the compliment.

Zara swiped a dish towel over the counter, worrying a speck that looked ingrained in the Formica. "I'm not really. I just followed instructions. I'm glad you like it."

"How are you feeling?" he asked, trying to convey his concern over what had transpired between them with as little words as possible.

The pink color suffusing her cheeks heightened to fuchsia. She cut her gaze to Will, then back to him. "Fine, thank you. And you?"

Daniel lifted anther forkful of pie off his plate and gave her what he hoped was a meaningful look "Better than fine, now that I know you're all right."

Scanning the room, he finished chewing before he said, "Things look pretty quiet around here. You want to come over after your shift? The night looks like it will be a clear one."

"Could you?" Will interjected. "We could watch television until it's time to sit on the overhang. We get the Sci-Fi Channel on our dish, and sometimes they have really cool shows."

Zara glanced around the diner. "I'm not sure. I still have to sweep the floor and wipe down the tables, then refill the condiments. There's the trash to take out and—"

"I can help." Will swiveled around to face his father. "Please, Dad. I've done it before. It won't be dark for a while yet, but I bet there'll be some really neat stars out later tonight."

Zara's gaze widened as she focused over Will's head. Tabs and money in hand, Jack, Frank, and Chuck had sidled to the counter. After giving a polite nod, Frank set down his check and a ten-dollar bill. "Thought that was a telescope we saw sitting on the deck over your back porch the other day. You two like to watch the stars?"

Always eager to spout off about the sights he viewed through the Meade, Will grinned. "Uh-huh. Dad and I try to get a good look most evenings."

"What a coincidence. Astronomy is a hobby of mine, too. I wonder, did you see anything interesting about a week ago, right before we came to town? I heard there was some kind of meteor shower toward the southeast."

Jiggling a foot, Will sat straighter on his seat and rubbed at his nose. Gauging the pleading look in his eyes, Daniel automatically guessed the boy's problem. "We see interesting sights almost every night. Will is hoping he'll discover a comet or maybe a new planet and the powers that be will name it after him. Isn't that right, son?"

"Um, yeah. That would be cool." Obviously relieved his father had kept him from lying, he downed the last of his milk.

"What about you, Zara?" Frank raised a bushy brow as he shifted his gaze. "Farley tells me you're interested in panning the stars for unusual sights, too."

Scrubbing at the same invisible spot on the counter she'd worked over a few minutes ago, Zara kept her eyes downcast. "Why, yes. I mean, doesn't everyone like to look at the stars?"

Jack Farley propped himself against a stool. "Whadda'ya say, Will? Maybe sometime you'll let me come over and take a peek through that telescope. If you like, I'll even tell you some really great stories about the aliens I've tracked."

"Aliens?" Will's eyes grew round as dinner plates. "You've seen aliens?"

"Well, not face-to-face, of course, but I've managed to take a few interesting photos. I have a friend at the NASA tracking station over on Wallop's Island who lets me know when there've been sightings."

"NASA? Wow."

Frank thumped Jack's back with a little too much enthusiasm. "Come on, Farley. Everybody knows the government doesn't take an interest in those cockamamie stories anymore. Stop pulling the boy's leg."

His gaze crestfallen, Will furrowed his forehead.

"Are you just teasing, Mr. Farley, or do you really have pictures?"

Jack let out a derisive snort. "I sure do. Maybe someday your dad will let you stop by the laundry and we'll go over them together. Would you like that?"

"Yeah. That'd be great. Could I, Dad?"

Daniel had been listening to the discussion with only half an ear, noticing instead that Zara had gone strangely quiet. Shuffling from foot to foot, she was acting as if she wanted to disappear. But what was it she hoped to run away from? Since it certainly couldn't be these men and their nonsensical talk about aliens, it had to be from him and his invitation.

Clearly, last night hadn't meant as much to her as he'd hoped, Daniel thought, suddenly annoyed. Well, if Zara didn't want to see him again, that was just fine. There were plenty of other things he could do with his time.

"Probably." He put a hand on Will's shoulder and forced out a smile. "Since Zara is too busy to join us, maybe the three of you would like to come over for a beer. We could find a ball game on the dish and Will could show you the Meade. What do you think?"

Will's mouth froze into a confused frown. "But I want to help Zara—"

"That's okay, Will. Maybe another night," Zara answered quickly, her breath coming out in a little huff.

Daniel stood. He didn't need a kick in the head to know when he was on the receiving end of a brush-off. Better he should use the time to pump a little more information from the surveyors and get his mind off of the contrary woman all at the same damned time.

Slapping his Stetson onto his head, he waited for Will to climb down from the stool. Without a backward glance, he guided his son to the door as Frank, Chuck, and Jack trailed behind.

Frustrated, Zara folded her arms under her breasts. The door slammed and it took all her self-control to hold back a loud shout of "good-bye." The female explorers she'd questioned before leaving for this mission had warned her most earthmen were full of themselves, but until this moment she hadn't quite understood what that meant. *Let Murphy go off with his male friends,* she told herself. In a few more hours she'd find out whether or not she was pregnant and, if she was, good riddance to him.

Besides wondering why Murphy had changed his name, she'd spent the entire day worrying about whether or not he would want to mate with her a second time. Now here he was, treating her as if she was a hat he could try on and discard without a second thought. Couldn't he tell she was anxious over what had happened between them? Had he lied when he'd told her he wanted to see her again? After everything that transpired, why was he acting as if she didn't exist, just because she didn't jump at his offhand invitation?

Yes, he'd asked if she was all right, but it was such a small stupid question to describe how she'd felt about the physical act of procreation. *How she felt about him.*

"You gonna' finish cleaning up around here, or you plan to stare a hole in that door?"

Zara jumped, embarrassed that Miss Lucy had managed to catch her unaware. "Hm? Oh, clean up, I guess. And I wasn't staring."

Lucy nodded a little too smartly. "Sure you weren't. Just the same, I think you ought to know somethin'."

She dropped her gaze to the counter. "What's that?

"Daniel Murphy wouldn't play fast and loose with a woman, then toss her away like a broken dinner plate. He's a man, like all the rest, but he's better'n ninety-nine percent of 'em. I'd swear by it."

Raising her chin, Zara sniffed. "What Mr. Murphy does or does not do with his damaged dishes has nothing to do with me. He can go eat dirt off a paper plate for all I care."

"That's the spirit. Let him play cards and drink beer with the rest of those fellas. Just remember what I said. If he's found enough nerve to sit in your saddle, he's the kind who'll be man enough to tell you if he doesn't want another ride. You're the one who's got to decide whether or not you're gonna give it to 'im."

Surprised by the older woman's frank words, Zara's cheeks grew warm. Was nothing sacred in Button Creek? Did people know, just by looking at her, that she and Daniel had been intimate? And why should she be embarrassed by a mere biological function?

Worse, those surveyors who she'd first thought were so friendly seemed to be stuck in a rut about gazing at the stars and watching for aliens. It was bad enough Jack Farley thought himself some kind of expert. Now Frank and Chuck were getting into the act, talking about the shower of light that had accompanied her descent to Earth.

It was impossible for anyone to recognize her as anything other than human. Several hundred years ago, when her people first realized the two species had evolved in a similar manner, they had shuttled settlers here with the hope of an alliance. Because her planet was more advanced, its elders decided to wait for the right moment to interact and tucked the planet Earth into a holding pattern.

Right now, Earth's scientists were on the brink of the very same discoveries that had led to her own planet's near downfall. Unfortunately, it would be generations before they realized that cloning and gene manipulation were dangerous. If Earth continued to experiment, uniting their two worlds would be the only way for both species to survive.

Lost in thought, she didn't hear Lucy trundle from the kitchen with the condiment refills until the tray she was carrying hit the table with a thud.

"Come on, girl, I'll give you a hand. If I know Dan'l, those fellas won't be allowed to stick around too long. By the time we're finished here, I'll bet he and Will'll be alone. You go on home and pretty yourself up, then have a look-see."

# Ten

Zara paced the confines of her cabin, suffused with a strange inner heat. Three hours had passed since she'd left the restaurant. Checking the clock on the stove, she knew it was past Will's bedtime. Had Lucy been correct when she'd said Daniel wouldn't keep the men around for long? Did she have the courage to walk across the street and climb the back stairs to his apartment?

And climb the stairs, she must. Because, according to her instruments, she was not pregnant.

It had been optimistic to think she would conceive on her very first try, but she'd been hoping. Getting pregnant last night would have solved a whole list of problems. She could avoid the pitfalls of continued contact with Murphy and pretend the entire en-counter was a mistake . . . pretend the sound of his voice or the rumble of his laughter didn't make her weak. If she went politely about her business, she'd never need to be intimate with the obstinate man again . . . never feel the touch of his hands or the warmth of his lips or . . .

She sighed. She had to find a way to get back in his good graces. A perplexing thought to be sure, as she'd had little practice handling people with the quixotic personality quirks he'd displayed that night.

Sitting heavily on the worn, plaid sofa, she thought back to when she'd first been tested for compatibility to an Earth male. After her scientists realized what their experimentation had wrought, they had searched closer galaxies for a solution, but no species had been found as compatible as the people of Earth. It was then the elders decided to use this planet's males for continuing the existence of her people.

After she'd been found fertile, she'd been sent to the Project Rejuvenation training center with hundreds of other women lucky enough to be capable of reproduction. Following extensive testing, she received news that she had been chosen for the mission and given a course in life on Earth. Though she'd been warned that coupling with a human male could be emotionally taxing, no one had told her it would try her patience or her sensibilities.

For some reason, she had made Murphy angry. To ensure the success of her mission, the only thing she could do was find a way back into his arms. The thought was daunting and, if she was truthful, made her afraid. He had changed his name, something an honest person wouldn't normally do. Was he in hiding? Had he committed a crime? Should she be physically wary of him?

The thought brought a smile to her lips. Daniel had shown himself to be a kind, caring man. Deep down inside, she knew the only reason she had to fear him was because he made her feel things she'd never imagined. Things she'd been told by the elders were forbidden on this quest.

Standing, she shoved her doubts to the back of her mind. Slipping into her shoes, she straightened her shirt, then ran her fingers through her hair. On her planet, physical enhancements were frowned upon, but the women here seemed to use cosmetics freely. If she wore lipstick, this would be the right time to apply it, but she didn't even own a tube of gloss. Murphy had liked her well enough without feminine embellishments last night. If she was lucky, tonight he would feel the same.

Marching to the front door, she swung it open and charged outside—

Straight into Daniel's arms.

"Sorry. I didn't mean to startle you."

Murphy grabbed her elbows and Zara caught his heady, soap-scrubbed scent, so potent it caused her to suck in a breath. Fighting the urge to linger, she took a shaky step back.

"Daniel. I was just coming to see you."

Setting his lips in a straight line, his eyebrows drew together over his hawklike nose. "You were? Why?"

Though the force of his gaze held her captive, Zara folded her arms and tried to maintain eye contact. If

Murphy wanted an argument, he was going to have to push a lot harder than this.

"To talk. I got the impression you were angry."

He raised his hand and propped it against the doorframe, the glow from the hanging lamp suspended over the kitchen table shrouding his features in pale, eerie light. "Why would I be angry? Will and I invited you over—you declined because you had a job to do. End of story. There was nothing to get mad about."

Zara wanted to believe him, but his sharp, clipped tone telegraphed his annoyance. Pulling back her shoulders, she gave him one of her brightest smiles. "Oh. Well, I'm glad you understood. Where is Will, by the way?"

"Home asleep, but I told him I was leaving when I tucked him in. Don't worry. He knows enough not to get out of bed to answer the phone or door."

"Do you have time to come in?"

Looking suddenly contrite, he removed his Stetson and twirled it between his fingers. "Do you *want* me to?"

Stepping back, she swung the door wide. "I do as long as you promise we won't argue."

He huffed out a breath. "I don't want to fight with you, but I don't want you to think I came here for— I don't want to be any trouble."

Zara turned and headed for the refrigerator. *Trouble?* It was all she could do to hold back a giggle. Letting Murphy invade her private space would be nothing but. The last thing she wanted was to send him away. She'd been drawn to him from the moment they'd met, even when she thought he was the wrong man. Now that she knew he was the right one, there was no way she could let him leave.

The snick of the lock and the sound of boots tapping against the worn linoleum had her heart skipping in double time. Looking for a task to still her trembling hands, she tucked her hair behind her ears and searched for refreshments.

"I'm afraid I don't have much to offer. Bottled water or a piece of fruit? I have apples—they're my favorite—or I could put out cheese and crackers—"

She glanced over her shoulder and caught Daniel ogling her backside, his face set in a silly grin. For some reason, the purely male act made her smile. The men on her planet had lost the urge to flirt ninants ago, which made his admiration all the more empowering.

Daniel met her amused gaze and cleared his throat. Setting his hat on the table, he pulled three smallish packets from his pocket. "No need. I brought you a peace offering."

The heady scent of chocolate filled her senses, bringing back the night of their first kiss. She'd seen this particular candy, a caramel-filled concoction said to be bittersweet and delicious, advertised on the television. Reaching out, she took it from him, letting their fingers touch.

"Thank you for thinking of me," she said, her smile still firmly in place.

"It's one of Will's favorites, so I stock it in the

store." He set the other two on her table. "Want me to open it for you?"

He was making amends with a gift so trivial, yet so thoughtful it made her heart ache and, she suddenly realized, not just for the taste of chocolate. The exotic aroma sent a shiver down her spine, almost as if Daniel were stroking her.

Eagerly, she passed the bar back to him. "Yes, please."

He tore into the wrapper and broke off a section. She held out her palm and he stepped closer, a little-boy look of mischief lighting his eyes. "Nu-uh. Open wide."

The idea of what he suggested registered like a thunder clap. She'd watched movies that showed men and women feeding each another as a precursor to the sexual act. If that was what Daniel had in mind, it was obvious she wouldn't have to do much to convince him to mate with her a second time.

Female explorers had been right. Earthmen could be incredibly easy.

She did as he asked, and he slipped the small, dark square between her lips, then broke off another piece. "Your turn," he whispered, placing the treat in her hand.

Getting comfortable with the game, Zara did the same, but before she could pull away he closed his lips around her finger. The glint in his eyes darkened to the color of the chocolate as she removed her hand. He chewed while she savored the slowly dissolving sweetness of her own piece.

Moving closer, he forced her to take a step of retreat, then another, and another, until her lower back hit the edge of the countertop. "First you fed me cherry pie, now candy. You're spoiling me," he murmured.

Electricity sizzled through her veins. Fighting to catch her breath, Zara stared at the front of his shirt. The memory of his well-formed body gleaming in the moonlight shot a tremor straight to her womb. How her fingers itched to separate the metal snaps one by one, until she could touch the finely sculpted muscles she knew lay hidden underneath.

"You were the one who brought the chocolate, remember?" Unaccustomed to the sexual banter, she fumbled behind her back until she found a glass. "It's making me thirsty."

He snatched the tumbler away and set it back on the counter. Catching her hand, he held tight, sending a jolt of desire to her midsection. "Me too. But not for water."

With deliberate smoothness, he snaked his arms around her waist, then slipped his palms under her T-shirt and up her back. Pulling her to his chest, he let his hands slide to her rib cage so his fingers could cup the bottom of her breasts through her bra. Tilting his head, Daniel's breath fanned her cheeks, warming her to the tips of her toes. Gently, he moved his lips over hers, until she thought she would melt. Opening his mouth, he drew her inside where his sweet, chocolaty taste filled her with longing.

A wave of primal desire washed through her. She'd been warned to keep her emotions in check when she found her target, but she was willing to bet the elders had never met anyone as compelling as Daniel Murphy. It was time to admit that for the short while she was on Earth, she would be completely entangled in his life. She only hoped she would be strong enough to leave him when the time came.

Cursing silently, Daniel fought against the kiss and everything it implied. He'd come here with a simple flag of truce for being such a jerk and leaving the diner mad. But the instant Zara opened the door, he knew he'd been wrong, which had made him even more angry. He'd wasted three hours with a group of men he didn't give a pig's whistle about, just because he refused to believe this woman had found a way to tunnel through the wall he'd so carefully constructed around his life.

Rebecca had been his graduate assistant, so sleeping with her had made him more than a little uncomfortable. When she'd disappeared, it had been almost a relief. Being with Zara was nothing like spending time with Rebecca. Touching her, feeling her body shape itself so perfectly to his, slammed like a fist to the gut. When they were together, he felt as if they were soaring high in the stratosphere, among the stars and planets he'd so often dreamed of exploring. Next to having sex with her, this inexplicable pull was the most unbelievable thing he'd ever experienced.

The sound of her whimper, a small moan of need, spurred him on. Lifting her breasts in his hands, he nestled his knee between her thighs, determined to make his intentions clear. If she pushed him away, if she sent out one negative signal, heaven help him, he would do the sensible thing.

He would leave.

Her hands traced the contour of his shoulders and came to rest on his chest, and he groaned his frustration. Ruing his hasty vow, he closed his eyes and cleared his throat. "I'm sorry. I don't know what—"

*Snap!* The pop sounded loud as a gun shot.

His eyes shot open in surprise. "What are you doing?"

*Snap!* "Something I've been wanting to do ever since I first saw you in this shirt." *Snap! Snap!* One by one, she undid the metal tabs holding the fabric in place.

Pleasure flared when her fingers brushed his skin. Leaning back, he gave her room. Her look of concentration was quickly replaced by one of reverence as the shirt gapped open. After popping the final snap, she ran her fingers to his stomach and lower, until she reached the button on his jeans. "One more to go," she murmured, undoing the straining clasp.

Daniel swallowed past the lump in his throat and placed his lips on her forehead. "Are you sure? Because once that zipper goes down, all bets are off. There's no way in hell I'll be able to walk out the door."

With time-stopping slowness, the final barrier to their intimacy rasped open. Like a match to gasoline, her searching touch set him on fire. *Spontaneous combustion*, he thought, filling his hands with her breasts.

If he didn't get them skin to skin soon, they would both go up in flames.

Her breasts swelled in his palms, her nipples turned rigid. Pushing upward, he slid off her shirt and bra and flung them behind him in one impatient motion. Tugging, they struggled out of their jeans and shoes, finally free to explore each another at will.

"This is crazy," he moaned. Grasping her bottom, he pulled her against his groin. "If I don't get myself inside of you, I'm going to launch like a rocket."

Zara's fingertips feathered against his jaw. "Me too. But I'd always heard this was something better done in a prone position."

His lips devoured hers, his hands branded her with need. Seconds later, they fell onto the bed. Daniel rolled beneath her so she could sit on top, nestled firmly against his erection. Reaching up, he teased her nipples until she groaned. Taut as a bowstring, she arched her back and gave a soft cry. Wanting more, he slipped a hand between her thighs and slid first one, then two fingers inside. When he found her hidden core he circled the hardened bud, fondling until her eyes closed and her body rocked in rhythm with his palm.

"Daniel . . . I can't . . ."

"You can. Just lift up a little—" He adjusted his length and arrowed into her hot, silky wetness. Tugging her hips in an up-and-down motion, he showed her the movement needed to pleasure them both.

"Oh, my." Zara bent forward to rest her hands on his shoulders, and he tongued a beaded nipple.

She shuddered, and he knew she was close to climax. He rolled over, until she lay beneath him, her moans primal, her flesh quivering.

"Wrap your legs around me, sweetheart, then hang on tight."

When she did as he asked, Daniel bent down and claimed her lips in an openmouthed kiss. Drinking her cries of surrender, he pumped into her until she clutched his back and stiffened in his embrace.

And when her cries faded, he took her over the edge a second time, finally letting the flames consume them both.

A dog barked. Somewhere in the distance a baby cried, waking Zara from a light, peaceful sleep. Daniel's muscle-corded arm lay possessively across her breast and stomach, while her back nestled against his front with her bottom tucked tight into his thighs. A feeling of perfect harmony swept through her, and she closed her eyes, fighting the sting of tears scratching the back of her throat. In a flash of remembrance, she heard the voice of her mother, a woman who had her own take on this mission, and the words of advice she'd given before Zara left on her journey.

*Be careful, my child, and be not ruled by your emotions. You've been entrusted with a sacred mission, one in which you must listen to your mind, not your heart.*

Fitting herself more closely to Murphy, she sighed. Of all the tests she'd taken in order to be chosen for this quest, objective reasoning was the area in which she scored the lowest. Somehow, her mother had known how difficult it would be for her only daughter to remain impersonal when it came time for her to mate with a man. Now, the sage words had returned to remind Zara of her own weakness.

She had been a healer her entire adult life, well versed in science but always guided by her heart. She'd never meant intentionally to deceive the selection committee. When they had pointed out their concerns and told her they thought she might not be objective enough for the trip, she had promised them she was capable of keeping her emotions in check.

Still, to admit their misgivings had merit, that she was flawed and unable to compartmentalize her feelings, was a blow to her sensibilities. She didn't want to be a failure.

Daniel stirred, and she bit back a sigh. Soon, he would wake and go home. Will was alone, and the man beside her was too good a father to allow him to remain that way for long. He was too good at everything.

Butterfly kisses trailed across her nape, tickling her ear. Squirming, she felt laughter rumble from Daniel's chest. "Sorry to wake you," he said, his breath soft against her neck. "But I have to get back."

She turned in his arms. "I know, and I don't want you to leave Will alone again. Next time, find a sitter for him, or have him spend the night with a friend."

Daniel raised a brow while amusement filled his eyes. "Is there going to be a next time?"

If tonight's coupling hadn't gotten her pregnant, there would have to be. And even if it had, she would want him again and again. "I guess that's up to you."

"I think you already know my answer." His mouth lifted into a full-blown smile. "Why do women always want the words, when men think their actions are enough?"

"Because, sometimes, it's just nice to hear them." She threaded her fingers through his hair. "You need to get home to your son."

"Too bad Will's not older, so you could come to our place, but I don't think that's a good idea."

"It's a terrible idea," she agreed.

"He's at a very impressionable age. You know what he asked me yesterday afternoon?"

"No. What did he ask you?"

"He wanted to know why women showed their breasts on the Internet. Seems he walked in on Ricky and that half-wit friend of his surfing a porn site and thought the women flashing their boo—" Embarrassed at his slip, Daniel swallowed. "Uh—their breasts—were getting ready to feed a baby."

Hiding a grin behind her hand, Zara asked, "What did you tell him?"

"Hell, I was ready to explain the whole darn shooting match, until he informed me that breasts were boring. Took a load off my mind with that comment."

"I'll bet it did." Rolling to her back, she watched his eyes glaze over at the sight of her chest. "But I get the idea you don't think the same?"

Daniel leaned forward and ran his tongue over her nipple, and she felt the pull all the way to her toes. Inhaling a breath, she let herself float away on a burgeoning cloud of desire. How easy it would be to lose herself in this man and his life. How easy it would be to love him.

Moving his lips to her mouth, he gave her a long, drawn-out kiss. "I hate to go, but it's getting late."

She cupped his face in her hands. "I know, and it's fine."

He rolled away and walked to the kitchen, giving her a tantalizing view of his taut buttocks and work-hardened thighs. After slipping into his jeans and tugging on his shirt, he sauntered to her side of the bed and sat down.

"I hear Miss Lucy's auditioning a new waitress tomorrow morning. Sally Zetmer?"

Zara nodded. "Lucy says my presence has brought so much extra business to the restaurant, I deserve a lighter schedule. I get to sleep in a whole extra three hours four mornings a week. I can't wait."

"You deserve it." Bending down, he nuzzled his nose against hers. "Five o'clock is way too early for a body to start work. I'll be there around eight for breakfast. Think I could be your first customer?"

"I think that can be arranged."

Daniel stood and headed for the door. "Don't get up. I'll lock it for you. Good night."

He doused the kitchen light, then opened the door, turned the lock, and left the cabin. A tear slid down her cheek, and she brushed it away, refusing to analyze the emotions bubbling up from inside.

Torn between the duty of needing to be pregnant and the desire to stay in Daniel's arms, she sat up and pressed her face into her hands. Why had no one ever explained to her how much it hurt to care for a man, to feel his joy and his pain and never want to leave his side? Was this one of the reasons the scientists of her world had resorted to conception in a test tube—because this type of emotion was too difficult to handle.

Her mother and father loved each other, as did most of those who'd shied away from having their children conceived in a laboratory. Years ago, her parents had been a source of amusement; it was only in the past generation that such unions were being given respect. When she returned carrying a male child, she, too, would gain that respect, even if she would have it alone.

She had to stay determined and concentrate on the job she was sent to do. The future of her world depended on it. When the time came for her to leave, she would not look back. Daniel's child would be enough.

He would have to be.

## Eleven

*D*aniel sat on a stool at the counter in the luncheonette, his lips itching to lift in a grin. It was five minutes to eight, and he expected Zara to arrive at any moment, a fact that had his stomach tied in knots. He'd gone sleepless most of the night, wondering what he was supposed to do, how he was supposed to act around her. Right now he felt like a fourteen-year-old with his first crush.

He'd been so absorbed with thoughts of Zara that he'd barely listened to Will this morning when the boy had babbled about hearing strange noises in their apartment last night. Instead of grabbing his baseball bat and investigating the creaks and whispered footfalls as he'd wanted, Will assured his father that he'd been obedient and stayed put, but Daniel could tell that the kid had been frightened.

Chalking up the tall tale to Will's being left alone in

the house at too young an age, he vowed to find a qualified sitter before he spent any more evenings away from his son. He'd also promised the boy that he would never be left alone again, then he encouraged Will to spend the day working on the school computers. Finally, he'd called Pepperdine's to ask if Jay could spare someone to mind the gas pumps while he went to the luncheonette for breakfast.

Over the past week, it seemed his mind had divided into two parts with neither half willing to relinquish control. Most of the time his sensible side warned him to steer clear of Zara, while the reckless, lustful side couldn't get enough of her. After last night's intimate encounter, reckless and lustful had won out big-time, and he decided to keep his word and come to the diner for his morning meal.

His situation would be downright depressing if not for the fact that he'd spent the past few minutes watching a prizefight between Lucy and her new waitress. Right now, Lucy and Sally Zetmer were sizing up one another over the kitchen pass-through while they prepared for round three.

"Don't go tellin' me that's not what you ordered, missy." Pointing at a plate piled high with flapjacks, Lucy pushed her sleeves up to her dimpled elbows and glared over the serving ledge. "If you knew how to spell, I wouldn'ta got it wrong."

Sally stomped a dainty, booted foot. "I wrote down what Gil ordered, clear as newsprint, Miss Lucy. Here, see—" She thrust the slip in Lucy's frowning face. "Three eggs, a side of ham and potatoes."

"The word I see is pancakes, Sally. Even that dim bulb Dan Quayle could spell potato better'n you."

Holding the paper to her nose, Sally blew out a breath. "Pancake—potato—what's the difference? Besides, you should have known it was potatoes, 'cause that's what comes with the eggs."

"I might have," Lucy answered, waving a dented metal turner, " 'ceptin' I happen to make the world's best flapjacks and Gil's been known to order 'em a time or two as a side with his eggs. Check the menu and you'll see 'em listed. I told you to familiarize yourself with the offerings before you started taking orders, didn't I?"

"Well, golly, it was a simple mistake. You sound just like my mother, always yelling at me." Sullen-faced, Sally lifted the plate and strutted around the counter.

Lucy raised her eyes to heaven. "Lord a'mighty, what the heck are they teachin' in school these days when a child can't write or spell worth a swallow of spit?"

She dropped her gaze and found Daniel grinning. "Don't you be sittin' there so smug and malelike, Mr. Know It All, or I just might decide to leave this French toast of yours on the griddle too long. And Tomas had to take Maria and the baby to the doctor this morning, so you can forget about the warm maple syrup."

Daniel shook his head, more to clear it of thoughts of Zara than anything else. "Now, Lucy, don't be mean. You have a way in the kitchen that puts most cooks to shame. There's not a customer here who isn't happy you're at the stove instead of Tomas, me included."

Lucy gave a disgruntled hmmph. Sliding a plate overladen with golden brown French toast onto the pass-through, she slapped at the pickup bell. "Order up!"

Sally winced at the racket as she came around the counter, grabbed Daniel's breakfast, and set the food down in front of him. "Hey, Mr. Murphy, I meant to tell you I started baby-sitting this summer. I'd be happy to watch Will for you on the nights you visit with Zara."

Daniel smothered his toast in syrup, more annoyed than shocked that this sassy teenager knew how he was spending his private time. Besides her smart-mouthed attitude, Sally's pierced eyebrow, spiky, blue-black hair, and shiny, bloodred lipstick was exactly what he didn't want for Will. A sitter with the Goth look was not a proper role model for his son.

Holding back a grimace, he said, "I appreciate the offer, Sally, but I really don't see her that often."

"Oh, well, that's not what I—"

Loud as a train crossing signal, the pickup bell dinged out another rapid staccato, startling the girl into a nervous jump. "Jeez, Miss Lucy, I'm not deaf, ya' know."

"These orders belong to Frank and Chuck. Now I suggest you stop tryin' to drum up baby-sitting customers and concentrate on the task at hand." Thumping a second plate onto the ledge, Lucy gave her an approving grin. "You're doin' a fair-to-middlin' job, this morning, missy. With a bit of training, you might be as good a waitress as Zara someday."

Sally scooped up the plates and turned. Rolling her eyes as if to say *not in this lifetime*, she carried the meals to the surveyors.

With no new orders waiting, Lucy waddled from the kitchen, patting at her hair. "Kids. Don't know where they get their nerve these days—or their fashion sense."

Daniel sipped at his coffee and decided it might be a good time to work a little damage control on the gossip raging about his love life. "Lucy, I'd appreciate it if you would do your best to keep the talk about Zara and me to a minimum. We're still exploring a—a—"

Hell what was it they were exploring, anyway?

"Relationship?" said the older woman, filling in the blank.

Not sure that was the right word, he frowned. "I'd hate for everyone in town to know how we felt about each other before we knew ourselves."

Slyly, she smiled. "Too late, Dan'l. Hattie Zetmer asked me a whole passel of questions this mornin' and I have to confess that at four-thirty in the morning my brain was still asleep. She wanted to know if you and Zara were keepin' company, and I was too dumb to play dumb. Sorry."

"There's nothing going on between us." He frowned for emphasis. "We're just friends who enjoy each other's company."

"Uh-huh." After taking an inordinate amount of time wiping down the counter, she rested her elbows and gave a mulish laugh. "What are you so afraid of, Dan'l? You and Zara make a fine-lookin' couple. It's only natural for a single woman and a lonely man to gravitate to one another."

Daniel smacked his coffee mug down with a sharp-sounding *thwack*. "Lonely! Who says I'm lonely?"

Lucy's grin turned motherly. "Half the town, that's who. Hattie and Dolly and Jay Pepperdine—"

"Jay has a hand in this gossip? For Pete's sake, Lucy, cut me some slack."

Leaning into the counter, she poked a stubby finger at his shoulder. "Don't you be layin' a guilt trip on me for caring about you, Dan'l Murphy. I cut you slack the day you moved here. Accepted you and Will and didn't ask a single question, not about you missing a wife or why you decided to settle into town so sudden-like or anything. When you shied away in the beginning, everybody suspected you were hidin' something. It was obvious from day one that's the only reason an educated fellow like yourself would bother comin' to an invisible dot on the map like Button Creek in the first place."

Swallowing hard, Daniel tried to dredge up the words to argue, but couldn't think of any. And here he thought he'd been so smart, getting away with his deception all these years.

"Lucy, I—"

"You don't have to say a thing. Whatever your secret is, it's safe with us. Button Creek protects its own. You oughta know that by now."

She touched his hand, which was still wrapped in a death grip around his coffee mug. "No need to say another word. Just give us a little leeway with our fantasies while we watch you'n Zara have at each other. We only want to see you and that boy of yours happy."

Daniel's gaze locked with Miss Lucy's, but before he could speak the bell above the door tinkled out a greeting. They turned in unison as Tomas and Zara strolled into the diner arm in arm.

Zara saw Daniel sitting at the counter and called out a hello as she ducked into the kitchen. He was here, just as he'd promised, reinforcing her belief that the man was a menace to her mental well-being as well as her heart. And from the pensive expression on his face, she guessed he'd been thinking hard about last night.

Well so had she. Unfortunately, she hadn't found a solution to her problem. As of this morning, she still wasn't pregnant.

She tied a clean apron around her waist and stepped aside to let Tomas grab one of his own. Seconds later, Lucy strolled in wearing a huge grin on her lined face. "How's my little namesake this morning, Tomas? Did the doctor give her a clean bill of health?"

"Lucetta is perfect. Maria and I, we are so happy that our baby is doing well. And we owe it all to you and Daniel. I don't think we'll ever be able to repay either of you for your kindness."

"Don't think a thing of it," said Lucy. "All I did was catch Lucetta when she slid outta the chute. It was Dan'l who knew the fancy medical stuff. Besides, if I remember correctly, Maria was the one who did the hard work."

"Still, we are grateful."

"How about you, Zara? Did you get enough rest this mornin'?" the older woman asked. Her expression neutral, she leaned back against the doorframe. "Noticed the lights were on awfully late in your cabin last night. Guess you found somethin' interesting to watch on TV, huh?"

Zara kept her gaze trained on her toes. How was she supposed to answer embarrassing questions when Daniel continued to follow her with that we-have-to-talk expression of his? "I slept very well, thank you. It was wonderful to get up with—with the sun already in the sky."

She glanced toward the counter, intent on giving Daniel a smile, and instead locked eyes with the younger of the two surveyors. The hair on her arms prickled at his suspicious gaze.

Lucy reached out and placed the back of her hand against Zara's cheek. "You feelin' all right, child? Lord a'mighty, you're white as a sheet. Maybe you should go back to bed."

"I'm fine. Just not awake yet, I guess. How did Sally do this morning?"

The girl in question sauntered into the kitchen, untying her apron as she walked. "Hey, Zara, I heard about what you did for Will at the campout. Can you teach me that meditation stuff sometime? It sounds awesome."

Pushing the prickle of fear to the back of her mind, Zara gave the teenager a polite smile. She'd met Sally once before and been intrigued by her manner of dress and makeup. If the elders on her planet ever got a good look at the girl, they would faint on the spot, but as far as she could tell Sally was completely normal for an Earth adolescent.

"Maybe some night when I get off early and you're free. How would that be?"

"Cool." Sally hung her apron on a hook and patted at the front pocket of her jeans. "But not tonight, Mom promised to take me to a mall to celebrate my first day at a real job. I made enough in tips to buy a new CD and a shirt I've been wanting." As if taken by a stroke of genius her baby blue eyes sparkled. "Say, how would you like to come with us? I'm sure Mom wouldn't mind."

Before Zara could answer, Lucy stepped in. "That's the best idea I heard all week. I'm gonna take a little snooze and get back here by four. Zara, you can have the night off to go shoppin' with Sally and Hattie. You haven't been out of town since our trip to the produce stand. It's about time you took a break for yourself."

Even if the thought of escaping Murphy for a night was tempting, Zara wasn't sure a trip to an unfamiliar place was a good idea. "Oh, but I couldn't ask you to do my job for me. It wouldn't be right."

"Nonsense. Evenings in the middle of the week are slow. I can handle things here." Lucy nodded to Sally. "Tell your mamma that'd be fine. The two of you can pick up Zara at about four-thirty. I'll see that she's ready."

"Great," Sally called, trotting out the restaurant door. "See you then."

Zara inhaled a gulp of air. Had Murphy heard their discussion? Did he care that she'd made plans without him? She shifted her gaze to the pass-through. His expression unreadable, Daniel shrugged and pointed to his watch, then to his gas station, signaling he had a customer. She waved and he mouthed "later," then headed for the door.

Frank held open the door of Zetmer's Hardware, which also doubled as the town's post office, and waited for his partner to join him on the sidewalk. Though just 9 A.M., the May air was thick and sticky and had both men sweating, a true testament to the severity of late-spring temperatures in Texas.

"Aren't you going to open it?" Chuck asked, indicating the Next Day Delivery envelope Frank had tucked under his arm.

Instead of answering, Frank continued his march down Main Street to their cabin. Once inside, he walked to the window air-conditioning unit and turned the dial to high, then pulled out a chair. Sitting down, he placed the packet on the desk in front of him and stared.

Chuck balanced on the edge of his desk and reached over, but before he could snag the letter, Frank snatched it up and zipped it open. Inside was a single sheet of paper, which he extracted and began to read.

"So what does it say?"

"See for yourself," Frank finally said, his mouth

curled in a satisfied smile. He sat back and watched while Chuck moved his lips as he read.

"This—this can't be right," the younger agent stuttered, tossing the report on the desk. "Something's not kosher. It can't be."

"Sorry, but government labs are rarely wrong. I think the big brass would be miffed if we arrested the woman for polluting the creek with a coating of harmless protein and other biodegradable substances, don't you agree?"

Chuck plopped into his chair. "Well, shit, the report has to be worth something. It says right here they never saw a compound like it."

Frank pulled a tissue from a box on his blotter and swiped at his forehead. When was the pup going to learn a little protocol? They needed hard evidence before they could make an arrest. If they jumped the gun and spooked whoever the alien was, this assignment was over.

"Can't you read? That paper says that goop was nothing more than a combination of ordinary proteins with a few amino acids and normal chemical compounds thrown in for good measure. They could identify all but 10 percent of the substance, which wasn't enough to worry them."

"Not enough to—What are they—idiots? The report only adds to the proof that we had an alien lifeform landing here. And I'm still betting on that waitress." He folded his arms and leaned back in the chair. "You should have seen the once-over she gave me this morning when I stopped at the counter to pick up a paper."

"Oh, for chrissake." Frank rolled his eyes. "Her giving you a strange look doesn't mean a damned thing. Instead of concentrating on the woman, we need to get busy canvassing the local ranches and farms. If she is the alien, we have a little leeway, because I don't think she's planning to leave anytime soon."

Chuck blinked his surprise. "Does that mean you've decided to at least consider her as a suspect?"

"I never said I wasn't considering her." Frank hunched forward in his chair. "I know she hit town the week we got word this was our target area. I also heard through the grapevine she doesn't have a driver's license and no one ever seems to mention her last name. And remember, I saw her with that bracelet."

"Okay. So what do we do about her?"

Frank shrugged. "I'm examining a few possibilities."

"And Murphy?"

"What about him?"

Chuck set his elbows on the desk. "I thought we agreed to open a file on him."

Sighing, Frank tilted his head. "Look, I'm willing to admit the man acts as if he's hiding something. Considering that he spent the last few nights in Zara's pants, maybe it's time we found out what."

"Now you're talking," said Chuck, still frowning.

Frank thought a second before giving a direct order. "Then wrap up that glass and those beer bottles we took from his place and get them to the mercantile so the fingerprint guys can tell us if Murphy is trouble. After that, I want you to go to the lake like I asked and see what you can dig up."

"But—"

He stood and headed for the door. "While you're gone, I'm going to find a way to corner Jack Farley and see if he knows anything concrete. It's damned sure we aren't going to get any information from the people in this town, and we've torn up the countryside without finding a single crumb of evidence, so I'll admit we need to dig deeper."

"Then you believe me about Farley, too?"

"I gave it some thought, and if he's looking for the same thing we are, it wouldn't hurt to check out who he is and what he knows. The man's so full of himself, I bet I won't even have to reveal who we are to get a bit of information."

Daniel stood with his shoulder propped against the open garage door. He'd stripped off his sweat-stained denim shirt after lunch and worked in a sleeveless T-shirt most of the afternoon just to keep even with the heat. Swiping a hand over his brow, he checked the foot-high white-enameled Pennzoil thermometer hanging on the cinder-block wall and noted that the mercury had climbed to ninety, about average for late May in north Texas. He'd need to hook up the fans soon. The inside of the garage was going to be an oven in a couple more weeks.

God, but he hated hot weather.

If he'd had his head on straight six years ago, he

would have found a job up around Duluth or gone to Canada, where the summer temperatures rarely rose out of the eighties. But he'd been in such a hurry to cover his tracks, he hadn't thought about the climate. Back then, his goals had been simple: set up a new identity for himself and Will, disappear from New York City as quickly as possible, and get his son settled in a stable home environment.

Stumbling onto Button Creek and finding this business for sale had been almost too good to be true. If he'd known then that the locals were such busybodies, he would have arced in a northerly direction faster than a shooting star. Of course, he could put the station in someone else's hands—Jay Pepperdine's for instance—make up an excuse, and take off running. But he doubted running would be the best thing for Will.

Or was he thinking only of himself?

He was still amazed that a woman like Zara had practically dropped into his lap. He'd always been the kind of guy who never had much luck with the opposite sex. As a full-fledged member of the geek squad, he'd rarely dated in high school, and it wasn't because he'd been acne prone or ugly, either. Teenage girls just weren't drawn to members of the astronomy club or debate team. When his SAT scores earned him a full scholarship to a good college, he'd spent most of his time studying or repairing friends' cars to earn spending money. He'd lost his virginity as a sophomore, but since he could barely remember the girl's name or face, he'd always thought it a nonevent.

After his parents died within a few years of one other, each from a different kind of cancer, he'd immersed himself in his classes and focused on his doctorate. Before teaching at Columbia, he'd only been involved in two serious relationships. When Rebecca applied for the job as his assistant, it had taken several months for him to think of her as anything more than a graduate student. After a three-month affair, during which time it seemed they never saw eye to eye on anything, he suspected her interest stemmed from a desire to irritate her parents more than find a loving partner. When she disappeared at the end of the semester, he'd chalked it up to his usual nonluck with women and didn't give it another thought.

There were times when he shuddered at the idea of where he and Will would be right now if Rebecca hadn't had the decency to send him that letter.

Until a few weeks ago, he'd given up on ever bringing another woman into his life, even if it might have been beneficial to Will. A child needed a mother, but only if she was stable and dedicated to parenting. Daniel had always figured he would be enough for the boy, exactly as he thought Will would be enough for him.

Since he'd rescued his son from the Warfields, Zara had been the first person he'd actually allowed into their select circle. The thought was so unsettling, he almost wanted to stop the relationship before it had a chance to go any further.

Almost.

Daniel fixed his gaze across the street. For the past

twenty minutes Jack Farley had been firmly ensconced on the front porch of the Feed and Grain, methodically snapping a camera while he chewed the fat with Jay's century-old grandfather. Dressed in traditional cowboy garb with an eagle feather he swore he'd swiped from a full-blooded Comanche tucked in his hat brim, the old man was a wealth of information about anything having to do with the Native American tribes of Texas and the surrounding states.

He didn't blame the photographer for spending time with the guy. Farley could probably build an entire coffee table book around Jeremiah alone, without ever speaking to another soul in town. The Feed and Grain itself was an interesting mix of brick, cinder block, and wood shingles that would fascinate anyone unfamiliar with the look of a rural business. Since their family had been a fixture in the area for over a century, Jack had been smart to start his digging with the Pepperdines.

From a distance came the rumble of the school bus engine. Daniel waited while the orange-and-black behemoth pulled to a stop at the corner and coughed out its passengers. Ricky and Grunt jumped from the bus and scampered across the street like a pair of newly freed rabbits. Then came Will, who stepped down slowly and walked to the garage.

"Hey, Dad." He skipped the last few steps across the worn pavement. "I finally found some decent vegetarian recipes for Zara." Will thrust out the papers. "Which of these do you think she'd like best?"

Typical of Will to stick to a project until he saw results, thought Daniel. "Give me a second to read them first." He grabbed the sheets, folded them in half, and tucked them in his back pocket. "I'll get to it after supper, okay?"

"Hey, Will, just the man I need to see." Jack Farley's New York twang cut over the noise of the battered pickup that pulled alongside a gas pump. "Think you have time to escort me to the creek? I'm curious about that one-lane bridge, and Jeremiah said you probably know the fields back there better than anyone."

"He did?" It was obvious from Will's ear-to-ear grin he felt honored to be thought of so highly by the older man.

"Yep. If you care to come along, I'd like to do a little exploring." Jack turned to Daniel. "What do you say, Murphy? Can I borrow the boy for the rest of the afternoon? I promise to have him back by suppertime."

Unable to find a logical reason to decline Farley's request, Daniel nodded. "Just be careful. One of the reasons that bridge isn't used much anymore is because the underpinnings have started to rot. If those TXdot men ever decide to do the job right, it should be the first thing the state takes care of around here."

"We'll watch our step, won't we, Will? See you later," said Jack, as they sauntered to the back of the building.

Daniel went inside, where he rang up a gas sale, then busied himself restocking canned goods. When he heard another vehicle pull up to the pumps, he walked to the register. A few minutes later, Jay Pepperdine stepped into the store.

"Murphy. How you doin' today?" He handed Daniel two twenty-dollar bills.

"Fine. Anything else I can get for you?"

Jay pushed the brim of his hat up a notch. "Got a tractor that needs an overhaul. Think you can handle it?"

Daniel cringed, not afraid to let Jay know how he felt. Tractors were a bitch, and not just because of their size, but the rancher had given him too much business to turn down the man's request. "Sure, but it'll probably take a good two days, and I might have to borrow one of your men to help with the heavy work. Next Monday and Tuesday are light. Can you get it over here by then?"

"I'll see to it. How's Will doing?"

"You mean how is he doing after that asthma attack?"

"He's a good kid, Murphy. I wouldn't mind if he and Ricky spent more time together, even if he's younger."

"Thanks," said Daniel, pleased Jay thought that highly of his son.

Jay shuffled his feet as Daniel handed him change. "Mind if I ask you something?"

"What do you need?"

"I was just wondering if you've gotten any weird vibes from that photographer fellow—Jack Farley."

*Weird is putting it mildly*, thought Daniel, *but why would Jay care?* "We've talked a few times. He's off to the creek with Will right now, as a matter of fact. Told me Jeremiah said the boy was the perfect choice to take him there."

"Yeah, I heard the conversation. In fact, I heard just about everything Farley was asking the old man. First he bragged about all the magazines and newspapers he'd worked for, then started in on the book he's planning. But you know what I think he's really after?"

"I haven't a clue," Daniel answered, still puzzled by Jay's concern.

"Aliens."

"Aliens?" Between the surveyors and Jack Farley, extraterrestrials were becoming a mighty popular topic around town. Maybe too popular.

"Yup." Jay tucked the change into his back pocket. "He spent most of his time asking Jeremiah if there'd ever been any reports of spaceship landings in the area. Even asked him about Indian legends—did he know of any that centered around beings from the heavens visiting Earth. Wanted to know if Jeremiah had seen anything peculiar lately, too, like in the past two weeks. Personally, I think the guy's certifiable. Tell Will to be careful what he says to the man, just in case Farley's a little soft in the head, okay?"

"The guy already knows Will and I spend a lot of time gazing out of a telescope, so he has to know the boy is interested. Still, thanks for the warning."

Daniel watched Jay climb into his Land Rover and pull away. Aliens. Now there was a topic Will could really get his teeth into. If Farley was dumb enough to start another conversation on space creatures, the kid would probably bend his ear so bad the man would take the next bus out of town without finishing his project.

Will had sworn to stay mum about the lights they'd tracked—ditto the goo that showed up the morning after their last sighting. If Daniel knew his son, Will would never discuss either incident with a guy like Jack Farley.

He thought again about Jay's friendly warning. Maybe it was time to get the slime in his freezer to a lab after all.

*Twelve*

Sally Zetmer assessed her shopping companion through wide blue eyes. Twirling her stubby, black-lacquered index finger like a miniature tornado, she directed Zara to turn in place. "I just knew you'd look totally awesome in that top."

Zara raised her gaze to the full-length mirror and blinked back a shudder, pulling the stretchy purple fabric up to her collarbone. After a second, the clingy material did a quick slide back to the top of her bra-less breasts.

"Are you sure this thing is supposed to be so . . . revealing?"

"It's a tube top, silly. You wear it with shorts in the summer, when it's really really hot."

Zara thought of her planet's more temperate climate as she dabbed at the droplets of perspiration dotting her forehead. The temperature controls in the mall had to be set on frigid, but she was definitely in a sweat over the way she looked in this scanty bit of nothing.

"You mean it's going to get warmer than it did today?"

Sally fisted her hands on her hips and tossed her a look of impatience. "Well, *duh*, this *is* Texas. Most summers it stays above a hundred for weeks in a row. What planet have you been living on?"

Biting her lower lip, Zara added to her list of failures. Why hadn't she paid more attention to the weather programs while she descended to Earth? Besides daydreaming over the man with whom she'd been selected to mate, she'd been so enthralled with the beauty of this new universe, its shifting stars and their alignment with its planets, she'd simply forgotten to concentrate on the more basic things she needed to know.

"I'm from north of here, remember?" she muttered, hoping that would satisfy her self-appointed fashion consultant.

"Oklahoma is too close to count as north of here. And it gets just as hot there. I know because my cousin Paige lives in Tulsa. Paige and I—"

Zara let the young girl ramble as she glanced around the crowded store. Black, yellow, and red painted walls held rows of shelves filled with disorderly piles of unisex clothing. Garish track lighting strobed to the beat of ear-shattering music. Teenagers of both sexes pawed the racks of shirts like eager puppies searching through trash. To quote Sally Zetmer, NX Generation was a really happening place.

*Happening* for anyone between the ages of twelve and twenty, Zara told herself, tugging again at the clingy top that dipped farther down her chest. If she wore something like this back home, her friends would laugh themselves sick—but not before they made sure she was in her right mind.

"So, what do you think?" Sally tapped Zara on the shoulder. "One each in purple, black, and maybe hot pink? Then we'll find you some shorts—"

"Sally, I don't think that's a good idea," Zara argued. "I'm a grown woman, not a teenager."

"Oh, come on. You have a fantastic figure. All the guys say so. I bet Mr. Murphy thinks so, too."

*Mr. Murphy?* Would seeing Daniel's reaction when she showed up wearing this less-than-respectable bit of clothing be worth the embarrassment?

Heaving a sigh, she set her lips in a thin line. "All right, but just one top and one pair of shorts. And nothing like those." She nodded toward a tall, red-haired salesgirl wearing strips of metallic silver fabric no wider than a place mat. "Maybe something midthigh in a nice sedate beige?"

Sally wrinkled her nose. "If you say so. But you'll have to buy them in a department store. We're supposed to meet my mom at Foley's. You'll probably find what you're looking for in the old lady department."

Connecting with Sally's irreverent humor, Zara rolled her eyes. "Give me a minute to change, then we can pay for this and find Hattie."

Back in her pale pink T-shirt and jeans, Zara walked beside Sally, who talked nonstop as she window-shopped, giving her opinion on what was in fashion and what Zara should buy next. Zara decided that when she left for the rendezvous site she would see to it the teenager received whatever was left of her Earth currency to thank her for the fun she'd had tonight. Even Hattie had been generous, treating her to gooey cheese pizza and a waffle cone filled with soft ice cream, delicacies she hoped could be re-created back home once the scientists figured a way to replicate a few of the ingredients.

Maybe she'd start a business marketing some of the more unusual foods she'd discovered here. The elders had plans for her and her child, but she'd been assured she would be allowed to raise her son and make all the decisions necessary in his life. They would be residing in a government research facility constructed to resemble a home, and would be free to visit her parents and friends and live as normally as possible, even if her child was going to be extraspecial.

Focusing on her mission reminded Zara that she needed to stick to the plan and keep her thoughts on a strict, scientific level. She had yet to conceive, but when it happened she would have to make some important decisions. With some time to go before meeting with the mother ship, she had to think about Daniel. Once the two of them created a viable lifeform, would she be able to resist the indefinable connection she felt for the man? Would she be able to stop herself from mating with him again and again?

The quandary was so painful it filled her with a stab of longing. The memory of his hard-muscled body as it loomed over her in the moonlight made her quiver. The way he treated his son, with such care and gentle discipline, made her sigh. He was a good parent and a wonderful lover; the perfect father for her child. The perfect partner for her.

But having sex with him just to gain pleasure would be deceitful. How was she going to cope when they were destined to be forever apart?

Lost in thought, she ignored Sally's chatter until they arrived at the department store cosmetics department. Like a heat-seeking missile, the teenager zeroed in on a brightly hued display and began sorting through tubes and palettes of face paint.

"This shade is perfect for you." Sally dabbed at Zara's mouth with a tube from the sample case.

Zara adjusted a mirror and studied her reflection. "Isn't it a little—red?"

"Trust me, red is in this summer. Besides, you wouldn't look good in what I'm wearing."

Raising her gaze, Zara inspected Sally's carefully outlined purplish black lips. "Uh . . . no, I guess not."

Sally pulled out an array of tubes and pencils until she found what she wanted and held it up for approval. "Eye shadow and liner. We'll use mocha frost for the lid and plum berry to line it. You are going to look totally awesome."

"Care to try our newest fragrance?"

Overwhelmed at the array of pots and potions arranged on the counter, Zara didn't think to answer. In a half second she was enveloped in a cloud of smelly mist. Perfume wafted in front of her face, covering her hair and shoulders.

Immediately, her nose began to twitch. "Ah-aah-choo!" A second sneeze escaped, this one more ferocious than the first.

"Bless you," Sally said with a giggle.

"Oh, I'm so sorry, my finger slipped," chimed the clerk. "I'm supposed to wait to spray until you say it's okay, just in case there's an allergic reaction." The woman's mascara'd eyes opened wide. "Oh God, please tell me you aren't allergic!"

Since cosmetics weren't the norm in her world, Zara had no idea whether or not her system was compatible with the cloying fragrance. She opened her mouth to speak, but no sound came out. In fact, her tongue suddenly felt three sizes too big for her mouth.

"Aah-choo! Aah-choo! Aah-choo!" Rapid-fire sneezes filled the air like exploding miniature hand grenades.

"Zara, are you all right?" Worry lines etched Sally's brow. "You look kind of green."

"Miss?" The saleswoman grabbed her elbow. "Do you need to sit down?"

"Ah . . . ah . . . blmph," was all Zara could squeeze past her swollen tongue. She felt another series of sneezes building and shook her head. The effort sent her stumbling into the counter, and she grabbed on for support.

"Jeez, you don't look so good. I'm going to find Mom."

Inhaling a huge gasp of air, Zara clutched at her throat. Why hadn't she listened earlier, when common sense warned her not to visit a strange place? Why hadn't the elders counseled her on the dangers of a shopping mall?

The room began to spin. Her lungs ached with the effort to breathe. She had healing stones in her bracelet, but how could she use one here, in front of the saleswoman and customers who had gathered to watch her folly?

Thinking she might be dying, Zara gurgled out a laugh. This would give the residents of Button Creek enough gossip to last a ninevar.

She heard the clerk call frantically for assistance, but the woman sounded as if she were speaking from a tunnel. Her knees buckled, and she sank to the floor.

Zara woke to a whisper of voices, their soft cadence surrounded her, humming in her ear like gently buzzing insects on a summer afternoon. She was at her favorite quiet place, floating on a lake of cool lapping water, meditating on life and the world around her. She'd been accepted for Project Rejuvenation and would soon report for training to the mission center. There she would meet her earthly biological match so that they could create a new, stronger life-form—

The rumble of a deep, commanding baritone pulled her quickly to reality, confirming that she was not at home waiting to begin indoctrination. She was already on Earth and had, in fact, been jostling along in Murphy's pickup truck only minutes earlier.

"See to it she gets plenty of rest and lots of plain old H-two-oh," said a gruff voice from far away.

"That's all you can recommend?" growled Daniel. "Water and rest?"

"For now."

"Christ, Doc, look at her. Zara hasn't moved since I laid her on the bed. There has to be something—"

"There is, but since you refuse to do as I suggest and take her to the nearest emergency room, I've done everything I can. The dose of epinephrine has eased her breathing, but I'd advise you to reconsider and drive her to Denton if she isn't awake and coherent in a half hour or so."

"You're supposed to be a doctor," Daniel choked out. "You helped me with Will when we first moved here."

"All I did for your boy was make an educated guess on his condition and send you to an allergist friend of mine. I'm a vet, Daniel, not an MD. I'd like to do more, but I can't."

Zara smiled to herself, relieved that Murphy had listened when she'd begged him to bring her home instead of the hospital. If the doctors here recognized that she was *different*, they might have called the authorities. She'd read up on the incident at Roswell, had studied enough of Earth's history to fear the scientists who claimed they wanted to contact an alien.

Instead, he had asked Doc Mayberry to evaluate her condition. As far as she knew, the kindly old man was an expert with dogs, cats, and pregnant mares. If she were staying on this planet, she might have gone to him for prenatal care. From the sound of it, he'd done the best he could to help her, given the circumstances.

Murphy's deep voice pulled her into the present. "All right, Doc, and thanks. I'll stay with her and do like you said. Will, you're going home with Jay."

"But—but Zara might need me." Will sounded as if he'd been crying, a fact that struck a chord in her heart, but Zara couldn't find the energy to muster a smile.

Lucy's motherly concern filled the air. "Zara's my employee, so she's my responsibility. I'm the one who's spending the night, so y'all can git."

"Lucy. I'm staying." Murphy's usually steady voice came out in a harsh rasp.

"But I'm the one who took her to the makeup department in the first place. I should be the one to stay."

Sally, Zara realized, was actually worried about her. They were all worried. How sweet.

"You, missy, can be the one to cover her shift tomorrow. Now, everybody—"

"Out!" shouted Daniel, drowning Lucy's order.

Murmurs of grudging capitulation echoed through the room. Above the noise, Zara heard Jay Pepperdine quite clearly.

"I'll send a man over to mind the garage tomorrow morning, Murphy. You take all the time you need here."

"Well, all right then," Lucy stated imperiously. "But I'll be sendin' over my homemade vegetable soup by the gallon. It'll be your job to see that she keeps it down."

After another burst of hushed conversation, Zara heard shuffling feet and, finally, the slamming of a door. Then nothing but blessed silence.

She wanted to open her eyes, but her lashes felt like the business end of a broomstick. A tear slipped from beneath one sticky eyelid, and she tried to brush it away, but her hand refused to come out from under the bedcovers.

The mattress shifted. Something soft as a feather touched her face. It took a second to register that Daniel was sitting at her side, wiping her cheek with a tissue.

"You awake?" he asked, stroking gently.

"What happened?" she managed to whisper, relieved to find her tongue had returned to its normal size.

"Severe allergic reaction," came his gruff response. "Some ditz in the cosmetic department sprayed you with perfume, and you started to sneeze. When you couldn't catch your breath, you collapsed. Scared everyone out of ten years' growth, including the store manager. I took his card, by the way, in case you wanted to pursue it legally."

"Legally?"

"You know—sue."

"Sue?"

"Never mind. We can discuss it later."

Was she imagining it, or had Daniel's palm just brushed the hair off her forehead? "I remember some of what happened. But I thought I was dreaming."

He gave a muffled snort. "Then it was a dream with

a cast of hundreds. I chased everybody away, but Dolly and Lucy are probably waiting out front, most likely with half the town."

"Could I have some water. Please?"

She struggled to sit up and his firm hand pressed her back against the pillow. "I'll get it. You stay right there and don't move a muscle."

*As if she could.* The bed bounced as he left, and Zara felt a flash of panic. "Daniel?"

"I'll be right back."

The refrigerator door opened and closed. She heard the tinkle of ice cubes and the gurgle of water hitting a glass, then he was beside her again. His palm slipped behind her shoulder and gently eased her into a sitting position. The glass touched her lips and she sipped greedily.

"Easy now. Go slow."

Exhausted, she sank back onto the mattress and sighed.

"Hey, you going to sleep on me?"

A smile tugged at the corners of her mouth. Daniel was worried about her. She could tell by the inflection in his voice and the gentle touch of his hands. "That's what my body is telling me it wants to do."

"All right. If you're sure you feel okay."

"I'm getting better by the nin—minute, but can I ask a favor?"

"Can't it wait? You've had a busy night."

He had to be leaning near, because she caught the scent of his minty breath as it fanned her face. Funny how she could have such a disastrous reaction to a simple spray of perfume, yet feel so comforted by Murphy's manly scent. The elders had said they would be ultimately compatible, but she hadn't realized how true the statement was until this second. She licked at her parched lips, and the glass touched her mouth again.

"Here, take another sip, then get some rest. We'll talk in the morning."

This time, when she sat up, she took a deeper swallow, enjoying the cool liquid as it slid slowly down her throat. Breathing was easier now. With Daniel beside her, everything seemed easier.

Before she had a chance to think, the words slipped out. "Stay with me—here on the bed?"

A second passed before he muttered, "I'll sleep on the sofa. You can call if you need me."

"Please. I'd feel safer if I knew you were at my side." Could she sound any more needy or pathetic?

"Um . . . I don't know if that's such a good idea. I might roll over on you and crush you or—something."

His words fell like soothing rain onto her questioning heart. Daniel wanted her in the most basic way, but he was too polite to say so.

"I think it's a wonderful idea. And I promise not to jump you, if that's what you're worried about."

He laughed. "Phew, that's a load off my mind."

At peace, Zara let herself drift back to the lake on her parents' property, only this time Daniel and Will were floating alongside her on the gently undulating water.

Daniel came out of the bathroom and gazed at the

woman on the bed, relieved to see her sleeping. According to Doc, rest was good. For a while there he'd had a real crisis on his hands, and the thought had practically scared the shirt off his back.

Christ, but she was something else. Even in the aftermath of a serious health scare, Zara looked serene and composed and so unbelievably beautiful. And she wanted him to sleep beside her on the bed.

How in the hell was he supposed to comply with her request and fall asleep at the same time? He was only human. Just a man doing his best to watch over a woman who didn't have enough common sense to stop an overanxious perfume clerk from spritzing her to death.

When he'd overheard Sally and Lucy convince Zara to take a night off, he wanted to kick himself. He should have been the one to ask her out—on a real date. He could have brought her to the mall, taken her to a movie or dinner, instead of her women friends. Lucky for him, Will had torn his best jeans, because that gave him the perfect excuse to take a trip to the shopping center in hopes of running into her.

Will had damn near started to cry when they'd pushed through the crowd behind Sally and Hattie and seen Zara crumpled on the floor. His own heart had just about stopped beating, too. She'd looked pale, yet her face seemed to have a sickly greenish cast he'd never seen on a human before. By the time the store manager had arrived and offered to call an ambulance, Daniel already had Zara in his arms and was heading for the exit. The manager stuffed a card in his shirt pocket and shouted that he should call with any of the medical bills, but Daniel hadn't bothered to answer.

Right now, it didn't look as if Zara needed a doctor, but he had toyed with the idea of driving her to an emergency room in the first few seconds after he'd loaded her into his truck. When he'd told her what he planned to do, she'd gotten agitated, mumbling nonsense through her swollen lips as if in terror. *No hospitals and no strangers.* As soon as he'd understood the gist of her plea, he'd promised to bring her straight home, which quieted her down immediately.

Once they arrived at the cabin, he'd sent Sally to get Doc Mayberry. After that, it hadn't taken long for the room to fill with concerned citizens. Now that he'd managed to send everyone home, he could finally sit back and take a breath.

He'd made a mountain out of a molehill. Zara had experienced a simple chemical reaction to an unfriendly substance. She hadn't gone into shock or lapsed into a coma, but merely been overcome by the fumes of a bottled odor—unusual, but not unheard of in this day of pheromones and the latest scientifically engineered scents. Her fainting spell had been, to put it simply, an extreme reaction.

Daniel went to the bed and bent over to make sure she was breathing properly, then sat on the other side of the mattress and slipped off his boots. Careful not to jostle her, he lay on his back and focused on the ceiling, willing his hormones to take a break and go dormant for the night.

Zara made a soft sound of protest and turned, nestling against him. Automatically, he put an arm around her and pulled her close. Her head fit perfectly into his shoulder while her palm crept up to rest against his heart. He yawned, trying to remember if he'd ever slept an entire night with a woman at his side.

Reaching around, he pulled her against him, frowning when she breathed a moan of contentment. Damn if she hadn't managed to burrow under his skin, directly to the spot he'd worked so hard to protect after Rebecca's betrayal. With Zara by his side, he felt as if the little bit of something he'd always thought was missing from his life had been set in place, like the final piece of the puzzle needed to complete his world.

Being with her made him think there was hope for him and Will. Hope for a normal life and a future. A family.

The enormity of what he'd just realized hit him like a supernova, and his breath caught in his throat. After all his careful planning, he'd gone and done the most stupid thing he could. He'd fallen in love with a woman he barely knew and who, he felt certain, was keeping a secret.

Now what the heck was he supposed to do?

Feeling warm and well rested, Zara turned on her side and snuggled under the covers. A smile built inside of her when she realized she could breathe normally. She knew from the hard wall of muscle resting beside her that Daniel had done as she asked and spent the night.

She opened one eye and focused on his beard-shadowed jaw and tempting mouth, both relaxed in sleep. Lips she knew to be firm yet gentle and capable of driving her to instant passion with a sigh or a touch, and she held herself back from pressing her own mouth against them. His nose, with its small bump at the top, had character and presence. His brows, thick and straight, sat over eyes the color of chocolate.

In a way, Will resembled him, though the boy seemed more delicate and fine-boned. Will's nose was smaller, his eyelashes almost feminine in their length, but when viewed side by side, anyone could tell the two were father and son.

Who, she wondered, would their own son take after?

She rolled to her back and stretched sore muscles. The perfume had taken its toll on her system, and the fall hadn't helped. Her shoulders ached as did the side she'd hit on the counter on her slide to the store floor. Struggling to a sitting position, the need to use the bathroom struck, and she swung her legs to the edge of the bed. A hand, large and gentle, clasped her wrist and she stilled.

"Where are you off to at this hour? The sun's not even up yet."

"I have to use the um . . ."

Daniel chuckled. "I guess that's okay. Do you need help?"

Heat flooded her cheeks. "Uh, no, thank you. I'll manage." But when she rose to her feet, her knees wobbled, dropping her to the mattress with a plop.

"Sure you don't need my help?" he asked, a touch of amusement lacing the worry in his voice.

"Yes, I'm sure. Just give me a minute." Muttering, she planted her feet under her and stood. Taking one step at a time, she rounded the bed, stopped at the bottom, and tossed him a grin. "See, I'm fine. Just needed to get my bearings."

Daniel sat up and the coverlet fell to his waist, revealing his hardened chest covered in a dusting of dark hair. "You do look better, but be careful. And call if you need me."

She swallowed. She needed him all right, but not for his help with this particular bodily function. The need she felt was visceral, more primal than anything she'd ever experienced, and went deep, penetrating her very bones. She needed Daniel, the lover—the father—the man.

Sighing, she headed for the bathroom and took care of business. After that, she washed her face and brushed her teeth, then took a good look at herself in the mirror. Greeted by red-rimmed eyes, wildly mussed hair, and a too-pale complexion, she shuddered. If this was better, she must have terrified half the town last night. No wonder they'd all been so concerned.

She turned on the taps in the bathtub and went to the linen closet to grab clean clothes. "I'm taking a shower," she called before she went back into the small bath, set her things on the counter, and slipped through the curtain.

After lathering her hair, she raised her head and let the warm water stream down, hoping to rinse the misgivings from her mind. What else could go wrong on this planet, what other simple experiences might cause the same reaction as the perfume? She had to be careful for the remainder of her stay, just in case another unusual scent or strange taste upset her system or, worse, harmed her baby once she conceived.

The shower curtain parted, and she jumped. Daniel, naked and grinning, stepped over the edge of the tub.

"I assume you know there's a water shortage in this state?"

Zara held the washcloth to her breast. "No, I mean yes. What are you doing?"

He took the soap from its holder. "Conserving water. It's the first rule of a drought."

She shivered in spite of the hot spray. "A drought?"

"Yep." As if they bathed together every day, he took the washcloth from her hand and worked it into the soap until it foamed. Then he began scrubbing her shoulders, moving the cloth in lazy circles, going lower until he was washing her breasts. Her nipples beaded to hard points, and he studied them as he ran the soapy cloth down her rib cage to her belly. Bending forward, he licked at a hardened nub, and she felt a quiver in her womb.

Her hands rose to his shoulders. He stepped closer and leaned forward to suck at her breast, until she thought she would puddle and follow the water down the drain. The cloth slid lower as he washed her belly while his tongue flicked at the nipple, sending jolts of heat zinging to her toes, making her woozy with desire.

He stopped when he heard her moan and gazed into her eyes. "I was worried about you standing in a tub while you were still unsteady on your feet. Did you know that falls in the bathroom are the most common of all home injuries?"

Fisting her hands in his hair, she shook her head. "You are a wealth of information this morning."

"If my being here is too much, just say the word, and I'll leave."

"Daniel." She sagged against him. "I can't . . . we can't . . ."

"We already are." The hand he held against her navel dipped lower. "Spread your legs."

Powerless to disobey, she did as he asked, clutching at him when the washcloth parted her feminine folds and massaged intimately. His seeking fingers moved up and inside of her, touching her in the one spot that mattered most, and a whimper escaped her lips.

"Shh," he whispered when she moaned. "Let me take care of you." Slipping his hand down her thigh, he raised her leg and rested her foot on the edge of the tub. "That's good, real good." He slid his fingers back inside of her.

She raised herself on tiptoe, and he kissed her, long and slow, using his tongue to mimic the movements of his hand. Then he trailed his lips down her collarbone and breast, until he found her nipple again and began to lave it with his tongue. Sipping at the water sluicing over her skin, he nipped and licked. Circling inside her, he drove her to the edge of sanity, until she sobbed against his chest.

Daniel pressed her against the tiles, hoisted her up and shifted his legs, centering her over his thighs. Then he let her slide slowly down the wall as he impaled her on his iron-hard staff.

Zara shuddered in his arms, and he knew she was close to climax. Her nipples scraped his chest like points of fire, and he cupped one in his hand, plucking until she moaned.

She bit at her lower lip and he smiled. "This may take a bit of fancy maneuvering, but I feel up to the challenge. How about you?"

She opened her eyes. "Anything, just do it, please."

He caught her around the waist and lifted her against the wall. Squirming, she hitched both of her heels onto the edge of the tub. Sliding her up the tiles, he positioned himself to take her weight and guided his aching erection farther inside of her, driving to the hilt.

"That's the way," he said in encouragement.

Together, they soared to a fever pitch. Daniel murmured encouragement, while Zara raised and lowered herself. Beating at his chest with her fists, she screamed, and he levered into her, harder and faster than before. Her head rocked from side to side with the force of his pumping, but he kept up the jackhammer staccato of his hips. His orgasm built to a crescendo just as she grabbed his shoulders and dug her nails in with a desperation he felt to his very soul. Pounding into her, he took them both to the edge of heaven and beyond.

*Thirteen*

Cooling water brought Zara to sanity faster than a shooting star. Gently, Daniel helped her slide to her feet.

"That was amazing," he said, brushing wet hair from her forehead.

When she tipped up her chin, he kissed her, teasing her lips with his tongue. "I'll get out and dry off. Knowing Lucy, she'll be here any second to make sure I did my duty as your protector."

He slipped from the shower before she could respond. Seconds later, the door closed, and she was alone. As though in a trance, Zara rinsed and washed quickly. Then she dried off and wrapped her damp hair in a towel.

The enormity of what they'd just done was almost too much to face. How was she supposed to act? What was she supposed to do now that they'd engaged in this new intimacy? Everyone in town knew Daniel had spent the night. Would they assume the two of them had done more than occupy the same room?

Suddenly queasy, she rested her hands on the sink's edge and bent her head. An aftereffect of the incident at the perfume counter, she told herself as she leaned into the sink. Her stomach heaved, and she clutched the sides of the basin. Good thing Lucy didn't expect her to work today, because there was no way she could stay on her feet when she felt like this.

She heard voices and smiled through the discomfort. Daniel had been right. The sun was barely up, and the older woman was here, checking on both of them. Pulling herself together, she heaved a breath and swallowed down the nausea. Reaching up, she rubbed the towel into her head until her hair was almost dry, then took down the blower contraption, turned it on, and ran her fingers through the tangled strands. Using a brush, she managed to tame her curls into order. Then she dressed.

Feeling a bit better, she stepped into the living area. The scent of cooked vegetables surrounded her, and her stomach rebelled. Hesitantly, she walked around the bed and peered into the kitchen. Daniel stood with his back to her, stirring a pot on the stove. Feeling weak, she slid a chair from the table and plopped down.

"Good thing you took your time," he said, turning to face her. "Lucy knocked about two minutes after I got dressed. She must have started this soup before she went to bed last night, otherwise it wouldn't have been ready this early."

Zara swallowed an answer, afraid that if she spoke she might embarrass herself in front of him.

Raising a brow, he walked over and put a hand to her forehead. "You feeling all right? You have that look about you again, as if you just smelled something sour."

"I'm okay," she managed to say, drawing back her head. "Do I have to eat that?"

"You don't have to do a thing you don't want to do." He walked back to the stove. "But I know from taking care of Will when he has the flu that you should eat. I can fix tea and toast. How does that sound?"

"Like something I can handle," she muttered. *If my stomach behaves.*

"Then tea and toast it is."

Zara watched as he busied himself at the counter. Working efficiently, he turned on the kettle, then put bread in the toaster. Digging through the cupboard, he pulled out a box of herbal tea.

"How does something soothing sound? Chamomile, or maybe Sleepytime?"

She nodded. Suddenly, she wanted to be back in bed more than anything. The toast popped. Daniel spread it with butter and brought it to the table. Then the kettle boiled, and he filled a mug with hot water.

"Here you go." His mouth turned down at the corners. "You still seem a little raw around the edges. Eat that, then I'd advise you get back in bed."

"I don't need to—"

He grabbed the back of a chair and his fingers clenched white. "Damm it, Zara, but you do. I won't say that I'm sorry about what we did in the shower, but I never should have forced myself on you like I did—I see that now. You weren't ready for more than a calm, relaxing shower, and I barged in and—"

She reached out and clasped his hands. "Made me feel wonderful," she insisted, completing his sentence. "I'm sure that once I've eaten I'll feel good as new."

Releasing his fingers, she leaned back, dunked the tea bag, and set it on the side of the plate. She took a sip of the steamy liquid and it slid easily down her throat, instantly calming her stomach. Feeling brave, she tried a bite of toast, then another, until she finished everything.

Daniel nodded his approval as she ate. "Okay, time for bed. No arguments," he warned, when she opened her mouth to protest.

Oddly, her eyelids felt heavy, so heavy she could barely keep them open. Pushing from the table, she stumbled, and he rushed to her side. Lifting her in his arms, he carried her to the bed and set her down.

His eyes darkened with concern as he ran his gaze to her clothing. "Let's get you out of those things."

He undressed her as he would a doll, unzipping her jeans and sliding them down and off her legs. Then he raised her back and gently eased her out of her shirt. After tucking the covers around her, he neatened the bed so that it looked freshly made. Gathering her clothes, he bent and kissed her on her forehead. "You get some rest. I'll stand guard."

Daniel called himself every rotten name in the book, as he walked to the linen closet, folded her things, and set them on a shelf. He'd been an idiot, thinking only of his wants this morning, practically accosting her in the shower. It was obvious from Zara's ghostly complexion and weakened state that she hadn't been ready for sex or any kind of physical activity, and he'd taken advantage. He was a jerk.

A soft tapping on the door had him on full alert. Walking past the bed, he saw that she was already asleep. Poor kid, she was exhausted. Opening the door a crack, he smiled when he saw Jay Pepperdine and Will standing on the cement slab that made up the cabin's front porch. Jay held a napkin-covered basket in his hand; Will a stack of magazines.

"Murphy," said Jay.

"Dad, can I see Zara?" asked Will.

He inched out the door and closed it behind him. " 'Fraid not, son. She was up for a little while, but she's still pretty tired. She took a shower and changed, but it wore her out. She's sound asleep."

"My housekeeper thought she might like some homemade cinnamon buns." Jay offered him the basket.

"And I brought her these." Will handed him the magazines. "So she can read while she gets better."

Daniel checked out Will's clean jeans and T-shirt. "You going to school today?"

"Uh-huh. The bus should be here soon."

"I'll see to it he comes to my place after school, Murphy, and don't worry about the Last Chance. I've freed up a few of my boys to man it all day. You just make sure Zara gets well."

"Will do. And thanks, I owe you one." He juggled the basket and magazines, then ruffled Will's hair with his free hand. "You doin' okay?"

"Yeah. But I miss you and Zara. Do you think I can see her when I get home?"

"I'd expect so. You have a lunch?"

"Housekeeper took care of it," said Jay. He set a hand on Will's shoulder. "We'll see you later."

Daniel watched them disappear down the path between the restaurant and the last cabin. Sighing, he slipped back inside. After he set the food on the counter, he made himself a cup of tea and indulged in a sweet roll. Then he picked up a magazine and a kitchen chair, carried both to the front porch, and sat down. He had a feeling he was going to do little more than play butler today, answering the townsfolk's questions while he tried to keep them from interrupting Zara's sleep.

Gut instinct honed from years of being on the run told him she needed protection, either from someone in her past or someone in the here and now, though he wasn't sure which. More than ever, he had questions for her that needed to be asked, because whether he liked it or not, he was involved with Zara right up to his eyebrows. If they were going to have a future together, he had to tell her the truth about his past.

He only hoped she cared enough to tell him about hers.

* * *

Jack Farley sat at Frank's kitchen table nursing a cold beer while he watched the man assemble their lunch. He had a good idea why he'd been asked to the cabin, and he wasn't sure what he was going to say when the pseudosurveyor posed the inevitable question, so he'd decided silence was best.

Finally, Frank turned and set two plates piled with chips and a sandwich on the table. Taking a seat, he smiled. "Bought the fixings at Murphy's yesterday. Ham and Swiss with mustard. If you're as tired as Chuck and me of the luncheonette food, it should hit the spot."

Farley eyed the meal with a raised brow.

"Go on, dig in. It's not poison, if that's what you're worried about."

"Where is Chuck, by the way?" Jack scooped up the sandwich and took a bite.

Leaning back in his chair, Frank folded his arms and stared as if pondering his answer. "Took a trip north—should be gone for a day or two."

"Good sandwich," said Jack. Biting into his lunch, he waited to hear the rest.

"He had some business to attend to." Frank finally started on his sandwich. "Official business," he added as he chewed.

"I take it you're not talking about TXdot," said Jack, voicing what he suspected almost from the moment he set foot in town.

Frank barked out a laugh. "Can't put anything past you, can we?"

He'd run into Frank's type before—men who had

to act like know-it-alls because they felt they were on a fruitless mission, doomed to the lowest rank on the government totem pole, a laughingstock in the department and in the eyes of most Americans. Flying saucer chasers. Alien hunters. Weirdos who believed in life from another planet.

"No, you can't," he said plainly. In a roundabout way, he and Frank were on the same side. Jack just had a more personal reason for doing what he did. Aside from being a bit shortsighted, the men would lead him to his goal. "So you might as well lay your cards on the table."

"You first," said Frank, around a mouthful of food.

"It's your party," countered Jack. Of course, there was a slim chance he was wrong. The last thing he wanted was to be on the receiving end of a derisive snort.

Frank downed the last of his beer, then gave his guest another once over. "Chuck and I are in this one-hole shitcan excuse of a town for a specific reason, and I suspect you already know it has nothing to do with roads or bridges. We're on a scouting mission from Washington."

"Go on," encouraged Jack, not giving an inch. He wasn't about to be the first to say it, unless he had no other choice.

"We're looking for a UFO."

Jack bit back a smug smile. "A UFO, or its passengers? Because I've combed every inch of this town and the surrounding area and haven't seen one thing that could lead me to an interstellar vehicle."

"Then you're searching, too?" answered Frank. "Chuck and I thought so, but we had to be sure."

"Be sure," Jack said. "I have friends who report directly to Washington, just as I suspect you do. I headed out of DC the moment I heard from my source that a series of alien landings had taken place around the country. Button Creek was one of nine sites pinpointed by their tracking system."

"Is that so?" asked Frank, his face an open book of amazement. "And who is this *source*? Is he in the bureau?"

"A good reporter never reveals his contacts. You know that," Jack reminded him. "Let's just say the tipster is reliable and sits at the top of the division."

"Lucas Diamond?"

Lucas Diamond was the man who ran every aspect of NASA's Division of Interstellar Activity, but the lone wolf's name was rarely mentioned. Contrary to many popular television series, most people scoffed at there actually being such a section at work in the government.

Jack forced out a half smile. "Hell no. Diamond is out to debunk the myth, not reinforce it."

Shock registered before Frank was able to mask his features. "He's head of Operation Roswell. Diamond would only be hurting himself if he kept us from producing a subject."

"So they're back to calling it that again, are they?" Jack quirked up a corner of his mouth. "Interesting."

"What do you mean? It's been OR ever since I joined the agency twenty years ago."

"That's what they'd like you to believe," said Jack, his pity for the agent clear.

Frank leaned into the table. "How do you know so much? What's in it for you?"

"Simple. I'm a photojournalist hoping for the story of the century, hell, the biggest story in the history of the world. The man who breaks the news is going to be famous, a Pulitzer Prize winner and a millionaire all at once. With the help of a friend, I intend to be that man."

"I see. Then the two of you are in it for yourselves?"

Jack shrugged. "Isn't everybody?"

"Tell me what else you know about Diamond."

"Not a hell of a lot." Jack swallowed the last of his beer. "But according to my sources, Diamond's definitely more a hindrance than a help."

"You're *friend* is wrong. He's an agency man, I'm sure of it. Sits in his plush chair in a big corner office and gives orders like a dictator. He'll look like a damned savior if one of us manages to strike gold and actually find an alien."

"That's where *you're* wrong," said Jack. He really loved setting these government geeks back a peg or two. What they didn't know about the stuff going on in their own division could fill Lake Michigan. "His goal is to prove that no alien life-forms have ever visited Earth. He's just more clever at it."

"I suppose your *friend* told you that, too?"

Jack didn't answer.

"At least tell me if the source is male or female?

"I can tell you they're human," said Jack with a laugh.

"That wasn't the answer I was looking for," Frank snapped. Picking up their plates, he carried them to the sink, then retrieved two more beers from the refrigerator and brought them to the table. "Okay. Since you seem to know so much, where do you think our visitors are?"

Jack twisted the top of his bottle and took a long swallow. "I thought this was a two-way street. I'd show you mine, and you'd show me yours," he drawled. "Seems to me, I've been the only one to face my hand."

"You're forgetting one important thing, Farley." Frank set his bottle down hard. "You don't cooperate with us, you could find yourself arrested and tossed in a federal prison. If that happens, you can kiss that Pulitzer good-bye."

"Don't threaten me, because I meant it when I said I know people," Jack shot back. "I'll cooperate, but only if you do the same."

A glimmer of annoyance flashed in Frank's eyes. "All right. We've given it a lot of thought, and we're looking at several suspects. Our best guess is that waitress. Zara."

Jack tried, but he couldn't contain his laughter.

"You got any better ideas?" Frank snarled.

"You think that woman—" Jack swiped a hand over eyes, but he couldn't stop the chortle, "is an alien? No wonder you and your buddy are batting triple zero."

"Haven't you heard about what happened to her last night? It's one more reason to suspect her, as far as I'm concerned."

"You mean her fainting spell at that department store?" Jack asked. "Hell, happens to females all the time. Probably just her time of the month."

"That's not what I heard," said Frank. "Miss Coombs said the woman was out cold, and her skin was practically green. That's not a normal reaction to a spritz of perfume, not by a long shot."

"The old lady was probably exaggerating," scoffed Jack.

"I got the same story from a half dozen people. Every one of them swore Zara's complexion was green as spring grass. Even Doc Mayberry said he'd never anything like it on a human before."

"Doc Mayberry is a horse doctor, not an MD. How the hell many people with allergic reactions do you think the old fool has treated?" Jack countered. "If that woman is an alien, then I'm an astronaut."

Frank huffed out a breath. "All right, if Zara isn't who we're looking for, then who is?"

Jack held up his hand and counted down, finger by finger. "Jay Pepperdine hired three new hands last week, same day word of the sightings reached Washington. Zetmer's rented a place to a trucker the day after, and the man hasn't left his room since. No one knows he's in town, except the Zetmers. I managed to wheedle the info out of Sally when I stopped by the store. According to her, he's a very spooky guy."

"Who told you about the new men at Pepperdines?"

"That old geezer who sits on the porch all day. Jeremiah. Haven't you talked to anyone?"

"We've run our own investigation. We've taken samples of soil and a few of the trees, plus sent a few fingerprints to the lab in Quantico—yours included," Frank said, as if to let Jack know he was being watched.

"Good for you. So what have you found out?"

Frank drew his mouth taut. "Haven't got the results back yet. But we will. And Chuck is up at that campsite at the lake. We'll find them."

"You say *them*, yet you suspect one little waitress? What do you think she's doing, supporting a half dozen aliens inside of her like some caricature from *Men in Black*?"

"Make jokes if you want, but we have reasons for suspecting her."

"And those might be?"

"How about we take a ride to Pepperdine's ranch and have a look around. I suddenly have a feeling that the feeder road running behind the Triple P might need to be monitored for traffic flow. On the way, I can tell you about Zara."

"Hey, Zara. Dad said he thought you'd be waking up soon."

Will's hesitant voice tugged Zara from her reverie. She'd managed to keep down a bowl of vegetable soup for lunch and doze away the rest of the afternoon. Aside from warming the soup, Murphy had come and gone like a spirit, righting covers, setting fresh water on her nightstand, even arranging a bouquet of wildflowers on the kitchen table without her ever seeing him. In her haze, she'd heard him at the door from time to time, speaking in a low, protective tone. He must have let his son in and gone to the Last Chance to check on his business.

"Hey, yourself," she said, sliding up on her pillow. "I didn't hear you come in."

Will studied her so intently she thought she might have grown a second nose. "How are you feeling?" he finally asked.

"Better. Practically back to my old self. I'm sure I'll be able to go to work tomorrow."

That brought a flicker of worry to his eyes. "You should let Sally cover the morning shift. And come home and take a nap in the afternoon. Doc Mayberry said you need lots of rest."

She smiled. "Sounds like you've had the flu before."

"The flu?"

"I figure I must have caught some kind of twenty-four-hour virus. I hope I didn't give it to anyone in town."

"I thought you had an allergic reaction to perfume?" Will wrinkled his brow. "Allergies are bad. I know because I was tested, and the doctors said so. They said I'm lucky I just have asthma, and I'm not allergic to pollen or stuff."

"I'm certain it was the flu," she assured him. "Lots of travelers come and go in the diner. I probably caught something from one of the truckers who stopped for a meal, that's all."

Will shuffled from foot to foot, and she took pity on

him. "Why don't you get a chair from the kitchen and sit down? I could use the company."

Grinning, he retrieved one and sat it next to her bed. "Did you like the magazines?"

"I slept most of the day, so I haven't had a chance to read them." She glanced at the pile of astronomy periodicals and stargazing journals stacked on the side table. Will had brought a stash of his favorite reading material, just for her. "I plan to look them over after dinner. I'm not much for television."

Will didn't seem upset that she hadn't found the time for his precious magazines. "It's hard to get local stations up here. Dallas is too far away, and Denton doesn't have much. That's why Dad and I have the satellite dish."

The mention of Daniel reminded her of how much she missed him. "Where is your father?"

"At the station. He said I should take his place watching you." Will sounded very proud of the job entrusted to him. "I'm supposed to keep people from bothering you."

Just then there was a knock at the door. "I'll get it," he said as he jumped from the chair.

Zara raised a hand to halt him, but he didn't notice. She imagined she looked a fright, and she had to use the bathroom. Besides Will, the last thing she wanted was another visitor. Unless it was Daniel.

Will flung the door open with enthusiasm. "Miss Lucy." He stepped back to let the older woman in. "Zara's up."

"I can see that." Lucy set a square, covered pan on

the table and walked to the foot of the bed. Her mouth opened and closed. Strange, because Zara couldn't remember a time Lucy was at a loss for words.

Finally, the older woman said, "Say there, missy, you look a mite pale."

"Pale?" Zara ran a hand over her hair. "But I'm feeling fine."

Lucy raised an eyebrow. "That's good to hear. It's probably just my tired eyes, is all." She nodded in the direction of the kitchen. "Business is slow, so I figured it was a good time to bring you a little supper. Made you a vegetable and rice casserole."

"Thank you." Lowering her voice, Zara waited for Lucy to come closer. "I didn't want to say this in front of Will, but I have to go to the bathroom, and I'm not properly dressed under here. Do you think you could—?"

"Just a second. I'll take care of it."

After giving her another subtle once-over, Lucy ambled from the room. Zara's bed was set back in a corner, but she could make out the front door and a section of the kitchen table. She heard whispers, then Will left the cabin.

"He's going to the luncheonette to ask Tomas for a teapot, so I can make you a proper cup of tea," Lucy said, craning her neck around the dividing wall. "Ought to take a good ten minutes, so you can do your business and get dressed if you've a mind. I'll just serve up the casserole."

Zara waited until Lucy disappeared before slipping out of bed. After stopping to gather fresh clothes, she headed for the bathroom and dressed. A quick glance in the mirror explained Will's and Lucy's confused expressions.

Her eyes, a usually dark, sedate blue, had turned a brilliant, jewel-like aqua. They didn't look unnatural, just . . . striking . . . and more than likely startling to anyone who knew how they'd looked before. Could her reaction to the perfume have caused the change, or had something else happened to her system?

What would Daniel say when he saw her?

She sank onto the commode and rested her cheek against the sink, hoping the cool porcelain would magically provide an answer. The solution came to her, and she smiled. People on earth still had problems with their vision. Many wore glasses and some had surgery to correct the defect, but a great majority wore contact lenses. *Colored* contact lenses.

It was a logical explanation. She could say she carried contacts with her because of a slight debility, but didn't always need to wear them. After her illness, her vision had blurred so she decided to insert the lenses. Surely, when she was back to perfect health, her eyes would return to their normal color.

A murmur of voices brought her to her feet. She ran a brush through her hair, tucked the sides behind her ears, and took a breath. For her ruse to work, she had to appear completely natural. There would be time to figure out the reason for the shocking change later.

She walked to the kitchen, where she found Daniel speaking to Lucy. Both of them grew quiet when they saw her standing in the doorway.

"Daniel, hello," she began. "Everything all right at the station?"

He searched her face with a quizzical gaze. "Yeah, fine." His eyes shifted quickly to Lucy and back. "How about you? I hope Will's chatter didn't talk you into a relapse?"

"Not at all. He's great company." She pulled out a chair and sat down. "Lucy, that casserole smells wonderful. I can hardly wait to taste it."

The woman took down plates from the cupboard. "There's enough for three, if Will and Dan'l don't mind a heap of veggies."

Before Daniel could answer, there was another knock at the door. He opened it, and Will walked in, carrying a teapot painted with brightly colored flowers. He handed the teapot to Lucy.

"Tomas had to climb a ladder and get it down from a cabinet above the refrigerator."

"Thanks, now how about setting the table?" Lucy opened a drawer, then began to assemble the tea. "You and your dad can sit a spell while I serve supper, then I'll head back home."

Continuing to gaze at Zara, Daniel took his seat. "So you're feeling better?"

"Fine, but my eyes were a little blurry earlier, so I had to put in my contacts."

"Your contacts?" He sat back in the chair. "I didn't know you wore them."

"Dad wears contacts, too." Will placed forks and napkins on the table. "But yours are way cooler."

She fumbled with her napkin, hoping to hide her surprise. "You do? I mean you never said."

"They're the disposable kind. Wear them two weeks and throw them away. No fuss. I get them through the mail. Mine are clear, not so dramatic as yours. I haven't noticed you wearing them before."

"I don't usually need them," she lied. "But sometimes, when I'm stressed, I have a problem with my vision. I know the color is a bit much, but they're all I have right now."

Lucy turned and set full plates on the table. "Have a niece who got colored lenses. Made her eyes look like bottle glass. Yours are prettier." She gave Daniel an encouraging grin. "Ain't that so, Dan'l?"

"I've never met your niece, so I can't compare, but yes, Zara's eyes are stunning." He met Will's smiling face. "Of course, we thought they were nice the other way, too, didn't we, son?"

The boy flushed pink and dug into his casserole.

Zara thanked Lucy for the dinner and ignored her curious gaze as the older woman let herself out of the cabin.

# Fourteen

"*I* heard about what happened to Zara last night," said Frank, standing in the doorway of her cabin. "Thought I'd come by and see how she was doing."

Murphy loomed like a sentinel, blocking his entrance. "She's better, but not completely, and she's had a long day. She needs her rest."

"So I heard. But Lucy said she was up to visitors. Dolly told me she'd stopped by after dinner, so I thought I'd do the same."

"I'll tell her you were here." Daniel settled himself like a rock against the doorjamb. "Maybe you can talk to her tomorrow."

*Or not.* At least not if Daniel Murphy has anything to say on the subject.

"Frank." Zara seemed to appear from nowhere as she peered at him from around Murphy's broad shoulder. "Come on in."

Frank had to hold himself in check to keep from laughing. Murphy glared at him, then Zara, then took a step back, his hand still on the door. "You need your rest. He can stop by to shoot the breeze when you're feeling better."

"I'm fine now. I plan to be at the luncheonette tomorrow," she said with a smile.

"No, you don't."

Zara folded her arms and gave a determined nod. "Yes, I do."

"Zara, we've talked this out until we're out of breath." He turned fully, unblocking the door. "Sally can take your morning shift, and Lucy can handle lunch. You need to stay in bed another day."

Frank took the opportunity to slide through the door and prop himself against the counter.

"I'm going to get all the rest I need for a full recovery tonight. Besides, Sally is spending the night at your place, looking after Will. She's going to be too tired to take my shift."

"Then I'll take it."

She arched a brow. "You're joking."

"Does it sound like I'm joking?"

"I'd talk to Lucy before I showed up in an apron if I were you, Daniel Murphy. With that cranky attitude of yours, every customer will be gone by 7 A.M."

"I can be charming if I have to," he growled back.

"Like you're being right now?"

Frank watched the exchange with amusement. Murphy sounded protective but loving, in a crabby-yet-teasing sort of way. Zara reacted to him playfully, almost as if they were an old married couple, and she knew exactly what buttons to push. He studied Zara the way he would any beautiful woman. And then he blinked. Besides the pallor of her skin, there was something else different about her—something he couldn't quite put his finger on. Until she swung around fully to face him.

"What do you say, Frank? Who would you rather have wait on you, Daniel or me?"

*Holy hell! What the heck was up with her eyes?*

"I . . . uh . . . why you of, course," he stuttered out. "Murphy's too darned ugly."

"Thank you—I think." She gave him a smile.

Murphy rounded on him, as if he'd just realized Frank was in the room. "Say your piece, then, and go home. The woman is impossible."

"Would you like something to drink?" Zara asked, playing hostess. Frank was certain she did it only to irritate Murphy.

"No, thank you. I just wanted to be sure you were okay. I can see myself out."

Frank heard Zara's muffled *good-bye* as the door slammed behind him. Suspicion swirled in his mind while he walked to his cabin. What in the hell was going on with the woman? Had Chuck been right, after all?

He entered the cottage and blew out a breath as he locked the door behind him. He and Jack Farley had managed to talk themselves onto the Triple P and inspect the area the bunkhouses were located in without a problem. Jay Pepperdine's housekeeper was a friendly sort and, since Jay had taken a drive into Denton, had no problem allowing them to check out the road that ran along the back of the ranch.

He and Farley had done a quick search, but hadn't found anything unusual. Thanks to the affable foreman, they'd even met the new hands. Two of them were eager, fresh-faced kids just out of high school, looking to make money before they started college in the fall. They seemed too normal to be anything other than cowhands. The third man, a grizzled fellow with a limp and a penchant for chewing tobacco, had been in the area for years and, according to the foreman, picked up work whenever he needed a few extra bucks. Again, not a stellar candidate for an alien.

He and Jack hadn't made it to Zetmers to check out the new boarder, but he planned to do that first thing in the morning. Now he didn't think he would have to. It was obvious Zara hadn't fully recovered from her ordeal. She was paler than he'd ever seen her, with dark circles under her eyes. He hadn't thought there was enough evidence to bring her in for questioning on her healing skills and glowing bracelet alone, but this latest oddity had moved her to the head of the list.

His cell phone rang, and he pulled it from the holder on his belt, eyeing the number screen. "Yeah?"

"Nice greeting, Frank. How'd you know it was me?"

Frank took a seat at the table and huffed out a breath. "I have caller ID."

"Oh, yeah. I forgot," mumbled Chuck.

"So, what have you got to tell me?

"Nothing. *Nada*. Zip. There isn't a thing going on up here, besides an influx of families and their squalling kids who've come for vacation. No one has seen anything or met anyone out of the ordinary. The owner of the biggest campground says so far all his customers are repeaters, ditto most of the smaller ones. And the newcomers are all family groups, as well."

"Hell."

"You took the word right out of my mouth," said Chuck, echoing the sentiment. "Now what?"

"Come on back. I've spent some time people watching with Jack Farley."

"And?"

"Let's just say he's on our side and leave it at that."

"Great. Now what?"

"We use him. I just have to figure out how. He's not hot on your idea of the waitress, by the way."

"Neither were you, when I first suggested her." Chuck waited a beat. "Don't tell me your feelings have changed?"

Frank recalled what he'd heard of Zara's mishap at the mall. He'd laughed when a couple of folks had said she looked "green around the gills" as if they meant it. Now, there was that hinky business with her eyes . . .

"Things have taken an odd turn. I need some time to check it out. Just get back here first thing in the morning."

"Remember, do what Sally tells you and go right to sleep."

"Yes, sir."

"Sally, you know where he keeps his inhaler?"

"You showed me twice already, Mr. Murphy."

"I left a list of numbers on the kitchen table. You can call the luncheonette before ten if you need me, after that call Miss Lucy at home, and she'll come get me."

Sally held up the sheet of paper. "Got it."

"And Will's not allowed on the overhang alone."

"I know that."

"He can have juice if he's thirsty, but nothing after eight o'clock, cause then he'll have to get up and—"

Sally rolled her eyes. "I understand."

Will moaned at the same time. "Da-aad. Jeez."

"Okay, then," said Daniel, standing at the top of the stairs. "I'll be on my way."

He reached out and ruffled his son's hair. "Be good."

"Good night, Mr. Murphy," said the teenager, an amused tone lacing her words.

"See ya," called Will.

Turning, Daniel pounded down the stairs before he said something else stupid to embarrass his boy. He checked the locks on the station before he crossed the street, just in case he thought of another fact Sally should know to help the evening go smoothly. When nothing came to mind, he sighed. Sally had looked at him as if he was a lunatic, and Will—Hell, the boy would probably never forgive him for making a fuss.

But he wasn't about to leave his son with a girl only six years his senior without setting a few ground rules.

Reseating his hat, he started across the highway. Jay Pepperdine slowed his SUV and waved, a smug grin etched in his rugged face. Otis Zetmer called a friendly greeting. Daniel passed the restaurant, and two of Pepperdine's cowhands made a loud comment about how some men had all the luck.

Talk about living in a fishbowl.

Worse, he'd only been gone from Zara's cabin for an hour, and he missed her already. But he'd needed the time to instruct Sally, and Zara needed time to shower and get ready for bed.

Ready for him.

*Scratch that,* he ordered himself. His randy actions in the shower had exhausted her. It was going to be hands off until she recovered. The most he would let himself give in to was some cuddling—maybe a make-out session. He was a grown man, not a sex-crazed teenager. Zara needed rest, and he was going to see that she got it.

He rounded the restaurant and walked past Frank's cottage. Was he imagining it, or did the curtains at the front window flutter as he passed? And why had the surveyor been so insistent on visiting Zara in her cabin, when he could have just as easily waited until morning?

Daniel rapped on her door, then opened it and went inside, locking the door behind him. The light over the sink was on, and there was a soft glow coming from the living room. "Zara? It's me," he called out. "You decent?"

He turned the corner and found her in bed, munching on a chocolate bar while she flipped through one of Will's astronomy journals. Covered to her neck in flower-sprigged white cotton, all Daniel could think of was female body armor. But where had it come from?

"I think I'm more than decent," she said with a smile. "When Lucy found out I was sleeping in my panties and bra, she brought over one of her nightgowns. I feel as if I'm wearing a parachute."

Daniel took off his hat and placed it on the table in front of the sofa. "Remind me to thank her in the morning."

Zara's aqua-colored eyes grew huge. "Don't you dare. It's bad enough the whole town knows you're spending the night here. Lucy's only trying to protect my reputation."

"Or give me a good kick in the pants."

She closed the magazine and set it on the nightstand, along with the wrapper from her candy. "This thing is removable, you know. All I have to do is slip a few buttons and tug it over my head."

Frowning, Daniel walked to her side of the bed and sat down. "Leave it be, Zara. I made a promise to myself that I wouldn't touch you tonight, and God help me, but I'm going to keep it."

Her pale face blushed pink, a sharp contrast to her oddly colored eyes. "Oh. I see."

"I'm afraid you don't." He tucked a strand of hair behind her ear. "I was a jerk this morning. You needed to stay quiet and sleep, and instead I followed you into the shower and acted like a randy gopher. I'm not going to do that to you tonight, or tomorrow. I'm not going to make love to you again until you're one hundred percent better."

Disappointment filled Zara to her very core. She'd been too distracted and too tired to check and see if she was pregnant. A small part of her hidden deep inside didn't want to know. If she was carrying a child, there would no longer be a need to mate with Daniel. If she didn't know, she could continue to tell herself she was sleeping with him for her mission.

Not her heart.

She had two more chances to conceive before she had to leave for the rendezvous site. If she didn't become pregnant, she would go home despondent, not only because she was barren, but also because she hadn't taken every advantage to give Daniel as much pleasure as she could. Sex after she conceived wouldn't hurt the fetus. Their time here together was precious. She owed him that much.

"But you will share the bed with me?" she asked. At least she could sleep in his arms tonight.

He turned off the bedside lamp, then stood and walked across the room. "Only if you promise to behave."

Daniel stood at the living room windows, a tall, determined figure. Unbuttoning his shirt, he tugged it free and draped it over the sofa arm. After pulling his belt from his jeans, he toed off his boots. Locking on to her gaze, he headed back in her direction.

Moisture beaded her forehead. A knot of desire coiled low in her belly. With his wide shoulders, sculpted chest, and tapered waist, Daniel was the most beautiful man she'd ever seen. Everything about him set her on fire. His chest hair was dark, his small nipples brown and erect, his stomach muscles taut and corded.

"Aren't you forgetting something?" she asked, licking her lower lip.

"Am I?" he answered, lying beside her on the bed.

She turned on her side and grabbed at the snap of his jeans. His erection strained behind the zipper, and she took pleasure in letting the metal slide slowly down.

Daniel covered her hand with his. "I thought you were going to behave?"

"Your words, not mine," she whispered, nipping at his chin.

Joining their fingers, he brought their hands up as he rolled her to her back. Kissing her deeply, he let his tongue answer her smart retort. Still on top of the covers, he settled over her and joined them from shoulders to belly to hips, making them one.

"You're welcome to come under the covers," she said when he drew back. "It would be warmer."

Sudden concern etched his face. "Are you cold? I can turn down the air conditioner if you're chilly."

"I'm fine. I like it cool. What about you?"

He smiled boyishly. "Me too, but being here with you makes me hot as a Texas road in August."

"Then slide under the covers. If you won't make love to me, please hold me through the night," she pleaded. *At least give me that to remember you by.*

"I meant what I said, Zara. No sex until I know you're fine." He tugged at the coverlet and slid beside her. She turned to snuggle into him and he studied her face. "Don't you have to take those contacts out before you fall asleep?"

Her heart skipped inside her chest. "Um . . . no. They're the kind you can sleep in."

"Just checking," he answered, pulling her closer.

Zara sighed. There was nothing but lies between them. Lies that would bring him pain. And with the pain would come loss. Loss that would wound them both.

At the first sound of tapping, Daniel sprang from the bed. Snagging his shirt from the sofa on the way to the kitchen, he shrugged it on and zipped up his jeans before inching open Zara's cabin door. Sally Zetmer, dressed in a skinny strap, bright yellow T-shirt, and purple miniskirt, stood on the stoop bathed in the emerging dawnlight. Fully made up in bloodred lipstick, black mascara, and spiky hair, the girl was so put together she must have been awake for hours.

"Hey, Mr. Murphy."

"Sally. What time is it?" Waking at a civilized hour was one of the things he missed most since moving to Button Creek. Truckers, farmers, and cattlemen started their day at the crack of dawn.

"Early. I just wanted you to know that I left Will sound asleep. I have to get home to shower and do my nails before I get to the diner and take the lunch shift."

Daniel ran a hand through his hair. "Okay, thanks. I'll be over with your money before you leave."

"No hurry. I'm on from eleven to one." Sally peeked around his shoulder. "How's Zara doing?"

"Still asleep. She had a quiet night, so my guess is she'll wake feeling fine. I doubt it will be necessary for you to look after Will tonight."

"Okay, but I don't mind. You know . . . in case you want to stay over again."

Daniel ignored her sly grin. "I gather Will was no trouble?"

"Nah. He's a nice kid. We had fun."

"No problems at bedtime?"

"Not a one."

"Great. I'll see you later."

Sally hoisted her overnight bag onto her shoulder. "Tell Zara I stopped by, and if she's still feeling crummy, let her know I don't mind working lunch by myself. Ditto watching Will—in case—you know," she repeated, giggling.

Daniel closed the door. What the hell was with kids these days? That girl was definitely too smart for her own good. On the way to the bathroom, he stopped at the foot of the bed. Zara was sleeping peacefully. With her hand tucked under her chin, she looked barely older than a teenager herself. Though he'd kept his word and done nothing but sleep beside her, it had been a long and restless night.

Whenever he'd turn away from Zara, she'd fit herself to his backside. If she flipped over, his body followed like steel filings to a magnet. They'd been so drawn to each other that when they settled face-to-face, she snuggled into his chest while he wrapped his arms around her and rested his chin on the top of her head. He'd been contemplating the tender-yet-frustrating torture before Sally's knock, while she had slept like a stone.

Once in the bathroom, Daniel took a good look at himself in the mirror. No wonder the girl had stared with that sassy grin. As a complement to his day's growth of dark beard, his unruly hair stood straight up on the top of his head. After patting it down with water, he opened the medicine chest to borrow a comb, but there wasn't much on the shelves: a bottle of aspirin, a tube of toothpaste and a toothbrush, a styptic pencil, and a falling-apart box of Band-Aids. No makeup, no box of protection for *that time of month*, no fancy creams or jars of goo most females used to make themselves look good.

He closed the door, ready to walk away when something nagged at his brain. Opening it again, he took a closer inventory. Drawing his brows together, he searched for whatever *hadn't* caught his eye, until he realized what was missing.

Contact lens solution and a storage case.

He checked the top of the commode, then edged toward the narrow linen closet. The top shelf held an extra set of towels and sheets; the middle shelf, an array of cleaning supplies, a box of tissues, rolls of toilet paper and a hairbrush; and on the bottom shelf, Zara's neatly folded clothing.

Daniel ran a hand over the back of his neck. He'd

worn his lenses to bed, but as soon as he arrived home
he planned to take them out and let them soak while
he got Will ready for school. People who used the disposable kind, as he did, needed to store and rinse
them when they weren't being worn, even if they got
tossed out after a week or two. He'd read about the
kind of lenses Zara claimed she had on, the kind that
could be worn twenty-four hours straight, but even
that type needed to be stored and changed regularly.
Either Zara was down to her last pair, or she'd lied
about wearing contacts.

But why would she do that? And if she did, what
could have caused the change in her eye color?

The mattress creaked, and he closed the closet door.
Zara walked around the bed, straight into his arms.
Hauling her against him, he pushed his misgivings
aside. She felt so good, so right, molded to him like
this, as if they were two interlocking pieces of the
same puzzle.

"Good morning." She kissed the underside of his
jaw. "Been up long?"

He inhaled the clean scent of her hair, smelled the
womanly fragrance of her curvy body, and fought the
urge to drag her back to bed. Unable to stop himself,
he stared into her eyes. "A few minutes. Sally stopped
by to say that she'd left Will sleeping and was on her
way home."

"Lucy's at the farmers' market, so I think I may
play lazy and take a nice hot bath before I go in."

"You're feeling better, I take it?"

Lowering her eyelids, she sidled past him into the

bathroom. "Like my old self," she said, closing the door.

He sat on the sofa and slipped on his boots. Maybe Zara was back to her old self, but it was clear her eyes were not. If she'd lied because she didn't have a logical explanation for the color change, she should have just said so.

She came out of the bathroom, stepped to the linen closet, and pulled out a towel. "I'll probably make the diner by noon. How about you?"

"I'm going home to make breakfast for Will. Ricky invited him over this afternoon, so I'll stop by for lunch—if you promise to wait on me."

Clutching the clothes to her chest, she turned. "Don't you have work at the station?"

Instead of coming across as self-assured, the eyebrow she raised only made her look nervous. He tucked his hands into his pockets to keep from walking over, gathering her up in his arms, and soothing her fears. The quirky eye color had to bother her— hell, it was driving him crazy.

Unless she was telling the truth . . .

Unfortunately, he couldn't come right out and confront her about the missing storage case and solution. Snooping had put him between a rock and a hard place, and that was no way to hold on to a relationship, especially when he wasn't even sure they had one.

"It's already arranged, Zara. Jay's sending a hand to the Last Chance so I can take care of you."

"Take care of me?" She shook her head. "You're going to be bored sick, sitting at the counter and staring at me all day. Go to work, Daniel. If I need you, I'll have Lucy or Sally come get you."

"I don't mind being bored. Besides, Will would never forgive me if you had a relapse. I can bring over my ledgers and balance the books at the counter. When you take a break, you can join me."

She put her clothes back in the closet, marched over, and placed her hands on his shoulders. Playfully turning him, she pushed him through the kitchen. "Go home and see to Will, then we'll talk."

At the door, he spun around and drew her near. "I'll be over in a couple of hours. If you get dizzy or feel peculiar, I want you to sit and have Lucy call me, understand? I can spend the night again, if you need me."

Without answering, Zara rose up and kissed him fully on the mouth. Plastering herself to his chest and groin, she showed him exactly what she needed. The feel of her tempting body pressed so intimately against his sent a rush of heat straight to the area below his belt.

He pulled away before he did something foolish. "This isn't a good idea."

Stepping back, she gave a shy smile, almost as if she couldn't believe what she'd just done. "Neither is thinking that I'm going to get dizzy or feel *peculiar.* Now go."

Zara gave him a final shove and closed the door. *What had she just done?* The man made her doubt her own sanity. First, he kept his promise and slept beside her through the night without making love to her, when she wanted nothing more than to lose herself in his embrace. Then he fussed over her as if she were a child. Standing in front of Daniel while he gazed at her with a purely male look of possession was more than she could bear.

None of the men on her planet would ever dare to be so controlling, and none of them would have been so solicitous of her health. Daniel Murphy was truly one of a kind, just not her kind.

No matter what transpired between them, no matter how many times they had sex or made love, he never would be.

*Fifteen*

"*W*ow." Sally gave Zara's eyes a second long inspection. "Incredible. They almost make me wish I needed contacts. Only the pair I got would be tinted purple."

"I thought you'd be impressed," said Lucy. "Kinda took me by surprise, too."

Not wanting to add to the list of people to whom she had already lied, Zara simply smiled. Now that she was back to feeling normal, she'd truly thought her eyes would return to their sedate and ordinary blue. One glance in the mirror told her that hadn't happened. Until it did, she had to accept the curious looks and questioning comments politely.

The first wave of lunch customers passed, and the three women stood in the kitchen taking a break. To show her appreciation to Sally for starting the shift, Zara had manned the counter and let the teenager wait tables, where the tips were better. It also gave her a chance to make certain she could handle the rigors of being on her feet without calling any more attention to her eyes than was necessary.

"You doing okay?" asked Lucy, propping her bottom on a kitchen stool.

"I'm fine. Sally can go home if she wants."

Sally sipped at a cup of tea. "I might do that after Mr. Murphy gets here with my money—if you really feel all right."

"I think that's a great idea," Zara said.

"Did you eat this morning?" asked Lucy. "'Cause you gotta keep up your strength after an illness. How about Tomas makes you something while there's a little downtime?"

The bell over the door rang, and Sally rushed to take care of the customer. Lucy shook her head as the girl raced past. "She's turning into a right handy young lady."

"Remember to tell Hattie so, when you see her. I've heard mothers love it when people compliment them on their children."

"I will. Now how about some lunch?"

Zara didn't usually eat at the diner, but the suggestion of a meal had her suddenly salivating. "Would it be too much trouble to have Tomas fix me some soup? Or maybe a grilled cheese sandwich?"

Lucy waved a hand at her cook. "Tomas, ladle out a bowl of that vegetable soup and put a cheese sandwich on the griddle for missy here, would you?" She slid from the stool and took Zara by the arm. "Just sit yourself down and eat. I'll take care of the counter until you're through."

She did as commanded. Tomas handed her a bowl of steaming soup, and she nodded her thanks. Uncertain how her stomach would react, she hesitantly took the first spoonful. The noodles and fresh vegetables warmed her from the inside out. Just as she emptied the bowl, Tomas served her sandwich, and she took a bite of the crusty bread with its creamy filling. Everything tasted incredibly good, so good she was tempted to ask for seconds.

The bell above the door rang, and a rush of voices warned her the diner was about to get busy. She finished her meal and set the utensils in the sink, then righted her apron and left the kitchen. Sally was taking care of two tables, Lucy a third, and there was a new customer at the counter.

"Can I help you?" Zara asked a pleasant-looking man reading a menu.

"Coffee," he said, still studying the offerings.

She poured him a cup and set it down. He was a stranger, and she could tell by his clothes he wasn't a cowboy or a trucker. "Anything else? We make a great bowl of chili, and there's fresh vegetable soup."

"The chili sounds good." He set down the menu. His light brown eyes crinkled at the corners. "And crackers, please."

Zara turned and placed the order on the serving ledge. The door opened, and Jack Farley sauntered in.

"Zara, glad to see you're up and around."

She poured Jack his usual. "I'm much better, thanks. Just a touch of the flu."

"Flu, huh?" His smile turned to a look of amazement when he caught the full effect of her eyes. "Whoa, what the—You're wearing colored contacts, right?

"Do you like them?"

"They're startling, but yeah, I do. They suit you."

"Thanks." Hoping the matter was closed, she asked, "So what can I get you?"

"A burger and fried onions, and top it with some of that fresh chili." He added a dollop of cream to his coffee from a small metal pitcher on the counter. "So when did you get them?"

"Get them?" She continued to write on her notepad.

"The lenses. You haven't worn them before. Believe me, I would have noticed."

She passed his order to Tomas. Maybe explaining to Jack would help spread the word, so there would be less gawking. "I've always had them. The prescription isn't very strong, but it helps if my eyes are tired. My eyesight got a little fuzzy while I was sick, so I put them on."

She refilled the stranger's coffee cup, and he nodded his thanks. "Your food will be right up."

"No rush." He poured sugar into the cup. "I noticed a sign in the window that said there are cabins for rent. Know anything about them?"

"Just that they're clean and comfortable. Lucy Coombs is the owner. I'll let her know you're interested."

Lucy came around the counter and passed Tomas

another order. The overhead bell rang, and a trio of ranch hands from Pepperdine's walked in and took seats at the counter.

"Lucy, this gentleman is interested in a cabin," Zara told her as she headed toward the cowboys. By the time she finished taking their selections, the newcomer's food was ready.

Then Murphy walked in.

When he removed his hat and smiled, Zara's heart thumped in her chest. He'd showered and put on fresh clothes. His dark hair curled over the collar of his shirt; tight jeans conformed to his lean hips and long legs.

He took a seat at the counter, and she poured coffee into a cup, positive no male from any planet in the universe could look as handsome as Daniel did at that moment. "Hi," she managed to stutter. "Hot turkey sandwich, right?"

One black brow lifted in amusement. "You're getting to be as bad as Lucy, reading a man's thoughts before he gets a chance to open his mouth."

"You order it every time you stop in for lunch," she said with a smug smile.

"I do?"

"The last three times," she informed him.

He shrugged. "I guess I do. I just didn't realize you paid attention." He took a sip of the hot brew as he scanned the diner. "Who's the new guy?"

Zara glanced at Lucy, who was still talking to the stranger, while Jack listened openly to their conversation. "I don't know, but I think he wants to rent a cottage."

Daniel almost dropped his cup as he cut a sideward glance down the counter. "That so?"

"Yes. Why?"

"No reason. Did he say what type of business brought him to town?"

Zara leaned forward to keep the conversation private. "No—and I didn't ask. Why are you so curious?"

"Just wondering," said Daniel, his voice low. "You see anything of those TXdot men today?"

"They haven't showed so far." The order bell rang, and she said, "Hang on a second."

Daniel focused on the new customer from the corner of his eye. Wearing worn jeans and a tweed jacket, the middle-aged man seemed like a regular Joe, but the back of Daniel's neck prickled anyway. Just what he needed: another stranger showing up to muddy the waters. He'd lived in Button Creek almost six years, and in all that time Lucy had never had so many occupied cabins. It was good for her profit margin, but it played havoc with his built-in alarm system.

At least the newcomer wasn't ogling Zara.

She brought his sandwich to the counter. "I expect you to finish eating and go to work. As you can see, I'm doing just fine."

"You might *look* fine, but it's how you feel that counts," he teased. "No dizzy spells, sore muscles, or queasy stomach?"

"No. I even had some soup and a sandwich."

"All that? You must have been pretty hungry."

"I was. I might even have a second bowl of soup if things slow down."

"Good. Remember to get off your feet whenever you can. And call me if you need me. I think you should take a nap when the crowd thins out."

"That's exactly what she's gonna do," said Lucy, adding her opinion. "I can handle the few folks who come in before dinner, and Zara can come back around five. Tomorrow's Sunday, so she can sleep late."

Zara folded her arms. "I don't appreciate the two of you setting my nap time and work schedule."

"Just live with it for another day or so," Daniel said, grinning. He turned to Lucy. "Did you rent another cabin?"

"Sure did. Fella's name is Lerner and he's from back East somewhere. Says he's on vacation and thought to poke around here a bit. Him and Jack got to talkin' and seemed to hit it off, so I took the man's money and left the two of 'em jawin'."

Daniel digested the information along with his meal, but it didn't quell the feeling of unease that had settled in the pit of his stomach. "Does he have a car?"

"Don't know, but I'd imagine so."

He pushed his plate away. "Did he pay by check or cash?"

Lucy dug a hundred-dollar bill from her apron pocket. "Paid cash for three nights." She held the bill to the light streaming in through the plate-glass window. "You don't think Mr. Franklin here is funny money, do you?'

Daniel watched Zara refill coffee mugs and chat with the cowhands. Farley and the stranger—Lerner, was it?—were still talking.

He set his money on the table, plus an extra bill. "I doubt it. Give this twenty to Sally and tell her it's from me for minding Will, then tell Zara I'll stop by later to check on her, okay?"

"I'll take care of it," said Lucy, pocketing the twenty.

Zara raised her gaze and smiled.

He tipped his hat and headed outside.

With her smile frozen in place, Zara cleared the last table of dishes. She was afraid that if she stopped grinning she would collapse on the spot—not the best way to end her first day back on her feet. After sleeping soundly through the afternoon, she woke refreshed, but that had been several hours ago. Saturday night was the diner's busiest time, and she now realized she hadn't been prepared for the amount of work.

She had to keep up her spirits and her strength. If she let slip that she was exhausted and ready to drop, Murphy, Lucy, and every other one of her concerned keepers would strap her into a bed for the rest of the week.

"You're lookin' a mite peaked, missy," whispered Lucy, sidling to the table with a tray of dirty dishes. "Why don't you let Dan'l walk you home, like he's been wantin' to do for the past hour? I can finish up here."

Zara kept her back to the counter as she wiped down the table. "Tomas asked permission to leave early, remember? He put in extra hours while I was out sick, and he was hoping to spend time with his wife and daughter. I can't leave you here to do all the work."

"Sure you can," said Lucy, her voice low. "This here is my place, so it's my responsibility. If I lose you to a relapse, I'll be in a worse fix than just havin' to tidy up by myself for a night."

"I can sleep late tomorrow morning, when the luncheonette is closed," Zara insisted.

The older woman set her tray on the table. "I know you don't like being fussed over. You ain't a complainer, either. But you got a man who's just plain dyin' to take care of you, girl. It wouldn't hurt to put him out of his misery and let him see to your needs for one more night."

"It's not that simple, Lucy. If I let Daniel do that, he'll expect . . . more." *More than I can give.* "I don't want to lead him on."

Lucy put a hand on her hip. "Are you telling me you're not in love with the man? Landsakes, gal, he's completely over the moon about you."

Zara sighed. "I just don't . . ." She swept a strand of hair behind her ears. "It's complicated. I can't explain it."

"Well, I'm a mighty fine listener, if you need to talk it over with someone." Lucy picked up her tray. "And I can keep a secret, if there's one to tell."

"I don't have a secret, not really," Zara lied. Lucy

had become more than an employer during her time in Button Creek. If there was anyone with whom she thought it might be safe to confide, it would be the motherly older woman. "Like I said, it's complicated. But thank you for the offer."

Lucy nodded, as if satisfied with her answer. Together, they walked past the counter and into the kitchen to unload their burdens. Zara felt Daniel's gaze boring a hole in her back, even after she gave him a bright smile. He'd sent Will home with Sally several hours ago, and started work on his books. She knew he was waiting to walk her to the cabin, not for sex, but simply because he cared.

Maybe talking things out with Lucy was a good idea. The woman was right about Daniel. Saying farewell to those you loved was always difficult. Saying good-bye to him would be impossible. Lucy might have a few suggestions on the best way to handle the heartbreaking task.

Tomas dried his hands while the women set their trays down. "Lucy, I have cleaned the griddle and washed the pots and pans. If possible, I would like to go to my family." He took off his apron and dropped it in the laundry hamper.

"Of course you can go home," said Lucy, opening the dishwasher. "We'll see to things here."

Zara almost felt guilty. Since her strange reaction to the perfume, she'd gotten enough rest for two women, and she still craved more sleep. So many people had covered for her or helped in some way, just so she could recuperate.

"I'll stay, Tomas. It's the least I can do to say thank you for all the extra time you put in while I was sick."

Together the women righted the kitchen and divided the remaining chores, with Lucy tackling the trash and Zara the condiment refills. On the way to the dining area, she stopped at the counter to talk to Murphy.

"I'm going to be here a while. Why don't you go home?"

Daniel frowned, something he seemed to do every time she carried a heavy order or stood on her feet for too long. "Sally is staying with Will. I don't mind."

"Lucy's already asked, and I promised she could." Zara had no idea where the words came from, but they made sense. If Daniel knew she was in good hands, he would be less inclined to hover. And Lucy had offered to keep her company.

His mouth hitched up at one corner. "Are you telling me you're throwing me over for Miss Lucy?"

"Not exactly. But I would like to talk to her about a few things. Please say you understand."

He huffed out a breath. "Yeah, I do." Taking her hand, he kissed the center of her palm. "You sure you're feeling all right?"

"I'm fine." She touched his cheek. "Really. Spend the night with your son, and we can get together in the morning. I'll even let you cook my breakfast."

His dark eyes lit with pleasure. "Now there's an idea that will set my boy on a tear. Will's been begging to try out a recipe for a vegetarian omelet he found on the Internet."

"It sounds wonderful. Tell him I'm looking forward to it."

Daniel peered over her shoulder, then leaned forward onto the counter. "How about a good night kiss?"

"Here?" She grinned. "In front of Lucy?"

"Lucy isn't looking, but it wouldn't matter if she was. Since just about every person within a five-mile radius knows we're keeping company, one kiss won't make the gossip any worse than it already is."

The sentiment was so sweet, Zara decided to meet him halfway. Their mouths touched, and she let her lips linger. Daniel tasted like apple pie and ice cream, the dessert she'd served him earlier. When his hand caressed her nape, she fell into the kiss with heartfelt longing. The man told her he wanted her with every word and glance, each movement of his body . . . and she wanted him.

"Ahem!" The sound of Lucy clearing her throat echoed from the kitchen. "Zara, you almost done out there?"

Reluctantly, they separated. Smiling, Daniel shook his head. "Lucy's about as subtle as an eighteen-wheeler."

"I know. It's one of the things I like best about her."

He rose from the stool, still holding her captive with his gaze. "I'll see you in the morning. Nine o'clock sharp at my place."

He ambled from the diner and closed the door. Zara stared, holding her fingers to her lips. If this was the way she felt when they bid a simple good night, how would she be able to tell him good-bye forever?

"Did I hear you right? Am I coming to your place for a chat?" said Lucy, rounding the doorway.

"Um . . . if you want." Zara ran a trembling hand through her hair. "I didn't mean to lie, Lucy, I just don't want Daniel to waste time watching over me. Not when we can't have a future together."

"Sounds to me like you mean that."

Zara sidestepped the statement and headed for the kitchen. "Let's finish cleaning, so we can have a cup of tea at my cabin."

"Looks to me like Murphy's not spending the night with our suspect," observed Chuck as he watched Daniel cross the street to the Last Chance. He'd been peering out the window of their office for a while, taking in the crowd at the honky-tonk on the corner opposite the luncheonette while he and Frank waited for Jack Farley to show. With the lights set at low and the van parked at an angle in front of the building, it was the best spot to monitor pedestrian traffic without being noticed.

Frank took a long neck from the minirefrigerator at the rear of the room and sauntered back to his desk. "Move away from the window before someone sees you."

"Nobody's going to see me," Chuck countered. "There are so many couples, cowhands, and single women milling around the parking lot of the Hole in the Wall, I doubt anyone is paying attention to this string of closed-up stores. Even Murphy didn't look our way when he came out."

"We can't be too careful where he's concerned," groused Frank. "Maybe that new guy will pique his interest, and he'll get off our back for a couple of days."

"You mean Lerner? Know anything about him?"

Frank powered up his laptop and waited for the machine to go through the start-up process. He rubbed his hands together, relishing the chance to track a subject on-line. "Just give me a second to connect to headquarters."

"While you're there, check to see when the rest of that fingerprint information will arrive."

Frank didn't acknowledge Chuck's request. Instead, he fiddled with the keyboard and waited for the dial-up connection to hold. A series of keystrokes took him to the automated site. "I'm in. Just give me a minute to get to the right directory." He tapped in the license plate number of Lerner's rental, did a little more fancy typing, and smiled.

"Okay, here we go. There's only one Lerner who picked up a car from that rental company in Dallas in the past twenty-four hours. Gave his name as Michael J. with a New York City driver's license. Hang on while I get the info."

Chuck shook his head at his superior's enthusiasm. "I still can't understand why you'd rather sit at a machine instead of doing fieldwork. We could just as easily have slipped into Lerner's cabin while he was having supper and helped ourselves to the information."

"You've been watching too much television." Frank squinted at the monitor. "What if the guy was smart and carried everything of value on his person? We'd have nothing, and have opened ourselves up to a whole lot of questions when he came back and found us snooping. Might even call the sheriff."

"Okay, have it your way. But I still prefer hands-on instead of surfing the Net." Chuck blinked. "Lights just went out in the diner. The door's opening. Looks like Lucy Coombs and Zara are headed for home."

"Is the Coombs woman going to her trailer?"

"Nope, turned the corner with the suspect. Maybe they're going to spend a little time together at Zara's."

"Well, well, well," muttered Frank, intent on the computer screen. "Interesting."

Chuck was hesitant to leave his post, but he hated when Frank knew more than he did. "What?" he said, with a hint of impatience.

"Looks like Michael James Lerner is a private investigator, licensed to carry—the works."

"Are you sure?"

"The profile gives his PI number right along with his picture and the name of his company: Lerner and Jackson, Private Investigators. They have offices in New York and Trenton."

Chuck stood at attention. "Farley's headed this way. Maybe he knows."

"I just hope to God Lerner's not another self-appointed alien hunter come to get underfoot and steal our thunder."

After a series of staccato knocks, Chuck opened the door.

"Evening, fellas," said Jack, annoying in his good humor. The sound of country western music trailed after him into the room. He stared at Frank's beer. "Got another one of those?"

Frank jerked his thumb in the direction of the minifridge.

Chuck locked the door, then walked past the desks and accepted one of the bottles Jack offered. "Where have you been all day? You were supposed to be here right after dinner."

"I ate at the bar and people-watched for a while. Didn't know I was punching a time clock." Jack took the only other seat in the room, a metal folding chair with a dent in the center. "Where'd you find this thing? The city dump?"

"It came with the office," Chuck stated, grinning. "This was never meant to be a three-person assignment."

"It doesn't have to be," sniped Jack. "If you two don't want to cooperate, it's fine by me. I'll just make a call to my contact in Washington and tell him so."

"I heard all about your so-called connection, and until you tell us who it is—"

"Will you two stop bickering?" Frank couldn't concentrate when there was conversation going on in the room.

"You find some information on that waitress?" he asked before he took a drink.

"Not her, though I've tried. According to headquarters, the glass we sent them—the one that was supposed to have her prints on it—came up blank."

"Blank? As in—her prints aren't on file?" asked Jack.

"There were no usable prints on the glass, at least nothing they could identify. The markings they found don't match any of the dozen known swirl patterns used by the experts."

Jack let out a low whistle. "No kidding?"

"No kidding. By the way, did you have a chance to take a look at her eyes?"

"I looked all right, and I'll admit the color is weird . . . even for contacts."

"She doesn't wear contacts, Farley. I know, because I searched her room."

Jack took another swallow of beer, then gave an almost feral smile. "I say we've found our alien."

"Just like that?" Chuck narrowed his gaze. "I thought you didn't agree with my—our theory?"

"I didn't then, but I do now. I've given it a lot of thought since yesterday. Zara is too perfect to be a human. She's always perfectly groomed, not a hair out of place. She's beautiful, yet she doesn't wear cosmetics. She's a hard worker, treats a gas station attendant like a king and his kid like a prince. She's having sex with Murphy, yet she has every male in the room thinking she could be his. She's just the kind of woman an alien race would invent for a cover."

"You're talking about her as if she wasn't human or humanoid. Like she's some kind of robot or android."

"She might be. How would we know?"

Chuck frowned. "A physical, blood tests, X rays . . . an autopsy?"

"Our orders are to bring her in alive," said Frank.

"I know. I'm just answering the question by listing the various ways that might be used to . . . verify the species."

"I think you boys are forgetting something. There's a new guy in town, and he's asking lots of questions," said Jack. "I tried to find out why he's here, but all he'd say was that he's on vacation, and while he's here he wants to look for a friend of his son's. Someone named Robert Lotello."

"Robert Lotello? Doesn't sound like anybody from this shit hole." Frank turned his laptop in Jack's direction. "Lerner's a private investigator."

"He showed me and a couple of people at the bar a photo," Jack said, "but it was so dark inside no one could help him. Since he didn't ask about aliens, spaceship landings, or anything we're searching for, I say we forget him. I just brought him up because he's a new face." Jack folded his hands on the table. "It's time you told me your plans, gentlemen, or I make my phone call."

Frank and Chuck eyed one another over the desk, then Frank spoke. "First off, we're going to watch Zara like a hawk. Monday morning, when Murphy goes to the doctor with his boy, we'll bring her in. If she tries to leave town before then, we take her down."

# Sixteen

"*I* don't know what's wrong with me. I'm hungry again." Zara put the kettle on the burner as soon as she walked into the kitchen, then opened the refrigerator and peered inside. "Can I get you something to eat?"

Lucy pulled out a chair and sat down. "Didn't you take a dinner break tonight?"

"Tomas warmed me another bowl of vegetable soup and one of those homemade wheat rolls, and I ate standing up." She pulled out peaches and a wedge of cheese and brought them to the table. "Then I had a slice of apple pie with a scoop of ice cream . . . or was it two? I forget."

"Did you now?"

"I guess I'm making up for all the food I didn't eat while I slept the past few days." Opening a cupboard, Zara took down a box of whole grain crackers. After retrieving plates and knives, she set the fixings on the table and stood back to admire her handiwork. "Everything I served tonight looked so good, I almost let Tomas talk me into a bowl of chili. Can you imagine?"

"Fancy that," said Lucy, raising a brow. Grinning, she surveyed the table. "Sure you don't want fries with that Happy Meal?"

Zara smiled when she caught the joke. The kettle whistled, and she turned. "What kind of tea do you want? I have Earl Grey, chamomile, Sleepytime."

Lucy propped an elbow on the table and rested her chin in her palm. "Chamomile sounds nice. I got some paperwork to do when I get home, so I have to stay up a while longer."

"You have more energy than I do." Zara puttered at the counter and returned with their tea. "I'm exhausted."

"Are you now? Maybe it's because you're still not up to snuff." Lucy dunked her tea bag and set it on her plate. "Once I leave, you can sleep and dream about Dan'l."

"I wish it were that simple," said Zara, doing the same with her own teabag.

"It could be—provided you're not married or anything."

"Married? Of course not. Whatever gave you that idea?" She bit at her lower lip as she took a piece of cheese and placed it on a cracker. "There are other things that can complicate a relationship besides marriage."

"Don't see what," Lucy mumbled around a bite of fruit. "Unless you're runnin' away from someone? Say an abusive man?"

"I don't have a boyfriend."

"Parents?"

"I'm very close to my mother and father, and old enough to be on my own."

Lucy sipped at her tea, her gaze dark. "What about the law?"

"Is that what you think, that I'm some kind of criminal? I've never done a dishonest thing in my life."

*Except lie to Daniel. And you. And the entire town.*

"Then I just don't get your problem. Dan'l Murphy is head-over-heels crazy about you, and so is his son. They're a ready-made family just waitin' for the right woman to come along and make 'em her own. A girl could do a whole lot worse for herself than lovin' those two men."

Lucy's insightful words seared Zara's insides, burning hotter than the tea she'd just swallowed. "I know."

"Then what's the problem?" Lucy chewed the last of her cracker and helped herself to a slice of peach. "What are you afraid of?"

Zara sliced into the cheese so she wouldn't have to look the older woman in the eye. "You don't understand."

"Okay, then. Explain it to me."

Sick of the lies and the interrogation, Zara sighed. "What if I told you that because of a duty—call it a debt of honor—I can't stay in Button Creek much longer?"

"I'd say, 'come back when the debt is paid.'"

"I keep telling you, it's not that simple. Once I leave here, I'll never be able to return."

"How far do you have to go, girl? Another planet?" Lucy chortled at her witty remark.

The urge to confess blossomed in Zara's chest. She quickly gulped a mouthful of tea, almost choking. "Another planet? That's nonsense." Heat rushed to her face and she knew she was blushing. "I'm tired, Lucy. I don't mean to toss you out, but it's time I got to bed."

Lucy's grinning expression turned wary. "I thought I was here 'cause you had something to say?" She continued to stare. "Zara honey, I promise there ain't a thing in this world I won't understand. Tell me what it is that's so bad you can't talk about it."

"I can't." She grabbed a paper napkin and dabbed the tears welling in her eyes.

"Does this have something to do with your past, or the present? And tell me again about them contact lenses you're supposed to be wearin', 'cause I changed the linens in here this afternoon, and you don't have any of the stuff I know goes with 'em, not in the closet or the medicine chest."

Zara blew her nose in the tissue. "It was the only thing I could think of at the time. I thought it had some-thing to do with that reaction to the perfume. We don't use it, where I come from . . . I mean . . . where I used to live."

"Where you come from?" Lucy's eyes narrowed. "Shoot gal, where exactly do you call home, and don't tell me it's Okalahoma, 'cause I won't buy it, just like I won't buy the gag about you comin' from another planet."

Unable to think of another lie, Zara stared at her fingers. Time hung suspended, until all Zara heard was the sound of her own sobbing and Lucy's sharp intake of breath.

"Well, I'll be," Lucy muttered after a few more seconds. "I watch television, I even read books about it, but I never thought I'd live to see the day." Her brows drew together as if she was thinking hard. "Let me guess. Folks don't drive where you come from, leastways not cars?"

Zara shook her head, then blew her nose.

"And they don't have last names?"

"We have a citizen's identification number encoded on a chip that's implanted behind our right ear at birth. It's so small, even your airport security arches wouldn't detect it We don't even know it's there."

Lucy's face paled to white. "Lord have mercy, girl. Are you sayin' what I think you're sayin?."

Zara gave a feeble grin. "Not to sound trite, but I come from a galaxy *far, far, away.*"

Pursing her lips, Lucy pointed a finger to the ceiling.

Zara simply nodded.

"I see." The older woman cleared her throat. "What do you call this . . . ah . . . place you come from?"

"You wouldn't recognize the name. It's in a star system your scientists have been watching, but it's too far for them to investigate without more sophisticated equipment."

Lucy raised a brow. "Uh-huh."

"I don't blame you for not believing me," said Zara. "Let's pretend we never had this conversation, all right?"

"Hang on a second, missy. I never said I didn't believe you. I was just wonderin' how you learned to . . . um . . . be like us? I mean, you look just like a human being."

"We are human, almost exactly like your species. But our planet is older, so my people have been around longer; therefore, we're more developed. The biggest difference is that we've learned to use more of our minds."

"How could you come from . . . where you come from . . . and talk like us?"

Zara touched the diamonds in her earlobes, then held up the wrist with the bracelet. "We've thought of a few simple inventions to help smooth the way."

"I always wondered why a classy gal like you arrived in town with hardly a stitch to her name, yet had such fancy jewelry." Lucy ran a hand over her face. "So, um, how much longer are you here for?"

"Not long. I've got to leave you, and Murphy and Will, and return to my world very soon. The longer I stay here, the more chance there is I'll be found out."

Lucy's eyes shot open in a burst of recognition. "Holy Hannah, girl! You're the one them government men have been searchin' for."

"Government men?" Zara shook her head. "Are you talking about the surveyors?"

"Them's the ones."

"I've heard them talk about the stars and aliens and all that, but I never thought—"

"That fella Farley's in on it, too." Lucy frowned. "I'd bet my last dollar you're the reason all three of 'em are here."

"Jack Farley? He's from the government?" Lucy's revelations were getting worse by the second. "Are you sure?"

"I didn't say he's with the government, but I know he's lookin' for somethin', and it's a lot more involved than shootin' pictures. The way him and those surveyors have been snugglin' up to each other, I wouldn't be surprised if they joined forces."

Zara closed her eyes and heaved a breath. She needed to leave Button Creek, tonight if possible, even if she wasn't pregnant. Her world wasn't ready for Earth to know of her people's existence. Not yet.

"If what you're saying is true, I have to get out of town as soon as possible. Will you help me?"

"I'll try, but first I need you to answer a question."

"If I can," Zara said. It was the least she could do for the woman.

"Why did you come here in the first place?"

Zara licked at her bottom lip. Tears flowed freely down her cheeks and she swiped them away. "I had to find someone and . . . befriend them on a personal level."

"Someone, as in Dan'l Murphy?"

"Yes. But I didn't know it was Murphy at first. You see, Daniel isn't who he says he is."

"Lordy, don't tell me he's from another planet, too?"

"No, no. But he is hiding something. I came here to find a specific person, and I found Daniel instead. He's the right man, but he has the wrong name." She held her hands to her head. "I told you it was complicated."

"What did you want with Murphy?"

Zara sniffed, composing herself. "My orders were to—interact with him—and get him to—"

"You were supposed to make him fall in love with you?" Lucy asked wryly. "Alien or not, that's a pretty low trick. Getting a man like Murphy to give his heart away, just so you could stomp it into the dust, and leave him behind while you fly back to who knows where."

"I didn't mean for it to happen that way. I just needed him to take me to bed."

"Well, you sure succeeded, now didn't you?"

Pain knotted in Zara's chest when she recognized disgust in the older woman's eyes. "I know I did a terrible thing, but I wasn't—we weren't—Daniel was never supposed to fall in love with me. I was just supposed to—"

"Get pregnant?" Lucy shifted in her seat. "Then I guess congratulations are in order."

Zara blinked back a fresh wave of tears. "What are you talking about? I'm not pregnant."

Lucy shook her head, a look of pity in her eyes. "Honey, I was with Maria and two of my sisters when they first found out they were carrying. I know the signs, and you have all of them. Call it experience or woman's intuition, but I'd bet my last nickel on it. You are pregnant."

* * *

Juggling his accounting books, Daniel plowed through the heavier-than-usual Saturday night crowd spilling into the parking lot of the Hole in the Wall. The headline band was local, which meant they were from somewhere north of Austin. Since they'd just cut their first record, he guessed the extra customers were in attendance to offer support and get in on the ground floor of the group's rise to fame.

Daniel knew he would find his son in bed. His trust in Sally had risen to new heights, thanks to her cheerful and efficient behavior, even if she continued to grin at him as if wise beyond her years. Thanks to the teenager, he'd be able to think a while without being interrupted by Will before he turned in. The evening sky was clear. After he dismissed Sally, he planned to sit on the overhang and use the Meade to gaze at a few of the farthest constellations. If he stared hard enough, maybe he could lose himself in the stars and stop dwelling on Zara.

*Yeah, like that could happen.*

He had carted his ledgers to the restaurant, hoping to get a little work done while she covered her shift, but he'd barely managed to balance the week's register receipts. The urge to act like a love-struck fool whenever he was within twenty feet of her was damned disconcerting. The sound of her laughter, the sparkle in her oddly colored eyes, the mere fragrance of her skin and hair as she walked past, tied his stomach in knots and sent his blood supply flowing straight to his groin. After tonight, he had no doubt of his feelings for her.

Zara had written her name on the wall of his heart, and there was no way it could ever be erased.

He still wondered how she'd ended up in Button Creek and why she'd lied about wearing contacts, but the reasons no longer mattered. It was time to tell her the truth about himself and Will, then confess that he loved her. He only hoped she would love him enough in return to accept his past. After that, they could handle anything.

Crossing the street, he walked to the rear of the station and took the stairs to the apartment. He hung his hat on the hook next to the kitchen door and set his books on the counter. Before he made it to the living room, Jay Pepperdine ambled in, his expression guarded.

"Murphy."

Taken aback, Daniel stared. "Jay. What are you doing here? Where's Sally?" His heart began to race. "Will!"

Jay placed a hand on his shoulder. "Not to worry. I paid Sally and sent her home. Will's fine, sound asleep in his bed and breathing easy."

Still wary, Daniel turned. "Even so, finding you here like this doesn't give me a warm fuzzy feeling. Let me rustle up a couple of beers, and we can go into the living room to talk."

Jay sat sideways at the table and stretched his long legs out in front of him. "Let's stay in the kitchen. I don't want your boy to hear what this is all about."

Daniel swallowed his surprise at the man's somber tone. The rancher had never invaded his privacy before, so whatever he had to say was probably important. He popped the caps off two long necks, took a seat, and slid a bottle in Jay's direction.

"Since I'm in the dark over this meeting, how about you start?"

Jay gazed at the beer as he spoke. "I spent a couple of hours at the Hole tonight. Place was packed, still is from the sound of it."

"I saw the crowd," said Daniel. He gulped down a swig of beer, hoping it would help wet his suddenly dry mouth. "Don't tell me it's time for another lecture on how I can make more money by staying open late on the nights Hank hires a live band. It's not my problem if those cowboys are too stupid to fill their gas tanks before they leave Fort Worth."

"Nothing that simple." Jay rested his arms on the table. "There's a stranger in town by the name of Lerner. Have you had a chance to meet him?"

"Not officially," Daniel said. "I was at the restaurant when he showed up for lunch, and I heard he was looking to rent the last of Lucy's cabins. I spent the day working, but he didn't come into the station."

"He went north to the campgrounds today. He'll get to your place soon enough, and I want you to be prepared."

Forcing a bland expression, Daniel leaned back in the chair. "Prepared for what? Is he going to try and rob me or something?"

Jay gave a half smile. "He's looking for someone,

and he has a picture of the guy, but it's dated—about six or seven years old. He spent part of the night flashing it at the honky-tonk, asking folks if they'd ever seen or heard of the man."

The past rose up and clamped an icy hand onto the back of Daniel's neck, shaking him hard. "And this would concern me because . . . ?"

"The man he's looking for is named Robert Lotello."

Daniel tamped back the rush of panic bubbling in his chest. "I still don't see what that has to do with me."

"You will, when you get a gander at the photos. The man in the first one has short, dark hair, and he's sporting a mustache and glasses. Took me a while, but I recognized him."

"I see." Daniel sipped at his beer, determined to remain in control.

"Of course, half the people Lerner asked were either from south of here or so hot on dancing they didn't care. Plus, the Hole is dark and smoky. It's difficult enough to see the person standing next to you, let alone make out faces in an old black-and-white photograph."

"I still don't get the point to this—"

"The man he's looking for is you, Murphy."

Daniel gave his best imitation of a smile. "How can it be me, when that's not my name?"

"Maybe you ought to hear the rest of it, before you say something you'll regret." Jay's lips flattened to a thin line. "He had a second photo, and that one is clear. It's a picture of a little boy, about eighteen months old with curly brown hair, big brown eyes, and a dimple in his right cheek. First thing I thought when I saw it was *this is a photo of Will.*"

The urge to bolt was so strong, Daniel had to grip the arms of the chair to hold himself in check. He'd often thought about this day, especially when he was lonely or depressed, and always managed to convince himself it would never come. That's what he got for believing a fool.

"What do you want me to say?"

"Hell, Murphy!" Jay smacked his bottle on the table. "I want you to tell me the truth!"

Leveling his gaze, Daniel stared at the closest person to a friend he had in town, a man who'd only been honest and fair with him. He was going to need help, and right now, Jay was the only one he could turn to.

"It's a long story."

"I've got all night."

"First, clue me in on what you told him," said Daniel.

"I said I didn't recognize either person, just like everybody else did. Of course, I doubt any of those other yahoos knew it was you and Will to begin with."

Daniel blew out a breath. "You're sure about that?"

"Pretty sure. Even that photographer fellow, Jack Farley, acted as if he didn't have a clue. Course that guy's so intent on himself, I doubt he'd recognize a picture of his own mother. Lucky for you, I guess."

*Lucky?* Daniel gave a snort. *My luck has just run out.*

"Did Lerner say *why* he was looking for the man and boy?"

"No. But I don't think he's the law, if that's what you're asking. He's wearing a shoulder holster, but he didn't flash a badge. He said the man in the picture was a friend of his son's, and he'd promised to look this Lotello character up, but lost the address. All he has are the photos and a name."

"Where's Lerner now?"

"I left him nursing a drink at the bar. When he realized he wasn't going to get anywhere with that crowd, he got into the music. I saw him put the pictures in his pocket."

Clenching the bottle, Daniel leaned into the table. "What I tell you has to stay in this room, Jay. Promise me that, then give me a dollar."

"A dollar?" Jay smiled. "If that's a bribe, it's a piss poor one."

Daniel stood and went to a drawer. After pulling out a legal pad, he sat back down. "I'll explain in a minute. Just give me the damn money."

Jay took out his wallet and passed over a crisp dollar bill. Daniel tucked it into his shirt pocket and scribbled for a minute, then passed the tablet to Jay, who read it with raised brows.

"What the hell is this?"

"It's a bill of sale for the Last Chance and everything that goes with it, including the surrounding acreage. We can go to Zetmer's tomorrow and get Otis to notarize it, so it'll be legal. Will and I have to leave town as soon as possible. I'd appreciate it if you'd give me title to one of the extra trucks you have at the ranch, something low-key that runs well."

"Are you crazy?" Jay pushed the pad back across the table. "I can't accept this."

Daniel shoved the tablet in the opposite direction. "Sure you can. And it's nice to know you're feeling guilty, because that means you'll keep your promise."

"What promise?"

"The promise you're going to make right now. That you'll have the entire parcel appraised, and pay me fair market value the next time I get in touch with you. Then I need you to promise that you'll wire the money to whatever bank I tell you, under the name I give you."

"So that's it. You're running away."

"Give me your word, Jay. Say that you'll do what I'm asking."

"Aw, hell," Jay growled out. "Okay, you have my word. Now trust me enough to let me know what's going on."

Gathering his thoughts, Daniel heaved another sigh. He'd never told the story to a living soul, and hadn't planned to until his son was old enough to understand.

"The less you know the better, so I'm going to give you an abbreviated version. Will is my child and his mother is dead. Her parents had custody but wouldn't let me see him. Things got ugly, so I took them to court. When I realized I couldn't win, I kidnapped him, changed our names—"

"And took off running." Jay finished the sentence

as he shook his head. "Everyone in Button Creek figured you were hiding out for a reason, but that was the last thing I would have guessed."

"I did what I had to do to keep my son."

Jay's befuddled expression transformed into one of commiseration, as if the cattleman was thinking of his own boy. "What do you suppose this Lerner fellow wants?"

Daniel swiped a hand across the back of his neck. "Isn't it obvious? The Warfields hired him to find their grandchild. When he does, I'll be arrested for kidnapping, child endangerment, the whole nine yards. They'll see to it I'm incarcerated for so long, I'll be lucky to get out in time for Will's college graduation."

"You're sure about this?" asked Jay. "It's been how many years? Maybe the grandparents just want to make amends."

Daniel gave a derisive laugh. Knowing the Warfields as well as he did, he'd bet money the word *atonement* was not listed in their personal dictionary. "Yeah, right. Those people raised their daughter on a steady diet of greed, neglect, and elitism. I couldn't even talk them into visitation privileges. They'd never let me have custody."

Frowning, Jay tugged on his lower lip. "What about Zara?"

Daniel muttered the words before he had a chance to think. "I'm going to ask her to come with us."

## Seventeen

Zara stared at her face in the bathroom mirror, joy filling her from bottom to top. She'd taken the required pregnancy tests immediately after Lucy left, never doubting it would be anything but positive. She had succeeded in her mission and done her duty to her world.

She was carrying Daniel's child.

Everything was so clear now: her exhaustion, her sudden bouts of queasiness interspersed with her huge appetite, even her turquoise-colored eyes. The scientists at home had mentioned such things might happen, as the bodily mechanics of pregnancy on her planet were almost identical to those on Earth. Her mother had described a few scenarios, as well, but Zara had never expected the changes to appear so quickly.

Unfortunately, the elation she felt was overshadowed by a terrifying revelation. According to Lucy, the very worst had occurred. A government agency knew of her existence.

In preparation for their journey, the scientists heading this mission had advised her and the others to expect the unexpected. They knew that certain groups in the United States and other countries monitored the sky, watching for any sign of intergalactic activity. The elders were also aware that the people of Earth were more frightened than curious of the idea of aliens visiting their planet.

If Lucy was correct, and Zara had a strong sense that she was, she had to leave Button Creek. She couldn't stay there and wait for the theory to prove itself. Fortunately, the elders had set up a contingency plan if any of the women thought they were in danger. She had to put that plan into action as soon as possible, without arousing suspicion.

She needed time to think. If Jack Farley or Chuck or Frank knew she was aware of their reason for being in town, she might lose her one chance to escape. If Daniel found out she was leaving, it would be worse.

A knock startled her, and she raced to answer it, positive it was Lucy. The woman either had more questions or another dose of advice.

Instead, she opened the door to Daniel.

"I saw the light, and figured you were up. May I come in?"

Zara placed a hand on her throat and felt the frantic beating of her pulse. He seemed so serious, so solemn, almost as if he knew what she'd been thinking.

"I . . . um . . . I'm tired. I was about to go to bed."

His dark gaze raked her from head to toe. "You're still in your work clothes."

"Lucy just left, and I haven't had time to change."

His body language insistent, he leaned into the room. "Please."

Zara stepped back, unable to say no. This was Daniel—the father of her child. The man to whom she'd given her heart. *The man she was sworn to deceive.* Careful to keep her distance, she walked to the table and sat down.

"Who's with Will?"

He took a seat across from her. "No one. But he was sound asleep when I left. I don't plan on being here long."

She folded her hands tightly in her lap to keep from touching him. "What did you want?"

Daniel cleared his throat. "I have to ask you a question. I'd hoped to do it when we knew each other a little better, but something's come up, and I no longer have any choice in the timing."

"I'm listening."

"First, I have to—I need to tell you—" Laughing softly, he shook his head. "This is tougher than I thought it would be." He cleared his throat. "I never meant to deceive you, or any of the people in this town. Before I ask you the question, I owe you honesty. I don't want you to answer until you know the complete truth."

*Deceit. Honesty. Truth.* Zara cringed inwardly at the words. "What is it you're trying to say?"

Inhaling a breath, he plowed his fingers through his hair. "I have a confession to make. Will and I—we're not who you think we are."

"That doesn't make sense." But it would explain why he no longer called himself Robert Lotello.

"Hear me out, and you'll understand. I'll begin by saying that I am Will's father in every sense of the word, even though I never married his mother."

"You already told me that. It's not important."

"There's more." He fisted his hands on the table. "Will is mine, but I don't have a right to him legally. I kidnapped him from his grandparents six years ago, and we went on the run. We've been in hiding ever since."

"You kidnapped your own son?"

"I had to. His grandparents refused to give me custody or visitation rights. They threatened to have me put in jail if I tried to see my own kid."

"But—but why?"

"Their daughter Rebecca was my graduate assistant. I'm not proud of the fact that I slept with her, but it happened. She quit school and disappeared without a trace after our one semester together, and I thought I'd seen the last of her. I didn't hear from her again until about two years later. She wrote to tell me she'd given birth to a son—my son—and to inform me she was dying. In the letter, she asked me to come and claim the boy. It seemed she had an epiphany on her deathbed, and didn't want Will raised by her parents. School was on hiatus, so I was on vacation. By the time I received the letter and went to find her, Rebecca was already in the ground."

Zara's heart turned in her chest. Daniel's face held little expression, but his eyes mirrored his pain.

"I made an appointment to talk with her parents, expecting to meet my son, but they refused to let me see him. When I showed them Rebecca's letter, they threw it in my face, told me that at the end she was delusional, and it would be a cold day in hell before I got custody. Then they had me tossed out of their apartment. I tried to reason with them, but they got a restraining order, so I took them to court."

"Surely you won? You had the letter, and I assume you took a paternity test. What happened?"

"I forgot to mention that Rebecca's father is a state supreme court judge with a lot of pull. Somehow, he was able to bribe the lab that did the DNA testing, and he got the results switched. Then he prevailed upon his good buddy, the judge hearing the case, to throw the petition out of court. My attorney advised me to forget taking the matter further; the legal fees would break me, and it would only hurt my boy. So I let them think I'd dropped my suit."

"Then how did you get Will?"

"I cleaned out what was left of my bank account and bought new identities for the two of us, then I made friends with his nanny." Daniel closed his eyes, as if remembering the day. "I snatched him in broad daylight. It was dicey, but I had everything arranged, and I toughed it out."

"What about Will?"

A smile lit Daniel's face. "He was the sweetest little guy—loved everyone he met. I'd seen him off and on when I stopped to flirt with the nanny, so he knew I was a friend, even held out his hands to be picked up when he saw me. The nanny and I began to meet whenever she took Will to the park. I figured I'd get my chance if I was patient, and it paid off. One afternoon, she had to run an errand, and I convinced her to leave Will in my care. Once I took him, I never looked back."

Zara broke her unspoken rule and covered his hands with hers. "How terrible for you, to have been living in fear all this time."

"It was pretty bad in the beginning. Once I found this place I relaxed a little. Until today."

"Today?"

"Jay was waiting for me when I got home from the diner. You know that guy Lucy rented the last cabin to? Lerner?"

"The man who showed up at breakfast?"

"That's the one. Apparently he has a picture of me from my college days and another of Will as a baby. He checked the campgrounds, now he's at the Hole in the Wall asking people if they recognized the faces in the photos."

Zara sucked in a breath. "What did people say?"

"You'd have a hard time matching me to the picture of the nerdy guy with short hair, glasses, and a mustache, but the one of Will is a dead giveaway. Jay saw the resemblance right off. He said no one blinked at the photos except him. Thank God he was smart enough to keep quiet and talk to me first."

"Maybe the man is looking for you and Will for a different reason."

"I have no family, Zara. There's no need for anyone to search for me unless the Warfields hired Lerner to find us."

"Why did it take so long for him to get here?"

Daniel shrugged. "I did a good job covering my tracks, so who knows. He might have been on my tail all this time and finally got a lead. The Warfields are righteous and wealthy beyond belief. I can see them paying the guy to hunt me down, even after Will turns twenty-one."

Her own troubles forgotten, Zara asked, "What can I do to help?"

Daniel gripped both her hands, and gazed into her eyes. "I know you have a past, Zara, and you're running, too. Otherwise, you wouldn't be holed up in this one-horse town waiting tables at a diner. Now that we've been found, Will and I have to leave. I want you to come with us."

She swallowed down a wave of sadness and tried to concentrate on her mission. "You're leaving Button Creek?"

He cupped her jaw in his palm. "Not right away. I need time to get another set of false identification papers for Will and myself, and Will has an appointment with the doctor on Monday. I don't want him to miss it, in case he needs a new prescription."

"But that man—"

"As long as no one lets on I'm the guy in the photo, we'll be fine. In the meantime, Jay's going to order his hands and the people in town to freeze Lerner out. No one will say a word if they hear it from Jay."

"Then he'll move on, and everything will be—"

"No, Zara, it won't. If Lerner found me, someone else will, too. I'm not going to live here waiting for the other shoe to drop. I'll go to Canada or Mexico if I have to, but I'll be damned if I'll lose my son." He used his thumb to wipe away the tear that washed down her cheek. "I don't want to lose you either."

"I—I don't know what to say."

Daniel smiled then, and she felt his hope, his pain, his love fill her from bottom to top.

"That's an easy one. Just say you'll come with us."

*Eighteen*

*B*alanced on his toes, Will stood at the stove and peered into the skillet. Seeing him so eager, with his dark hair in tousled curls and his face shining bright, Daniel couldn't help but think of Rebecca, the woman who had given him the incredible gift of a son.

In the past, he had alternately cursed and revered her, first for hiding her pregnancy, then for having the decency to write and send that letter. He would regret always that she'd died, but would never be sorry he'd rescued the boy from his mean-spirited grandparents. It was time he put Rebecca from his life for good. There was no need to let another woman enter his mind when he had Zara.

He'd left her last night positive she was at least *thinking* of his proposal. He'd told her the truth about his past, and she hadn't lectured or accused him of a crime. Instead, she'd shed tears while she listened to his story. Though she didn't come right out and agree to accompany them, she was on his side.

Daniel had no doubt Zara was harboring a secret from her past, but he didn't want to lose her in his future. Though he had yet to tell her he loved her, he was certain she returned his feelings. Slow and steady was the way to win her heart. Once he found them a safe haven, they could settle in a new place. There, he would confess his love, and they would marry and become a real family.

He would share today's plan with Zara when she arrived for breakfast. Tomorrow, after he and Will returned from the doctor, he'd hide the boy at the Triple P. Then he'd drive to Dallas and locate the shady ID salesman Tomas had told him about. After that, he'd pack up the truck Jay promised to park behind the station. Once night fell, they could head north to Canada. All that remained was hearing Zara say the words he desperately wanted to hear.

"I think the eggs are getting brown on the bottom," said Will, interrupting Daniel's thoughts.

He sauntered over and finger-combed his son's curls. "Looks like. How about you give me that turner so I can flip the omelet while you set the table?"

Will did as ordered, and Daniel took care of finishing the eggs. A knock sounded from the stairwell, and he smiled when he heard Zara's greeting.

"I'm coming up and I'm hungry. Whatever you're cooking, Will Murphy, it smells delicious."

Will slid to the top of the stairs, a grin splitting his

face from ear to ear as he followed Zara up the steps with his eyes. "Dad said I was old enough to use a paring knife, so I chopped the green onions and peppers by myself. Then I mixed the cheese, eggs, and milk, and poured everything into the pan."

Zara arrived on the landing carrying the magazines Will had given her when she'd been ill. "It sounds like you did all the work." She offered him the bundle. "Thank you for lending these to me."

"Dad made toast and coffee." Will set the books on the counter. "It looks pretty good."

"I'm sure it will be perfect." She gave Daniel a hesitant smile. "So, when do we eat?"

"Patience, woman," he teased, enjoying the possessive tone. "Have a seat, and I'll bring it to you."

Will pulled out a chair, and Zara sat down. Resting her chin in her hand, she waited until he went to the refrigerator before she said to Daniel, "How did you sleep last night?"

He divided the omelet into thirds and handed her a plate. "About as well as you'd imagine under the circumstances. How about you? Did you come up with an answer to my question?"

Instead of responding, Zara cut into her breakfast.

"Here's juice," said Will, setting a glass in front of her. He passed one to his father. "I'm starving, too."

Daniel wasn't worried about Zara's failure to speak. He knew she was sensitive to Will's presence, and probably had a few questions of her own to ask that she hadn't thought of last night. No problem there. He would answer every one as honestly as he could. He didn't want there to be any secrets between them, at least on his side.

Will chattered as he ate, and Zara complimented him on the recipe. Every so often, her gaze locked with his, and Daniel flashed a grin of encouragement. When they finished the meal, he asked Will to bring their laundry basket from the bedroom to the kitchen in preparation for a trip to Dolly's, and the boy hurried to obey.

"You're going to the Washeteria, as usual, right?" Daniel asked, when Will left the room.

"My basket is at the bottom of the stairs. Why?"

"Because I figure that's the next logical place for Lerner to show his face. Since he's not looking for you, I was hoping you'd do our wash and hang around for a while. Then you'd have an excuse to listen in on what he has to say and see if you can get him to drop a clue."

Zara thought Daniel made perfect sense. Spending time in the laundry would give her something to worry about besides her own problem. Aiding the two of them in their getaway was the least she could do before they separated forever. Once she knew Daniel and Will were safely away, she could implement the plan she'd been given for her own escape.

"I think I can manage it, but what are you going to tell Will? I'm sure he'll want to go to Dolly's."

"He won't be able to tag along when he finds out I'm starting inventory today. He'll give me grief about having to count canned goods and toilet paper, but I can't risk Lerner seeing him. According to Jay, even a blind man can tell the kid in the photo is Will."

"Do you want me to come to the station when I'm through?"

Daniel hitched up a corner of his mouth. "I thought I'd stop by your place after dark, and we could hash over what you learn. I'll get Sally to sit with Will and we can . . . discuss things."

Zara bit her lower lip. She knew exactly what *things* Daniel was referring to. He wanted to make love to her and ask her again if she would leave with them.

Laundry basket in hand, Will walked into the kitchen. "Are we going to Dolly's with Zara?"

"'Fraid not, son. It's inventory time in the store, and I need your help. Zara volunteered to do the wash for us."

"Aw, Dad," Will moaned. "I hate inventory. It's boring."

"I know, but it has to get done."

"Zara needs help, too. I can carry the basket for her and—"

"Maybe some other time, but not today. Now say good-bye and go put on your old clothes while I take care of the dishes. Then we'll get started."

Will forced a disgruntled, "Bye, Zara. Guess I'll see you later," and shuffled from the room.

Zara stood and picked up their laundry basket. Daniel walked to her side and enfolded her in his arms. "I don't know how I'm going to repay you for everything you're doing." He nuzzled the sensitive spot behind her ear. "But I'm sure I'll find a way."

Burdened by the weight of her deceit, she ducked from the embrace. "You and Will belong together. Jay, Lucy, anyone in this town would do the same."

"You're not just *anyone*." He gazed deep into her eyes. "You're special, Zara . . . to both of us."

Before Daniel said another word, she turned and walked down the stairs.

Barely aware of the awkward load, Zara entered Dolly's with a laundry basked tucked under each arm. The relief she felt when she confessed to Lucy was overshadowed by the knowledge that she'd lied to Daniel twice in less than twenty-four hours. Standing in the laundry, where she was sure to be confronted by Jack Farley, or Frank and Chuck, as well as the man named Lerner, had her ready to snap, but she had to be strong. She had to do this for the men she loved.

As Daniel predicted, the Washeteria was crowded with locals perusing the video rack, doing laundry, or merely hanging out to eat pastry and gossip. She spotted Jack as soon as she arrived, holding court in a far corner while he efficiently logged out videos and immediately feigned interest in the soap dispenser, but she felt his gaze stab her in the back, just the same.

After sorting the dirty clothes into washers at the front of the store, she inserted the necessary number of quarters and set the machines to humming. The thought that this was the last time she would ever do the mundane task suddenly filled her with a rush of sadness. Tears welled when she realized she would never again dance the two-step or ride in Miss Lucy's rusty truck or carry a tray emitting the fragrant aroma of maple syrup over a toasted pecan waffle.

No more would she sit on the overhang and watch the stars with Will.

Never again would she make love with Daniel.

Dolly handed her a tissue. "You doing all right today?"

Zara accepted the kind gesture with gratitude. Sniffing, she dabbed at her tears. "I think it's allergies."

Dolly nodded. "I know what that's like. The late Mr. Hingle had a terrible time with pollen. The poor man doctored himself silly with medication every spring and fall. I may have some leftover pills in the medicine chest. You want me to take a look?"

"No, thank you." She didn't dare ingest any kind of medication after her reaction to that perfume, especially when she didn't need it.

"Well, then, I'll just fix you a nice hot cup of herbal tea," said Dolly. "Have it here in a jiffy."

Before she could refuse, the woman trundled off in the direction of the pastry table. Resting her bottom against a washer, Zara sighed.

"You're looking glum. Anything I can do to cheer you up?"

The sound of Jack Farley's deep voice made her scalp prickle. Stiffening her spine, she ordered herself to remain calm. "I'm fine. Just my allergies acting up."

"You sure seem to have that problem more than most," he said, closing in on her right side. "First there was that run-in at the perfume counter, now what? Soap, pollen, the air?"

Tucking a strand of hair behind her ear, she forced a pleasant tone. "I'm not sure what it is."

Jack zeroed in on her wrist and raised a brow. "I keep meaning to ask about your bracelet. It's sure is a beauty. Mind telling me where you bought it?"

"Bought it?"

"Yeah. I'd like to get one for my girlfriend. She's always been into gemstones, and yours is one of the nicest I've seen. Unusual too."

"It was a gift," said Zara. "I have no idea where it was purchased."

He clasped her hand and raised it to the light to better examine the stones. Staring at the diamonds, he let go a long whistle. "Wow, someone spent a pretty penny. Those rocks are real, aren't they? Is the setting white gold or platinum?"

Masking her disgust with an expression of innocence, she eased her wrist from his fingers. "I don't know. I never thought to ask."

"How about you let me take a look? There should be a hallmark stamped inside the band."

"Sorry, but I promised the . . . person who gave it to me I'd never take it off."

Just then, Dolly came over with her tea. "Hope this helps. You're looking a little pale."

"I'm just tired. Yesterday was my first day back on the job." Zara closed her eyes and inhaled the comforting aroma. "I'm going to take a nap as soon as I'm finished here."

The door opened, and the man she now knew was named Lerner walked in. Scanning the crowd, he brightened when he saw the coffee and baked goods and headed for the back of the room. " 'Scuse me," said Dolly. "I'll just go see to the new customer."

"For a small town, this place sure gets its fair share of newcomers, doesn't it?" asked Jack, following Lerner with a sharp gaze.

One of her washers stopped spinning, and Zara turned. "I really haven't noticed."

"I understand you got here just a day or two before I did?"

She reached into the washer and began pulling out clothes.

"That's right."

"What was it about Button Creek that made you decide to stay? Forgive me for saying so, but this doesn't look like the kind of place a woman such as yourself would want to live."

Hefting the basket, she raised her brow. "I'm not sure I know what you mean by that."

"You know, attractive, smart. The second I met you I thought you were out of place here." He dogged her steps as she moved to the next washer. "Think you'll stay in town long?"

"It all depends. Why do you want to know?"

"I never did get the chance to show you my photographs," said Jack. "Just thought you'd like to see them before you . . . go back to where you came from."

"Sorry, but I really need to nap this afternoon." Ignoring the churning in her stomach, she emptied the last machine and faced him. "Maybe next weekend."

"Sure, if we're both still here." He reached for the basket. "Say, can I carry that for you?"

"No thanks, I've got it."

All smiles, Jack took the hint and returned to manning the video rack. Zara walked to the wall of dryers and blew out a breath. She hadn't really cared much for Farley when she first met him. Now that she was aware of Lucy's suspicions, he made her skin crawl. After sorting the wash and putting coins in the dryers, she stopped at the pastry table and purposely stood next to Lerner.

"You're sure you've never seen either of the men in these photos?" Lerner asked Dolly, who gazed at the pictures with a sour expression.

"Sure as I can be," the older woman answered. "Maybe you should ask Zara, here. She waits on just about everybody that stops in town."

His face split into a grin. "Well, hello. I'm Mike Lerner. We met yesterday, when you served me lunch."

"I remember." Zara looked over the pastries, studying her choices. "Dolly, may I have one of those powdered sugar donuts?"

"Mind if I ask you a question?" Lerner continued.

She dropped a few coins in a box on the table and accepted the napkin-wrapped pastry. "What can I do for you?"

"I'm looking for someone; hit all the busy spots in the area, but so far I haven't had any luck." He held out the photos. "Do either of these two people look familiar to you?"

Her heart thudded in her chest, but Zara did her best to show only a casual interest in the photos. Jay had been correct. Though the boy in the first one was barely past infancy, his brown curly hair and adorable dimple marked him as Will. The blurry photo of Daniel was less obvious. Only someone with imagination would connect him to the unremarkable man with short hair, a mustache, and wearing black-rimmed glasses.

Keeping her expression one of mild curiosity, she stared at each picture in turn. "What a sweet little boy. Who are they?"

"The man's name is Robert Lotello," offered Lerner. "That's his son. Ever hear that name before?"

Zara stared at the photos, then shook her head. "Sorry, no. Why are you looking for them?"

"They're old family friends, but we lost track of them and thought they may have moved to this area." Lerner held the snapshots higher. "Sure you haven't seen them?"

"I'd remember a cute little baby like that one," she assured him.

"The boy would be quite a bit older now, eight or so, and Lotello might have shaved his mustache or changed his hairstyle."

"Where'd you say they were from?"

"I didn't." Lerner was about to tuck the photos back in his pocket when Jack strolled over.

"You still looking for your son's friend?"

"Yeah. Why? Did you remember something?"

Zara held her breath, but Jack failed to show an interest in the pictures. "Nope, but like I said at the bar, I'm not from around here."

His comment didn't seem to deter the man. Lerner simply sipped at his coffee and gazed about the room as if scanning for someone else to question. Finally, he focused on a group of cowboys at the video rack. "Well, thanks. I guess I'll see you for breakfast tomorrow morning, young lady."

Hoping to avoid another confrontation with Farley, Zara bit into her donut and headed for the dryers.

"Hey, Zara?"

She turned at the sound of Jack's voice.

"Where are Murphy and Will today?"

"I really wouldn't know," she answered smoothly.

His smug smile told her he knew she was lying. "Just thought you might, seeing as you're doing their laundry."

## Nineteen

$\mathcal{D}$aniel kept busy in the store, coming out from between the aisles only when he had to ring up a gas sale. After he and Will tallied every item on the shelves twice, he sent the boy to the storeroom to count unopened cases of canned goods and paper products. He knew Will was antsy, especially since it was a nice day, but he couldn't take the chance of Lerner seeing either of them.

Instead of concentrating on the pretend chore of taking inventory, he'd been mentally planning their escape. With most of the details taken care of, his next worry was how to explain their hasty departure to his son. Honesty was always an option; he only hoped the boy was mature enough to handle the truth.

Now, at just a few minutes before closing, he breathed a sigh of relief. He'd already made arrangements for Sally to baby-sit tonight so he could visit

Zara. Will was happy because Sally had promised to bring a video he had not seen in the theater. Tonight he'd collect their laundry and get a report on Lerner. Tomorrow he'd take Will to the doctor and pick up their false IDs. They'd be gone from Button Creek in a little over twenty-four hours.

The door opened, and Daniel turned. He hadn't heard the pumps running, so he figured it was Jay, coming to check on his plan. When he saw that it was Lerner, he sucked down the urge to bolt and busied himself at the cash register.

The man took an aisle to the rear of the store, where he checked out the freezer case. Daniel waited, alternately inhaling air and holding his breath. Had someone ignored Jay's warning and purposely sent him here, or was Lerner simply shopping for a meal while on his hunt for information?

After making his selection, the man wandered back up the aisle and set a lone frozen dinner, single serving dessert, bag of chips, and can of soda on the counter.

"Lucky for me you're still open," he said jovially. "I didn't realize this town closed up tight on a Sunday."

Daniel kept his gaze on the cash register as he scanned and bagged each item. "Not much happens here on the weekend."

"I see that," said Lerner.

He pushed the plastic bag across the Formica. "That'll be six dollars and forty-two cents."

"I don't believe we've met. Name's Lerner." He reached into a back pocket, pulled out his wallet, and handed Daniel a ten-dollar bill. "Mind taking a look at something for me?"

Daniel deposited the money in the cash drawer and made change. "I'm about ready to close."

"It'll only take a second." Lerner placed two photos on the counter. "I'm trying to locate a father and son. Do either of those two look familiar?"

Daniel stared at his likeness and recognized it as a picture from his first year at Columbia, when he'd been a geeky, boyish-looking assistant professor. He'd grown the mustache because he thought it would gain him more respect. Only someone who knew him well would see the resemblance.

Swallowing, he shifted his body language into neutral and slid his gaze to the second snapshot. He'd never seen the photo, so he imagined it came straight from the Warfields's personal stash. It was Will all right; no mistaking that megawatt smile or his big brown eyes.

"Nope, haven't seen them." He kept his eyes downcast. "Sorry."

Lerner sighed. "You're sure?"

"When was it they were supposed to have come through here?" Daniel found himself asking. *How did you know where we were?*

"Anytime from a few years ago until now. I've been searching for a while, and I'm starting to get the feeling I'm on a wild-goose chase."

Just then, Will walked into the rear of the store and started up the center aisle. "I counted the last cartons of canned corn twice, Dad, and I still come up with eight cases of paper towels. Now can we go make dinner?"

"Will!" Daniel realized he'd shouted and gave himself a kick. "I'll be right there. Go back in the storeroom."

Will stopped in his tracks and smiled at Lerner, his dimple flashing like a beacon. "Hi." He turned to Daniel. "But I'm finished. Besides, it's lonely in there. When's Sally coming over?"

Daniel trained his eyes on his son. "Later. If you're done, go up to the house."

"But—"

"Now."

"Can I call Sally and ask her what time?"

"Yes, but do it upstairs." He softened his tone. "I'll be there as soon as I close up."

"Okay." Will stuck his hands in his pockets and shuffled out the side door to the garage.

"Kids." Daniel shook his head. "At least he listens from time to time."

"These days you've got to be firm." Lerner followed Will with his eyes, then picked up his bag, but he left the photos on the counter. "What is he— seven—eight years old?"

"Almost nine," Daniel lied. "He's small for his age."

"And bright. Sounds like he could argue you into the ground. What grade is he in?"

"He'll start fourth this fall."

The older man cocked his head, as if counting the years. "You don't seem to have the Texas twang I hear from the rest of the people in town. You from around here?"

Daniel deliberately slid the pictures in Lerner's direction to let him know he was through talking. "We've lived here since my son was born, but I'm originally from California."

"Now there's a crazy state." Lerner raised a brow. "What made you move to this godforsaken place?"

"Peace and quiet." Daniel placed his hands flat on the counter. "If you'll excuse me, I have to make supper."

The man retrieved the photos and tucked them in his shirt pocket. "I should tell you I haven't been totally honest about why I'm looking for these two. I've been hired by an attorney from Manhattan to locate them, because there's an inheritance involved. But don't spread that around."

"Then I hope you find them," said Daniel. He walked to the front door and held it wide. "Good luck with the search."

Zara sat at her kitchen table and finished dinner, grateful her appetite was almost back to normal. She had no idea when her stomach might switch to starvation mode, but vowed not to be surprised if it happened again. Even though she'd come home from the laundry in a near panic, she'd managed to fall into a restful sleep. Now that she was awake, the day's events rose in her mind. One by one, she separated the thoughts, determined to put each detail in the proper compartment of her brain.

The appearance of the man named Lerner; Jack's probing questions and his sudden interest in her bracelet; Daniel's plan for leaving town and his request for her to come with; even her confession to Lucy, and the woman's suspicions about Frank and Chuck, all paled when she thought of her primary focus.

*The baby she carried and her duty to her world.*

She expected Daniel to arrive soon and prepared herself for the heartbreak of letting him go. It was better to have him leave her than the other way around. Staring at her bracelet as the last rays of afternoon sun faded from her cabin, she felt a measure of security. Daniel was clever and knew how to take care of Will; his child's safety had to be his first concern. As was hers in taking care of her unborn baby.

Zara cleared the table and washed her utensils. Sitting on the sofa, she used the remote to turn on the television, hoping to pass the time. Settling on a newscast, she let herself doze. It was dark when she heard the sound of tapping. After clicking off the TV, she stumbled through the kitchen and opened the door to Daniel. His grim expression told her nothing about his situation had changed from this morning.

Sweeping her into his arms, he pulled her to his chest and walked her backward until she was pressed against the counter. "Don't say a word. Just let me hold you."

He slanted his head and fused his lips to hers in a searing kiss. Molding her to his thighs and hips, he devoured her mouth, sucking the very breath from her body.

Taken by surprise, she fell into the embrace, giving herself up to his ardor. His fingers worked their way from her waist to her shoulders and up to her jaw, where they held her in a trembling caress.

"God, but I missed you today," he said, when he finally broke the kiss.

She forced a smile, the bittersweet moment one she would cherish forever. "I can tell." His eyes turned liquid in the moonlight, and she clung to his wrists. "What happened?"

Stepping away, Daniel ran a hand over the back of his neck. "Lerner stopped by the store."

She switched on the overhead light. "What did he want?"

"Supper fixings and information. I gather you saw him at the laundry?"

"He was there, and he had the pictures. Jay was right about the photo of Will, but I don't think you need to worry about the one he has of you."

"What did you tell him?"

"Exactly what I heard everyone else say. I was at Dolly's for a while, and aside from giving the pictures a quick inspection, no one seemed to pay him any mind."

"Thank God for that. I only wish I could say the same." He heaved a sigh. "He saw Will."

"How did that happen?" Zara whispered.

Daniel jammed his hands in his pockets and began to pace. "Will wandered into the store by accident. After I sent him upstairs, Lerner asked how old he was. I lied. Said he was nine and small for his age."

"Do you think he believed you?"

"I doubt it."

"How do you know? Children grow at different rates. Maybe he was just curious or—"

"Because right after that, he asked me how long we'd lived in Button Creek. Said he could tell by my accent I wasn't a native."

"Maybe you should leave tonight," Zara said. "You'd be miles away before he realized you were gone."

Daniel whipped out a chair and sat at the table. "Believe me, it was all I could do not to race upstairs and drag Will to the pickup." He raised his head, and she took a seat next to him. "It was strange. He said something so odd, I'm still trying to make sense of it."

"What was that?"

"He said he was looking for Robert Lotello because of an inheritance."

"Inheritance? But I thought you didn't have any relatives?"

"That's just it. I don't. I'm also aware that putting out the word there's money involved is an old trick if you're hoping to flush someone from hiding. But he said it as if he meant it. And he acted as if I was the only one he'd told so far."

"That could be true. I never heard any mention of money in the Washeteria."

Daniel raised her hand to his mouth and grazed her knuckles with his lips. "Even so, I can't take the chance. All the money in the world won't mean a thing if I lose my son." He gazed into her eyes. "I don't want to lose you either."

His tender words twisted a knife in her heart. Zara realized her deception was complete. If Daniel learned that she was taking his unborn child away, he would never forgive her. No matter what else he learned about her, her pregnancy was the one thing that had to remain a secret.

"My plans haven't changed. I'm still taking Will to the doctor tomorrow, then hiding him at Jay's. When I come home from Dallas, I'm packing the truck Jay said he'd give me and leaving. It's the only way I know to keep my son safe."

"What are you going to tell Will?"

Daniel shrugged. "The truth, after we're far enough away. Until then, he's going to have to trust me." His steely gaze softened. "I'm hoping you'll do the same." Reaching out, he cupped her jaw. "We need you, Zara. Come with us."

The sound of someone beating on the door hard enough to shatter the hinges bought her a reprieve. A man's voice, sounding fearful and anxious, loudly called her name.

Daniel rose to his feet. "Who the hell can that be?"

Zara flung the door open to find Tomas, his eyes panicked, pacing the stoop. "Tomas? What's wrong?"

Tomas grabbed at her hands and pulled her outside. "It is Lucetta. You must come now. Please."

"Your baby? What's wrong with your baby?"

"It is the fever. Maria and I, we have done everything—given her baby aspirin, baths, and cool water to drink. She is burning up."

"What about her doctor?"

"He is not available. Lucy says we should go to the hospital, but I'm afraid there is no time."

She squeezed his hands. "Go back to the trailer. I'll be right over."

"Hurry, please." With a final, pleading glance he raced into the darkness.

Zara turned and bumped into Daniel.

"I heard." He headed out the door.

"Where are you going?"

"I want to check on Will and let Sally know where I'll be. Go to the trailer. I'll meet you there."

All of her problems faded in that moment. In her heart, Zara was a healer; she had taken an oath to care for those in need. Though every use of her skills on this planet might put her at risk of detection, an innocent life was in danger, and she could ignore it no more than she could forget to breathe. Composing her thoughts, she walked out of the cabin and across the gravel lot.

The trailers sat about twenty feet from the restaurant on a small patch of fenced-in grass. The larger of the two, a gray behemoth mounted on cinder blocks, was Miss Lucy's. Next to it and slightly behind, was a smaller, more streamlined unit. The Herreras lived there as part of Tomas's salary for being the diner's cook.

She pushed at the half-open door and stepped inside. The first person she saw was Miss Lucy, folding a pile of clean cloth diapers on a small metal table jutting out from the wall. "Thank the Lord you're here. I've tried everything I know, but I can't get Lucetta's temperature down. Thought before I loaded up the truck and drove them to the emergency room, I'd have you take a look. After what you told me about— you know"—she raised her eyes heavenward—"I figured you could help. Tomas and Maria are waiting in the bedroom down the hall."

Zara threaded her way through the kitchen and living areas. She passed a full bath and a bedroom before stopping in the doorway of a dimly lighted room filled with yellow-and-white-painted baby furniture. Tomas was standing near the crib, while Maria, a dark-haired woman-child of no more than eighteen, sat in a rocking chair cradling Lucetta and crooning softly.

Tomas swiped a hand over his too-bright eyes, then said something to his wife in Spanish. Maria clutched the baby closer to her breast. Zara tugged at her right earlobe, which activated her translator chip, and spoke in fluent Spanish.

"I need to hold Lucetta, Maria. Please, it will only take a minute. I promise I won't hurt her."

Tomas leaned forward and reached for the little girl. Maria raised her luminous eyes and let out a cry of protest, begging him to be certain they were doing the right thing. The cook didn't waver as he reminded his wife of the time Zara had taken care of Will.

Maria heaved a sigh. Resignedly, she stood and

kissed Lucetta on the forehead, then handed her to Zara. "She is all we have. Be gentle, I beg of you."

The second Zara touched Lucetta, she knew something was terribly wrong. The baby was burning hot, her skin dry to the touch, as if she was on fire from within. Searching her memory bank, she sifted through her encyclopedia of illnesses. In her world, she ministered mainly to those who, like her, had been born without gene alteration. Even with her planet's progress, people still suffered an occasional headache or stomach upset, even a cold, but rarely did they need her for anything serious. She had never tended a baby; had never come across something her senses told her was such a life-threatening problem. Raising her gaze, Zara drew the child to her breast. If Maria and Tomas saw what she planned to do, they would make it impossible for her to succeed.

"Please, I need to be alone with the baby. Wait in the kitchen and try to relax. Tomas, ask Lucy to brew a pot of tea. I'm sure Maria could use something soothing right now."

Tomas put his arm around his wife's shoulder and led her from the room. She waited until Maria's sobs faded, then carefully settled the diaper-clad baby onto her thighs and covered her with a thin cotton blanket. Lucetta's tiny chest barely moved, while her face looked flat and doll-like. With her dark hair plastered to her forehead and her eyes puffy slits, she seemed almost comatose.

Zara raised her wrist and removed one of the ruby

crystals from her bracelet, then popped the stone into the clasp. Immediately, the disc began to brighten, signaling it was activated and working properly. Gently, she lifted Lucetta and held the little girl to her breast, enveloping the child with as much of her body as she could. The tiny form shuddered and gave a soft, sick-kitten mewl, and Zara felt a ray of hope. The feeble protest told her that a spark of life still burned in the limp, exhausted body.

After crossing her arms behind the baby's back, she inhaled several deep breaths and focused all her energy on the glowing clasp, letting the power of the energy-charged stone commingle with her own until it filled her body and her mind.

Bursting with the pure, healing light, she transferred the energy to Lucetta. Then, shaking with the effort to control the power, she gave herself up to it in one shuddering moan.

"Dan'l." Miss Lucy folded her arms across her ample bosom and stared. "What are you doing here?"

Daniel took the final step into the trailer. "Where's Zara?"

"In the back room with Tomas and Maria and the baby. How'd you know she was here?"

"I was with Zara when Tomas banged on her door. I wanted to check on Will and let Sally know where I'd be if she had to find me." He glanced around the room, noting its well-kept but sparse appearance. He'd only been inside the trailer once before, when he helped with Lucetta's birth. He didn't know the Herreras well, but they'd always been kind to his son. "How long has the baby been sick?"

"Most of the evening, but I've only been here 'bout an hour. Maria and Tomas are beside themselves. They knew Lucetta was ailin', but they ain't got a lick of insurance. And I'm not too sure Maria has a green card, either. I told 'em I'd do what I could, but when I saw that baby I knew it wouldn't be much."

"So you decided to let Zara try?" He sat at the small dining table and stretched his legs in front of him, taking up most of the floor space in the kitchen.

Lucy sat next to him and snorted out a sigh. "Couldn't think of anything better. She took care of Will's asthma, didn't she?"

"That she did, but the hospital—"

"Is an hour away. If anyone can help that baby, Zara can. If not, I'll drive the three of them to Denton."

Daniel covered both of Lucy's work-reddened hands with one of his own. "I know you have faith in Zara, Lucy, but this might be more than she's capable of."

Her expression determined, Lucy stuck out her chin. "Trust me, the woman knows what she's doing."

Before he could ask Lucy why she felt so positive about Zara's healing abilities, soft voices and shuffling footsteps came from the hall. Tomas guided Maria into the kitchen and helped her into a chair. When she was seated, he put his hands on her shoulders and began a slow massage.

"Miss Lucy, do you think you could boil water for tea? Maria is exhausted. Zara thought it might help."

"Now there's the best idea I've heard all night." Lucy stood and retrieved the kettle from the stove, then crossed to the sink.

"Tomas, Maria," Daniel began. "How are you holding up?"

Maria threw him a weak smile. Dressed in a plain cotton blouse and faded jeans, she looked weary and frightened, and much too young to be a mother. Tomas bent low and wrapped his arms around his wife. "Me, I am fine. It is my girls I am worried about. You are good friends with Miss Zara, *sí*? Do you truly think she can help our Lucetta?"

Daniel recalled the night he and Zara had first been intimate, when she'd cured his whopper of a headache with the mere touch of her fingers. And Will's asthma attack had been severe, yet she'd handled it amazingly well. Though he had his doubts as to how she managed her *relaxation techniques*, she definitely had more than a passable rate of success. Maybe Lucy was right to have faith in her.

"I don't want to get your hopes up, because there's no rational way to explain how Zara gets results, but I'd say Lucetta is in good hands."

The kettle whistled, startling Maria. As if waking from a stupor, she raised her teary eyes. "What is taking so long?"

Tomas patted her shoulder, but his gaze fell on Daniel. "Zara told us she needed privacy and asked us to leave. Maybe I should see what is happening?"

Lucy placed a variety of chipped but colorful mugs on the table, as well as a carton of milk and a sugar bowl. "You just sit yourself right there, Tomas, and let Daniel go. You need to get off your feet."

Maria clutched at his hand, a look of sheer panic in her dark brown eyes. "*Por favor, Señor Daniel.*"

Standing, Daniel edged his way from behind the table and headed slowly down the hall. After all the time Will spent here, he didn't remember his son ever describing the Herreras' living conditions as cramped or less than average. Will usually went on and on about how much fun it was to talk to Maria or play with the baby. Lurking like this, he found it hard to ignore the frayed, thirdhand furniture or the way the trailer reeked of pungent smelling spices underlaid with a sweet, baby-powder smell.

Times like this, he remembered all that he'd missed of his son's childhood, and he cursed the Warfields anew. He'd found a community he liked, a good place to raise his boy. Thanks to the judge and his wife, he had to uproot his family and go on the run again.

For the hundredth time, he wondered how he was supposed to explain it to Will. It had been fine when the boy was a toddler who went blithely to anyone with a ready smile and a gentle hand. There would be no way to spin a believable story after living in Button Creek.

Running a hand over his jaw, he stopped two feet from the bedroom doorway. Strange, but he'd thought it would be a lot darker back here while Zara was meditating over Lucetta. He hadn't expected to see the bright white glow spilling from the baby's room and out into the hall.

He took a step closer. Blinking against the light, he rounded the doorframe. Once his vision adjusted, he zeroed in on the old-fashioned rocking chair in a far corner. Rubbing at his eyes, his heart rate tripped in double time as he took a long look at Zara and the baby. What the hell was going on?

A full thirty seconds ticked by in silence before Daniel calmed enough to view the scene rationally. Zara's eyes were closed, the baby nestled snugly against her breast. Brilliant light radiated from the bracelet on her wrist, just as he'd thought it had the night he'd found her in his field. Her body, her very flesh, seemed to shimmer, as did Lucetta's. The glow reflected outward from their skin and back into the room in a wave of near-blinding whiteness.

He couldn't believe his eyes. He wanted to call to her, but the words stuck in his throat. He moved to walk to her side, and his feet refused to move. Over the past few weeks, he'd begun to wonder if Zara wasn't his own private miracle. Now he was positive of it.

At first, Zara felt, rather than saw, Daniel's disbelieving stare. When she was in healing mode, her every sense was supercharged, so even while she concentrated on her subject, she was fully aware of her surroundings and the presence of others. Most of the time, she could ignore it, but right now was not one of them.

Lucetta's fever had disappeared several minutes ago. Though she could have diminished the power of the stone at any time, she'd wanted to stay connected with the little girl just a bit longer to make certain she hadn't missed something that might take hold later. She should have known better than to be so foolish. She'd counted on the Herreras and Lucy to respect her wishes, but Daniel had said he would be over. Leave it to him to barge in and catch the show.

Slowly, she shut down the energy field, all the while trying to think of a logical way to explain what he'd just witnessed. Unfortunately, the drain to her senses had turned her mind blank. She couldn't even come up with a lie that sounded convincing enough to her own ears, let alone his.

Standing, Zara ran her lips over the baby's brow, smoothing back the dark, downy hair. The little girl let out a weary sigh and snuggled closer to her chest, as if recognizing the safe haven. Inwardly, she smiled at the blissful joy Lucetta's trust inspired. Bending down, she placed the girl in the crib and covered her with the cotton blanket, then patted her raised bottom to ensure the baby was truly at rest.

Inhaling a deep breath, she straightened and walked to the door. "Daniel. What are you doing back here?"

He placed a hand on each side of the molding, effectively blocking her escape. "Watching you. I told you I'd be over after I checked on Will, remember?"

"How was he?"

"Sound asleep. I told Sally I'd be home in a bit."

Not meeting his curious gaze, she turned sideways, but when she wedged herself between his solid mass and the door it only brought her lower body into intimate contact with his hips. Stuck between the molding and his muscular thighs, she tamped down the rush of dread commingled with sexual desire roiling in her stomach.

"Excuse me." She frowned and sidestepped again. "I need to speak with the Herreras."

Daniel did a quick pivot and grasped her upper arms. "Zara, what the hell just happened in this room?"

Letting her backside rest against the wall, she relaxed her stance. If she kept her composure, she might be able to bluff her way out of the situation, at least until she could think up a believable lie.

"Tomas and Maria should be told Lucetta is fine first, don't you think? We can talk later."

He blew out a frustrated breath, fluttering the damp tendrils curling at her temples. "I think we need to talk now."

Zara pulled from his no-nonsense grip and tucked the strands of wayward hair behind her ears. "The Herreras are probably worried sick, and I'm exhausted. Please let me pass."

The almost electric pull of his gaze set her insides to simmering. His glare traveled from her eyes to her mouth and back again, filling the space between them with enough sizzle to singe her eyebrows.

"You're stalling. And I'm trying to figure out why."

"You're imagining things. We can discuss this tomorrow, after you get back from the doctor with Will."

He ran a hand through his hair. "That will be too late. We need to settle things tonight."

"There's nothing to settle. I'm tired, and you have to get home to your son."

"You still haven't answered my question. I asked you to come with us when we left."

"I haven't decided—yet," she stuttered. "And if you keep pressuring me, I doubt the answer will be yes."

Daniel raised his hands and stepped back. "Sorry. It's just that—You do realize the way it looked when I stood in the doorway, don't you?"

Instead of answering, Zara headed down the hall and into the kitchen. Tomas and Maria rose to their feet, and Lucy handed her a mug of tepid tea. She gulped greedily, while Tomas laid a palm on her shoulder and Maria clutched her free hand. Smiling at the young couple, she passed the empty mug to Lucy.

"Lucetta is fine. Go in and check on her, but let her sleep," she said in Spanish. "She's been through quite a bit of trauma tonight."

The Herreras spoke rapid-fire as they hugged her, then raced down the hall. She turned in time to see Daniel jump aside to avoid a collision. Still glaring, he sauntered into the kitchen and leaned against the counter, commandeering, it seemed, most of the oxygen in the room.

"I knew you'd take care of it, but we were worried just the same." Fussing, Lucy pressed a clean diaper to Zara's brow. "You're dripping like a broken faucet. Are you all right?"

Zara took the cloth and turned from Daniel's penetrating stare, dabbing at her cheeks and neck. "Just tired. I'm not sure what was wrong with the baby, but she's fine now. If you don't mind, I really need to get to bed."

"Seein' as it's late, I think you and Tomas ought to take part of the day off." Lucy turned to Dan'l. "Tell Sally I'll need her as soon as she can make it in the morning, would you?"

"I'll pass her the message." Somehow he managed to cross the kitchen and put a hand on her elbow without Zara's ever sensing him move. "I'll walk you to the cabin."

She kept her voice polite but distant as she headed for the door. "I'm perfectly capable of seeing myself home."

Ignoring her chilly response, Daniel took her elbow and steered her down the stairs. "Good night, Lucy," he called, pulling the door closed behind them.

Zara lurched from his grasp and walked at warp speed. Daniel settled his Stetson on his head and let the brim shutter his eyes. More nervous than angry, she stomped over the ruts in the lot while he trailed after her, muttering under his breath. She reached her front stoop and tried to slip through the door, but he stuck his hand on the frame.

"Hold it right there. We need to settle this—"

"Tomorrow. I'm too tired to talk now."

"Why didn't you tell me you spoke Spanish?"

"I didn't think it mattered." She blew out a breath. "Please let me go inside."

His gaze scoured over her in a rush of heat and

longing. Somehow, some way, she had to come up with a lie that would satisfy his curiosity. She just needed a little more time.

"Please, Daniel? Let it . . . let me rest for the night."

Slowly he straightened and pulled away from the door. "I don't mean to bully you, I just want to understand."

"I can't give you answers tonight—about anything."

He heaved a sigh. Cupping her cheek with his hand, he leaned forward and brushed her lips lightly with his. "Okay, get some sleep. We'll talk tomorrow."

Zara closed and locked the door, then watched out the front window until he crossed the parking lot and disappeared around the corner of the diner. Resting her forehead against the cool glass, she exhaled a breath. She was in a terrible mess, and it was of her own making. She'd let her heart rule her head, just as her mother had warned against, and now she was paying the price.

Holding back a sob, she walked to the bed and tumbled fully clothed onto the mattress. Just about everything that could have gone wrong had: Daniel had witnessed a healing; she'd exposed herself to Lucy; and, worse, she'd fallen in love with the father of her child.

She had to leave at dawn.

## Twenty

Zara checked her backpack a final time. Along with a lightweight blanket, flashlight, and emergency cash, she had a map of the area surrounding her destination, a supply of bottled water, and enough fresh fruit to last several days. At the last second, she added the remaining chocolate bar she'd received from Daniel. It would be a small reminder of the time she'd spent here with the Murphys.

Opening the cabin door, she stepped into the darkness and focused on her goal: reaching the covered bridge by sunrise. The bridge would take her to a two-lane road where she hoped to catch a ride to a sparsely populated area in southeastern Oklahoma. There, she would activate her bracelet and send a signal to the mother ship, alerting it to her emergency. After the craft picked her up, she would stay on board and wait out the return journey.

Heading around the far end of the row of cabins, Zara crossed the street to the string of offices housing the veterinary clinic, where several paths fanned out across the field and led to the bridge.

Approaching the building, she glanced over her shoulder and noted that the diner was still dark. Soon Tomas would heat the griddle, then Lucy would wait on the first customer of the day. She wouldn't find Zara's farewell note until well into morning.

Her thoughts drifted to Daniel, still asleep in his apartment over the garage. She'd left him a note, too, though she doubted he would understand its meaning. But she took comfort in knowing his plan was sound; he and his son would be safe. In time, he would forget about her and find another woman to love. Someone who could give him and Will the care and devotion they deserved.

Someone who was free to give her heart.

Plowing forward into the dawn, Zara slammed against a wall of muscle, and felt herself clasped in a punishing grip. She pulled back, only to be blinded by a beam of light. Willing her heart to stop pounding, she raised her head and stared into a pair of glittering green eyes.

"Well, well, well. We thought you might be headed out of town today."

"Chuck!" She sucked in a breath, cloaking herself in a mantle of false bravado. "What are you doing out at this hour?"

The light washed over her, bringing its owner near. "Frank. I didn't realize you started your job so early."

His expression blank, Frank blurted, "Don't make a fuss, and we won't tranquilize you. Go inside quietly."

Before she could speak again, he grabbed her by an elbow and they escorted her to the rear of the building. Frank opened the door and stepped aside, giving her a clear view of Jack Farley. Aiming his camera, Jack took a series of photos as she was pushed none too gently into the office.

Her steps faltered, and Chuck squeezed her shoulder, steering her ahead of him. Spinning around, she stomped on his instep, hoping to break free, and he answered with a string of curses and a bone-jarring shake.

"Here now, none of that," growled Frank. "Don't do anything stupid, and you won't get hurt."

"Turn her in this direction," said Jack, his tone eager. "I want to get a clear shot of the first alien capture."

Another round of lights flashed, and Zara swallowed her fear. Forcing a laugh, she relaxed her stance. "Alien capture? Is this a joke?"

Chuck dragged the backpack off her shoulders, then shoved her forward. "No joke, now get moving."

"Hey, take it easy," Frank ordered. Snagging her arm, he snapped a pair of handcuffs on her wrists. "There's no call to damage the merchandise."

Jack kept his camera at the ready. "Sit her down so I can get a few more pictures."

Zara gazed at Frank, who seemed to be in charge. "Am I under arrest?"

"The agency would prefer to call it *protective custody*."

"For leaving town? And what agency are you talking about?"

"The United States government," said Frank, scowling. "And you know the reasons as well as we do. Shall I read the list?"

"You have no right to do this—"

Frank held up a hand, ticking off her transgressions. "You showed up out of nowhere the day after an unidentified spacecraft breeched Earth's atmosphere and sent a raft of smaller ships throughout the U.S. You have no legal form of identification, and your fingerprints are unrecognizable as human." He nodded toward her cuffed hands. "Not to mention the strange bracelet on your wrist, or the fact that your eyes changed color after an odd reaction to a simple perfume. Shall I go on?"

"You're serious about this? You really think those things qualify me as a being from another planet?"

"How about you take out those so-called contact lenses and let me see them?" She opened her mouth, and he held up a hand. "And before you deny anything, you should know that we watched you through a window in the Herreras' trailer last night."

Unable to respond, Zara closed her eyes.

Frank toed a chair in her direction. "Have a seat, Zara. If that's really your name."

"Yes, it's my name," she snapped.

She sat down and waited, her mind swimming in a sea of ideas. Chuck opened the backpack and pulled out the blanket, scattering fruit, bottled water, and the rest of the contents across the desktop. After turning the bag inside out, he dropped it on the desk.

"Hold up her hand." Jack took a step closer. "I want to get a shot of that bracelet."

Jerking her elbow, Chuck grabbed her fingers and moved the handcuff aside, giving Jack better access.

Jack finished another series of photos, then balanced the camera in one hand and raised a brow. "Don't mind me. You two handle this the way you normally would. I'm just here to record it for posterity."

Frank cut his gaze to his partner. "That could be a problem. We've never captured an alien before today."

Chuck gave a disgusted-sounding sigh. "We're trained agents, Frank. We handle this like we would any other takedown." A smug smile marred his face as he pulled out his gun. "There's nothing unusual in her carryall, so I say we just remove the damned bracelet. It's all she has that's out of the ordinary."

"Chuck's right." The photographer held the camera high. "She wouldn't let me near it in the laundry yesterday, so it has to be special. Probably her communicator, or whatever the hell they call those things."

Zara feigned interest in their discussion while she tucked her hands between her thighs. Squeezing her legs together, she maneuvered her fingers around an energy stone. If she could slip one into the clasp and release its power . . .

Chuck waved the gun when he caught on to what she was doing. "Grab her hands, before she uses that thing to zap us!"

Jack jumped back, holding the camera out in front of him like a shield. "You heard him, Frank. Get it off her!"

Frank pulled at her forearms, but she locked them in place.

"I wouldn't do that if I were you," Zara threatened, amazed at how easily she'd learned to lie. "I'm the only one who can remove it safely."

"Okay, take it easy." Frank stepped back, his hands raised high. "Don't do anything you'll be sorry for."

"If I agree to give you the bracelet, then what?"

"We'll escort you to the van and drive out of here before folks in town get suspicious. We have an office in Denton, and I'll alert them we're coming."

Zara jutted her chin. She'd managed to lock a gem in the clasp. She only hoped it was the right color stone. "I don't think that's a good idea."

With his gun aimed at her chest, Chuck hoisted a hip onto the desk. "Why don't you stop playing games and confess? It'll go a lot easier if you just tell us where you're from and why you're here."

Frank made another grab for her wrists and Zara pressed the clasp down. The power of the gem flowed through her arms, raced up her neck and into her mind. Closing her eyes, she visualized a safe scenario. She didn't want to hurt her captors, but she had to keep them occupied, at least until she was far away.

The room grew silent, the air still, while she breathed deeply and centered her thoughts. Though Frank's hands continued to rest on her arms, the pressure he'd exerted was gone. Focusing on the present, she found his face only inches from hers. The frantic darting of his eyeballs told Zara he had just realized he was frozen in place.

Carefully, she slid the chair back and slipped from his grasp. Then she stood and inspected Chuck, who exhibited the identical eye action while he perched statuelike on the desk. She walked to Jack, who crouched with the camera covering his face. He, too, had the same look of panic in his one visible eye.

Zara sighed. She'd been told that anyone she immobilized would have full function of their sight, hearing, and reason. Only their ability to move and speak would be impaired.

Filled with a sense of giddy relief, she patted the photographer's stony face. "The next time you decide to brag about your expertise with beings from outer space, Jack, I hope you'll remember this moment."

Moving to the desk, she waved a hand in front of Chuck's terror-filled eyes, resisting the urge to pinch him as payback for all the pain he'd just caused her.

Turning to Frank, Zara felt his pockets and retrieved a set of keys. After unlocking the handcuffs, she let them drop to the ground. She was behind schedule and had to hurry. This might not be the optimum time to learn how to drive an Earth vehicle, but she had no other choice.

"Tell your superiors we're a peace-loving people, Frank. We didn't come here to threaten national security or harm anyone. Our planet needs something the Earth has in abundance, and we didn't feel the time was right simply to ask for it."

Pale rays of morning light brightened the front window. Zara picked up her backpack and stuffed whatever she could gather inside. At the door she turned, looking to give a small measure of comfort. "You should be back to normal in a few hours."

Then she remembered her manners. "By the way, it was a pleasure meeting all three of you."

It only took Zara a few minutes to start the van and drive it around the building and across the field, zigzagging as if she'd consumed too much alcohol. Unfortunately, the boxy machine was low-slung and the ground a sodden mess, making it difficult to steer.

Reaching the road, she checked for oncoming traffic while she thought about her predicament. She had no doubt that the second Frank and Chuck were mobile, they would find another vehicle and come after her. Turning her wheels to the left, she lumbered onto the two-lane road in the wrong direction, then executed a series of turns on the pavement that pointed her the way she wanted to go. To anyone examining her muddy tracks, it would look as if she'd headed the opposite way, which might buy her more time.

Concentrating on the road, she thought about Daniel. Her heart already ached because she'd left him. She didn't want to think of how empty her world would be when she was home. And Will had found a place in her heart as well. She had to protect her child, the one small bit she had left of both men.

Feeding the van just enough fuel to keep it moving at a sedate pace, she drove until she crossed into Oklahoma, then searched one-handed through her backpack. When she didn't find her map, she used the road signs as a guide. If they were accurate, she would be at the safe site soon.

She passed the time drying her tears and reading markers, while she focused on her goal: finding the pickup site and contacting the mother ship.

A short time later, the vehicle slowed. When she pressed on the accelerator and the engine coughed in protest, she checked the instruments and saw that the van was out of fuel. She'd passed a gas station several miles back, but hadn't thought of stopping. Lucky for her she'd just crested a hill, because the downward movement gave the van enough forward momentum to roll to a clearing that turned out to be a rest stop.

Zara left the keys in the ignition, grabbed her backpack and stepped onto the gravel. Opening her carryall, she took out an apple and ate it while she checked the immediate area. A series of signs informed her she was nearing her final destination: Pine Creek Lake.

The park seemed deserted, an optimum situation for her rescue, but she was certain that by now, Frank, Chuck, and Jack were on her tail. The men were a bit dense, but they wouldn't be fooled by the maneuver she'd made back at the field for long—especially if they had gotten a good look at her map.

Resting at the base of a tree, she ate another apple while she set an emerald green stone in her clasp and checked it for accuracy. When she pressed a series of small tabs at the side, the stone flickered and locked in place. All she had to do was walk until the pulsing stopped and the light remained steady, which meant she was at the site. There she would sit and wait.

She consoled herself with the knowledge that, by now, both Murphys were well on their way to Canada. She imagined Daniel was furious with her for leaving Button Creek with nothing more than a note, but she'd had no other choice. His fury would help him forget her and make him more determined to get as far away with Will as he could.

The depressing thought brought more tears to her eyes. She would never have enough anger inside of her to wipe Daniel from her mind. To her, their baby would be a constant source of joy and sorrow. She could only hope the joy would overshadow the misery of losing him and help her to remember the kind of man he'd been: a friend, a lover, and the father of her child.

Standing, she dropped the apple core and continued toward the lake.

Thanks to a patient cancellation, the doctor saw Will ahead of schedule, which allowed father and son to return to town early. Daniel drove straight to the restaurant to inform Zara that after he dropped his son at the Triple P, the two of them were going to have a private chat.

Between the incident in the Herreras' trailer and all the other things he *didn't* know about her, he'd been up half the night. Her use of that bracelet to heal Lucetta, and her sudden ability to speak Spanish had him flummoxed, but he was most upset by the fact that she had yet to agree to leave town with him and Will.

He ordered his son to sit tight, left the truck engine running, and hurried into the diner. Checking the room, he saw Sally carrying a tray and Lucy waiting on customers at the counter.

"Lucy." He took off his Stetson. "Is Zara in the kitchen? I need to talk with her."

Lucy's eyes opened wide. She threw a sideways glance at Lerner, who was busy stirring his coffee, and joined Daniel at the far end of the counter. "I was just going to her cabin."

"You mean she hasn't shown yet?" He lowered his voice. "How late is she?"

"'Bout an hour." Lucy hunched forward. "And that fella down there is still askin' folks a whole passel of questions, only now they're about you and Will."

Daniel refused to give Lerner a thought. "Yeah, well, it'll have to wait. Do you have a key to her cabin?"

Lucy dug into her apron pocket and pulled out a ring of keys. "Sure do, but you're not going there without me." She trundled from behind the serving bar. "Zara mighta had a relapse, or another bout of . . . of whatever's ailin' her. If so, she's gonna need a woman's touch."

Only half-hearing Lucy's comment, he took off for the door.

When he trotted past the truck, Will jumped to the ground. "Dad, where you goin'?"

"Stay in the truck, son." Daniel made a beeline for Zara's cabin. On the front stoop, he pounded on the door. "Zara! Zara, you in there? Open up, it's me!"

Lucy and Will reached him at the same time. "Here now, no cause to break the thing down." She turned the knob, and the door opened, then she stepped inside ahead of Daniel. "Zara! You all right?"

Daniel raced past Lucy, through the living room into the bathroom, but there was no sign of her. Staring at the bed, stripped of its linens with the coverlet folded neatly on the mattress, a ripple of foreboding filled him. He walked back to the kitchen and surveyed the stack of precisely arranged bills and coins aligned next to a sheet of paper printed with Sally's name. His gaze came to rest on Lucy, who was sitting down with an envelope in each hand.

"She's gone, Dan'l." The older woman sniffed back tears as she slid an envelope addressed to him in neat, rounded script across the table. "She left us these."

"Zara's gone?"

Will reached for the note, but Daniel snatched it up. He blew out a breath as he tore into the plain white envelope.

*Daniel,*

*By the time you read this, I'll be far away. I didn't want to leave you, but I would have hurt you if I stayed any longer. Please believe me when I say that I*

*love you and Will more than you will ever know. Take*
*him and find your happiness, as I too shall try to do.*
*Trust me, it's better this way.*

*Yours always,*
*Zara*

He looked up to find Lucy crying while she
folded her letter. "Damn fool woman," she muttered. "This here proves there ain't no intelligent life
in the universe."

"Dad?" Will clutched at his arm. "What does Zara
say? Why did she leave?"

Daniel crumpled the letter in his fist. Clearly agitated, Will tried to pry it from his fingers, but he
raised his hand in the air. "Later."

"But—"

"What's going on, Murphy? I thought you were
bringing Will to my place?"

Spinning on his heel, he spotted Jay standing in
the doorway. Lerner appeared beside him, and
Daniel's mouth turned dry as dust. "What's he doing here?"

Jay stepped into the room. "I came to the diner to
find you and got cornered by Mr. Lerner. I think you
ought to listen to the man. What he has to say is important."

"Not now," Daniel spat out. "I've got to find Zara."

"Why? What's happened?"

Waving the note, Lucy sniffled loudly. "She's gone,
Jay. Just upped and left for home."

"Home?" Daniel glared at her. "Let me see that."

The older woman tucked the letter behind her back. "Read your own danged note, Dan'l Murphy. This one is private."

"Murphy," Jay began, "I know Zara means the world to you, but you need to take a second to talk to Mr. Lerner. He really does have something to tell you."

"He's right, Mr. Murphy, or should I say Mr. Lotello." Lerner held out a newspaper clipping and a parcel of papers. "All I'm trying to do is explain—"

Daniel stared at the offerings. "If you're here to haul me to jail, it'll have to wait."

"Not jail, but I do want you and your son to accompany me to New York." He smiled at Will. "Read these documents, and you'll see what I'm talking about."

Taking a protective stance, Daniel wrapped an arm around Will's shoulder. "What the hell are you saying?"

The man handed him the papers. "The Warfields were killed in a car accident four years ago. Their attorney thought you might have heard and returned to New York. When it became apparent you weren't going to show, they hired me to locate you. Will is the Warfields' sole heir."

Flipping through the packet, Daniel inspected copies of the death certificates, read the date on the obituaries, and scanned papers from a legal firm in Manhattan.

"Are you telling me I'm no longer a wanted man?"

"In a manner of speaking. About a year after you kidnapped your son the Warfields had a change of heart. They decided that if you came back of your own accord, they'd be willing to work through the custody issue." Lerner took back the papers and stuck them in his pocket. "There's still an outstanding warrant for your arrest, but the lawyers assured me that because you're named as Will's legal guardian, it should only take a single court appearance to clear you of all charges. The two of you will soon be free to enjoy the good life. As I said, he's a wealthy young man."

Jay clapped him on the back. "Hear that, Murphy? You're free. There's no need to run away."

Daniel rubbed at his neck. The enormity of what he'd just heard overwhelmed him. He could go back to teaching astronomy. Will was legally his. They were free.

Then he stared at the letter fisted in his hand.

Without Zara to share it, neither the money nor his freedom meant a thing. He might as well still be on the run, because he and Will would find no peace, enjoy no life without her.

"Let me read your note, Lucy. Please."

Lucy swiped at her tears. "All right, but promise me you'll keep an open mind. Zara had to go, but I know she didn't want to, 'specially with her carryin'—with her bein'—"Aw, hell." She thrust the paper at him. "Here."

Daniel read the letter twice. Confused, he gazed at the ceiling. Lucy's note said a lot more than his did, but nothing was any clearer.

"I don't get it. What is she talking about—being true to her mission—meeting with a ship and traveling back to her home?" He shook his head. "Anyone reading this would think she's some kind of visitor from another planet."

Jay plucked the sheet from his hand. Daniel walked to the open door, his heart in a vise. According to Lerner, he was free, but that was a lie. He'd never be free, not if he lost Zara. From the tone of the letter, she was determined to disappear. If that happened, he might never find her.

"Holy hell, Murphy. Did you pay attention when you read this? I don't want to believe it, but—" Jay stood next to him and touched his shoulder. "She's saying she was sent here from another world, and she's on her way back. Is that possible?"

Daniel locked gazes with Jay and marked the rancher's shocked expression. He remembered the questions he'd amassed about Zara, all the times he'd tried to question her and received no answer. He'd been prepared to handle any secret she threw at him, even something as upsetting as running from a husband or committing a crime . . . or what had happened last night in the Herreras' trailer

He and Will had often discussed the idea of intelligent life in other solar systems. He was a scientist, well aware there was much more to the universe than had been revealed. To think that the one woman he'd fallen in love with might come from another planet, that she wasn't even human . . .

Walking to the table, he pulled out a chair and grasped Lucy's clenched hands. "Please, if you care for me and Will at all, tell me everything you know about Zara."

# Twenty-one

Daniel blasted out of the cabin, jogged around the diner, and crossed the highway with Will, Jay, Lucy, and Lerner on his heels. The black van that was usually parked in front of the building was gone, but he banged on the surveyors' door anyway. If Lucy was correct, these bozos knew something about Zara's disappearance, and he was prepared to beat it out of them.

"Hey, now." Doc Mayberry poked his head out of his office, located a door down. "Murphy. What's all the racket about?"

"Doc, have you seen those surveyors this morning? Have you seen Zara?"

"Haven't seen your pretty little friend, but those TXdot boys were at my door a while ago. Seems someone stole their van, so they asked to borrow my truck. That photographer fella was with 'em." He scratched at his jaw. "Thought it was odd they didn't call the law about their missing vehicle."

"We could always break the door down," said Jay.

Daniel ignored the suggestion and headed around the building, where he found the back door to the survey office open wide. He charged inside, followed by his posse, which now included Doc, and took stock of the untidy room. Ducking, he spotted something under the desk and crawled to retrieve it.

Jay nosed around the other side of the office with Doc, while Lucy held Will to her side.

"What are they doing?" Will asked her.

"Lookin' for clues," whispered Lucy.

Lerner folded his arms and shook his head, stepping farther into the room. "It sure looks like something odd went on in here. Chairs overturned, papers scattered to kingdom come." He righted the chair, found a set of handcuffs, and dangled them in the air. "Isn't this interesting?"

Daniel backed out from beneath the desk, clutching a map and a chocolate bar—the same candy he'd brought to Zara's cabin the night after they'd first made love. When Lerner handed him the cuffs, his gut heaved. Those TXdot men had better pray to God they didn't run into him; ditto Jack Farley.

He spread the map on the desk and spotted a section circled in red. Jay hunkered down alongside him, with Doc, Lucy, Will, and Lerner following suit. "How well do you know that area?" Jay asked, pointing at the circled area.

"Will and I visited the lake a time or two. There are

campgrounds to the north, but the southern end is fairly isolated."

"Isolated enough to cover up a spacecraft landing?" returned Jay.

"What the hell—sure—why not?" Daniel shook his head. "I never thought I'd be involved in a scenario like this one, but I can't think of anything else that makes sense."

"It appears she's the one who stole their van." Jay smiled. "The woman has guts, I'll give her that."

"There's no tellin' that's where Zara is headed," Lucy offered. "This map could be one Frank and Chuck used in their survey work."

Daniel folded the map to the front side and showed her a price stamp. "The candy is from my store, ditto the map. I loaned it to Zara when we talked about camping." He flipped it back the way he found it. "This has to be where she's going."

Doc nodded. "Now that you mention it, them fellas drove around the back of the building when they left and headed for the bridge instead of takin' the main highway."

"Makes perfect sense to me," murmured Jay. "That route leads straight to the feeder road into Pine Creek Lake. If it's as isolated as I think it is, it would be a perfect spot to—

"Make contact with a spaceship," murmured Will. "Wow."

Daniel stuffed the map into his rear pocket and grabbed Will by the hand. "We're going after her."

"I don't want to put ideas in your head, Murphy,

but I think you need to take a little firepower," cautioned Jay.

"I'm way ahead of you," cried Daniel over his shoulder as he hurried out the front door with his son in tow.

Jay paced the room after Daniel left. "I have a shotgun and shells in the rear of the SUV. Think Murphy would mind if I borrowed a tank of gas?"

Lucy fisted her hands on her hips. "And what if he did? He's gonna need help if he plans to rescue that gal."

"That's what I'm thinking," said Jay. He scrambled to the door and turned, giving the rest of the group a grin. "From the sound of it, the next couple hours are going to be exciting. I never thought I'd live long enough to spot a flying saucer."

"A flyin' saucer?" Scratching at his jaw, Doc stared at Jay's retreating backside. "Feel up to takin' a little spin this afternoon, Miss Lucy? You can fill me in on the ride."

"Fine by me." Lucy turned and bumped smack into Lerner. "Get outta my way or come along, don't matter none to me. But I wouldn't miss this for all the tea in China."

Daniel vaulted into his truck and rammed it in reverse while Will scrambled in on the passenger side. Luckily, he'd filled the gas tank before they left for the doctor. Will bounced in his seat, as if preparing for a roller-coaster ride, and Daniel remembered how this type of excitement played havoc with the boy's asthma.

"Got your inhaler?"

Will patted his pocket. "Yes, sir. Are we going to look for Zara?"

"We are." Backing out of the parking space, he caught Will's eager expression. He could only imagine the crazy ideas going through the boy's head. "You do understand what we talked about back there? You realize that Zara told Lucy she's an—that Jay thinks she's—that there's evidence Zara is from another planet?"

"Yeah, and I can't wait to ask her if she got here in one of those shooting stars. I bet she knows all about the goop in our freezer, too."

"I guess I should have paid more attention when you said those lights were important," said Daniel, feeling like a fool. "You said all along those stars carried visitors from outer space."

"Who knew?" Will said magnanimously. "And she's our friend. That is way cool." He leaned forward in the seat. "I just hope we can find her before those other guys do."

"Don't worry, we'll find her." Daniel cleared his throat. He'd kept too many secrets from his son, for too long. It was time he bit the bullet and confessed. "Zara is more than a friend, Will. She and I are involved—like grown-ups. I'm . . . in love with her."

Will threw him a lopsided grin. "Well, duh. Like the whole town doesn't know that already. Sally said—"

"Never mind Sally," Daniel ordered, muffling a groan. "Just fasten your seat belt."

Intent on taking the same route he assumed Zara

and the phony surveyors had, he steered toward the string of offices. He spotted Jay filling up at the Last Chance, while Lucy and Doc speed-walked toward him, engaged in heavy conversation. And damned if Lerner wasn't dogging their steps like a hound sniffing after a bone. He sighed, waiting for the next round of questions. Will didn't disappoint him.

"What did Mr. Lerner mean when he said there was a warrant out for your arrest? Why did he call you Mr. Lotello? And if I'm really a wealthy young man, can we buy a computer?"

The truck sped around the building and jounced over the field. Daniel rolled his eyes, not sure which issue to tackle first. Turning right, he headed west toward the lake. He should have found the courage to tell Will the truth long before then . . . even if it wasn't something to be proud of. Between explaining his past and worrying about how to keep Zara safe—

"Dad . . . ?"

"It's a long story, and it happened when you were a baby. I'll tell you all of it, as soon as we settle things with Zara. How does that sound?"

Will thought a few seconds before he said, "Cool."

Daniel had broken every posted speed limit as he made tracks to the park, while Will glanced at the few side roads that whizzed by. If what he suspected was true, Zara had taken it slow on her journey. Besides never driving a car, she had no license. Getting caught by the law would have been the last thing she wanted.

Now inside the confines of the park, Daniel noted it was almost empty. He careened down a hill and sped past a rest stop, noting the signs that pointed him in the direction of Pine Creek Lake.

"Dad! Stop!" Will swiveled in his seat and pressed his nose against the window. "I think that's the van!"

Daniel screeched to a halt, made a U-turn, skidded into the parking lot, and pulled alongside a familiar black vehicle. "Good going, son." He swung his door wide. "Let's take a look before we make our next move."

He climbed out of the truck, and Will did the same. Daniel peered into the front passenger window. "Keys are in the ignition, so Zara's on foot from here. Question is, which way?"

He strode to the edge of the lot and scrutinized the hiking trail that, according to posted signs, led to the southern end of the lake. Walking a few feet onto the packed dirt, he bent over and plucked an apple core from the ground. Apples were Zara's favorite fruit, and the remains hadn't been there long.

He scanned in a circle. There was no trace of Doc's truck, and no sign of other hikers. Where the hell were Chuck, Frank, and Farley? If they had a breakdown, he and Will would have passed them on the highway. Had Zara laid a false trail that sent them in the wrong direction, or did they plan to come at the park from another angle?

Back at his pickup, he pulled down the rear gate, hoisted himself into the bed, and opened a side compartment. After taking out a battery-powered lantern, rifle, and a box of shells, he eased to the ground and loaded the weapon.

"This could get dangerous, son." He rested the rifle in the crook of his arm with the muzzle pointed downward. "You have to promise that from here on out you'll do exactly what I tell you, no matter how it sounds. That's the only way you're coming with me. You understand what I'm saying?"

"Yes, sir." Will swiped at his nose. "I don't want anything bad to happen to Zara, Dad. If those TXdot men are from the government, they probably want her so they can do bad things to her—you know, like they did to those aliens who landed in Roswell."

Daniel shook his head, the weight of the handcuffs heavy in his front pocket. "That's speculation, but I agree Frank and Chuck are up to no good." He gazed at the setting sun. "I'm going to do everything I can to keep her—to keep all of us out of trouble."

Daniel locked the truck and held the lantern out to Will. The boy took it, and, together, they stepped onto the trail.

Zara reached the emergency site and found cover in a stand of trees. Propped against a pile of boulders, she removed the blanket and flashlight from her backpack. Hoping to keep the beacon from alerting anyone to her position, she draped the material over her wrist. It was only a matter of time before the mother ship locked on to the signal.

Once that was done, she leaned back into the rocks and took stock of her surroundings. The sun was just beginning to set. Ahead of her stretched a large, grassy area that ran to the tip of the lake. The spacecraft wouldn't land, but it did need an unimpeded spot in which to hover, and this field was perfect.

She placed her hand low on her stomach and daydreamed about her time on Earth. How much would Lucy reveal when people realized she was gone? Would anyone believe she was a space traveler? Would the citizens of Button Creek understand that she'd meant them no harm, or would they listen to Chuck and Frank?

The letter she'd written to Lucy had explained as much as she dared, but not once had she mentioned the baby. If Frank and Chuck had found out she was pregnant, they would have been even more determined to capture her so they could take her baby away. It was another reason she couldn't have gone with Daniel and Will. Her presence would have doubled their danger.

A snapping sound echoed in the darkness, bringing her to attention. Crouching, she scrabbled behind the boulders and narrowed her eyes. Lights bobbed in the distance, and she froze in place, her only hope to remain perfectly still. If they found her, she would have to rely on one of her last two energy stones, but she would have to disrupt the locator's signal to use it.

Muffled whispers carried over the quiet of the night, sending a ripple of fear slithering up her spine. The lights separated, and she counted three individual beacons coming toward her from the lake. She clutched the blanket hiding the transmitter beam to her chest, determined to hold her position.

Watching the lights float in the darkness like disembodied spirits, her stomach heaved. Three lights could mean only one thing. Frank, Chuck, and Jack were here.

Zara shrunk farther against the rocks, willing herself as small as possible. Another rustle, this one from behind, made her suck in a breath. There were others.

She was surrounded.

Daniel made a motion for Will to douse the lantern. The boy obeyed, and he took Will's hand. He'd spotted a trio of lights and knew they meant trouble. He had to find Zara before Frank, Chuck, and Jack did.

He kept Will close as they walked toward a small copse of trees ahead and to their right. It was there he hoped to find a place to take cover, instead of venturing into the open field in front of them. Taking one step at a time, he and Will inched their way into the woods. Ghostly white boulders, pushing from the ground like huge tombstones, loomed only a few feet ahead. If they could make it to those rocks, they could hide.

Agonizing seconds later, Daniel pressed into a boulder. Will made like moss and flattened himself against a second rock. Twigs snapped. Measured footsteps sounded in the quiet of the night as the hunters walked a wide arc around the area. So far, the bad guys had stayed on the perimeter, but it was only a matter of time before they tightened their circle.

And very near, Daniel heard the indrawn breath of another.

He gave Will the silent command to stay put, set his rifle on the ground, and held his hand in the air. Will nodded and hunched lower. Daniel put each foot down, heel to toe, and sidled around the pile of rocks. The soft breathing tapered to one indrawn gasp. He smiled when the aroma of fresh apples and another familiar scent assaulted his senses.

Clasping Zara's mouth from behind, he drew her against him. She quivered in his arms, her fear a living thing, and he whispered in her ear, "Shh. It's me. Don't say a word."

The air seeped from her lungs as she nodded and collapsed into his chest. Daniel enveloped her from behind and kissed her ear, the nape of her neck, whatever part of her he could reach.

She turned and touched his cheeks, his mouth, his chin, with trembling fingers. Even in the dark, he could see her expression of surprise and the brightness of her smile.

He placed a hand to her lips and she nodded. Huddling closer, he mouthed, "Are you all right?"

"Yes, but how—Why are you here?"

Again, he touched her lips. "Later." He slanted his head, his voice a bare whisper. "Frank and Chuck are out there."

She sighed. "And Jack."

"We have to get away from here."

She closed her eyes.

He grasped her shoulders and shook her gently,

until she stared at him, her beautiful face filled with sorrow.

"You're leaving." It was a comment, not a question. She shrugged.

"Dammit, Zara. You can't go."

A tear trickled down her cheek, glistening in the pale moonlight. Daniel leaned forward and kissed it away. "I don't care where you came from, just don't leave."

"I'll always remember my time here with you and Will." Her voice, so small and sad, tore at his heart. "But it's impossible for me to stay. Please, tell Will how much I loved him—how much I loved both of you."

He pulled her into his arms. "We'll go to Canada. I'll keep you safe—"

Will's frightened voice cut through the darkness. "Dad?"

# Twenty-two

Lucy glared at the rancher and the other men clustered around the rear bumper of Jay's Land Rover. She and Jay had driven convoy style until her truck blew a tire. Instead of fixing the flat, they'd left the vehicle at the side of the road and piled into Jay's SUV. When they passed Daniel's pickup and the black van, they figured Murphy had things covered on foot, so they decided to drive farther into the park and hit the area circled on Zara's map from the other side.

"This here is Doc's truck; that means them bozos are somewhere nearby," she said, eyeing the vet's vehicle. "I say we just walk right in and try to find 'em."

"We need a plan," muttered Jay. "And excuse me for saying so, but you and Doc are a little too old to be traipsing through the woods. If one of you fell, you'd not only give us away, you'd ruin the element of surprise."

The older woman scowled as she raised her Smith & Wesson. "I got all the surprise I need right here."

"Now, Lucy," Doc said, always the voice of reason. "You know very well Jay is right."

Lerner pulled out his own gun, a small snub-nosed revolver. "Whatever you decide, I'm in."

Jay paced a few steps, then turned. "How about we split up? You and Doc each take a lantern and pick your way—carefully, mind you—on the trail, while Lerner and I cut through the brush. We'll get there ahead of you, but you'll catch up eventually."

"And miss out on all the action," snorted Lucy. "I don't like the sounda that."

Doc held her by the elbow. "I suspect Jay and Mr. Lerner are much more accustomed to this type of scenario than we old fools are. Our main concern needs to be Zara, Daniel, and Will."

Lucy swiped at her eyes, which had been watering on and off since she'd left Button Creek. She tilted her head to Jay. "Promise me you'll try and hold 'em until we get there . . . unless you need to do something to save Zara. Her and the baby have to come first."

The three men gasped as one.

"B—baby?" stuttered Lerner.

"Zara's pregnant?" mouthed Jay.

"Well, I'll be," muttered Doc.

Lucy grinned. Finally, she had the upper hand. "Yes, and it's a secret. Even Dan'l don't know. Zara came down here because the men on her planet can't get the job done, if you get my drift. Murphy did us proud."

Jay set his rifle in the crook of his arm. "Certainly puts a whole new spin on things. I take it that's the reason she has to go home?"

"You got it," said Lucy. "She was on a mission, and she did her duty. She didn't want Dan'l to find out 'cause she didn't want him to be hurt."

"Hurt! If anything happens to her or the baby, he'll be devastated," said Jay. "God, what a mess."

"And He's gonna take care of it, mark my word." Lucy waved her pistol. "Now let's roll."

Zara and Daniel rose slowly to their feet. Chuck stood next to Will on the other side of the boulders, his gun pressed firmly against the boy's temple.

"Come on out from behind there, nice and easy, the both of you."

Daniel growled deep in his throat. "Hurt him, and you're a dead man."

"We don't want your boy, Murphy. We just want to make a trade. Your little alien friend there for your son."

Daniel lurched forward, but Zara clutched his hand. "I'll come willingly—just let Will go."

Chuck shook his head. "Not so fast."

"That's right, Zara," Frank hissed. He stepped from the trees and set his lantern on the rocks, then moved to Will's other side. "Before you take another step, remove that bracelet and put it where I can see it."

Zara pulled her arm from underneath the blanket, unclasped the bracelet, and placed it on top of the nearest boulder, but not before she noticed that instead of a steady beacon, it was pulsing rhythmically.

"What the hell is it doing?" asked Frank, bending down to get a better look.

"It's signaling my ship. My people will be here soon to take me home."

"No kidding." A flash brightened the night as Jack moved into the circle. Wielding the camera, he swooped in for a close-up. "This is going to take over the headlines for weeks—and make me a very rich man."

"Well somebody better turn the thing off," said Chuck. "We're only asking for trouble if her buddies get here. We're not prepared for that kind of thing."

"Can't you call for backup?" asked Jack.

"It's too late now." Frank glared at Chuck. "Somebody insisted we could do this on our own."

"We caught her fair and square," snapped Chuck. "We don't need anybody else from the agency horning in on our success. We can do this."

"Sounds good to me." Jack's smile, his entire demeanor, reeked of greed. "The last thing I want is the government confiscating my camera or impeding my right to market the photos. I'll have enough pictures to keep the tabloids, NASA—hell—the whole world busy for a year. It's my ticket to fame and fortune."

"Then let me go," said Zara. "I told you we meant no harm. You'll have the bracelet and the pictures for proof, and my people will take me away. What more do you want?"

"You're not leaving me." Daniel tugged her back to his side and glared across the rocks. "And let go of my boy."

Chuck ignored his demand. Frank grabbed the bracelet and held it to the light, clicking at the tabs.

"Are you crazy?" Chuck's voice wavered. "Press the wrong button, and we could all be blown up, or turned to stone again."

He met Zara's smiling gaze. "That was a nasty trick you pulled, by the way. We told you we weren't going to hurt you."

She crossed her arms. "Really? That's not the impression I got back in your office."

"Stop bickering," demanded Frank. He dropped the still-pulsing bracelet on a boulder. "I'm going to send the boy to you, Murphy. I expect Zara to walk over here when I do."

He clasped Will by the shoulder and pushed him in their direction.

Zara jerked her hand from Daniel's and took a step forward.

The sound of a shotgun blast split the night. Six bodies froze in place, their eyes on Jay Pepperdine.

"Will, go to your father. Nobody else move a muscle, or the next time I aim for someone's ass."

Will ran to Daniel and clung to his side. Zara inhaled a breath to stop from shaking.

"All right, everybody hand your weapons to Mr. Lerner," said Jay, cool as glass. "He'll take care of them."

"Do you know who we are?" asked Chuck, reaching into his back pocket.

"Stop right there," warned Jay. He stepped into the lanternlight. "I imagine you're the FBI or some such federal agency intent on keeping our skies safe from alien predators. Well, I'm not impressed."

"You won't get away with this, Pepperdine," said Frank. "You're interfering with a top-priority United States government project. We answer directly to the president. We're the law here."

Jay muffled a snort. "Well, here in Texas, the man with the biggest gun is the law—and that's me. Now do like I said and give your weapons to Lerner, slow and careful." He smiled at Jack. "You, too, Mr. Photographer. Put your equipment on the rocks."

Jack held the camera behind his back while Lerner collected the weapons. "Hey now, Jay, there's no reason to blame me for this mess. I'm not working for anyone but myself." He inclined his head toward Zara. "The way I see it, it doesn't matter if she's captured or set free. All I want are the final rights to my photos of the first alien to land on American soil. Bonus shots of a flying saucer and the departure of our visitor are fine by me. I'm even willing to split a part of the profits. What do you say?"

"He says no!" Lucy barked. Everyone turned toward the two lanterns heading their way. Doc and the older woman neared, and Lucy aimed her gun directly at Jack. "Now do like Jay told you, Mr. Farley."

"Lucy." Zara rushed to her side. "What are you— how did you get here?"

Lucy grinned. "In my rust bucket,'til it blew a tire. Then we piled into Jay's SUV. Are you and the ba— are you doin' okay?"

"I've been better, but we're—I'm fine."

Lucy followed Zara's hesitant gaze across the pile of boulders. "Hey there, Will, Dan'l. You boys all right?"

Daniel hugged Will to his side, but he focused on Zara. "I'll be a hell of a lot better after you convince my woman to stick around."

Unable to look Daniel in the eye, Zara swiped at the tears streaming down her cheeks. "Lucy, I expect you to keep your promise when I'm gone."

"What promise?" Daniel asked through gritted teeth.

His raised voice was drowned by the sound of a million insects humming. With her heart beating in triple time, Zara searched the sky. Snatching the bracelet, she snapped it onto her wrist and scanned the heavens a second time. Jay and Lucy followed her gaze, as did the rest of the men.

Brilliant, strobing pinpoints of light filled an area above and in front of them so wide it seemed as if a football stadium were coming to Earth. The lights began to pulse in rhythm with the bracelet as the huge expanse swept across the heavens in a wide arc, then circled and hovered, coming to rest over the center of the field.

Jack aimed his camera and started shooting. Lerner clutched the weapons to his chest, smart enough to know this was not the time for gunfire.

Zara turned and stared at Daniel. He and Will walked to her side. "I have to go," she said, tears still running freely down her face.

Will grabbed her around the waist. "No! You can't. You love us. My dad said so."

Zara bent and placed her lips on the top of his head. "I do love you, Will, more than you'll ever know. But my people need me. I promised them I'd return. I can't break my word."

"Zara." Daniel cupped her jaw and wiped her tears with his thumb. "What can I say to make you stay?"

She shook her head. "There's nothing you can say. You and Will have to go to Canada and—" Her gaze shifted to Lerner. "Why is he here?"

"Because I've been given a reprieve," answered Daniel. "Will and I are free. Stay, and I'll tell you about it."

"That's wonderful. I'm happy for you."

The buzzing noise increased as the ship's lights brightened the surrounding area. Will covered his ears, as did Lucy and the men, but Daniel's gaze never left her face.

"Please, they're calling me. I have to go," she cried to him. "It's for the best."

He grabbed her, his eyes pleading. "If you leave, my life won't be worth living."

"You don't understand." She jerked backward, but he held her tight.

"Then make me understand. Tell me why we can't be together. Tell me you don't love me."

She pried his hands from her arms. "You have to let me go."

Turning, she bolted for the ship. Daniel watched her, his eyes, his very heart turning to ashes inside of him. The ground trembled beneath his feet, and, finally, he raised his gaze. The spacecraft was more than he'd ever dreamed possible, big and bright and mind-boggling, it seemed to encompass the entire sky.

But it couldn't erase the pain of Zara's running across the field and away from him.

"Dad, do something," Will sobbed above the racket. "You can't let her leave."

Daniel set his hands on Will's shoulders, hoping to absorb his son's misery. They'd both had so many losses in their life, this was almost too much to bear.

"What other choice do we have?"

Will's gaze darted from Zara to Daniel. Then he broke away and took off after her. In shock, Daniel shouted, "Will, stop! What are you doing!"

The boy turned, stumbling backward, but still running. "I'm going to ask if we can go with her. Come on, Dad, hurry!"

Sucker punched, Daniel grinned. *Well, hot damn. The kid is definitely smarter than I am—and a hell of a lot braver.*

He took off at a sprint just as Zara stopped under the ship, shouting at the top of his lungs. "Zara, wait. For the love of God, don't go."

She turned and raised her hand, but when she saw him and Will, she put her fingers to her mouth. Will reached her just as a beam of light shot down from the craft and bathed her in a brilliant glow.

"Zara, we want to come with you!" Will called, racing into the light beam.

"You do?" She looked up into the belly of the ship, and the light beam grew to encompass Will. "I—I don't know."

Daniel reached her side and enclosed both her and Will in his arms. "I can't believe we didn't think of it sooner. Ask them, Zara. See if they have room for two more passengers."

She blinked, then smiled. Daniel kissed her as if he would never let her go.

Will stared up between them at the bottom of the ship. "Hey, is anyone up there? Can you hear us? We want to go with you!" He tugged frantically on her shirt. "Ask them, Zara, please!"

Zara broke the kiss, but kept her eyes on Daniel. "I have no idea if you'll ever be allowed to come back."

"I don't care."

"But you'll have to leave everything behind. It will be a whole new world for you."

Daniel pulled her against his chest, crushing Will between them. "If it's what you want, then we—I— want it, too. I love you, Zara. Can't you see—I won't have a world without you."

She smiled and raised her gaze skyward. Closing her eyes, she concentrated. Then she cocked her head.

"They say yes. You're welcome to board."

"Ya-hoo!" Will turned and waved to Lucy. "We're goin' with you. Good-bye Lucy! We're going to outer space. Good-bye!"

Zara grabbed Will and clutched him to her side. "Hold on to me. This is going to tingle, but it's a great feeling."

Daniel raised his voice against the increasing roar. "Is there anything you want to tell me, *before* we go on board?"

"Just that I love you and Will." He continued to stare into her eyes, and she took his hand, pressing it against her belly. "And the baby we made."

His expression stern, Daniel raised an eyebrow. "You might have said something before all this."

"I never meant to deceive you. I'll explain in a minute." The light beam pulsed faster, the buzzing noise vibrating their bodies until it felt as if they might break apart. "Ready?"

Daniel pulled them close, wrapping his arms around Zara and his son. "I've loved you forever. I've always been ready."

She drew back her head and smiled a farewell to Lucy. The older woman waved, but her expression echoed her sadness.

The tingling started, and Zara stared into Daniel's eyes, giving herself up to the incredible sensation of his love.

Lucy watched Will jump like a swamp frog, saw Daniel and Zara kiss with almost unbearable passion. Even from this far away, she could feel the love the three of them had for each other filling the air around them until it matched the vibration from the spacecraft.

She'd seen an ocean liner once, down in Corpus; this ship was triple the boat's size or more. There was no true way to estimate, because the upper half appeared to melt into the heavens.

The light beam from the craft almost blinded her, but Lucy kept her eyes on the trio, waving until the very last second, when it seemed as if Daniel, Will, and Zara broke apart in fragments of dust and were vacuumed straight into the ship.

"Well, I'll be. Just like on *Star Trek*," murmured Doc.

Jay scrubbed a hand across his face. "If I hadn't seen it, I never would have believed it."

Still staring, Frank and Chuck shook their heads.

"Well, fuck. Now what?" said Frank, gazing at the behemoth as it rose into the sky.

"We go in with Jack's pictures," reasoned Chuck. "At least we have something to prove we're not crazy, and we did our job. Isn't that right, Jack?"

Jack kept snapping his camera, even though the sky looked normal and the air still. "Yeah, sure. I suppose I could lend you a few pics to show your superiors."

"*Lend* us a few?" Frank grabbed for the camera, and Jack raised it high. "I'm confiscating those photos in the name of the United States government. Now hand over your equipment."

Jay caught the gleam in Lucy's eye. With six inches of height over the asshole photographer, it was no challenge for him to reach out and jerk the camera from Jack's hand. Quicker than a lightning strike, he flipped open the back, pulled out a ribbon of celluloid, and let it flutter to the ground.

Jack turned a mottled red when he realized what happened, but Lucy and Lerner were too busy laughing to care.

Jay calmly set the camera on top of a boulder.

"I'll sue your ass, you fuckin' moron," screamed Jack, dropping to his knees to scrabble in the grass.

Holding the ruined film in one hand, he stood and

hauled back to take a swing with his other, but Jay beat him to it, landing a blow that sent the photographer sprawling.

Doc, Lucy, and Jay cast a final glance at the sky, breathtakingly beautiful, with a brilliant patina of stars and almost reverent stillness. Lerner joined them as they walked through the park toward Jay's truck, while behind them an argument ensued among Jack, Frank, and Chuck.

"I wonder if Mr. Lotello ... er ... Mr. Murphy knows exactly how much money he just lost," mused Lerner. "He's thrown away a fortune."

Lucy stopped in her tracks and grinned at each man in turn. Finally, she focused on the sky. "He knows, Mr. Lerner, believe me, he knows. It's just that he got a much better offer."

# Epilogue

Lucas Diamond charged into the hotel, intent on making it to his room, taking a hot shower, and slipping into bed in less than fifteen minutes. Riding the edge of the biggest discovery in the history of mankind, it had been three nights since he'd gotten any sleep. If he allowed the reckless schedule to continue, he wouldn't be worth shit come morning.

After pressing the up button, he crossed his arms. At this hour of the night, he'd expect all six of the upscale hotel's elevators to be ready and waiting on the ground floor. What the hell was taking them so long?

He felt a presence at his side and slid his gaze to the other guest. Hit by a wave of curiosity, he did a double take. The woman standing next to him smiled politely and turned her attention to the overhead panels counting down the elevators' snail-like approach.

He drummed his fingers on his forearm, resisting

the urge to speak. The woman, tall and curvy, with sinfully long legs and impressive breasts, ignored him. He cursed inwardly. *This is a hell of a time to get hit with a serious case of lust*, he thought, even as he felt his groin twitch to attention.

*What the hell is wrong with me?*

Finally, the elevator directly in front of them opened, and he stepped aside to let the woman enter first. Her heart-shaped rear, covered in black, clung to her like the skin on a grape. Long black hair cascaded to her shoulders in shining corkscrew curls. Dressed in black stiletto heels, she almost matched his own six-foot height. He couldn't help but think she was one heck of a package of formidable femininity. Watch out, Xena, Warrior Princess.

She rested against the back of the elevator, and he pressed the button for the penthouse. "What floor?" he asked, trying to keep his voice level.

"The same as yours."

Her deep, smoky voice brought his erection to full mast. "So we're neighbors?" There were only two penthouse apartments on his floor, and he'd thought the other one was empty.

"Not exactly," she answered.

He raised his gaze from her mesmerizing breasts, covered in some type of stretchy black fabric as tight as her slacks, to her arresting face. Immediately captured by her storm gray eyes, he swallowed. "Sorry, I'm not following."

Her wide, luscious mouth smiled, and he felt gut punched. Shaking his head, he tried to clear the haze, but all he could think about was getting close enough to touch her, to feel her satiny skin under his fingertips and taste the sweetness of her lush, ripe lips.

"I'm thirsty, and the bar is closed. I was hoping you'd have something cool to drink in your suite."

Bombarded by a dozen reasons why he shouldn't invite her in, Lucas shifted on his feet. The elevator continued its climb, but she didn't say another word, just set her mouth into a curving line and waited.

When the doors slid open, and she followed him into the hall, Lucas swallowed. Against every grain of common sense he could muster, he found himself saying, "Sure, why not?"

The best in romance can be found from Avon Books
with these sizzling March releases.

### ENGLAND'S PERFECT HERO by Suzanne Enoch
*An Avon Romantic Treasure*

Lucinda Barrett has seen her friends happily marry the men they
chose for their "lessons in love." So the practical beauty decides to
find someone who is steady and uneventful—and that someone is
definitely *not* Robert Carroway! She wants a husband, not a pas-
sionate, irresistible lover who could shake her world with one deep,
lingering kiss . . .

### FACING FEAR by Gennita Low
*An Avon Contemporary Romance*

Agent Nikki Taylor is a woman with questions about her past
assigned to investigate Rick Harden, the CIA's Operations Chief
who is suspected of treason. Yet instead of unlocking his secrets,
she unleashes a dark consuming passion . . . and more questions.
Now in a race against time, piecing together her history can get
them both killed.

### THREE NIGHTS . . . by Debra Mullins
*An Avon Romance*

Faced with her father's enormous gambling debt, Aveline Stoddard
agrees to three nights in the arms of London's most notorious rake,
a man they call "Lucifer." Once those nights of blistering sensuality
and unparalleled ecstasy are over, will Aveline be able to forget the
man who has stolen her heart?

### LEGENDARY WARRIOR by Donna Fletcher
*An Avon Romance*

Reena grew up listening to the tales of the Legend—a merciless
warrior who is both feared and respected. So when her village is devastated by a cruel landlord, she knows the Legend is the only one
who can rescue her people. But the flesh-and-blood man is even
more powerful and sensuous than the hero she imagined . . .

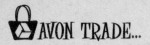